Praise for O

"It's rock'n'roll with a dash or two o̶ ... .at delves into the ugly side of fame. *Only One Survives* is devilishly fun, utterly addictive, and shockingly twisty—further cementing McKinnon as a force to be reckoned with!"

—Jeneva Rose, *New York Times* bestselling author

"A raw, honest exploration of female friendships, envy, and the price of fame. Both thrilling and moving, *Only One Survives* will keep you on the edge of your seat. McKinnon is an auto-read for me."

—Mary Kubica, *New York Times* bestselling author of *Local Woman Missing*

"Perfect for Daisy Jones fans who want an element of mystery and twisted suspense with their music, *Only One Survives* is a tour de force."

—J.T. Ellison, *New York Times* bestselling author of *It's One of Us*

"Like a relentlessly sinister version of psychological musical chairs, when this thriller's propulsive soundtrack stops, *Only One Survives*. Standing ovation!"

—Hank Phillippi Ryan, *USA TODAY* bestselling author of *One Wrong Word*

"A devilishly entertaining read that stabs at the heart of friendship, jealousy, and the relentless pursuit of fame. The thrills never waver in this gripping tale that sings with pulse-pounding suspense and spine-tingling twists and turns."

—Heather Gudenkauf, *New York Times* bestselling author of *Everyone Is Watching*

"McKinnon drip-feeds us clues, keeps us guessing, and shows herself to be a maestro of misdirection."

—Caz Frear, internationally bestselling author of *Five Bad Deeds*

"An absorbing, thrilling page-turner. Every twist left my jaw on the ground."   —Samantha Downing, internationally bestselling author of *A Twisted Love Story*

"Gutsy, original and hugely compelling, *Only One Survives* draws you in right from the very first page."

—B.A. Paris, internationally bestselling author of *Behind Closed Doors*

"McKinnon is a master at flipping the script with twists that will keep readers on their toes."

—Kimberly Belle, internationally bestselling author of *The Paris Widow*

Also by Hannah Mary McKinnon

The Revenge List
Never Coming Home
You Will Remember Me
Sister Dear
Her Secret Son
The Neighbors

For additional books by Hannah Mary McKinnon,
visit her website, hannahmarymckinnon.com.

ONLY ONE SURVIVES

HANNAH MARY McKINNON

/||MIRA

/Il MIRA™

Recycling programs
for this product may
not exist in your area.

ISBN-13: 978-0-7783-0547-7

Only One Survives

Copyright © 2024 by Hannah McKinnon

For questions and comments about the quality of this book, please contact us at CustomerService@Harlequin.com.

TM is a trademark of Harlequin Enterprises ULC.

Mira
22 Adelaide St. West, 41st Floor
Toronto, Ontario M5H 4E3, Canada

Printed in U.S.A.

For music & thriller lovers, everywhere

Various are the roads to fame.

PROLOGUE

42 days after the accident

Music Lovers,

I've guzzled three vats of coffee in record time. Could be why my mind's racing faster than a cheetah on steroids but it's more likely from the shock of what went down with the Bittersweet today. After failing to process the news, I came here to write a blog post. It was either this or a bottle of gin. To be honest, I'm not sure either will help make sense of it all.

If you've seen my recent posts, listened to my radio show *What's On NYC*, or visited my social media, you'll know I adore the Bittersweet, and you'll have read about my devastation after what happened to the band last month. Their accident was such an incredible, tragic loss.

Since they rocked their way into my world last year, I've played "Sweet Spot" a million times on air, in my car, and while jogging through my neighborhood. Spotify's profitability probably doubled because of me.

I've said this before and it merits repeating, it was time

another all-female pop-rock group hit the scene. The Bittersweet, aka Vienna Taylor, Madison Pierce, Isabel Riotto, and sisters Gabi and Evelina Sevillano, were the perfect blend of powerful women who sang, played instruments, and wrote their own tracks. In short: they were kick-ass.

They once told me their sound was influenced by Blondie, the Bangles, Lenny Kravitz, Elastica, Lush, Oasis, P!nk, Prince, the Go-Go's, and the more recent band The Beaches, but trust me when I say they were on their way to becoming legends in their own right.

I caught one of the Bittersweet's shows last fall. Yeah, I've raved about it multiple times, so I won't wax lyrical if you'll pardon the pun, but it was easily in the Top-10 best concerts I've seen. The quality of their live performance and their showwomanship were off the charts. More like a band that had played together for a decade, not a little over a year.

They came into the audience afterward and walked through the crowd, taking selfies, and signing every single autograph request until there were no more. Down-to-earth and friendly, totally approachable.

After watching them interact with each other, and having interviewed them on my show, the best way to describe their relationship is *united*. They gelled, you know? You could tell this band would go the distance. I'd have bet anything they'd be around for decades.

Thousands of us were heartbroken when the news broke about their car crash. Few details emerged at first, although we soon learned that after the single-vehicle accident on an isolated stretch of road in the Catskills, they'd been stranded overnight at an abandoned cabin during a major snowstorm.

Next came a report of fatalities. The fans (myself included) were freaking out, speculating about who had perished. Finally, the cops released pictures of Vienna, and confirmed another person who'd been traveling with the Bittersweet had also survived. With the heaviest of hearts, we concluded Isabel, Gabi, Evelina, and Madison had died...until the cops confirmed Madison was—and to this day still is—missing.

The police remained tight-lipped about the details, so naturally the whispers started. Words like *crime scene*, *perpetrator*, and *investigations*, as in plural, got thrown around. I figured it was nonsense. Clickbait for the gullible. No crime had been committed. I felt certain the accident would be ruled exactly that, an *accident*, after which we'd mourn the demise of one of the most exciting up-and-coming all-female bands in recent history.

Seems I was wrong. In case you missed it this morning, Vienna was approached by the police at a public memorial service for Gabi and Evelina in Queens. Taken in for questioning about their deaths.

You read it right and, in this instance, I'm not the only one who thinks *deaths* is synonymous with *murders*.

I was at the church along with hundreds of other gatherers, and we all had dazed and confused expressions on our faces. Couldn't believe it. Thought it was some kind of mistake, yet, sure enough, Vienna got into the cruiser, and they drove off.

But wait, there's more! Apparently, Vienna might be a suspect in Madison's disappearance (I can't believe I wrote those words, I mean, wtf?).

Now, it might all be nothing but rumors and speculation, but for the cops to show up outside the church in front of all of us and the press, and whisk a startled-looking Vienna away? We all know the saying about no smoke without fire. There's got to be substance there for them to risk doing this. But what?

In any case, whoever hadn't heard of the Bittersweet before certainly has now. This morning's sound bite of Vienna insisting she's innocent has been viewed thousands of times already.

Holy crap, I hope she's telling the truth because not only do I love the Bittersweet, but candidly I've been #TeamVienna from the start. She's cool, has this *I-don't-give-a-shit-what-you-think-about-me* vibe and her drumming skills are off-the-charts. It's like she's Meg White, Karen Carpenter, Sheila E., and Cindy Blackman rolled into one (read my prior *Best Drummers of All Time* post if you don't know who I'm talking about), plus she writes the Bittersweet's songs.

It might sound absurd, but someone so brilliantly talented can't be guilty of murder, can they? *Multiple* murders. Could Vienna have hurt her girls? Where the hell is Madison? It's been weeks since the accident and there's no sign of her. Is she hiding? If so, why, when she could exonerate Vienna by showing up? Unless Madison fled because she's the guilty one. Or they're in this together. After all, they've been best friends since high school.

As I said, my mind's spinning.

Tell me your theory about what went on in the Catskills. Could Vienna be a killer? What about Madison? Got another theory? Leave a comment, and if you hear anything, message me. We need to get to the bottom of the Bittersweet tragedy.

Stay tuned,
Melodie @musicalmelodiej

Comments (1,246—showing most recent)

@harry_dude92 Tragedy? Whatever. The Bittersweet sucked.

@georgiaonmym_ Four of them are dead, asshat. Shut up.

@harry_dude92 Being dead doesn't make them any better. Well, kind of, since they can't make more music.

@georgiaonmym_ You're so gdmn rude

@musicalmelodiej @harry_dude92 Stay respectful

@harry_dude92 STFU your blog and show suck

@musicalmelodiej @harry_dude92 has been blocked. I don't accept aggression.

@georgiaonmym_ Good! Btw I don't think Vienna's capable of murder

@bellybean56 I bet V killed them all #TeamMadison

@clefgalforever @bellybean56 How d'ya figure?

@bellybean56 It's her eyes

@clefgalforever @bellybean56 huh?

@bellybean56 Cold. Brr.

@susie_jessica_hugs #TeamVienna? No chance! She's 100% guilty.

@bellybean56 Agree. Whatever kicked off the Bittersweet shitstorm, I'll bet it brewed for years. Way before the cabin, which was creepy af btw. What was that? The Shining Part II?

@cg_sunshine21 I want the entire story, right from the beginning when Madison & Vienna met. Warts'n'all. Everything.

@susie_jessica_hugs Hell yeah. Someone get on it already.

PART ONE

Truth and oil always come to the surface.

—SPANISH PROVERB

1

The day of the accident

SOMETHING SCREAMS AT me to open my eyes. *Just open your eyes.* I don't want to. Darkness thicker than molasses surrounds me like a cloak. It feels safe. Comforting. As if my brain already knows I can't handle what I'll see. If I look, no matter how small or fast of a glimpse, I'll never forget.

As I press my eyes shut, trying to block out the voice in my head, long spindly shadows emerge from the depths of my mind. They beckon me to follow them, down, down, and I give in, ignoring the screaming as I let myself sink deeper and deeper into the stillness, a place of peace.

Vienna, open your eyes.

It won't go away. Won't leave me alone. A thought emerges from the thick fog swirling through my brain. The voice isn't mine. It's not inside my head. I raise a hand in a feeble attempt to bat the words away.

"Vienna, wake up," the voice says, clearer now. "Please, please wake *up.*"

It's a herculean effort to do as I'm asked, and as my eyes

flicker open, I turn my head, glance over my left shoulder. Madison's leaning forward and staring at me, her fiery red hair disheveled, her emerald eyes wild, wide with fear and a hint of what might be relief. I'm not sure what to make of the mixture. I'm not sure what to make of anything. I look away, but not before I see tears snake down her cheeks and drop onto her blue hoodie.

"Can you hear me?" she says.

My throat's dry, rough as sandpaper. I don't think I can speak but manage to push out a weak-sounding "Yes." I nod in case Madison didn't hear, and the movement brings a stabbing pain to the side of my temple. When I touch my head, I feel a tender lump beneath my fingers. Why am I hurt? Why—

Everything returns all at once. A sudden whoosh of thoughts and memories and fear—so much fear—banishing the darkness like birds startled from a tree.

Six of us were in my old Tahoe SUV. The Bittersweet—Madison, Gabi, Evelina, Isabel, and me—plus Libby, the documentary research assistant who's been shadowing us over the past few weeks. It's midafternoon in early December, and we were driving from Brooklyn to a holiday party in the Catskills hosted by our record label. A major event Madison insisted we couldn't miss, no matter what.

No matter the impending storm.

A sequence of images flashes through my mind. Gabi offering to drive because I was tired. The weather turning earlier than expected, and far worse than anything we'd anticipated. Whiteout conditions. Getting lost in the middle of nowhere. A steep, winding, narrow road up a hill. Slippery lanes. Me tightening my grip on the cup of coffee in my hands, opening my mouth to tell Gabi we were perhaps going a little too fast.

And then…

My fists bunch tight as I recall the sudden movement when the Tahoe slid. This is when the memories slow down. It's as if I'm watching the events unfold from above, all in slow motion. I remember the SUV getting closer and closer to the edge of the road. When I looked out of the passenger window, there was no asphalt left on my side, only the tops of snow-laden trees and a sharp drop below.

Renewed panic rises, making my heart pound. It leaps into my throat, threatening to choke me when I relive the sound of our collective screams as we crashed into the metal barrier.

There was a tiny moment of disbelief. A fraction of an instant when I truly believed we'd be fine, before the barrier gave way, and the Tahoe toppled over the edge of the road, right side first. One second, I thought we'd be all right, we'd be safe, and then we rolled once, twice.

After that...

I search my brain for what came next but there's nothing.

My coffee cup's empty, its contents spilled, the scent turning my stomach. At least the vehicle's upright now, which I'm grateful for, but the front passenger side where I'm sitting is severely crushed, the windshield and front window shattered, half-gone. Thumb-size snowflakes drift in through the holes, landing on my jacket. As I watch them soak into the fabric and disappear, I long to go back into the darkness. Pretend none of this has happened. Maybe if I escape for a while, everything will be back to normal when I wake up.

Except I know it won't.

"Are you all right?" I ask Madison, turning around again, and she nods.

I look at the others. Gabi's in the driver's seat, shoulders trembling, face pale, but she's not making a sound. Libby's in the back row, one hand over her mouth as she sobs. Evelina's slumped face down on the floor, her body twisted at an unnatural angle. There's blood on her jacket. My gaze searches for its origins but can't find it.

Madison leans over, touches Evelina's shoulder, but she

doesn't move. Was she knocked unconscious, too? Is that why it's taking her longer to wake up? My gaze sweeps the rest of the vehicle, my temple throbbing again. It takes me a moment to spot what else is wrong.

There are five of us.

Five.

There should be six.

"Wh-where's Isabel?" I say. "Where did she—"

"Look."

The tone of Gabi's whisper makes a shiver tear down my spine. She points to the broken windshield, and I follow her line of sight. At first, I'm unsure of what I'm seeing. A jumble of clothes at the base of a tree? It's what I tell myself until I register the bright teal color. The exact shade of the puffer jacket Isabel wore when we left Brooklyn. The coat she refused to take off, even after we cranked up the heat.

"No," I say, wrestling with my seat belt, breaking free. "No, no, no, no."

Scrambling, I heave myself up and climb over Gabi, hands yanking on the driver's door. Mercifully, her side opens, and I jump out.

Driven by pure adrenaline, all temptation of going back to the darkness banished for good, I run to the heap of clothes— the heap I know is Isabel—gasping as I fall to my knees at her side.

A tree branch thicker than my arm is embedded in the left side of her chest where her heart should be, her shirt torn and spattered with deep red. Her eyes are open, staring at the gray skies above, but she doesn't blink. She doesn't move.

A guttural scream rises from deep within me, and I put my head back to let it escape. Before it can emerge, the smell of smoke makes the noise wither and die in my throat.

The Tahoe's on fire. My friends are still inside.

2

4 years 4 months before the accident

LANDING AT THE principal's office two hours into the first day of twelfth grade had to be some kind of record. Considering I was a brand-new student at Rosemont High, and the aptly named, stone-faced Principal Mason didn't seem to have much of a sense of humor, I decided not to ask.

"I'm not impressed with either of you," he said, before turning to me. "Vienna, I understand you've just arrived in town but it's no excuse. Madison, I'm surprised to find you in this predicament. I'd have thought you'd know better."

Tuning out his monotone about decorum, expectations, and mutual respect, I snuck a glance at Madison. I didn't know her last name and didn't care. She was the reason we found ourselves in this mess. If it weren't for her, I'd be in calculus class. Although in a way she'd done me a favor as math was my least favorite subject.

Neither of us had said much, Principal Mason clearly enjoyed hearing himself talk. While I leaned back in my chair, Madison sat with a rod-straight spine, hands neatly folded in her lap, giving the occasional nod. Enviable, natural red waves tumbled past her shoulders, and she had choppy bangs, which emphasized her big green eyes and near flawless skin.

My gaze dropped to her perfectly manicured nails, and the Lululemon backpack by her feet. I'd seen her cute tan suede ankle boots at Portland's Maine Mall on Saturday, had quickly calculated I'd need over ten shifts at my ice cream parlor job to buy them, double if Mom's boyfriend found the money I'd hidden again.

I bet Madison never needed to save for anything. Her jean shorts were as trendy as her backpack and boots, and they were strategically ripped in all the right places. Not the DIY job I'd done on the pair I'd got from the local pawnshop.

At least nobody had the same ones, and I liked the fact mine were original whereas Madison was a carbon copy of all the other rich girls circulating around the building. The ones who air-kissed, flicked their hair, and pretended commoners like me were invisible. Girls who *summered*.

I wondered if this was the first time Madison had ended up in front of Principal Mason. She seemed too much of a goody-two-suede-boots to me. Her mom was probably head of the parent-teacher committee, baked treats for the staff to keep them on her side. Whatever consequences came our way, no doubt Little Miss Madison would shimmy out of them faster than I could say *blueberry muffins*.

"Are you going to answer me, Vienna?" Principal Mason's use of my name snapped my wandering attention back to him. "Or do you plan to continue sitting in silence?"

My eyes flickered over his fluffy dark brown hair, which reminded me of a duckling, and I took in his polyester-blend suit and Snoopy tie. Maybe he wore the latter to prove to himself he was a fun guy. He wasn't fooling me.

A knock on the door stopped me from answering his question. Principal Mason's assistant stepped into the office, a short guy whose desk nameplate read Harry Sweet. He didn't look much older than me and might've borrowed his dad's pine-green corduroy jacket to give himself an air of authority, but all it did was transform him into a kid playing dress-up.

"I made the calls to the parents," Harry said. "Ms. Taylor didn't pick up."

Unable to help myself, I let out a snort.

"Something you can share with us, Vienna?" Principal Mason asked.

There were a million things I could've said about my mother. My total lack of surprise at how Harry's quest to reach her had failed would've been as good a place as any to start. She'd ignored school phone calls pretty much since first grade, including the time I'd fallen off a stone wall and Grams had taken me to get stitched up.

Mom's excuse was her busy work schedule at the gas station in Falmouth where we'd lived until the beginning of this summer, except most days I could smell alcohol on her because she'd been at her local bar.

Maybe I should've told Principal Mason how Mom had never attended any of my school performances since I was eight, despite her knowing they were my favorite thing in the world.

Once you've seen one goddamn school concert you've seen them all, Mom told her boyfriend du jour when she hadn't known I was within earshot, or maybe she'd seen me and hadn't cared. *There's two hours of your life you'll never get back.*

She had no idea how wrong she was. My previous school's production of *The Addams Family* had been such a success, we'd added another date. Mom still hadn't come. Instead, she'd partied with Rick, her latest beau and the man who was the reason why I'd ended up at Rosemont for my senior year.

I hated how we'd moved from Falmouth to Portland's North Deering area, and now lived in his house. So did Grams, who seemed to loathe Rick more than I did, but at least we had a non-leaky roof over our heads and no longer shared a bedroom. I loved Grams more than anyone but sleeping in the same room was exhausting now her dementia had got worse and she confused the time of day, thinking it was afternoon when it was the middle of the night.

Principal Mason cleared his throat and raised his eyebrows as he waited for an answer. Was there something I *could* share? Sure. Something I *wanted* to?

"Nope." I omitted the customary *sir* to see if it would infuriate him, but to his credit, the guy didn't react.

"Mr. Pierce will be here any minute," Harry said, and as I glanced at Principal Mason, I noticed a twitch of his upper lip, a small widening of his eyes. This news clearly bothered him.

"Madison," he said, turning to my newfound nemesis. "Before your father arrives, would you please explain what happened at the cafeteria?"

Madison swallowed hard and took a deep breath. *Wait for it*, I thought, expecting a master class in how to wrap people around your little finger. What would she do? Go vamp and bat her eyelashes at the principal? Lean forward while subtly using her arms to push her boobs together as she insisted none of this was her fault? Maybe she'd wait for her father to rush through the door, and do a daddy's little girl routine, bursting into tears so he felt protective of her.

As I studied her, Madison looked straight ahead, raised her chin, and crossed her arms, her body language almost identical to mine. Her whole demeanor was interesting and…unexpected.

Principal Mason was about to speak when another man pushed past Harry, who immediately fled and closed the door behind him. I swear the temperature in the office dropped twenty degrees, making me sit up straight as if on autopilot.

The tall man I presumed to be Mr. Pierce wore a dark suit with a crisp white button-down shirt. Instead of a fun comic-strip tie, his was black, covered in silver spheres, and secured with the most precise knot I'd ever seen. I guessed him to be in his late forties, and whatever he did for work, it had to pay more than well. With his clothes, haircut, and shiny shoes, Madison's father oozed cash.

I'd never known my dad. Mom had me when she was twenty-one, another drunken one-night stand with an out-of-towner whose name she couldn't remember. She'd regretted him, and me, ever since.

"Mr. Pierce." Principal Mason held out a hand, fingers trembling slightly.

"Ronald," Mr. Pierce said as they shook. "What's going on?"

"There was an incident at the cafeteria," Principal Mason offered.

"What are the specifics of this *incident*?"

"Well, uh, Madison and Ms. Taylor here—" the principal gestured at me "—ended up in a scuffle."

Mr. Pierce whipped his head in Madison's direction, and she shrank into her seat, almost as if she wished it would swallow her. "You got into a *fight*? Explain."

"It was nothing," Madison said, her voice small now, her defiance gone.

"Which is why you ended up here," her father replied, waving a hand around. "On your first day back. Let's try this again. Tell me what happened. I rearranged a client call to be here, and I'd appreciate you not wasting more of anyone's time."

There had been a few occasions over the past years when I'd longed for supportive parents who'd come to the school. A few years ago, I'd been bullied by a girl named Patsy. She'd picked on me for whatever reason, and when I'd asked Mom for help, she'd instructed me to do whatever Patsy did to me but twice as hard.

Mom's idea hadn't gone down well—when Patsy kicked me in the shins, I'd done it back, and the teacher had spotted me.

Then again, Patsy had limped for a week, and she'd left me alone thereafter, so maybe Mom's approach hadn't been the worst idea. Still, it would've been nice to have her show her face from time to time, although looking at Mr. Pierce now, I was thankful for her lack of interest, and for the fact my dad wasn't around.

"*Madison*." His tone could've sliced Harry's metal nameplate in half. "I want an answer."

When I glanced over, my animosity toward Madison faded. She seemed terrified. Shoulders hunched, arms still crossed, chin now pointing to her chest.

"It was my fault," I said, and Madison let out a tiny gasp.

I don't know why I spoke up and chose to lie. Maybe it was because I saw part of myself in Madison, the way I'd been until I'd clued into building myself a suit of invisible armor, so nobody's jabs, taunts, or comments got beneath my skin.

Her father stared at me. "I don't believe I was talking to—"

"Who cares? You wanted an answer," I said, cutting him off, figuring it would be the easiest way to draw his ire in my direction and away from his daughter. I didn't have to live in the same house as him. In fact, I'd never see him again, so I didn't care what he thought. "I cut in front of Madison at the cafeteria. She pointed out the back of the line, and I told her to get lost. Things got heated."

"And who pushed whom first?" Principal Mason said, his authoritative tone making a comeback now he was talking at a student, not with an intimidating parent.

I shrugged. "I shoved her."

"Very well," Principal Mason said. "Thank you for being honest, Vienna. You're new to this school, but we don't take assault lightly here."

"Assault?" I said with a laugh. "Seriously?"

"I shoved her back," Madison jumped in, "which means technically I assaulted her."

"Madison." Mr. Pierce's blue eyes bored into her. "You're almost an adult. You most certainly know this is no way to behave."

As he paused, his gaze swept over me while a distasteful look he couldn't quite—or didn't want to—hide crossed his face. As he took in my edgy raven bob, the rows of silver hoops in my ears, my homemade ripped jean shorts, and the Joan Jett *Bad Reputation* tank top—the black one with the set of bright red lips—I knew exactly what he was thinking: *this one's trouble.*

"Principal Mason," he said, still staring at me, "I expect consequences for them both."

"Well, seeing as it's the first day of school and they spoke up, I think we should—"

"Start as we mean to go on? Quite." Mr. Pierce made his way to the door and pulled it open, rattling the gray set of blinds covering the window. Before stepping out, he turned and looked at each of us in turn before adding, "I trust you'll make the right decision, Ronald. Madison isn't busy this afternoon."

"That's not true, Dad," she said. "I have my audition for the orchestra after school."

He waited a beat. "Not anymore."

I watched as Principal Mason gave Madison a pained look while she clenched her fists and bit her bottom lip almost hard enough to draw blood. Seemed I'd been too quick to judge. A love of music and a shared hatred for at least one of our parents? Maybe we had stuff in common after all.

3

4 years before the accident

A SMASHING HO-HO-HOLIDAY CONCERT
by Eleanor Willis of the *Maine Daily*

You snooze, you lose rang true for some last night. Tickets to Rosemont High School's revered annual Winter Holiday concert were already in short supply weeks ago. Now, a day after the event, word in the school's corridors and beyond is anyone who missed out on the festivities is regretting their decision.

This should come as no surprise. Rosemont's concerts have long been hailed as the best in the Portland public school system, and close to professional quality. No fewer than four of the school's more recent graduates have gone on to perform with philharmonic orchestras around the world, including New York, Berlin, and London. However, Rosemont's traditionally classical renditions of holiday tunes weren't what raised the roof this time.

"We went in a slightly different direction this year and decided to add a modern element," Rosemont's head of music, Angie Choi, says. "After putting out a call for auditions via our daily announcements, we were approached by EmVee, and chose them almost immediately."

EmVee, a recently formed duo comprised of Rosemont twelfth graders Madison Pierce on guitar and Vienna Taylor on drums, wowed the audience with their vocal skills. They were scheduled to perform one song, the upbeat "Christmas All Over Again" by Tom Petty and the Heartbreakers, but after a standing ovation, Choi encouraged EmVee to add a second.

"We panicked, to be honest," Taylor says with a giddy laugh, adding that EmVee has only performed together since the fall and doesn't have many songs in its repertoire yet. "Because we both adore 'Wherever You Will Go' by the Calling and had practiced it a few times this past week, we went for it."

Their spontaneity earned them another standing ovation, longer than the first.

How was it for the teenage pair to bring the house down? "Incredible," Pierce says, the elation in her voice audible. "Performing music is what I want to do for the rest of my life. All I can think about is playing more venues with my best friend Vienna. I can't wait to see what we do next."

"We may have a few opportunities soon," Taylor adds. "It's too early to share anything, but we're excited and grateful."

And what do their families make of the runaway holiday concert success? Taylor says her grandmother has always been her biggest champion, giving her wooden spoons and plastic buckets to play on when she was a toddler before gifting her a secondhand drum kit a few years ago. For Pierce it's her parents, who encouraged her to take music lessons well before she entered elementary school. "They're unbelievably happy," she says. "They've always been so supportive, including of Vienna and me forming the band."

With yesterday's knockout performance, EmVee's fan base is sure to expand well beyond their loved ones and high school. No doubt about it, this is a band to watch.

Comments (11—showing most recent)

@maplesyrup_12 Great concert. Bravo, Madison & Vienna!

@flip_flop_22 They weren't as good as the Calling

@juicy_froot16 Duh! They're STUDENTS. They were fab.

@sandie_j56 Vienna sounds way better than Madison

@juicy_froot16 And she's cuter. I'm #TeamVienna

@jenjen_99 #TeamMadison all the way! Much better stage presence & she's prettier with that gorgeous red hair. And those guitar skills? Incredible!

@maplesyrup_12 @juicy_froot16 You said they're STUDENTS and yet you're judging them on their appearance? Yikes!

@juicy_froot16 Calm down. We're not hurting anyone. Who cares about a few comments?

4

The day of the accident

SURVIVAL INSTINCTS TAKE OVER, making me laser-focused. The need to keep everyone alive pushes away any fear I have. I scramble to my feet, conscious of the distinct smell of smoke in the air, and I search for its source. Spot the steady stream billowing from underneath the back of the vehicle.

"Get out," I yell as I run through the snow, trying not to fall. "Everybody out."

"Is Isabel all right?" Madison says when I reach them.

"Get out," I urge. "All of you."

"Evelina's hurt," Gabi shouts. She's in the back of the Tahoe now, the terror in her voice unmistakable. "Her hand's gone."

I look down, almost vomit when I see the torn flesh and shredded tendons at the bottom of Evelina's wrist.

Gabi's screaming again. "We can't move her."

"There's no choice," I say. "Move. *Now.*"

I'm aware of how stern I sound, but there's no time for niceties. Leaning in, I remove the key from the ignition. The engine isn't running but all things electrical might be, which could be dangerous if they cause a spark. Next, I reach for the small fire extinguisher tucked underneath the driver's seat. Nobody else has budged.

"Come on," I say, voice harsh because it needs to be. "Get Evelina out of here. The truck's on fire, you have to move." It's enough of a threat to make Libby and Madison react, and I hear them scrambling as Gabi attempts to help her sister.

I head to the back of the SUV. Crouching, I work quickly, pulling the pin on the extinguisher, aiming the nozzle low, and squeezing the lever. White powder shoots out, smothering the flames. Holding steady, I keep going, sweeping left and right, up and down as best I can until the canister's empty, and the chemical smell fills my nostrils instead of the smoke. The fire's gone but it doesn't mean we're out of danger, and if another starts somewhere else, we've nothing left to fight it with.

When I look up, I see Evelina has been pulled from the wreckage. She lies on her back between two small fir trees, her face whiter than the snow on the ground. Gabi's trying to wake her, begging her to speak, but there's no response.

I lift my head, see Madison walk over to Isabel. She lowers herself to the ground and hesitates before placing her fingertips on Isabel's eyelids and closing them. I wonder why I didn't think of it. Then I wonder if Isabel knew this forest was the last thing she'd ever see. If she felt any pain before the tree branch…

My mind won't go there, and I look around in a daze. We're in the middle of nowhere, at the bottom of a ravine, the road fifty, sixty, seventy feet up. The snow has intensified, and other than the winds, which are blowing hard, there's barely a sound.

I get up, walk to Gabi, and put my arms around her. Evelina looks as if she's asleep, but it doesn't mean there aren't other injuries we can't see. Should we try to find her missing hand? I quickly scan the area, but it could be anywhere.

Libby comes over with her belt and a clean pair of white socks. Gabi and I watch as she loops the belt around the bloody stump of Evelina's forearm and pulls it tight, a makeshift tourniquet to stop the bleeding. Once done, she gently slips a sock over Evelina's damaged wrist.

As Libby's putting the second sock in place, Gabi leans into me, her body shaking, and whispers, "This is my fault."

"It was an accident," I tell her.

"I was driving."

"It was an accident," I repeat, my voice more forceful as Madison arrives, her face streaked with tears.

"Isabel's…gone," she says, and Gabi lets out a moan.

"Gone?" Libby gasps. "She's *dead*?"

"Yes," I say, willing myself to stay strong, hold it together and think about how we'll get out of this situation. Once that's done, there'll be time to grieve. "Does anyone have cell service?" I ask.

I'm not hopeful as I pull out my phone, and sure enough there's no connection. I have no sense of direction, either. We're somewhere in the Catskills during a heavy snowstorm. We got lost about twenty minutes ago, increasingly confused after taking a few wrong turns when our cell service disappeared. I hadn't thought to bring a paper map. Who has one of those these days?

Gabi, Libby, and Madison retrieve their phones, locate Evelina's and Isabel's, too, point them at the sky. Not a single bar between us. The snow's falling thicker now, pelting my jacket, covering my red gloves. Flakes hit faster than my heartbeat but they're nowhere near as loud.

"We have to get back to the road," Madison says.

I point at the incline the Tahoe tumbled down. With the amount of trees, shrubs, and boulders, it's a miracle any of us survived. "It's too steep. We'll have to go around."

"Around where?" Libby says, voice going up a notch. "Maybe we should wait for help."

"We can't risk it," I say. "It could take forever for anyone to spot us, and it'll be dark soon. If we stay here, we'll freeze."

"Evelina needs help *now*," Gabi says, crying again. "We have to find someone."

"Vienna and I will go," Madison offers. "We'll try to get to the road. You two stay here and take care of Evelina. Grab the clothes from the bags and keep each other warm."

Thankfully we'd packed thick winter jackets, hats, and boots, and once we've ensured Evelina's as comfortable as possible, we drape a T-shirt over Isabel's face and torso. I hug Libby and Gabi before we leave, but Madison's already ten steps away, muttering as she evaluates which direction to take.

We try climbing the embankment but it's impossible. Both of us slip and slide, and when a jagged rock rips Madison's pants and she bangs her knee, we give up and head in what the compass on my phone tells me is a southerly direction. We're city women. Neither of us have outdoor or survival skills and my sense of orientation is horrendous, but I keep telling myself doing something is better than doing nothing.

No clue how far we walk, half a mile, maybe more—it's impossible to tell in these conditions—and we still haven't been able to find a place to climb up to the road. The cliffs are steeper now, sheer rock, which makes me shudder. If we'd fallen here...

Madison grabs my arm, points ahead. "A trail!"

The wind's blowing snow horizontally into our faces, but as I hold up a hand to shield my eyes, I think she's right. There does seem to be a path between the trees, heading upward. It's an incline, but at least it's not made of the same rock as what's on the other side of us.

We scramble, the soles of our boots slipping as we try to run, desperate to see where the apparent path leads. I hope we don't stray too far. We need to find our way back to the others. They need us. They're relying on Madison and me to get help, and the thought pushes me onward, one step and then another while I try to remember the different markers we pass.

A large, ogre-shaped boulder on my left. A lightning-struck tree, charred and black, on my right. Remember to go left when we return. We can't rely on our footprints because they're already partially gone.

After another hundred yards or so, this time I'm the one who grabs Madison. "A cabin," I say, and as soon as the words escape my mouth, I know it doesn't do the structure justice. This isn't a small hunting lodge, it's two stories tall and has basement windows. Maybe someone's home.

"Hello? Is anyone here? Hello?" Madison's cries are useless, blown away by the winds.

As she reaches the porch, she bounds up the steps and rattles the front door, cups her hands against a window. I hang back and take a moment to look at the place, a sense of foreboding I can't explain growing in my stomach.

If houses have energy, this one's tense. Angry. The windows are dark, many of the panes cracked and broken. It doesn't seem like anyone's been here in years. The tiny sliver of hope I had when I first saw the cabin slides down my legs and seeps into the frigid ground.

Nobody's inside. The place is abandoned. It's getting close to dusk, nightfall not far behind. I don't want to be here, but we have no other option. If we don't seek proper shelter, we'll die.

"Let's get the others," I tell Madison. "We can try to start a fire, keep warm for the night. At least we'll be out of the storm."

Madison nods as she takes a step to me, then stops. "What if we get lost trying to find this place again? Maybe you and I should stay."

"What? We can't abandon them."

Her green unblinking eyes pierce mine like the sharpest of daggers. "Yes, we can, Vienna. Maybe we should think about saving ourselves."

I wait for her to dismiss her words as a terrible lapse of judgment because she's terrified. She says nothing, and the way she's staring at me makes me shudder because it's as if she's trying to make me bend to her will. I met Madison when we were seventeen. Enough time to know she has a way of always getting what she wants. This time I won't let her.

5

3 years 10 months before the accident

IF SOMEONE HAD told me on the first day of twelfth grade that I'd be spending Valentine's Day evening sitting in Rick's detached, musty, and overflowing garage with Madison Pierce, I'd have laughed in their face. I definitely wouldn't have believed I'd turn down a date with a boy from my class, but the simple fact was that Madison had begged me to hang out with her, and there was nobody else I'd have rather spent the day with than my best friend.

Incredible how much things had changed in six months, especially considering how I'd been ready to write off my entire Rosemont High experience as a complete disaster right from the beginning.

I hadn't been eager to join a new school for my final year. I liked my old one, had been comfortable there. Never one of the popular kids, I'd had some friends, although since Mom and I moved in with Rick, they hadn't bothered keeping in touch other than the rare Snapchat message. It felt as if I'd moved to another continent, not a fifteen-minute drive away. So, landing in Principal Mason's office that morning hadn't filled me with the warm and fuzzies.

"Are you kidding me?"

Those were my exact words after Mr. Pierce had stormed out, and Principal Mason announced Madison and I were to remain at school at the end of the day and help the caretaker clean the cafeteria.

"Not even slightly kidding, I'm afraid," the principal had answered with a pained expression, making me roll my eyes because he was trying to play it off as if he had no choice. Then again, with the way Madison's dad had spoken to him, maybe he didn't. "Return to class. Report to Mr. Davenport at the cafeteria after last bell."

"How long do we have to stay?" Madison asked.

"It'll be at least an hour until you're done. Maybe longer."

She didn't reply, and after we trudged into the corridor, Madison walked off in the opposite direction, her tan boots click-clacking on the scuffed linoleum floor.

"You're welcome," I yelled when I remembered she hadn't thanked me for saving her ass by lying about pushing her first. In reality, she'd cut in front of me as I'd stood in line and I'd grumbled about her not going to the back.

"What's it to you?" she'd said. "Stay out of my face." Then she'd shoved me, hard, and I'd pushed her back. When a teacher intervened, we ended up at the office.

I was still seething at her overreaction when I reached math class and dumped my bag next to one of the empty chairs, apologizing to the teacher as she chastised me for being late.

Thankfully the rest of the day had gone smoothly. I met the head of the music department, Ms. Choi, who had a "Purple Rain" decal on the back of her phone and a passion for '80s and '90s bands rivaling mine. I liked her instantly.

When Ms. Choi learned I was a drummer, she let me play the Yamaha Stage kit the school had bought over the summer. Rosemont's music department was far better than the one at my old school. This drum kit sounded incredible and was light-years newer than the set Grams had bought off a friend and given me on my twelfth birthday, along with access to the online drumming school Drumeo. We'd briefly wondered if Mom would give herself a hernia from complaining about the noise but decided my mother wouldn't be home often enough to hear me playing anyway.

I'd barely used my kit since we'd moved in with Rick. Mom insisted I could only play when he was out, regardless of my stuffing everything into the cramped garage after I'd cleared a spot, which took ages because Rick was such a pack rat. She didn't care when I demonstrated he couldn't hear a thing while watching his prized *Survivor*, sprawled out on the sofa with a six-pack of tallboys.

It had already become abundantly clear that whatever Rick said, whatever he wanted, ruled. This was his house, Mom reminded me, despite the fact she paid rent, and he took my ice cream parlor cash whenever he found it.

Still, thanks to Ms. Choi, the music spark I'd forced to go dormant for almost a month came roaring back, especially when she praised me multiple times during class, and told me I had a real talent for percussion. My elation from her compliments lasted until the bell rang and I remembered I had detention with Madison Pierce.

I retrieved my phone and called Mom. "I have a group project, so I'll be late," I said. The lie was easier than telling her I had detention, which she'd no doubt scold me for despite not asking to see any of my report cards since fifth grade. If she knew I forged her signatures on those, and permission slips, she never said.

She clicked her tongue. "On your first day? You're supposed to watch your grandmother. You know how unsettled she is after the move." A languid sigh. "I guess I'll have to call work, but if I lose my job, it'll be on you, Vienna."

Barb Taylor's concept of motherhood was a complicated one and her fallback position often led to major guilt tripping. She wasn't on the gas station's roster until tomorrow, which I knew because I'd taken a photo of the schedule I'd spotted in her bag. No doubt she wanted to go to Rick's favorite bar early and keep an eye on him. Understandable considering he'd been involved with someone else when he'd met Mom.

The fact Rick had a partner at the time didn't faze my mother. For reasons I couldn't understand she saw him as a decent catch— her standards were low—so she'd got dressed up in a short skirt and a tight tank top, put on red lipstick and high wedge heels, feigned a problem with our car, and taken it to the garage where Rick had a job as a mechanic. Worked like a charm.

Now though, she worried he'd cheat on her, which would be a complete pain in the ass for everyone seeing as we lived with him. Then again, if Douchebag was up to something, I doubted he'd make it obvious. His wife had left him a few years ago (unsurprising), he didn't have any kids, and he liked having someone to feed him, do his laundry, and clear up his mess. My mother was okay with that because Rick had a larger and more comfortable house than the one we'd been renting, and it cost less. Overall, I couldn't decide who was using whom more.

"I'll be back as soon as I can," I said. "Couple hours."

Mom didn't bother with a reply and hung up, so I pocketed my phone and headed to the cafeteria where Mr. Davenport waited with two orange buckets, mops, and cleaning supplies.

As I walked up to him, Madison came in through the main doors, dropping a wireless earbud in the palm of her hand, the music still blaring. When she got closer, it sounded as if she'd been listening to "Our Lips Are Sealed" by the Go-Go's, one of my all-time favorite bands. I must've got it wrong because there was no way Snooty Boots had heard of them.

Ten minutes later and we were busy working. Mr. Davenport had instructed Madison to wipe the dozens of tables and chairs while I mopped the floors. I'd expected her to be slow, complain about the smell of bleach or how it was ruining her manicure, but she never said a word. After being told what to do, she'd stuck her earbud back in place and got to it.

As I moved a little closer, I heard Madison singing, and this time I instantly recognized the tune. "I Bet My Life" by Imagine Dragons. I tapped her on the shoulder.

"S'up?" she said, pushing a strand of red hair from her face.

"You like the Dragons?"

"Don't look so surprised. Just because I'm not wearing one of those—" she pointed at my Joan Jett shirt "—doesn't mean I don't know how to rock out."

I laughed. "Rock out? What are you, fifty-five?"

Madison turned up the volume, effectively tuning me out. Much like Principal Mason, she didn't seem to have a sense of humor. When Mr. Davenport told us to take a quick break half an hour later while he fetched more garbage bags, I was fully prepared not to talk to Madison until he returned. Madison, however, had other ideas.

"Is it true you play the drums?" she said when we were alone.

"Yeah."

"You any good?"

"Yeah."

Half expecting her to make a cutting comment about hearing is believing, or share the virtues of being modest, I couldn't help smiling when she answered, "That's super cool. What kind of music do you like, other than the Dragons?"

"Older stuff, mainly. Seventies, eighties, nineties."

"Same."

"Really?" I said.

"Yeah. I had a nanny for a while who insisted all great music stopped in 1995." Madison grinned. "Can't say I entirely agree with her, but we had this game where she'd play a few bars of a song and we'd guess what it was. She killed it every time, but I got pretty good in the end."

"She sounds fun."

"She was. What about you? Where did your passion for older music come from?"

"My grams," I said. "She had this huge vinyl collection, and we'd take turns choosing which album to listen to whenever I was at her house." I paused, didn't want to add how, after Grams had moved in with us, Mom sold all the records to make a fast buck.

"Do you play any instruments?"

Madison wrinkled her nose. "The piano since I was three. My parents forced me."

"You don't enjoy it?"

A shrug. "It's okay."

"What about anything else?"

"The electric guitar."

I sat up straight. "No way!"

"There you go again, acting all surprised."

I grinned at her. "Are *you* any good?"

Madison hesitated a little, said, "I don't know. I've never played in front of anyone."

"What, nobody? Not even your parents?"

"You met my dad, didn't you?" Madison scoffed. "They don't approve. I play when they're not around."

"Sounds familiar."

"How so?"

I was unsure if I should tell Madison anything else considering how we'd ended up cleaning the cafeteria. Then again, we were detainees together, and we both loved Imagine Dragons, maybe the Go-Go's, if I'd heard the song properly. "My mom, my grandmother, and I moved in with Mom's boyfriend over the summer."

"From the tone of your voice I'm guessing he's a dick."

Her frankness made me laugh. "Total douchebag, like, all the time. He's not a fan of my music, or any music. Never listens to anything."

"Weird," she said. "I couldn't exist without music."

"Same." I took a breath. "I'm sorry you missed your audition. Was it important?"

Madison grinned, an easy, sly smile lighting up her face. "My folks thought so." She made a circular gesture with her fingers next to her temple. "Reverse psychology."

Before I could ask more, Mr. Davenport returned, and I got up. Madison held out one of her earbuds. "It'll make the time go faster," she said. "Tell me if you don't like a song and I'll skip it."

Early the next day, we approached Ms. Choi and begged her to let us use the music room during spare periods and after school so we could practice our instruments together. The first time I heard Madison play the guitar and sing an acoustic version of "Sunday Morning" by Maroon 5, my mouth dropped. She sounded so grounded and wise. Sexy, sultry, confident, and I watched in awe as she swayed her hips to the music, eyes closed. I didn't dare move in case I broke the magic.

"You said you've barely had guitar lessons?" I asked when the last notes faded.

She pulled a face, dropped her chin. "Was I that bad?"

"No." I took a step and grabbed her hands. "God, *no*. You're amazing."

A hint of a blush crept up her neck and across her cheeks. "Thanks," she whispered. "It's your turn now. Show me what you can do."

We'd found an unexpected friendship as well as great harmonies. Now, six months later, we knew her father regretted demanding consequences for our cafeteria spat. He'd had no idea how replacing an orchestra audition she'd secretly never cared about and landing her in detention would lead to us becoming inseparable. If he had, Madison said he would've whisked her from the office and taken her for a slice of pie with extra whipped cream.

"Or a power grain salad," she'd said. "Barry and Lucinda Pierce don't *do* sugar."

Her parents seemed impossible to please. They weren't happy when we formed EmVee, the name a phonetic combination of the first letters of Madison and Vienna, and which we thought sounded close to *envy*.

I didn't tell Mom we'd been chosen to perform at Rosemont's Winter Holiday concert because I knew she wouldn't bother coming. In contrast, Madison remained vague about her involvement because she knew her parents would try to stop her. They were happy for her to play music, providing it was *tasteful*. According to them, our rock songs weren't, and both Madison and I sometimes speculated they'd fallen through a wormhole from two hundred years ago.

"They told me they've spent thousands of dollars on my classical music education," Madison said when we went for pizza after she picked me up from one of my shifts. "Dad says the Pierces of Portland have a reputation to maintain. Honestly, they're defense attorneys, not nobility."

"If they're worried about their reputation, how come you're not at a private school?" I asked, folding my slice of pizza in half, and wiping my oily fingers on my pants.

Madison smiled. "Because I refused."

"Why?"

"Because I didn't want to become like them."

"Didn't your dad have a fit?"

"Yeah, so did Mom, but they stopped when I threatened to deliberately fail my classes if they forced me to switch."

"Were you serious?"

"Nah, but they didn't know for sure." She paused. "And of course, their expectation is at least a ninety-six in every class."

Lucinda and Barry didn't mess around when it came to almost anything concerning their only daughter. They'd arrived at the winter concert expecting to see Madison play a piano recital, and Madison said she imagined her mother's face turning beet red when EmVee got on stage. After Lucinda read the newspaper article in which Madison claimed they'd supported her forming the band, they'd grounded her for three weeks.

Luckily, forging letters from teachers had long been one of my specialties. Unfortunately, while Lucinda wasn't on the school's parent-teacher committee, she knew most of the staff. I got busted when she called the office to verify the third note about Madison needing to stay at school for extra practice, which pissed us off for months.

"Do your parents still talk about me?" I asked Madison as I covered my legs with a blanket, our winter jackets and Rick's space heater not providing quite enough warmth.

"Only to remind me you're a bad influence," Madison said, taking a drag on her joint as another of her sly grins danced across her heart-shaped lips. "They insist I don't hang out with you anymore."

"Obviously, you listened."

"Obviously." Madison blew out a steady stream of smoke and indicated to the joint. "Want some?"

"No, thanks."

Drugs, booze, even cigarettes weren't my thing. Didn't need to search far and wide to see what too much of them could do to a person considering Mom was a walking warning for the latter two.

I hadn't told Madison how I felt in case she branded me a boring loser. At least every other week she'd drive across town and use a fake ID to get whatever provisions she wanted from the liquor store, and she swiped cash from her parents' wallets every so often—small amounts they wouldn't notice. There was a guy at school who sold her however much dope she wanted plus a bit extra because he was completely in love with her.

Everyone loved Madison. She had this invisible aura, a little like a force field, but instead of repelling people it attracted them into her orbit. Most of the time she seemed oblivious to it happening and occasionally I wondered why she'd befriended me, because it really did feel as if it had been her choice rather than mine, but I never asked.

"By the way, I saw you talking to Tessa Morris at break," she said now, leaning back and resting her head on the top of Rick's dusty old wicker chair. "Be careful there."

"Why?"

Madison looked at me, her face falling a little. "I wasn't sure if I should tell you, but she and her group of snitty friends talk shit about you sometimes."

"They do?" I said, my stomach dropping. "Like what?"

"You know, things like where you live, where you get your clothes, that kind of pretentious crap."

"Oh," I said, putting my head down. "I thought she was being nice."

"Forget about Tessa," Madison said. "You don't need her. Not when you've got me."

I gave her a smile, glad she always had my back, and vowed to stay away from two-faced Tessa from now on. "And we have EmVee," I said. "Don't forget about that."

"Never," Madison said as she stubbed out her joint. "I'm excited for our gig. Let's go over our set list again."

Nerves fluttered in my stomach. The newspaper feature after the school concert had generated a few local gigs for us, and last week we'd been asked to play at a woman's surprise fifty-seventh birthday party tonight. Her husband had specifically requested her favorite '80s hits, thankfully most of which Madison and I already knew. They weren't paying us much, but I didn't care. The fact they'd contacted EmVee was reward enough, even if we had to keep it a secret from her folks.

As we ran through the songs, I couldn't wait to get on the

stage for a few hours of freedom. Madison's parents were working late at the office on a difficult case, whereas Rick was with
his friends somewhere and Mom had taken Grams to a Valentine's Day bingo night, more than likely because the cocktails
were half price.

As I let out a yawn and stretched, Madison frowned. "Don't
fall asleep on me."

"No way. I'm just tired because of Grams."

"I can't believe she tried to leave the house in the middle of
the night again."

I nodded. "This time she insisted she needed to buy milk.
It was three o'clock."

"I'm sorry, Vee, that's got to be rough."

"It's fine," I said, brushing everything away because I didn't
know how to deal with it. Vocalizing how I felt about Grams' dementia to anyone, including Madison, wasn't something I handled
well. I generally kept the truth to myself. "We should get going."

Madison had talked a friend of hers into letting us borrow
his old hippie van for the night, and after loading our gear we
drove the short distance to Riverton, planning on arriving early
so we had plenty of time to set up. Things came to an instant
halt as we hauled my drum kit from the back of the vehicle.

"Madison, what are you doing?"

We spun around, came face-to-face with Barry Pierce, arms
crossed, eyes glaring, his entire body silently demanding an ex-
planation. I sensed Madison stiffen. My mom didn't care where
I was or what I was doing tonight. The only thing she'd hate
was my hiding how I'd earned money from a gig. Rick would
go ballistic for the same reason, immediately demanding half.
Madison's dad was a whole other story.

"She's helping me get ready for a gig," I said, staring at him.

Barry continued addressing Madison. "Answer me."

"What Vienna said," she mumbled. Her defiance had evap-
orated because, unlike the orchestra audition her dad made

her miss the day we'd received detention, she very much cared about this gig. "I'm here to help her get set up."

"You're lying," Barry said, tone glacial. "The husband of the woman whose party you're here for works at the local bakery. When your mother saw him three days ago, he mentioned how he was highly anticipating your performance."

"Three days?" Madison whispered.

"We thought we'd give you time to come clean," he said. "How utterly disappointing."

"Why won't you let her play?" I blurted out. "Madison's talented. Her guitar—"

"Madison, you'll call the man now and tell him you can't make it." Barry made a vague dismissive hand gesture in my direction. "She'll perform on her own."

Madison let out a gasp. "EmVee's a duo. It's what they're expecting."

"Such a shame when expectations aren't met," he said curtly.

"I'm not letting anyone down," she insisted. "EmVee's reputation—"

"*Reputation?*" he snapped, patience dangerously thin. "What reputation? You'll graduate high school in a few months and it'll all end anyway."

"End?" I said. "What do you mean?"

"Get in my car and call him," Barry said. "Now, Madison."

She threw me a defeated and apologetic look as she grabbed her bag, guitar, and amplifier from the van, stomped to Barry's car, and gently put her things in the trunk. Before she opened the door, she glanced at me again, placed one hand over her heart and mouthed, "I'm so sorry."

I gave her a nod and a small wave, refocused on Barry as she disappeared into the back. "She'll hate you for this."

He let out a puff of air as he made full eye contact with me for the first time since he'd arrived. "She'll be thanking me for making her understand what's important. Her studies, her future." He leaned in, lowering his voice. "Let it be known I'll ensure you're not in it."

"Why? What's it to you?"

"Amongst other things, my wife smelled marijuana on Madison the other night."

"Mrs. Pierce must've been mistaken because neither of us smoke."

His eyes narrowed. "I can't stop you from seeing each other at school, but I'll make it extraordinarily difficult for you to interact after class. Madison's going to be busy over the next few months with other activities. It's time for you to find more... *suitable* friends."

As he walked away, I wished I could burn holes in his back with my poisoned gaze. I knew he looked down on me because he was rich and I was poor, but screw that. As for finding other friends, not likely, especially after what Madison told me about Tessa. Connecting with people didn't come easily for me, and Madison said she never shared secrets with anyone the way she did with me. She trusted me completely, and she'd once told me she never wanted anyone to take her place in my life.

I watched the car disappear, wondering if her father's actions would succeed in killing our friendship. The answer landed via a message on my phone a few seconds later.

Garage at 11. Love, M xoxo

Making a silent vow, I promised myself Madison would always be my best friend, no matter what. Nothing, and nobody, would ever change that.

6

3 years 9 months before the accident

FOR THE NEXT few weeks, I tried to keep my head down at home as much as possible. Mom, Grams, and I had lived with Rick for less than a year, and I already knew he could be a selfish, misogynistic ass. However, one Friday afternoon in mid-March, I also discovered his cruel streak.

It happened as I walked home from school when I spotted a plastic bag moving in the grass next to the sidewalk. At first I figured it was a mouse or a rat until I saw the handles were tied together. I inched closer, heard the distinctive sound of meowing. I took another step, and the bag went still, so I knelt and gently undid the knot before peering inside.

A kitten was nestled at the bottom, a tiny gray fluffy thing who couldn't have been more than a few weeks old. It meowed again, melting my heart. I loved cats. They'd been my favorite animal since I was a kid. Mom had never wanted one, saying the food and veterinarian bills were too expensive. She wouldn't be happy about having a kitten in the house, but it was freezing, with another snowstorm set to start within the hour.

Mind made up, I gently popped the shivering animal into my jacket and held it close, googling *what should I feed a kitten* as I walked. My fingers soon turned numb, and my mind raced ahead as I thought about where I could hide my new pet, and how I'd get away with it.

Neither Mom nor Rick was at the house, so I went straight to Grams' room, frowning when the motion sensor door chime didn't go off. I'd bought one online a few weeks ago when I'd heard Grams rattling the front door just after midnight, and I'd installed it above her bedroom door. It was simple enough to use but Rick complained about it ringing and the jerk had already taken the batteries out twice.

"Come in," Grams said when I knocked.

She sat in her trusty old olive-green chair, an episode of the '70s cop show *The Streets of San Francisco* blaring on her TV. Michael Douglas reminded her of Pops, but I'd never met my grandfather because he died in a workplace accident the year before I was born.

"Hello, sweet pea," she said, eyes sparkling. Instead of wearing her usual attire of pajamas, housecoat, and memory foam slippers, she was dressed in her best sapphire pencil skirt, a cream shirt, and low black leather heels. She'd done her classic makeup of winged eyeliner, mascara, and blush, too. Grams was in her seventies, but on a good day she could pass for ten years younger.

"You look fancy." I gave her a hug and kissed the top of her head, taking in the scent of her lavender shampoo. "Are you going out?"

A wide smile lit up her face again. "Yes. Rupert's taking me to dinner and we're going dancing. I think I'll have steak and a twice-baked potato tonight. Yum."

"That's lovely," I said, my chest tightening.

I never knew what to do when she talked about Pops as if he were still alive. I'd upset her if I gently pointed out he'd been gone for almost two decades. The alternative was waiting for the pathways in her brain to reconnect and figure it out for themselves. Either option was unbearable for her whenever the realization hit that her husband was gone. How did it feel, I wondered, having to relive such acute grief over and over again?

Grams had already shown signs of memory loss four years ago, which Mom kept insisting was only because her mother was getting older. Except Grams wasn't *old*. Eighteen months ago, she'd left soup on the stove and gone out, almost burning her house down, so after that she'd come to live with us. These days, Grams spent most of her time living in the past, becoming frightened and confused when she reemerged from the world her mind had reconstructed. I hated seeing her in so much distress, and she'd recently been diagnosed with a heart condition, too. It wasn't fair.

"I'm sure you'll have a lovely time with Pops," I said, deciding to play along as I sat on the bed next to her chair. "Before you go, want to see a surprise?"

"Oh, yes," she said, clapping her hands. "I love surprises."

"It's a secret, too. You can't tell anyone."

Grams mimed zipping her lips shut and throwing the key over her shoulder, before putting a hand to her mouth as she let out a soft giggle. After instructing her to close her eyes I opened my jacket and lifted the kitten out, gently placing it in the palms of her hands.

In an instant, Grams' eyes flew open, and she gasped. Her fingers traveled over the tiny creature's shivering body, settling behind its ears. I swear the cat let out a sigh as it leaned in and purred, making Grams giggle again.

"I think it's a boy," I said. "What should we call him?"

Without missing a beat, Grams declared, "Pepper."

"Because of his gray fur?"

"Yes, and because of Sergeant Pepper. Have you heard of the Beatles?"

I smiled. "Once or twice."

"They're my favorite band."

"Are they really?"

She lowered her voice. "I love John Lennon the most, but don't tell Rupert when he gets home. I wouldn't want him to be jealous."

My heart pinched again. "I won't. Grams, didn't you see the Beatles play in Boston?"

She drew a breath as a flicker of uncertainty crossed her face. For a moment I wondered if she'd recall the concert or get muddled again, but when she spoke, it was with one hundred percent conviction.

"Rupert and I lied about where we were going," she said. "My mother wouldn't have been happy if she'd known her unwed daughter was driving all the way to Boston with a boy, so I fibbed and said I was going to church group."

I laughed. Grams' love of music had bypassed my mother—in that sense she and Rick were perfectly suited—and we'd always joked about me inheriting all of the passion instead.

"Boston Garden, September twelfth, nineteen sixty-four." Grams shook her head as she patted Pepper. "I remember it as if it was yesterday. Hardly heard any of the songs because of all the excited fans screaming. Me and Rupert included."

"It must've been wild. You and Pops were such rebels. Did you ever tell your mom where you'd been?"

Grams was about to answer, hopefully regale me with more stories about the concerts she'd been to because she'd seen so many legends, including the Rolling Stones and Queen, but the bedroom door opened.

Rick stood in the doorway, his eyes narrowed as he stared at us, and at Pepper who was now fast asleep in Grams' palms.

"What's that?" he said, pointing. "A goddamn cat?"

I wanted to make a quip about his observational skills being killer but managed to keep my mouth shut. No point antagonizing Rick when I needed to get him on our side. Judging by the look on his face, he'd be hard to win over.

"I found him on my way home," I answered, keeping calm. "This is Pepper."

"Don't care if it's Garfield. Get it out of my house."

Grams' back stiffened, her voice going up. "I don't like you. You're not a nice man."

Rick's mouth curled into a sneer, and I vowed there and then if he insulted Grams, I'd retaliate twice as hard. I didn't get the chance because Mom's head popped up behind her boyfriend's shoulder.

"What's going on?" she said, her voice frostier than his. No need to try and guess whose side she'd already picked before knowing what the argument was about.

"Your kid brought a cat into my house," Rick said, and Mom's eyes dropped to Pepper, who still purred gently, oblivious to the trouble caused by his tiny presence. "Make sure she gets it out of here, today." He turned, walked down the hall to the kitchen, and we heard the fridge open and slam shut, followed by the metallic click of a beer can. No doubt the first of many, another thing he and Mom had in common.

"He's nasty," Grams said, her voice determined. "He's not like my Rupert."

"Dad's dead," Mom said, tone overflowing with exasperation. "Remember?"

"No, he isn't. We're going dancing and he's taking me for dinner. I'm having steak."

Ignoring Grams, Mom turned to me, pinched the bridge of her nose. "Get rid of the cat."

"But, Mom—"

"Don't argue. Put it outside."

"Have you seen the weather? There's a storm coming. It'll freeze."

Mom pulled a packet of cigarettes and a lighter from the

pocket of her jeans. She lit up, smoke curling from her mouth. "Do it now, or I will."

"Fine." I jumped up, brushed past her, and pulled on my winter jacket. Once I had my boots, hat, and scarf on, I came back and placed Pepper on my chest, kissed Grams on the cheek, and turned to Mom. "Rick took the batteries out of the motion sensor again," I said. "Tell him to knock it off or I'll wreck his precious car." Without waiting for a reply, I headed outside.

The storm had arrived, thick snowflakes already coating the asphalt. Mom didn't let me drive in this weather, said I was too inexperienced, and she couldn't afford the repairs if I got in an accident. She also wanted gas money up-front, but I was flat broke as my shifts at the ice cream parlor had been cut days after I'd spent my savings on a new bass pedal for my aging drum kit.

Rick's black 1970 Ford Mustang sat in the driveway. He loved his car, proudly told everyone how he'd found the rusty carcass in an old barn and bought it for next to nothing, restoring it piece by piece over more than two years. He'd recently given it a sleek new paint job, bought a cover for it so he could *put her to bed*, and I suspected the money he'd taken from me had paid for part of it.

If I'd had the courage, I'd have carried out the threat I'd made—lifted the cover and gouged the paint with my keys, leaving a snakelike scratch, metal on metal, all the way down the side. Except he'd instantly know it was me and I had to live with him. I had my limits.

It was two miles to the animal shelter, so I set off on foot, tears from the stinging winds blurring my vision. I thought about messaging Madison, remembered she'd left school early and joined her parents in their quest to find a vacation home in the Hamptons.

I kept going, feeling like little Pepper. Alone. Abandoned. Unloved and unwanted by my family, except for Grams. I desperately feared the time when she'd no longer recognize me.

I didn't think it would be much longer. Maybe it was why she called me *dear* or *sweet pea* most of the time. A week ago, she'd asked how long I'd been her nurse. More and more often she saw me as a stranger, and once she was gone—mind, body, or both—I'd feel adrift forever.

It was no longer the wind making my eyes tear up as I dropped Pepper off at the shelter, although the owner assured me she'd find a great home for him because he was adorable. Actually, her kindness made it worse. I wanted Pepper to stay with me and Grams, for the two of us to live alone, in a place where we could be happy. That would never be possible. I had to make do with the situation and be there for Grams as much as I could as I waited for Mom to tire of Rick or the other way around.

Unfortunately, my hopes of Mom and Rick splitting up soon disappeared a month later when they returned from an impromptu trip to Niagara Falls with cheap rings on their fingers. I guessed there'd been copious amounts of alcohol involved in their decision to get married, and they probably still had whopping hangovers. Whatever the case, with zero warning, Rick went from being Mom's horrible boyfriend to my vile stepfather. If nothing else, it was a clear signal how things could only get worse.

7

The day of the accident

"YOU'RE IN SHOCK," I reply, taking a step back from Madison. We're standing in the woods, not twenty feet from the cabin, and I can't believe what she said about the two of us staying here. "I'm not abandoning the others," I continue. "They're counting on us to *do* something. If we don't go back, they could all—"

Madison grabs my hand, yanks me toward her. "Think about it. We—"

"No." I pull away. "We have to stick together. The Bittersweet are—"

"Finished," she says, and when she sees my expression, I swear she's about to roll her eyes. "You know it's true. Isabel's dead and Evelina's barely alive. She's missing a hand. We're over."

"Stop it. We—"

"Jesus, this'll be one hell of a story once the press gets hold of it," she says, her voice so low, I'm not sure if she's talking to me or herself. "Imagine the coverage we'll get."

I will myself to believe the shock's making her talk this way. Except she's calm. She's serious. She means every word.

Without another moment's hesitation, I turn and break into a run as best I can. When I throw a glance over my shoulder, Madison hasn't moved. She's staring at me, hands on hips, shaking her head as if chastising me. I wonder if she'll follow, and for the first time since we met, part of me hopes I'll never see her again.

Although I try to move faster, the thick snow that's accumulating slows me down, and it feels like forever before I get to the crash site. When Gabi sees me, her face fills with hope. "Did you find help? Is Madison bringing someone?"

"The cliffs were too steep. We can't get to the road but we—"

"We need *help*," Gabi shouts, standing up. "My sister needs medical attention, *now*. You were supposed to find someone. That was your *job*."

"I'm sorry," I whisper. "It's getting dark, and we don't know where we are. The last town was miles back and I'm not sure in which direction. Everything's so confusing, there's nothing to orient ourselves by. We found—"

Evelina lets out a small moan and Gabi's focus turns back to her sister. She drops to her knees, holds Evelina's remaining hand, and strokes her face as she murmurs words of reassurance about everything being all right.

Libby pulls me to one side. "Evelina's not doing well at all," she whispers. "She woke up only to pass out from the pain again. How did she lose her hand?"

"I'm not sure but she and Isabel didn't have their seat belts on," I say with a grimace. "There's so much jagged metal on the broken frame and the windows are shattered. At least Evelina stayed in the truck, but Isabel must've gone through the windshield before the tree branch…you know."

Libby's eyes well up. "Maybe if I'd said something—"

"This is nobody's fault," I say. "Listen, when Madison and I were in the forest—"

"Ouch." She winces, puts a hand to her head.

"Are you okay?" I ask.

"Headache," she says. "Do you have any pills?"

"Sure, I'll get them." I make my way inside the Tahoe and remove two round white pills from a generic bottle of acetaminophen I have in my bag. I hand them to Libby and as she swallows them dry, Madison's voice rings out.

"Did she tell you about the cabin?" she says as she walks to us.

Gabi gasps. "You found a cabin? Why didn't you say so?"

"It's abandoned, but I managed to break down the door," Madison answers before I get the chance. "At least we'll have shelter. Let's take as much stuff from here as we can, and—"

"What about my sister?" Gabi says. "She can't walk, she's not conscious."

"We'll have to carry her," Madison says, and I wonder if I'm the only one detecting the mild annoyance in her voice. How can she be so cold? So indifferent? Maybe it's her no-nonsense survivor mode, but to me, it's bordering on mean, although I guess at least she came back to help.

"How will we move her?" Gabi asks, desperate. "We could cause more harm."

"If we stay here, we could die of hypothermia," I tell her. "At least at the cabin we can try to get warm, maybe build a fire."

"A fire?" she says, sounding hopeful.

"It'll be really good for Evelina," Libby adds.

"As soon as the storm stops, two of us will go for help, I promise," I say. "Please, Gabi. It's only about twenty minutes away, but it'll take us longer carrying Evelina. We have to move before we can't see where we're going."

"I know how to make a stretcher," Libby offers.

"Great," I say. "Can you work on it while Madison and I

pick up whatever supplies we can carry? I know we have some snacks and water bottles."

"Does anyone have a first aid kit?" Madison asks as she moves toward the truck, and when I realize none of us do, I try not to cry.

"I only have these painkillers," I say, throwing her the bottle of acetaminophen. "Can you put them back in my bag or keep them safe somewhere?"

As Madison does what I ask, I push her words about leaving everyone here from my mind. She came back. That's what matters.

"What about Isabel?" Gabi glances at the body, looking guilty. "We can't leave her."

"We have to," I say. "She's gone, Gabi. Let's focus on Evelina."

Silence descends on us as we get to work. Libby finds two sturdy branches of equal thickness and length. As I search the bags for food and water, I watch her retrieve two jackets from the Tahoe. She inverts the sleeves, tucking them inside. Next, she threads the branches through the sleeves and removes the laces from the pair of sneakers she'd brought with her.

"Does anyone have laces they don't need?" she asks.

Nobody does, so Libby moves over to Isabel, whispering, "I'm sorry, I'm so, so sorry," as she kneels and unties Isabel's shoes. I turn away, unable to watch as I swipe the tears stinging my eyes. Later, I remind myself. There'll be time to mourn later.

"Where did you learn how to do all this stuff?" I ask Libby as she uses the laces to attach two shorter branches to the ends of the makeshift stretcher.

"Girl Scouts when I was a kid. I only went a few times, but we made jacket stretchers, and I never forgot." She glances at Gabi and Madison, who are preoccupied with collecting items to take to the cabin. "I want you to know I'm bringing my camera," she says, rushing on before I can answer. "I know I was showing Gabi how to use it earlier but don't worry, nobody's going to film anything, obviously, but I don't want to leave it behind."

"I understand. If I'd brought my drums with me, I'd probably want to do the same."

"Thanks," she whispers.

"Have you gathered everything?" I call out to the other two. "We need to get moving."

"Will it hold her?" Gabi asks as she walks over and points at the stretcher.

"Yes, I think so," Libby replies. "Gabi, you and I will take the front as we're about the same height. Vienna and Madison, you'll grab the back."

It feels good to finally be taking action, to make some form of progress. It takes us a while to decide how to best maneuver Evelina onto the stretcher and when we eventually lift her, she lets out another groan but doesn't open her eyes and barely moves.

My medical knowledge is more than limited, but Evelina's condition seems dire. Aside from the fact she's lost a hand, her face has gone from white to ashen, a line of sweat spreading across her brow, beneath the pink woolen hat Gabi has placed on top of her sister's head.

Evelina's slim—she's lost weight recently—but tall, and my back protests when we lift her. We sling our backpacks stuffed with supplies over our shoulders, and as we take baby steps through the forest, holding the stretcher in our gloved hands, dread curls around my legs like vines, climbing all the way to my stomach and chest, where it encircles me and pulls tight.

A terrified voice I desperately try to push away whispers inside my head, getting louder and louder, until it's impossible to ignore.

No one knows where you are.

Nobody's looking.

8

3 years 5 months before the accident

MY PREMONITION ABOUT things going from bad to worse came true a couple of weeks after our high school graduation. Madison and I generally hung out at her house when I didn't have a shift as her parents often worked late at their Portland office. When they were out, she and I had free rein over their huge house. It had four bedrooms upstairs, a finished basement, and a massive ground floor that boasted a living room and a formal dining room, a library, a cozy den, plus a chef's kitchen, although neither of us did much beyond warming stuff up in the microwave.

Their backyard was an oasis, an escape from the real world with its tall shady trees and humongous kidney-shaped swimming pool. They even had a pool house, a sure indication of how well Lucinda and Barry Pierce were doing for themselves. From what Madison had shared, her parents came from modest backgrounds, which they'd been desperate to shed. To their credit, they'd worked hard to afford the finer things in life. Shame they seemed to have forgotten where they came from.

In any case, I'd never been friends with anyone who had a whole other dwelling on the same lot, unless you counted a trailer. Madison's pool house was almost as big as Rick's entire home, and contained two large bedrooms, a generous living room, and another fully equipped kitchen.

There was another reason why we spent so much time there. On the few occasions when Madison had come home with me, Mom had slurred her words when it was midafternoon. Later, when Rick arrived, he'd given Madison the once-over, slowly, from her toes to the top of her head, his gaze lingering at her chest. It was embarrassing, and he was gross.

Still, on this particular day after the Fourth of July weekend, we'd decided to stop by Rick's house on our way to the mall. Summer temperatures had soared, making me desperate for my pair of flip-flops and homemade cutoff shorts.

"Mind if I use the bathroom?" Madison said when we pulled up in her car.

Mom had taken Grams to the podiatrist, but Rick's prized Mustang was in the driveway, making me hesitate. "Douchebag's here," I said. "Are you sure you want to come in?"

"It can't wait until we get to town," she said with a grimace.

"Let's sneak in through the back," I said. "Fingers crossed he's watching TV and won't hear us."

We walked around the house and stepped inside. The television was on, but Rick was moving around in the kitchen, the smell of coffee and toast in the air.

After a quick and whispered exchange with Madison, I hurried to my bedroom to change while she used the only bathroom in the house, which was down the narrow wood-paneled hall. I'd barely zipped up my shorts and was about to dig out my flip-flops from my closet when Madison stormed into the room with a furious expression on her face.

"What's wrong?" I asked.

"Douchebag," she said, her voice dripping with disgust.

"What happened? Did he say something?"

She shuddered. "Nope. He was waiting outside the bathroom, the creep. Said he saw my car and figured I was here. When I tried to get past, he brushed his arm against my boobs."

"He did *what*?" Rage ignited in my stomach, flowed from my core to every other part of me, burning me up from the inside out. Sure, we'd noticed Rick's lust-filled eyes follow her on the couple of times she'd visited, but for him to *touch* her? Hell no.

I stomped to the living room where Rick had settled into his knockoff Barcalounger and seemed to have already fallen asleep, an array of beer cans littered around his feet. Smoke wafted in the air, his hand two inches above the ashtray where one of his lit cigarettes still glowed.

"Let's go," Madison whispered, tugging on my shirt. "He's not worth it. Things are awful enough for you already. We'll only make it worse."

I didn't listen and crept over, nudged the ashtray and the burning cigarette until it was directly beneath Rick's pinkie finger. Before I made it to the door, he leaped up and let out a howl. Frankly, I hadn't known he was capable of moving so fast.

"What the actual fuck?" he said, rubbing his singed finger. "Did you…*burn* me? The hell is wrong with you?"

"Don't. Ever. Touch. Her. Again." My voice came out so hard and bitter, I barely recognized it as my own. Teeth clenched, fists balled, I added, *"Ever."*

"You bitch." He lunged, closing the gap between us in three powerful steps.

Before I could get out of his way, the force of his backhander sent me flying, and I landed with a thud against the sideboard, the wooden corner digging into my ribs, making me yelp.

Madison gasped as she helped me get up and shouted, "Leave her alone."

Rick didn't listen but moved toward me, hand raised, a malicious glint in his eyes.

I stood tall, defiant, ready for him to strike. "Go ahead," I said, tasting blood from my split lip. "But you'd better make sure I don't get up again because I'll be calling the cops and landing your ass in prison."

My words made him hesitate, take a step back as the front door opened and my grandmother's voice rang out, asking if anyone was home. Seconds later Mom came into the living room while I heard Grams shuffle off to the kitchen, unaware of the storm brewing in the next room.

"What's going on?" Mom asked.

"Rick touched Madison's chest," I said, deciding to go for it, tell her the truth and show her what kind of disgusting man she'd married.

"I didn't do shit," Rick said.

"Yes, you did," Madison said.

Mom's face fell but she recovered quickly. "You made a mistake, Madison."

"No, she *didn't*," I said.

"She sure did," Rick said, "'cause it never happened."

"It *did*," Madison insisted. "We were in the hallway—"

"That narrow thing?" Mom said. "There isn't room to swing half a cat in there."

"He touched her, and he backhanded me." I pointed to my lip, which felt as if I'd set it on fire. "He was about to hit me again when you and Grams came home."

Mom sniffed. "Well, I'm not surprised he slapped you. You deserved it after accusing him of doing a terrible thing."

Triumph gleamed in Rick's eyes. "Vienna did more than that," he said, holding up his hand. "She put the ashtray under my finger as I was nodding off. Burned me with my own cigarette. Can you believe it? What kind of a person does that?"

Mom glared at me, and not for the first time I knew I'd lost the battle and would never win the war. The man could do no wrong. Me? I was a deadweight she'd dragged around since before I was born. She once told me she wished she'd had an abortion. In my darkest of moments, I wished she'd had one, too.

"This is his house. Don't you forget it." Mom moved over to Rick and patted his fingers as if he were a child. A child she wanted. "If I catch you telling lies like this again, Vienna, you can pack your bags and leave."

"Let's go," Madison said quietly, grabbing my hand. "Leave things to cool down."

I shook her off. "Who'll take care of Grams if I'm not here, Mom? Because it won't be him. Or you. It'll cut into your drinking time."

"How dare you," Mom snapped. "My gosh, I took her to the doctor today."

"First time for everything."

"Don't speak to your mother like that," Rick said.

"Oh, go fuck yourself, you creep."

Mom grabbed his arm, holding him back as she glared at me. "Final warning. If you—"

"Don't bother. I'm going." I spun around and marched to my bedroom where I yanked a sports bag from my closet and shoved clothes inside as fast as I could. T-shirts, pants, a pair of shorts, underwear—whatever I could grab, color combinations be damned.

Madison had followed me into my room and put her arms around my shoulders. "I shouldn't have said anything. Maybe I was mistaken. Perhaps he didn't touch—"

"Don't," I said. "Don't apologize for what you know he did."

"Where will you go?"

"I don't know," I said. "To be honest, I haven't thought that far ahead, and of course there's Grams." I sank onto my bed. "What am I going to do? I can't leave her."

"Call your mom and Douchebag's bluff for one night," Madison said. "Like you said, they need you, so show them. Come home with me. Stay in the pool house."

"Really?"

"Yeah, it's perfect," she said, nodding eagerly. "Remember they took out the pool liner last week? The new one was supposed to be installed tomorrow but there's a two-week delay. Dad lost his shit despite the fact he barely swims, and neither of them go in the pool house unless we have guests from out of town."

"What if we get caught? You promised them ages ago we don't hang out anymore."

"Let them throw me out and we'll run away together," Madison said. "You're eighteen already so your mom can't do anything and my birthday's in September. We'll be free. We can go wherever we want. Down the East Coast, all the way to Florida or across the country to California."

Playing pretend for a day sounded like heaven, and I needed the escape more than anything. I ignored Mom and Rick, who were speaking in hushed tones in the kitchen, and went to Grams' room.

"I'm going out for the night," I told her, giving her a hug as I kissed the top of her head. "Will you be okay?"

"Right as rain, sweet pea," she said. "Will you be back? You're such a lovely nurse."

"Tomorrow, Grams," I said, trying not to cry. "I'll be back tomorrow."

Not long after, Madison and I sneaked into her pool house. As we lay on the king-size bed, quietly whispering to one another until way after sunset, Madison fell silent. At first, I thought she was asleep, but then I caught her staring at me.

"I have to tell you a secret," she said. "But I'm scared you'll hate me."

I rolled onto my side. "Never going to happen. You're my best friend."

As Madison's eyes filled with tears, I felt the panic rising in my throat. Was she sick? How bad? I couldn't imagine life without our friendship. It seemed worse than death.

"I accepted an offer from NYU," she blurted. "Engineering."

"What? But...but you said you weren't sure. You wanted to take a year off."

Madison let out a stream of shaky breath. "I did, but Mom and Dad wouldn't let me. I know you don't want me to go but...they bought me an apartment in Brooklyn."

"They *bought* you an apartment?"

"Yeah," she said. "It's really cute."

"Of course it is."

"Please don't be like that. Can't you see? I'll finally get away. I can leave them behind."

"But you're leaving me and EmVee."

"I have to go, but—" she grabbed my hand "—you can come with me."

"To New York?"

"Yes. It'll be you and me, only the two of us. Fuck everybody else. You can go to college. I bet we can find a music program for you."

"No way, I don't have any money, or the grades for a scholarship."

"Then come anyway and find a job. *Please*, Vee. Come with me. Live with me. The place in Brooklyn has two bedrooms. We won't tell anyone, and we'll stretch my allowance until you find work."

"I don't know, I—"

"Let me help you. We'll both get out of here, away from everyone."

I closed my eyes and imagined the life we'd have. The two of us—best friends—against the world. We'd explore New York City, walk across the Brooklyn Bridge, find the best pizza joints in each neighborhood, go there together or on double dates. I could see it, almost taste the freedom a life like that would bring, but then I tumbled back to reality, smashing into the ground when I thought of Grams. Her memory, her physical health would get so much worse over the next months and years. How could I think about going away when she needed me?

"I can't," I said, stifling a sob at the realization I was trapped, sinking, drowning in a situation I hadn't created and had no control over. "I have to…I have to go *home* tomorrow."

My heart exploded into a million pieces. Madison was leaving. No matter what she said, or how often I messaged or called, our lives were going in different directions. She'd move on, make new friends. In no time, I'd become the girl she once knew in high school. I was losing my best friend, my only friend. The one person in this world aside from Grams whom I loved, and there was nothing I could do about it.

9

3 years 5 months before the accident

MADISON ASKED ME to stay at her pool house for another
night. I didn't want to at first, but when I spoke to Grams on
the phone, and she sounded chirpier and more alert than she
had in months, I agreed.

Barry and Lucinda went to a work function, so Madison and
I spent another evening hidden away in the pool house with the
blinds closed and the curtains drawn, watching *Almost Famous*
and *Bohemian Rhapsody*. She left shortly before midnight, and
I fell asleep in the huge bed, wishing I could stay here forever.

A few hours later, my phone vibrated on the bedside table,
pulling me from my dreams. Disorientated, I rubbed my eyes
with one hand as I tried to grab my cell with the other, knocking it onto the floor in my haste. My phone had stopped ringing by the time I located it under the bed, and as I squinted at
the screen, I saw it was 4:00 a.m.

The missed call was from Mom. I presumed she'd drunk
butt-dialed me again, but when I heard the ping of a voice-
mail notification, and I listened to her message, panic coiled
inside my lungs.

"Where are you?" she barked. "Your grandmother's missing. The cops are coming. Get your ass over here, so you can help find her. *Now*."

I practically leaped into my clothes as I dashed around, gathering my things. Part of my brain wanted to delay my return to Rick's house because I was terrified of what had happened, the other part screamed at me to hurry, hurry, *hurry*. I sent Madison a message saying I'd be in touch when I had more news and ran home.

A police cruiser had already arrived and was parked in the road, its blue-and-red lights flashing. Rick's beloved Mustang stood in the driveway, but thankfully he wasn't outside. I presumed he'd either gone to or had stayed in bed, leaving my mother to deal with the crisis.

Sure enough, Mom was on the front steps with two uniformed officers. She wore a pair of microscopic white shorts and a crimson crop-top, her toned legs and midriff on full display. Unsurprisingly she stood near the male officer who had to be closer to my age than hers, looking up at him from underneath her long fake lashes. When she saw me, her face hardened.

"Where have you been?" she said, and without waiting for a reply added, "Officers, this is my daughter, Vienna. She just graduated high school."

"Where's Grams?" I asked.

"That's what we're trying to determine," the older officer replied. Her name tag read Cortez, and there was a gentleness in her eyes I wished I sometimes saw in my mother's.

"We're doing everything we can to find Mrs. Taylor as quickly as possible," the other officer, Rubin according to his name tag, added with a reassuring nod. He turned to Mom. "Mrs. Taylor-Cole—"

"Please, call me Barb," Mom said with a flutter of her eyelashes as she put a hand to her chest. She really couldn't help herself, was probably pissed neither of them had commented on how she must be far too young to have a kid my age.

"Tell me what happened," I said, my voice laden with impatience.

"It seems your grandmother left the house sometime between 9:00 p.m. last night and 3:00 a.m. this morning," Cortez said.

"Didn't you hear her?" I asked Mom. "Did Rick disable her door chime again?"

Mom raised her chin but said nothing, and Rubin spoke instead. "From what we understand, nobody else was home at the time."

"You left Grams alone?" I said. "What were you thinking?"

"How rich coming from you," Mom said. "You're the one who abandoned us."

"I didn't—"

"Where were you? I needed you to look after your grandmother. I can't believe you walked out, and—"

"Walked out?" I said. "Where were *you*? At the bar? You're certainly dressed for it."

"Ladies," Cortez said gently. "Let's focus on finding Mrs. Taylor. Vienna, do you know where she might've gone? Anything you can tell us would be extremely helpful. Maybe there's a place she likes to visit in the area."

"She hates it here," I said. "We came from Falmouth last year and she's not used to it."

"I see," Cortez said. "Let's go over her daily routine."

We spent the next few minutes answering questions about Grams. What she did during the day, her state of mind, her dementia, whether she'd gone missing before, seemingly endless questions about where she could've gone. As I was about to shout at them to hurry up and get a search team together, Cortez's phone rang. She listened for a moment before turning to me and Mom.

"A woman dressed in plaid pajamas and a white John Lennon T-shirt—"

"It's Grams," I said. "I gave her the shirt last Christmas. Is… is she okay?"

Cortez nodded and spoke into the phone again before hanging up. "An early-morning jogger found her near Mt. Sinai Cemetery. He called it in and stayed with Mrs. Taylor until the ambulance arrived. She's been taken to Maine Medical—"

"But you said she's all right," I said.

Rubin jumped in. "I'm sure it's just a precaution."

"We'll go to the hospital now," I said, and after we'd thanked the officers, Mom and I pulled out of the driveway with me behind the wheel.

"This would never have happened if you hadn't left," Mom said, making me bite my tongue so hard, I tasted blood.

Keeping my mouth shut, I decided I wouldn't get into an argument with her about who was responsible because she was partly right. If I'd come back after one night at the pool house, none of this would've happened. I'd never forgive myself if Grams had slipped, broken a bone, or worse. Was she okay? Would we get to the hospital only to be told she'd been hurt after all?

My anxiety didn't lessen until I saw Grams in the bland, fluorescent-lit room at Maine Medical. She was dressed in a hospital gown, propped up in bed, dark circles under her eyes, and a smudge of mascara on her cheeks.

"Grams," I said as I rushed up to her, hugging her gently, spotting the intravenous drip attached to her hand. "Where did you go?"

"Rupert was late coming to get me," she said, patting my arm. "I wanted to surprise him, so I headed to his house, but I couldn't find it."

"You and Dad lived in Falmouth," Mom said. "They tore

the house down years ago and replaced it with condos. I told you already."

"Don't be silly," Grams tutted. "Tore it down? I was there with Rupert yesterday."

From the expression on her face, I could tell Mom's patience was stretched phyllo pastry thin. Thankfully a man wearing a white coat with a purple stethoscope slung around his neck arrived. The guy was around Mom's age, tall, broad-shouldered, and had magnetic, deep brown eyes. Predictably, my mother's entire body language changed in an instant. Shoulders back, stomach in, chest pushed out a little. I looked at my feet.

"Good morning, I'm Dr. Mantero," he said with a Boston lilt, and as he stretched out his arm I saw a tattoo on his wrist, an ECG line with a heart and the words *salud es vida* underneath. "Are you Mrs. Taylor's family?"

"Yes," Mom said, her smile broader. "She's my mother, and this is my daughter. She just graduated from—"

"I'm Vienna," I said, cutting her off.

"Pleased to meet you both," he said, before turning to Grams and asking, "How are you feeling, Mrs. Taylor?"

"Do you know where Rupert is?" she said, wringing the sheets between her hands, eyes darting to the door. "He was late picking me up."

"Let me find out for you," he said, gesturing for Mom and me to follow him into the hall. Once we were outside Grams' room, he interlaced his fingers and rested them against his flat stomach. His expression was kind, patient, full of compassion. I wanted to cry.

"Is she okay?" I asked.

"Physically, Mrs. Taylor will make a full recovery," Dr. Mantero said. "She was a little dehydrated when she first arrived, which is why we administered an intravenous drip to replenish her fluids."

"How long before we can take her home?" Mom asked. The

concern in her voice surprised me until I wondered if she was thinking about the cost of the hospital stay. I couldn't blame her. None of us had any insurance or benefits, and we didn't have spare cash to cover what would surely be ludicrous medical fees. Grams' money from the sale of her house hadn't been much, and it was long gone.

"A few hours," Dr. Mantero said. "I'm concerned about her mental health. She's showing signs of—"

"Dementia," Mom said. "We know. Her family doctor already diagnosed her."

"Is this the first time she's wandered off?" he asked.

"I'm usually at home to look out for her," I said, guilt prickling the back of my throat, reminding me this was my fault. "But I spent the last two nights at a friend's house."

Dr. Mantero smiled. "You're in high school?"

"Just graduated."

"Heading to college?"

Mom jumped in. "She'll be getting a job. Working around here. Vienna will help care for her grandmother, properly this time."

"Respectfully," he said, looking directly at my mother, "taking care of a person with dementia can quickly become a full-time job for more than one person. There are other avenues you should explore. I can put you in touch with—"

"No need, I've already talked to our doctor about assisted living," Mom said, which was news to me. "We'll be discussing things in more detail now."

"Very well," Dr. Mantero said. "I'll come by in a few hours and I expect you'll be able to take Mrs. Taylor home. The nurses will check in a few times before then, just in case. Don't hesitate to ask if you need anything."

"Thank you, Doctor," I said.

He smiled. "You're welcome, Vienna. She'll be fine. Don't worry."

Once he'd walked away, I turned to Mom. "Assisted living? When were you going to tell me about putting Grams into a home?"

"Don't be ridiculous," she replied. "Do you have any idea how much it would cost?" My mother's eyes darted around the hallway, no doubt assessing who was within earshot, but it was still early morning, the place quiet. "I expect you to do your part and help pay for tonight. Like you told the cops, if you hadn't abandoned your grandmother—"

"Don't put this on me. You left her in the house alone."

"I didn't know she could climb out of the window. Christ."

I let out a gasp. "You locked her in? What if there'd been a fire? What if—"

"Enough," Mom said. "Do your part. Ask the ice cream shop for more shifts or find another job. Do you understand?"

What choice did I have? In an instant, more invisible shackles slid around my wrists and clicked into place, making me their prisoner.

10

MADISON LEFT FOR New York in August, a teary good-bye at her house one afternoon while her parents were out. We made promises about sending messages and FaceTiming every day, assurances I clung to and tried to convince myself would stay true. I'd hold up my end of the bargain but knew Madison would soon be busy with coursework and exploring Brooklyn and beyond with her new friends.

"Are you going to replace me in EmVee?" she asked.

"Never," I said. "EmVee is you and me, always will be."

"Good," Madison said, giving me another hug. "Because I'd be pissed."

While our duo was no more, during the early fall I got a few local gigs with some bands who needed a stand-in drummer. It wasn't the same without Madison. I was missing half of our energy, her entire soul and spirit, and everything she poured into our performances.

At one point I thought about starting a new band but didn't have time for practice sessions anyway. As my mother had instructed,

I'd found a second job at a grocery store, and whenever I was on a break, I sat on an upturned milk crate at the back and wrote songs.

Feel you tear yourself away
Never seemed enough for you to stay
Not much left for me to say
Think you're gonna leave me anyway

Was it about me? Madison? Grams? Probably all three. My grandmother was happiest living in the past, Madison had made a break for it to New York for her future, and I felt stuck in my same old present.

The feeling of being suffocated intensified when the astronomical hospital bill for Grams' short stay arrived. Mom demanded I contribute half of my income. Rick took another quarter for utilities.

With so much money gone, I barely saved a dime. I couldn't move out—leaving Grams in my mother's pseudo-care was deterrent enough—but I fantasized about it. Imagined the day I'd scraped enough cash together to get to Brooklyn and be able to support myself until I found work. This tiny nugget of hope kept me going.

Fall turned to early winter. I hoped Madison would come to Portland for Christmas, but her parents had organized a ski trip to Vail, and she wasn't flying back to New York until a couple of days before New Year's Eve.

"There's not much point coming to Portland, Vee," she said, and while I understood her not wanting to spend more time with her parents, her comment still felt as if she'd thrust a blade into my heart.

Christmas was uneventful, as it always had been with my mother, although Grams and I ate a turkey TV dinner and wore silly paper crowns while we drank sherry, which I knew was a festive ritual she'd enjoyed with my grandfather.

I'd also reduced my shifts at the grocery store in anticipation of Madison being home, and had the day after Christmas off, but instead of sleeping in that morning, I went to pick up the newest copy of *US Weekly* for Grams as a belated Christmas gift.

When I got back to the house, Rick and Mom were in the kitchen, the volume of their raised voices making them oblivious to my return. They'd been married eight months and didn't argue often because Mom complied with whatever Rick wanted, so I wondered what their fight was about. I sneaked down the hallway, stopping a few feet from the door, out of sight.

"Find another solution," Rick said. "I'm sick to death of her being here."

Ah, they were talking about me. I rolled my eyes. Rick might've been fed up with my presence, but he was delirious to take my cash. I was about to brush off the words when Mom replied, "She can't have much longer, Rick. Last week the doctor said her heart's not well, you know he gave her more pills, and her dementia's—"

"My uncle had dementia and he lasted a decade," Rick said. "Had someone feeding him every meal at the end. Changing his diapers. I don't want that in my house. It's not what I signed up for."

"What do you want me to do?" Mom said, defiant for the first time in ages, and I almost burst into the room to applaud her. "You agreed to the three of us moving in."

"I didn't know how bad she was," he said. "Not to mention you made her out to have money socked away, which was obviously a lie. Her pension barely covers her food."

"If we put her in a home—"

"*We?* This isn't a *we* situation, Barb. I'm telling you to deal with it."

I stormed into the kitchen, planted my feet, and squared my hips as I stood inside the doorway. "Grams is a human being,"

I said, teeth clenched. "One of the most caring, kindhearted people you'll ever meet."

"Shut up," Rick fired off. "This is none of your business."

"Yes, it is," I shouted. "You don't get to speak about Grams like that, you asshole."

His cheeks flushed, fists clenching and unclenching by his sides. At times I'd felt more than a little afraid of him, but not today. Not with the anger filling my body, heat coursing through my veins, turning my backbone to titanium. I felt superhuman, almost invincible.

He looked at Mom. "You're going to let her talk to me this way?"

"Tell him where to go, Mom," I said. "Stand up to him."

"Enough, Vienna," she said, voice raised. "Stop it."

"You don't need him," I said. "You're better off alone."

"Shut. Your. Mouth." Rick's words were filled with malice and spittle. "Shut it now or I swear I'll do it for you."

"Are you threatening me?" I said, taking a step.

"It's not a threat, *Vienna*," Rick said with a smirk. "Talk to me like that again and I swear it's the last thing you'll do."

I stared at Mom, who remained silent. "You're okay with *him* saying these things to me? Seriously?"

"Go to your room," she said without making eye contact, but I didn't move. "*Now.* Have some respect for your stepfather."

"He's not my stepfather," I yelled, walking out of the kitchen with one middle finger raised over my shoulder. "He'll never be anything but a douchebag to me."

Mom and Rick left a while later, meaning Grams and I had the place to ourselves. We spent the day listening to the Beatles and watching *The Streets of San Francisco* reruns, but I couldn't focus. Rick would be home soon, the animosity levels between us at DEFCON 1. He didn't want me here. I didn't want to be here. We were lions pacing a cage, waiting for the other to pounce.

At some point in the evening, I fell asleep on the living room sofa, waking up at 10:30 p.m. with the TV still on. I pushed myself up, saw I was alone.

"Grams?" I called out, fear rising as I thought about the time she'd slipped out and the jogger had found her near the cemetery. It had been early summer, the temperatures far more clement than the end of December. If she'd wandered off into the night, this time the outcome might be very different.

Jumping up, I rushed past the empty kitchen and straight to her room, my breath slowing when I saw her fast asleep in bed. I checked her daily medication organizer, saw she'd taken the ones I'd popped into the little green plastic square, including a pill to help her sleep. I needed a good night's rest myself, so I shut off the TV, brushed my teeth, and went to bed.

As I lay in the darkness, I knew we couldn't keep living like this. I didn't doubt Rick's earlier threat of hurting me was real, not when he'd already hit me once before. In one way I almost wanted him to thump me again, and if he did, this time I'd press charges.

A possible and dangerous scenario sped through my brain—me provoking him, him smashing his fist into my face. How much time might he get for assault? Would it be any? Rick often mentioned he had friends on the force, joked about one of them letting him off with a warning when he got caught speeding in his Mustang. What if his police buddies gave him a smack on the wrist for beating me, and dropped the case? How could I ever get Grams out of this house and take care of her? It felt impossible, insurmountable. Hopeless.

Sleep finally found me, and I didn't wake again until nine. I got out of bed, stretched, and threw on a pair of jeans and an old Animal from *The Muppets* T-shirt. Grams would be hungry, no doubt hoping for a boiled egg on toast with a generous ketchup smiley face on top, which she'd always made for me when I was a kid.

Opening my bedroom door, I listened to see if anyone was up. Maybe—hopefully—Rick had gone out because all was quiet, the two other bedroom doors shut tight. I crept to the kitchen, made a pot of coffee, toast and two six-minute eggs, just the way my grandmother liked them, and grabbed the ketchup from the fridge.

With everything placed neatly on a daffodil-patterned plastic tray, I tiptoed to Grams' room, cursing when the door chime didn't sound again. Balancing the tray on one hand, I pushed open the door, expecting to see my grandmother sitting in her chair, reading the copy of *US Weekly* I'd gifted her. Except she wasn't awake, but lay stretched out in bed on her back, the room dim as the curtains were still drawn.

Forcing joviality and sprightliness into my voice, no matter how gloomy I felt on the inside, I said, "Rise and shine, Grams. I have breakfast."

When she didn't answer, unease prickled my neck as a sharp chill snaked its way up my back. Nudging Grams' box of costume jewelry out of the way, I set the food on the dresser and slowly walked across the room. "Grams? Are you awake?"

I reached for the curtains and opened them up, sending light streaming in. As I turned to wake my grandmother, I let out a scream. Her mouth and eyes were wide open, her gaze empty and blank.

"Grams?" I said, reaching for her wrist. "Can you hear me? Wake up. *Please.*"

When she didn't respond, I sank to the floor with a soft moan because I knew she was gone. My knees hit the carpet with a thud as I wrapped my arms over Grams' torso, and I put my head on her soft belly, unable to speak, unable to do anything but sob.

I'd lost Madison to Brooklyn, and now the only person in my family whom I loved had left me, too. It was too much to take in, impossible to accept, and I didn't think I'd withstand the searing pain tearing me in half. I buried my head in the blankets, and, when the tears finally stopped, kissed Grams on the cheek before I called her family doctor on his cell phone to ask what I should do next, grateful when he said he'd come right over.

"Safe travels, I love you," I whispered to Grams, knowing I had to go find my mother.

She sat in the kitchen with Rick, both of them happily munching their way through plates stacked high with pancakes, bacon, and eggs, their cups filled with steaming coffee.

Neither of them had bothered checking on Grams, hadn't stuck their head through the doorway to see why she wasn't up, or why I'd screamed a little earlier. Rick not giving a crap was no surprise, but my mother's coldness, her disinterest, sliced my already festering wounds.

"Grams passed away," I said. "The doctor's coming. He'll help us take care of things."

Mom frowned. "What did you say?"

"Grams is dead."

She didn't move, then slammed her cup on the table, spilling half of its contents over the yellow Formica before pushing back her chair and running from the kitchen. A moment later we heard a yell followed by a few teary cries. Frankly, it was more than I thought her capable of.

Rick didn't get up, but continued to shovel food into his mouth, mopping up sweet-smelling maple syrup with a piece of pancake before licking his fingers, and I thought I saw a smirk cross his face.

I understood how he didn't care for my grandmother, but he seemed...*relieved*. I hadn't heard them come home last night, hadn't heard the chimes above Grams' room ring but I'd been so exhausted, a freight train couldn't have woken me.

I watched as he reached for more food. When he—the man

who hated music—started to whistle, I took a step closer, a million thoughts racing through my head. All of them bad.

"Did you hurt her?" I said.

"Huh?" Rick froze, full mouth agape.

"Did you hurt my grandmother?"

He narrowed his eyes. "The hell…? Watch what you're saying."

"Why? Are you worried I'll tell the cops how you said you wanted Grams out of here just yesterday?"

"I never—"

"I heard you talking to Mom. What do you think they'll make of that?"

Rick bit into his pancake. "Your grandmother was old."

"She was *fine*."

"Bullshit. She was not *fine*. She had heart problems and advanced dementia."

"I'm telling the cops you—"

"Tell them what?" he said. "You were here with her all of last night. Alone."

"But, I—"

"Maybe *you* hurt her. Got sick of caring for her." He shrugged. "It happens. I won't tell."

I couldn't take any more. Not a single insult. Lunging forward, I closed my fist and swung hard at his face. Something cracked beneath my knuckles—his bones or mine, I wasn't sure—and he let out a howl.

Jumping up, he covered the left side of his jaw with his hand and moved in, teeth clenched. I stepped back, was about to hold my arms in front of my face because I knew a blow was coming, but as I squeezed my eyes shut, Mom burst into the kitchen. She grabbed Rick's raised arm, pulling him away from me.

"Don't touch her," she said.

"You're defending the little bitch?" he shouted. "She punched me."

As he took another step in my direction, Mom held firm. "I

have to call the police about my mother," she said. "You can tell them Vienna attacked you."

He shook her off. "Ha. You want me to admit I got smacked by a girl? No, thanks. I'm taking care of this my way."

"Stop," Mom insisted. "She's not worth you getting into trouble, which you will if you lay a hand on her right now, and you know it."

Rick let his fists drop to his sides as his eyes bulged so hard, I thought they might pop out of his skull and roll across the floor. "Get out," he said. "Leave my house and don't come back."

Mom nodded at the door. "You heard him."

My body must've turned on its autopilot because I found myself backing out of the kitchen and going to my room, turning all of my other senses down until I didn't register them anymore. As I thrust my belongings into my backpack and a duffel bag, I called the only person who could help.

"Hey," Madison said when she picked up. "How are you?"

The connection from my mouth to my brain seemed to be malfunctioning, because I only managed a, "I… I'm…"

"What's wrong? What happened?"

"Grams…sh-she passed away."

"Oh, Vee. How are you? Where are you? What can I do?"

"Rick threw me out of the house."

"What? Why?"

"I accused him of having something to do with Grams… dying."

Madison drew a sharp breath. "You think he hurt her?"

"I don't know. He seemed so happy she was gone. I couldn't take it."

"We know the guy's a dick, Vee, but murder? I mean, the cops will definitely spot that. Is that why he's throwing you out, because you accused him?"

"Yeah, and I punched him."

Madison let out a laugh. "Obviously it's not funny given the circumstances, but good for you. He's had it coming since you got there. What are you going to do now? Where will you go?"

Sinking onto my bed I muttered, "I've no idea."

"I do," she said, her voice determined. "I'll Venmo money to you now. Buy a bus ticket to New York. Whatever you can get."

"But you're in Vail."

"Not much longer. A storm's coming so we changed our schedule and we're flying back today. I'll probably get home before you arrive."

"What about your parents?"

"They're going to check on the new house in the Hamptons. They want me to go but I'll talk my way out of it. Please, Vee, come to Brooklyn."

"I can't leave everything behind."

"Leave what, exactly?" Madison said, sounding exasperated. "Two jobs you loathe, a crap mother, and a guy you say may have hurt your grams? Why stay? What for?"

"What about the funeral?"

"Oh, Vienna, she's gone," Madison said quietly. "She wouldn't want you to stay."

"My drums. I can't leave them. I—"

"I'll buy you another kit."

"But—"

"Listen to me. Don't be scared. I'm here for you. Please, please, come to Brooklyn. I'm terrified bad stuff will happen to you if you don't. *Please.* I could do with the company. My exam results were so awful, I lied to my parents about them. Maybe you being here will help me, too. It's New Year's Eve in a few days. It'll be a fresh start for both of us."

I didn't need more convincing. Fifteen minutes later I'd packed my things, but I waited another five in my room until the doctor came. I didn't say anything about Rick after the cops arrived, too. All I wanted was to get out of here as the house swirled with emergency personnel, curious neighbors, and a few of Mom's friends. Watching her pretend to everyone how she was grief-stricken made me want to punch something.

Finally, after kissing Grams on the cheek for what would be the very last time, I slipped out of the house without saying goodbye. Madison was right. It was time for a fresh start, and the upcoming year promised so much more. A new life. A brand-new *me*. In Brooklyn.

11

The day of the accident

BY THE TIME the cabin comes back into view, the last of the light has almost faded. Darkness makes the place more ominous, as if a snow-covered giant is rising from the shadowy woods, ready to consume us whole. I'm shivering, but can't tell if it's from fear, shock, or the cold. Probably a mixture of all three.

I urge our group to keep going, one more step, and then another. As we move up the stairs and onto the cabin's rickety porch, I hope our collective weight won't send us crashing through it. Nobody else can get hurt. We need to survive the night and get help as soon as possible come morning.

The muscles in my arms scream with relief as we finally lower Evelina to the ground, and when I straighten up again, a gush of cold sweat rushes down my back. As Madison had said, the front door is open now, hanging lopsided like a gaping mouth as it rests on one hinge. She pushes it in all the way, and we pick up the stretcher again, tilting it a little to one side so we can fit through the entrance and into the hall.

The cabin's dark. It smells like a million years of dust and ne-

glect, but I'm grateful to get out of the storm and biting winds.
We move through the hall and Libby leads us to an opening
on the right, into what appears to be the main living room.

As my eyes adjust to the dimness, I see the room spans the
length of the house. A quarter of the windows in the space are
broken, letting in the cold. The cabin has sat abandoned for
more than a while considering the state of the place.

A few pieces of furniture were left here, including two
threadbare armchairs which might've been burgundy once,
but are now sunset pink, placed in front of an empty gray stone
fireplace that goes halfway up the wood-paneled walls. We set
Evelina on the floor, and once we're done, exhaustion takes
over, making me unsure of what to do next.

I spot the remnants of a kitchen at the back of the room.
Upper and lower Shaker-style cabinets, empty spaces where a
sink, fridge, and oven might have been. A few of the floorboards on the right-hand side are rotten, and when I look up I
see water damage and a broken board in the ceiling.

"Be careful over there," I say, pointing. "The floor's rotting through."

"Maybe this was a hunting cabin," Libby says, looking around
as she slumps into one of the armchairs, rubbing at her temples.

"What's going on?" I say when I notice how the color has
drained from her skin. My head's still throbbing, too, but not
nearly as much as before. "Is your headache worse?"

"A little," she says.

"Madison, did you bring those painkillers?" I ask.

"Shouldn't we save them for Evelina?" Libby says, but Madison's already retrieving the meds, shakes two pills into her palm
and passes them over with a water bottle.

"Take these," Madison orders. "We need you as fit as possible as soon as possible."

Libby gives in. "Thanks. I must admit it's got pretty bad."

"Probably from all the stress and exertion," I say. "Sit and rest. Hopefully you'll feel better soon."

"I'm going to see what else is in here," Madison says, pulling out her phone and muttering a few cuss words. "Still no connection, and my battery's getting low. How about anyone else?"

None of us can connect, and as Madison disappears from the room to explore, Gabi starts to cry. She collapses into the other faded red chair, a plume of dust shooting in all directions. I kneel next to her, hold her tight as she sobs, rocking her gently as if consoling a child.

She's the youngest of us all, barely twenty, and while I'm not much older, the Bittersweet is my band, my family. Although I tell myself it's irrational, and we're here because of an accident, I feel I've let them down. We got lost. We've been unable to find help after the crash. If I'd driven, maybe none of this would've happened.

"What are we going to do?" Gabi says, interrupting my thoughts.

"We'll get help once the storm stops."

"What if it lasts for days?" she asks. "We've barely got any food or water. And—"

"It's going to be all right," Libby whispers, kneeling on the other side of the chair. "First, we'll make a fire, here, in this room. We can melt snow in our water bottles if we put them near the flames. Not too close as they're plastic, but hopefully that way there'll be plenty to drink."

"We'll huddle in here and conserve the power on our phones as much as possible," I add, but given Gabi's expression, she's not reassured. "I think they said the storm would be done by tomorrow morning."

"What if it's too late for…?" she says, before covering her mouth with one hand, as if she's trying to push the words back into her throat, lest they become a self-fulfilling prophecy.

"We'll get through this," I reassure her. "We will."

"Vienna?" Madison's standing in the doorway. "Can you help me?"

I get up, follow her into the hall. On one side there's a bathroom with a stain-speckled toilet, and a built-in tub that has a few tiles missing on the front.

Backing out, I see another room on my left, and a narrow door to my right. I open the door, spot stairs leading to what must be a basement. It smells of wet dog, and the darkness emanating from below feels strange and creepy. I'm not ready to venture down there so I close the door again and keep going.

"Over here," Madison says, her voice impatient.

She's standing in what must've been another bedroom, empty now save for a single bed pushed up against the wall with an old, discolored mattress from which a spring has popped like a decapitated jack-in-the-box. The floor's bare, the rosebud wallpaper hanging off in random strips.

Madison takes a step and leans in. "What were you three talking about in there?" she asks in a sharp whisper, her hot breath tickling my hair, making me want to move away, but she grabs my arm, pulls me closer.

"Gabi was upset," I say, keeping my voice low. "We were trying to comfort her."

"Did you tell them what I said earlier? About not going back for them?"

"No, of course not."

"Good." She lets me go. "I didn't mean it."

"It's fine. Already forgotten."

Not true at all, in fact I can't shake her words or how she said them, but I try to convince myself we all react differently under pressure and dire circumstances. I remind myself of stories about drowning people who push their saviors underwater in a desperate bid to survive. That's what Madison's comment was, nothing more. Nobody got hurt. Still, a lingering feeling of disquiet settles in my bones. I'm finding it impossible to make it go away.

Madison gestures to the bed. "We can put Evelina in here."

"It's probably better if we move the mattress into the main room," I counter. "We'll be together, and it'll be more comfortable for her, especially when we get a fire going."

Madison doesn't argue and when we heave the mattress from the frame, we find an old camping light under the bed. I'm not hopeful when I turn the knob, but it's still working—barely—the batteries must be running low but it's more than we had a moment ago.

We grab the mattress and slide it down the hall. Gabi jumps up but Libby's slower, wobbly on her feet. I make her sit on the floor as the rest of us move the armchairs out of the way, making enough space to lay down Evelina's new bed.

Once we're happy the spot's a good distance from the still empty fireplace, we get Evelina settled, adding layers of clothing from our bags to keep her warm, being mindful of her injured arm. I put the lamp on the side; it's not doing much but at least we can see a little better now, and I don't feel quite as scared.

We sit down, our collective adrenaline levels ebbing. I'm exhausted and grateful to rest for a while as we decide how to best conserve the power on our phones. We'll use our flashlight apps one person at a time, and only when strictly necessary. As we're deciding this, an alert dings on Evelina's phone, which Gabi pulls from her own pocket.

"Do you have service?" I ask.

Her eyes widen as she mutters under her breath, but she doesn't answer me. She picks up Evelina's backpack and pulls out the contents. Clothes, a makeup bag, hairbrush, deodorant—things go flying. As I'm about to ask what she needs, and if I can help, Gabi gasps.

"Shit," she says. "Shit, shit, *shit*. Guys, I have to go back to the truck."

12

2 years 11 months before the accident

OWNER OF BURNING FALMOUTH CAR LOCATED

by Eleanor Willis of the *Maine Daily*

At 8:36 a.m. on Sunday morning, police and fire services responded to a report of a burning vehicle on Blackstrap Road in Falmouth. After the blaze was extinguished, emergency crews confirmed the vehicle had been empty. No injuries were sustained managing the incident.

According to a police report, the beyond repair black 1970 Ford Mustang was reported stolen by its owner Richard Cole, from Portland, late Saturday night. Cole hadn't noticed his vehicle was missing from his driveway in North Deering, as he and his wife, Barbara Taylor-Cole, were dealing with a death in the family.

"My mother-in-law passed suddenly in the morning, and with the stress and how shocked we are, I didn't see my Mustang was gone," Cole said, adding he assumed his stepdaughter had taken the car and gone for a drive because she'd lost her beloved grandmother and needed time alone. When she didn't come home or answer her cell phone, he notified the police. "Now we know why," Cole said. "She torched it. She's an angry person."

When the authorities informed Cole that his destroyed Mustang had been located, he said they didn't appear interested in what he thought had happened to his vehicle. As to why his stepdaughter allegedly may have committed arson, Cole said he doesn't understand, adding, "She knows how much love went into the restoration of my Mustang."

"It's not what you expect from your closest family," Taylor-Cole said when speaking about her daughter. "Rick and I have been nothing but good to her."

When asked if she was concerned for her daughter's well-being and would report her missing, Taylor-Cole replied, "She's an adult. And she's not missing. She took off after setting Rick's car on fire."

Portland Police Officer Amelia Cortez declined to comment on the case but says it's a good time to remind everyone there's been a steep increase in car thefts already this winter. She recommends people stay vigilant at all times, adding, "Don't put your keys near your front door, or leave your vehicle unattended when the engine's running, as it gives thieves an easy target."

Recovering stolen cars is often difficult as they routinely have their GPS tracking devices disarmed immediately or removed entirely before the vehicles are taken to shipping containers in various cities along the East Coast and into Canada, destined for profitable sales overseas.

Comments (12—showing most recent)

@jenjen_99 Fords suck. Burn them all.

@maplesyrup_12 How can he accuse his stepdaughter of arson when there's no proof of anything? I hope she's okay!

@kitty_paws11 And why is the paper quoting him on it?

@maplesyrup_12 Nobody believes in "innocent until proven guilty" anymore

@juicy_froot16 Who says she's innocent? No smoke without fire!

@maplesyrup_12 Congrats! You proved my point.

13

2 years 11 months before the accident

NEW YORK WAS a revelation. Like so many others, I'd only seen the city in movies and photographs, none of which did the place any justice. Long before I arrived at the Port Authority Bus Terminal, I'd fallen in love with the skyscrapers, the hustle and bustle, the sheer amount of people going about their day.

This place smelled of opportunity, of escape. Somewhere invisibility and anonymity were offered unconditionally, and in which I could envelop myself like a cocoon until I was ready to reemerge, reinvented and reborn.

As I stepped off the bus, I saw Madison in the crowd, waving at me, her gorgeous red hair shorter than I remembered. It had only been a little over four months since she'd left Portland, but it may as well have been years. I rushed over, threw my arms around her, and hugged her tight. I'd made the right decision to come. The city would be the answer to all my dreams, all my desires. Here, I had a future.

"God, I've missed you," Madison said, hugging me again as her face turned serious. "I'm so sorry about your grams. I know it's a ludicrous question, but how are you feeling?"

I looked down, cheeks flushing. "Guilty."

"Because you're not there for the funeral? We'll send flowers, and before you say anything, I'll pay. The next time we go back to Portland—"

"I'm never going back. Never, ever."

Madison gave me a single, solemn nod. "Then let's get you home."

Home. The word filled me with relief. As much as I'd miss Grams and my heart ached for her, she was free now, no longer suffering. Neither of us were. I'd meant what I'd said—I'd never return to Portland, and as the bus had made its way from Maine to New York, I'd pushed the images of the city, Mom, and Rick away, confining them to the forgotten depths of my mind.

Was it strange to be elated about never seeing my relatives again? Perhaps to those who had normal familial relationships, whatever those were. The saying *blood runs thicker than water* had never applied to me. Madison was my family now and I focused on the present.

I'd expected us to take the subway to Williamsburg, the Brooklyn neighborhood where Madison's apartment was—where I now lived—but she called an Uber.

The ride took forever with the traffic creeping more slowly than an aging caterpillar, but I didn't mind spending most of the time with my face pressed against the cool window, jabbering on about the architecture and counting the abundance of iconic yellow taxis. New York seemed to have a soul, a pulse, a life of its own. I could hardly believe I was about to become a part of it.

"Will we go over the Brooklyn Bridge?" I asked, fully aware of how excited I sounded, but unable to rein myself in.

"The Midtown Tunnel's faster," Madison said. "Don't worry, we'll walk across the bridge on the weekend. Let's go to Jane's Carousel as well. It's neat. I'll take you everywhere. We'll pretend we're tourists."

"I *am* a tourist."

"No, you're not," she tutted. "You're a Brooklynite now."

Her enthusiasm stoked more of mine until I remembered I had the grand sum of ninety-two dollars and sixty-three cents in my pocket, some of which I'd lifted from my mother's purse. I had no regrets taking her money, not a single one—other than the fact there hadn't been more bills in her wallet.

"I need to find a job," I said.

Madison waved a hand. "All in good time."

"But—"

"Relax, you got here half an hour ago. Take a few days to settle in."

This was one of the only things that had ever annoyed me about Madison. Our concepts about money were vastly differ- ent. When she said she had none, she meant her account had dipped below a few grand, not a hundred bucks, and her par- ents were somehow always willing to shovel cash her way, no matter what they fought over.

"I'm broke," I whispered. "Flat out *broke*."

"It'll be fine. We need to celebrate your arrival. Let's go out tonight." She raised a hand before I could butt in to say I couldn't afford to party. "I'll introduce you to a few people. One of my friends, Guy, manages an Italian restaurant near the apartment. He needs staff. Oh, before I forget." She stuck a hand in her bag and pulled out a small envelope, lowering her voice. "Fake ID to get into the clubs."

I couldn't afford that either, but still took the ID. "Viola Smith," I said with a chuckle. "Did you know she was—"

"One of America's first professional female drummers?" Madison winked at me. "Thought you'd get a kick out of it."

Over the next four months, I spent most of my time work- ing at a restaurant called Papa e Ragazzi. As promised, Madison had introduced me to the manager, Guy, the night I'd arrived in Brooklyn, and I'd started my first shift two days later.

The Italian hot spot served the best pizza Napoletana, caponata, and zeppole I'd ever tasted, and the place was always packed with tourists and locals alike, meaning Guy happily added more shifts to my schedule whenever they became available.

By the time I got home and during my days off, I was usually too exhausted to join Madison and her wealthy friends for another night out. Her lifestyle was far too expensive for me anyway. I'd expected Brooklyn to be pricey, but if I tried to keep up with Madison, I'd barely have money for food let alone the bit of rent I insisted on giving her.

It hadn't taken me long to work out why she'd bombed in her exams at the end of the previous semester, not with the amount of partying she did. I'd lost count of the number of times she'd woken up late for class or had missed one entirely, on occasion emerging from her room with a dude in tow, none of whom were ever around long enough for me to remember their name.

Still, living with Madison was awesome. I loved our cozy apartment with its wide-plank ash flooring, eggshell paint, exposed brick feature-wall in the kitchen, and the fire escape off my room, which I could sit on now it was April, and the temperatures were on the rise.

My mother had sent a few nasty messages since my abrupt departure, which I'd ignored, and the only thing I missed from Portland was Grams. I thought about her every day, felt a lump in my throat whenever a tune by the Beatles played on Papa e Ragazzi's sound system. A few weeks prior, as I'd walked home from work one afternoon, I'd found a cheap frame in a thrift shop and put a photo of Grams inside. It was the only sentimental item I'd brought with me.

I wished I'd been able to bring my drum kit to Brooklyn. After four months, the impulse to play was so strong, I constantly tapped my feet, banged out rhythms on my thighs with my fingers or on the kitchen countertop using pencils.

I hadn't yet mentioned Madison's comment about buying me a new set. All her money came from her parents, and while I didn't care for them, the request still felt unreasonable. It was an offer she'd probably made without thinking and had since forgotten.

It gave me another reason to stay home, squirreling away as much of my salary and tips as possible so I could afford a secondhand kit soon. I'd planned it all out, had already struck a deal with the doorman, an older gentleman from Lyon named Raphaël, who sported a d'Artagnan mustache and loved the French band Les Rita Mitsouko more than anything.

"You play the drums?" he'd said in his thick accent when we'd struck up a conversation about music while I'd waited for an Uber. "An excellent choice."

"I'm hoping to get a kit soon," I said. "Once I've saved enough money."

"Oof, I don't think Madame Graff in 3B will appreciate the noise."

I pulled a face. "I hadn't thought of that. Crap. Where will I practice?"

"Maybe I can help," he said, lowering his voice. "There's a half-empty storage room downstairs. Not big, but it has a lock."

"You'd let me use it?" I searched his face for the real reason behind his generosity. "Why?"

"Why not? Until someone says they need it, it'll be yours. Music should be encouraged. I wish I'd learned to play an instrument."

"Maybe I can teach you?"

He smiled. "Maybe for my granddaughter? She's twelve."

I wished Madison showed as much interest because it seemed she had little desire to resurrect EmVee. Whenever I raised the subject, she said she didn't have time, and while she hummed along when I shared my songs-in-progress with her, she didn't offer to work on them with me. Her guitar sat untouched in her room, gathering a layer of dust. She was in a rut.

Vowing I'd reignite her passion for our music, I splurged on tickets for Fleur de Lizzie, a popular local band who were playing in Brooklyn Heights on Friday night. I knew Madison liked their stuff because she had them on almost all her playlists.

"Remember I have a surprise for you this evening," I said when she left for class on the day of the concert. "It's in Brooklyn, but you need to be back by eight."

"I will," she said. "I'm excited. Will you give me a clue?"

"Nope," I answered with a grin. "You'll have to wait and see."

I spent the day at work, grateful Guy was an easygoing boss who'd given me the night off when I offered to work double time on Saturday and Sunday. When my shift ended at six, I pulled out my phone, saw Madison had sent a bunch of messages, most of them in the last five minutes.

Are you at work?

Can you talk?

Really need to talk

Call me. Urgent!!!

Vienna????!!!

I zipped up my jacket and waved goodbye to Guy before slipping out of the restaurant's back door as I dialed Madison's number. "What's up?" I said. "I hope you're not bailing on me."

"Where are you?" she said.

"Just left the restaurant. What's going on? You sound like you're having a panic attack."

"I *am*. My parents are in town."

"What? Here? *Now?*"

"Mom called half an hour ago. Said it was a surprise trip."

"More like they're checking up on you."

"Exactly. They're meeting me on campus after I fibbed about having a late lecture. I've stalled them, but I need you to go home and hide your stuff."

I let out a long breath. "Or…we tell them I'm living with you. Maybe they—"

"No chance," she said. "Who do you think they'll blame for my low grades?"

"Not fair, I—"

"Who said anything about fair? You know how they are. I'll suggest we go for dinner around here, but I know they want to see the apartment and Mom mentioned using the spare bedroom tonight."

"Seriously? How long are they here for?"

"One night, I think."

"Where will I sleep?"

"Can you get a hotel room?"

When I was close to what I needed for a drum kit and had spent a small fortune on concert tickets? Not likely. "I'll figure it out. Message me when I can come back."

"I'm really sorry, Vee. I know you had plans for us. I'll make it up to you, I swear."

After we hung up, I raced back to the apartment, my body turning into a whirlwind as I dashed from room to room, erasing any signs of my living there, pulling off my jacket and dumping it on the kitchen chair midway as I was boiling from all the running around.

My shoes and other clothes went into Madison's closet, tucked at the back. I blitzed through the bathroom, removing my toothbrush, makeup, and toiletries, and scanned the apartment for anything I may have forgotten. As I was in the hallway, dumping a bag of trash into the chute to dispose of any remaining evidence that two people lived in the apartment, I heard people coming up the stairs.

"How could Raphaël have been mistaken? He seems intelligent enough." Lucinda—there was no mistaking her distinctive, nasal voice or how she always sounded as if she disapproved of whatever, or whomever, she was talking about. Clearly Madison's plan of trying to get them to a restaurant closer to college hadn't worked.

"No clue," Madison said. "I told you, I invite friends over sometimes."

"We spoke about this," Barry chimed in, sounding irritated, which was his default mode. "You're in Brooklyn to study, not party."

"They're study buddies, Dad, don't worry."

I thought about heading up the stairwell and waiting until they'd gone into the apartment, but my jacket containing my phone, wallet, and keys was still in the kitchen. After dithering for a few precious seconds, I sped down the hall and made it through the apartment door moments before Barry, Lucinda, and Madison rounded the corner.

Without any time to waste, I grabbed my jacket and darted to what now really did seem like a spare room, devoid of any of the personal touches I'd made in the last four months. I slid the window open as quietly as I could, and climbed down the fire escape, feeling like a criminal.

Once on firm ground below, I decided I'd make my way to the concert, then find a cheap place to sleep. I put my hand in my pocket, expecting to feel my things, and swore out loud when I came up empty. Madison's jacket had been in the kitchen, too. I'd borrowed her coat so often she'd come home with the exact same one for me a few weeks ago, and in my rush to not get caught by the Pierces, I'd snatched hers by mistake.

This was a disaster. I couldn't return to the apartment. I couldn't get in if they left because I didn't have my keys and climbing up the fire escape while they were there wasn't an option. I'd never be able to swap coats unnoticed.

When the skies opened a short while later, dumping a deluge of frigid water on top of my head, I let out another colorful string of expletives. I didn't have many choices, so I walked back to the restaurant, not knowing what else to do unless I was prepared to spend a night on the street.

"Forget something?" Guy said as soon as I arrived, ushering me into the kitchen where he gave me a clean dish towel to dry my sopping hair. "What's up?"

"Long story," I said, and when he raised an eyebrow I added, "Madison's parents don't know I'm staying with her and they showed up tonight, unannounced."

"Are you serious?"

"Yup. I had to leave before they saw me."

"Wow, that sucks. If you need a place to stay, I have a sofa."

I was grateful he took instant pity on me, but felt terrible I wasn't there to support Madison when I messaged her using Guy's phone and she said her parents were losing it about her falling grades. Then again, she had a point—they'd blame me and make her life hell.

A few hours later, as I curled up on Guy's two-seater with a chenille blanket that smelled of lavender, reminding me of Grams' shampoo, I vowed I'd never be this vulnerable in my life again. I loved living with Madison, but I needed to be in a position where I could support myself. If I had to take more shifts or somehow fit in another job, I'd do it, except that meant my plan to make music a priority would have to wait a while longer.

The next afternoon, Madison came to the restaurant to bring me my phone, wallet, and a change of clothes. I asked Guy if

I could take a break, and when he agreed, Madison followed me to the rear exit, where we stood under a tiny ruby awning.

The temperatures had dropped overnight, and with the cloudy skies and wispy drizzle, it felt more reminiscent of early March than late April. A miserable day matching my equally miserable mood.

"I'm sorry, Vee," Madison said. "Really. It shouldn't have happened."

"It's okay. I already told you Guy let me sleep on his sofa."

"That's good of him."

"Yeah. Did your parents leave?"

She let out a long sigh. "Thankfully. I came as soon as I could."

"Was it awful?"

"Well, they bought me dinner, during which they read me the riot act." She pulled a face. "Basically, if I don't make it through the year they'll reconsider paying for my education, and the apartment. I'm not sure I believe them, but calling their bluff isn't the smartest idea. I need to study. I have a big assignment due Monday."

"Do you know why they came to town? Did Raphaël tell them I'm staying with you?"

"Not intentionally," Madison said. "You know how awesome he is, it's like we're his daughters. No, Dad called him to ask how I was—and this is a direct quote—*behaving*."

"Seriously?"

"Yup. Raphaël said I was doing great but mentioned a roommate. Of course, Dad asked him to describe said roommate, and she sounded exactly like you."

"They drove all this way to see if I was living with you?"

"Not exactly. Mom and Dad have a meeting with the decorators in the Hamptons today, so they made an impromptu pit stop."

"Holy hell, how sneaky."

"Tell me about it. They grilled me for ages, asked if you were living here, so I lied my ass off, insisted I have a friend who looks like you and often comes around. Thank goodness Raphaël has a few days off and the new guy doesn't know you yet."

"Did they buy your story?"

"I think so. I mean, the apartment had no trace of you, so they had to."

"But what now? If they ask Raphaël—"

"I took care of it."

"How?"

Madison smiled slowly. "Gave him another Easter bonus. Apparently, his overbearing parents are why he came to New York when he was eighteen. If anybody asks, he'll say I live like a nun, which I will, starting tomorrow. I'm going out tonight."

"Didn't you say you have an assignment due?"

Madison rolled her eyes. "Jeez, Mom, I thought you left town."

"But if you don't pass the year—"

Madison held up a hand, cutting me off. "It's fine. See you later."

The sharpness in her voice made her sound exactly like her father. While I was grateful she'd lied to her parents to protect me—and herself—deceit came so naturally to her. As she walked away, I wondered if she'd ever lied to me, and, if so, what about.

14

The day of the accident

"WHY DO YOU have to go back?" I ask Gabi, who's still crouched on the floor, going through Evelina's bag again. She doesn't answer as she turns it upside down and gives it another shake. A strawberry lip balm rolls across the floor, but Gabi ignores it, grabs another backpack, pulls out a toiletries case and unzips it before throwing it to the side, her movements frantic.

I walk over, put my hands over hers and she jumps, almost as if she's forgotten there are other people in the room. "Tell us what you're searching for so we can help."

"Evelina's insulin."

"Insulin?" Libby says. "Does Evelina have—"

"Diabetes," Gabi snaps. "Type one. She got diagnosed two months ago."

"That's rough," I say. "We had no idea."

"It's not as if she feels the need to announce it to everyone." The irritation ebbs a little from her voice. "The monitor on her phone says her blood sugar's really high. Can you help me find her insulin kit? It's a black-and-white polka-dot case the size of a small book."

"Doesn't she have one of those pumps?" Libby asks.

"No, they're expensive and we don't have insurance," Gabi says as she rubs a hand over her face. "I don't understand why she's spiking. She hasn't eaten anything."

"Maybe because of the accident?" I offer, but I really have no clue. The fact none of us has any kind of medical background reminds me of how alone and helpless we are, out here in the middle of the Catskills, who knows how far away from the nearest neighbor.

We spend the next few minutes examining each bag and Gabi insists on searching them once more. The result is the same—Evelina's insulin isn't here.

"Can we get it in the morning?" I ask, but before I've finished my sentence, Gabi's already shaking her head.

"No, she needs it now and—" she points to the window "—it's snowing harder than before, so finding the kit will already be more difficult. What if it freezes? I can't inject ice cubes into my sister."

"Do you have any idea where the pouch is?" Madison asks.

"No," Gabi says. "It must've fallen out as I was going through her stuff at the crash site. I can't believe I was so careless. I'm going back now."

"I'll come with you," Libby says, getting up, but she immediately grabs the back of the armchair to steady herself before slowly sinking to the floor again. "Whoa, I'm so dizzy I think I'm going to pass out."

"Stay here," Gabi says.

Libby starts to protest, and I cut her off. "Gabi's right," I say. "There's no sense in you going if you faint on the way. It'll put more of us in danger, and we can't risk it."

"You're right," Libby mumbles. "I don't think I can make it there and back. Gabi, I'll watch over Evelina in case she wakes up, tell her you're on your way if she notices you're gone."

"One of us should go with you," I tell Gabi, but she's already pulling out her phone, and switches on the flashlight app.

"It's not far and I know what I'm looking for." She gestures to Madison and me. "Can you two start a fire? Otherwise, we'll all be in trouble. It's freezing and it'll only get worse."

Madison jumps up. "There's got to be something around here we can burn. The whole place is made of wood. Come on, Vienna, let's see what we can find."

"I still don't think you should go alone, Gabi," I insist. "If you get lost—"

"I won't, and we need a fire." She holds out her hands. "Give me your scarves, I'll tie them around some trees so I can find my way back more easily." When Madison and I hesitate, she throws her hands in the air. "Come on. The longer you wait the thicker the snow and the darker and colder it's getting. Evelina needs her insulin. We all need a fire. Stop arguing and let's move."

This is a new side to Gabi. She's usually the quiet one, happy to follow Evelina's lead. Now, she's on a mission and it's clear she'll do anything to keep her sister safe, meaning whoever stands in her way had better move or risk being pulverized.

Without another word she loops the scarves we hand her around her neck, zips up her jacket, and heads for the front door, disappearing into the night. I'm uneasy about Gabi going alone, but she's right, it's so cold I can barely feel my fingertips despite my gloves. I notice Libby, who's lying on the floor behind one of the armchairs and closer to the doorway, curled into a ball, her eyes closed.

"Libby?" I say, tapping her shoulder. "Libby, wake up."

When she doesn't move, I suddenly remember in elementary school after I fell playing tag and hit my head on the metal climbing frame, the nurse said I might have a concussion. Libby hasn't vomited and she didn't mention blacking out after the accident, both of which can be signs of a head injury, but I can't be sure and asking might not be the best approach.

I don't want her to worry, but I'm now freaking out because I gave her two painkillers at the crash site and Madison handed her another two when we arrived at the cabin. Is acetaminophen okay if you have a concussion? Have I made her worse? I start panicking, need to find a way to calm myself down because if I lose it I'll be no good to anyone.

Making a swift plan in my mind, I decide I'll search the house for materials to burn as fast as I can before checking on Libby and then going after Gabi to ensure she returns safely. While I'm out, Madison can start the fire with the lighter she always carries with her.

"It'll be faster if we split up," I tell her as we move into the hall. "I'll go upstairs, and you search this floor. Check the kitchen cabinets for anything useful, or if we can burn the cabinets themselves. Remember to be careful of the floor. Stick to the outside perimeter. We don't want you ending up in the basement."

"Got it. Afterward we can search outside. Maybe there's a woodpile still dry enough."

As Madison turns to walk away, I grab her hand, tears prickling my eyes. "We're going to be okay, aren't we?"

"Everything will be fine," she says, but her voice and the curious look on her face tell me she doesn't quite believe it.

15

2 years 7 months before the accident

BOTH OF US were surprised when Madison scraped through her first year of college. At first, she thought about getting a job over the summer, and Guy said she could work at the restaurant with me. When Lucinda and Barry saw Madison's grades, they immediately vetoed the suggestion and hired private tutors to prepare her for the upcoming year instead. As we sat on our sofa one evening, hopping around Netflix, I asked if she felt controlled by their decision.

"No more than usual," she said. "I'd make a crap server anyway. Probably drop the plates and get myself fired."

"Not likely," I said. "Guy's completely enamored with you."

Madison waved a hand. "It's never been serious between us."

"Didn't he spend the night here again last week?"

"Yeah, but there's no future for us," she said. "It's sex. Great sex. And it's another reason for me not to work at Papa e Ragazzi. Anyway, if Mom and Dad want to pay for me to stay home and study, fine by me."

"You have such an odd dynamic with your parents."

She raised an eyebrow. "Oh, and you don't?"

"Sure, sure, of course I do," I said quickly. "It's glacial with Mom and nonexistent with whoever my dad is. Yours is more…indifferent than cold, held together by your perfunctory check-in call every Wednesday night."

"Oh, gah, don't remind me. I always need a large drink after those."

She meant *drinks*, but I said, "Can I ask you something?"

"Sure…"

"Why do you take their money despite not liking them?"

"It's payback for them treating me like a show pony." She sighed. "Classic poor little rich girl story, huh? I'll shut my mouth and be grateful."

"Or not take the money and claim your independence."

Madison gestured around the room. "Will my independence pay for this?"

I fell silent, wondering if I'd have spent my mother's money so easily had she been wealthy, but I valued my freedom and sanity too much. Then again, I'd always been poor, so not having much cash wasn't a huge deal. Madison picked up the remote and put on an obscure comedy show, and I let the subject drop.

Summer arrived, my first in Brooklyn, long and hot. Guy upped my shifts some more, and I made decent money with the tips I pulled in. Not nearly enough to get my own place, which I didn't want anyway, but it meant I could pay my way with food and bills, and give Raphaël a bonus here and there, ensuring he kept quiet if the Pierces asked about me again.

Whenever I had a day off and Madison had a break from working with her tutors, we'd head into Manhattan to explore the neighborhoods, searching for the best gelato, bagels, and pastrami sandwiches. With the pressure from being on campus and having assignments, tests, and exams gone for a few months, Madison was a different person—happy and relaxed, fun to be around.

"I'm sorry I've been so grumpy," she said as we walked up Fifth Avenue on our way to Central Park, lemon sorbet–filled cones in our hands. "I've been so stressed, it's unreal."

I decided to voice a question that had trundled around my head for a few weeks and which I hadn't asked because of Madison's mercurial moods. "Do you believe engineering's the best choice for you?"

"You think I'm not smart enough?" she said, and when she saw the panic in my face, she let out a chuckle. "Because you're not wrong."

"No, that's not what I meant," I said. "You're smart. Really smart. I've seen the textbooks lying around and it may as well be hieroglyphs for all the sense they make to me."

"Exactly how I feel."

"I guess you knew college would be hard. Everyone's grades drop compared to high school, don't they?"

"Not always. Some people in my year sneeze and get As."

I wanted to say they might not be partying most nights, but it felt flip and mean. Over the past few weeks Madison was opening up to me again, and I'd missed us being close, sharing secrets and talking late into the night. Truth was, I missed my best friend.

"Maybe engineering isn't right for you," I said gently. "What if you switched? A field you actually love. If you talked to your parents—"

Madison laughed but the sound had no warmth, and her expression told me I should tread carefully. "You know I can't discuss this with them," she said. "They made my career path options perfectly clear. Law, medicine, or engineering. I picked what interested me the most because blood makes me squeamish, and I'll be damned if I follow in their legal footsteps."

"But if you don't love—"

"Listen," she said, throwing the rest of her cone in the trash as she grabbed my hand. "Let's enjoy ourselves these next few months. The tutors promised they'll get me caught up over the summer and beyond. Mom and Dad will be off my back, and it'll be fine. Honest."

There didn't seem much point in arguing, and as we continued down the street, the sun beating down, she changed the subject to the movie we'd watched the night before, *24 Hour Party People*, indicating our college discussion was over.

After we'd walked another hundred yards, I wished I'd worn lighter pants than my jeans. I hadn't known how hot it would get, but the concrete jungle that is New York seemed to be intent on frying me alive.

I gulped down the rest of my sorbet, wiped my sticky hands on a napkin. Two more blocks and we passed Pattie's Pawn Shop. I'm not exactly sure what drew me in. Probably the combination of the kitschy yellow neon OPEN sign, and the memory of buying clothes at similar places in Portland. I could almost hear a pair of shorts calling my name, so I headed inside, and Madison followed close behind.

We explored the aisles, and I took in the racks of clothes, jewelry cases, and gaudy singing frog ornaments on the rows of spotless pine shelving. There was a stack of paisley shorts on the left-hand side, but I ignored those when I saw a saxophone, a banjo, and electric and bass guitars on the back wall. With a fluttering in my chest, I headed over to the store clerk, a lithe woman whose short, bleached hair reminded me of Annie Lennox from Eurythmics but whose name badge said Elyse.

"Excuse me," I said, anticipation building. "Do you have any drum kits?"

"As a matter of fact, I do," she said with a broad smile, and as she nodded, her red teardrop earrings wobbled. They were so big, trapeze artists could've performed on them. "One came in yesterday. Haven't had a chance to unpack it yet."

"Can I see it?" I asked, a grin spreading across my face. It'd been six and a half months since I'd played. Way, way too long.

She made big eyes at me. "You play the drums?"

"Yeah. Since I was a kid."

"Awesome." She turned, called out to a man wearing a three-piece suit that made him look as if he should be working at Tiffany's. "Hey, Earl, I'll be in the storage room. Let me know if you need me."

As I followed Elyse to the back of the store, Madison walked over. "Where are you going?"

"To see a drum kit."

She frowned. "Why? There's no space in your bedroom and with all the homework the tutors are giving me, you can't put it anywhere else, it'll be too noisy."

I grinned at her. "Relax, I've got it all worked out. There's a storage room in the basement Raphaël said I can use. I need to do this. I have to play."

I saw a flicker in Madison's eyes and wondered if I'd finally found a way to get her back into EmVee, but she said, "When will you have time?"

"I'll make time," I said, wondering why she sounded so jealous. Since I'd arrived in Brooklyn, she'd barely used her Spotify account. Why did she care if I played? "Music is my life. It's been long enough."

I walked ahead, and Madison followed. When we got to the back room, Elyse lifted a dustsheet. "Here we go," she said.

It took me a nanosecond to fall in love with the disassembled Ludwig Classic Maple set. The sparkling black wrap twinkled under the overhead lights, pulling me in like a seductive invitation. I forced myself to walk slowly, trying to not let too much eagerness show on my face.

"Not bad," I said, congratulating myself for my alleged muted interest. I wasn't sure how pawnshops worked in New York but guessed it wasn't any different from Portland. I had to hide my enthusiasm if I wanted this gorgeous equipment for a price I could afford, and I wanted it—*needed* it—badly. "Can I give it a try?"

Elyse grimaced. "Only if you come back later. I'll need time to set it up."

"Let me do it for you."

When Elyse hesitated, Madison said, "Vienna can do it in her sleep."

"Well, you'd save me some head scratching," Elyse said. "I haven't had many of these. I think it came with cymbals and a stool. Maybe some sticks. Oh, and there are travel bags, too."

Twenty minutes later the entire set, complete with crash, ride, and hi-hat cymbals stood in front of us, my heart beating fast as my throat went dry as dust. Taking a seat on the drum throne, I closed my eyes, smacked the drumsticks together, and burst into, "Running Up That Hill" by Kate Bush, one of Grams' and my all-time favorites.

As I played, Madison came over and joined in the chorus, making me grin so hard, it became almost impossible to get the words out. It felt as if we were back in Rosemont's music room, jamming together on our lunch break. At some point a couple of heads appeared in the doorway, but I was too focused on the exquisite pleasure of drumming again to pay much attention.

"You sounded amazing," Elyse said, giving us a round of applause as we finished. "You're in a band, right? You must be."

"We used to be," I said, glancing at Madison, whose flushed face practically glowed as she bounced on her heels. I hadn't felt her energy or seen her this excited in months. I wanted it to happen again, preferably every day. She was made to perform, to be wrapped up in music, not bogged down in the physics textbooks she hated so much. "How much do you want for the set?" I asked.

The three of us negotiated, hard. Elyse got less than her original so-called *firm* offer but I spent a few hundred more than I'd budgeted. Totally worth it, especially when she threw in transportation for thirty bucks because they were delivering other large items to Brooklyn the next morning. When we left the shop, with the receipt tucked in my pocket, I'm pretty sure I floated all the way home.

As promised, Raphaël let me set the kit up in the basement, and with the door shut, nobody upstairs could hear me play. Whenever I returned from a shift at Papa e Ragazzi, no matter the time, how tired I felt or how badly I needed a shower, I went to the basement and played a few songs, freedom and joy filling my veins. Despite Madison only coming downstairs a handful of times, I felt reborn, like I could breathe again.

When late summer approached, Guy introduced me to one of his friends who was a musician. Theo walked dogs, washed dishes, and did whatever he could to support himself while he played keyboard with a variety of bands—blues, jazz, and rock. Because he knew so many people, within a week after we met he'd hooked me up with a few bands. Soon I was filling in for drummers whenever they couldn't make a gig.

Not long after, one of the bands asked me to join on a permanent basis. I was excited at first, but when the guys instructed me to wear a sexier outfit than my usual attire of jeans and tank tops, I insisted they do the same. I never heard from them again.

It wasn't that I didn't want to be in a band, I did. *My* band, on *my* terms, and I was desperate for Madison to be a part of it, which wouldn't happen anytime soon because her second year at college had started off worse than the first.

A few days before a Thanksgiving gig I'd scored, Madison and I had an argument, this time about my relationship with Theo.

After what he and I had both assumed was a one-night stand, we'd started dating. Over the last few weeks, I'd spent most of my time at his apartment, mainly to stay out of Madison's way. With work, gigging, practicing in the basement, and Theo, I barely saw her, but that morning we were in the kitchen to-gether, me making coffee and a bagel while she nursed a mid-week hangover.

"Are you seeing Theo tonight?" she asked. "Again?"

"Yes, I think so. Why do you ask?"

She sighed. "Don't take this the wrong way but...I don't like him."

"There's a good way to take that?" I said. "You were happy for us to hang out at the beginning whenever you hooked up with Guy. You liked Theo enough then."

"Yeah, before you were dating him. Guy told me Theo has broken more hearts than there are hearts in Brooklyn. He's bad news."

"Good thing it's not serious then," I said. "Don't worry about me."

"Right." She tapped her fingers on the table. "But what are you going to do long-term?"

"With Theo? I don't know. It's only been—"

"Not with him. With work."

I felt my face scrunch up in a frown. "Huh?"

"What's the plan? The job with Guy was supposed to be a stopgap."

I tried to brush off the feeling this was some sort of inter-view, not a discussion with my best friend. "I want to make music, be able to live from it."

"Pah," she scoffed. "You know musicians are like writers and sculptors. Most starve if they don't have a real job. Or they become famous when they're dead."

Still digesting the *real job* comment, I said, "I have plenty of time to decide what I want to do with the rest of my life, thanks. I don't need a plan."

"God, you sound exactly like Theo. If you ask me—"

"I didn't."

"—he's bringing you down to the lowest common denominator."

"That's *exactly* what your mom once said about *me*."

"No, she didn't." Madison's face turned pink.

"Yeah. You told me she said I was driving you to Loserville and you didn't care about being in the passenger seat." I raised my chin. "Remember?"

"Maybe she had a point," Madison shot back.

"You don't mean that."

"Maybe I do. Ever since you arrived, my grades have gone down the toilet."

"You're blaming me for your academic failures?" I said. "Stop partying so hard and focus on your studies for a while. See what happens."

I half expected her to apologize, in which case I'd do the same, but she walked into her bedroom and slammed the door, leaving me with our spite-filled words hanging in the air.

I tried to rationalize Madison's behavior, see things from her perspective. I was mostly broke, but free from meddling parents and their pressure. I was involved in music, following my dreams, however slowly.

A series of light bulbs went off in my head. Madison was stressed and anxious about her coursework, yes, but she was also envious. Of me, my freedom, and although she could've told her parents to shove their funding up their backsides, she was afraid.

Being broke wasn't new to me. I could scrimp and save, eat pasta with ketchup to get by, clip coupons as I had with Grams. In contrast, Madison had been brought up on the finer things. A big house. An allowance. After-school activities. Skiing holidays. Summer vacations. Expensive restaurants. Her parents had a place in the Hamptons. Like she'd said not long ago, she was a poor little rich girl—unhappy, and without the right to complain.

I'd been envious of her lifestyle many times, and of the opportunities money provided. Now it seemed she felt the same about mine. Except, while I thought I understood her, I didn't know if it would make much difference to what was going on between us. I still loved Madison like a sister, but with a gnarly green-eyed monster growing between us, I wasn't convinced she felt the same.

16

MY SECOND WINTER in Brooklyn was colder than the first, and it valiantly fought any signs of an early spring with snow-laden storms and ridiculous temperature swings, making me pile on the layers one day, rip them off the next. The bigger surprise, however, was Theo inviting me to move in with him.

"Are you asking because your roommate left?" I teased as we lay in bed. I didn't have to work the lunch shift at Papa e Ragazzi, so we were indulging in a lazy Sunday morning, a rare opportunity to explore each other's bodies before feasting on a leisurely brunch.

"No, I'm not. I swear." His smile accentuated the cute dimples in his cheeks, and the way his long black hair fell over his eyes made me want to kiss him again. Theo leaned in and nuzzled my neck, ran his fingers up my thigh, making my skin tingle as he lowered his voice to a whisper. "Actually, it's because I want to have sex with you in every room."

"Ha, we already have. Well, except for what's now the spare room."

"We'll work on it. But first…will you move in?" His eagerness dissipated when he saw my face. "Uh-oh. Too soon? You don't want us to level up?"

"No, it's not that." It was the truth. While initially thinking our relationship wouldn't become serious, it had. Letting someone fully into my heart had always been difficult, but with Theo it felt easier than with anyone else I'd dated. He was funny, gentle, and kind. As another struggling artist who'd left his family behind in Alabama, he understood me, certainly more than Madison did these days.

"What is it?" he asked.

"Madison."

Theo rolled onto his back and put a hand beneath his head. "You're worried about how she'll take the news?"

"Yeah."

A year ago, I'd have thought Madison would be devastated if I moved out, but now I was unsure. It wasn't as if she needed the rent money I gave her, not when her parents still funded her entire life here, despite the fact she'd failed two courses in the first semester of her second year and would have to retake them during the summer. This new Madison was tense, on edge, and I never knew what might set her off. I was tired of tiptoeing around her, exhausted by always being the one who made an effort.

We'd argued again the night before last, this time about my allegedly using her expensive moisturizer, which I hadn't touched. When I'd refused to engage in whatever combat she was hoping for, she'd stormed out, hadn't returned until late, stumbling through the apartment as she made her drunken way to the kitchen. She'd thrown up, and I'd held her hair and rubbed her back, because despite our arguments, I believed in our friendship. It was a bad patch for her, a rough time I wanted to help her through.

I looked up at Theo. "She needs me."

"Does she? I think she uses you more than she needs you, to be honest."

"Maybe sometimes, but I don't want to lose her."

"I get it," he said. "And I'd never ask you to cut ties, it's not my place. I'm just wondering if there's a friendship left to lose."

"Of course there is. She's my best friend."

"Is or was?" He pulled me a little closer. "Sometimes we hold on to people because of the past when there's nothing left in the present, never mind the future."

"Whoa. When did you become deep and philosophical?"

Leaning in, Theo kissed the top of my head. "Always was. You're only noticing it now."

When I went home the next evening and gently broached the subject about Theo asking me to move in, Madison exploded. "You want to *live* with him? He's a total ass."

"That's not fair," I said. "Things are great between us."

"Things are great between *us*," she said, gesturing back and forth.

"Are they?" I asked. "Because it doesn't feel like it anymore."

Madison stared me down. "Whatever. Go ahead and move out then. I'll use the spare room to study."

The statement in itself was laughable, really. She hadn't cracked open her books more than twice since the semester began unless she was with one of her tutors, but her attitude, her indifference made the decision to leave a whole lot easier.

I still felt as if I was abandoning Madison, betraying her somehow, but perhaps we needed the distance if the shreds of our friendship were to survive. Packing my bags hurt my heart, but only until Madison left the apartment early on moving day the next weekend without saying goodbye.

Theo's place was in the Bed-Stuy area, south of Williamsburg and still in Brooklyn, which I'd continued to fall in love with since I'd arrived fifteen months earlier. His apartment wasn't flashy or modern like Madison's—the last time it had seen a new coat of paint had to be before either of us was born—but it was clean, and although longer, my commute to Papa e Ragazzi wasn't bad.

The one downside was Theo insisting we couldn't move my drums into the spare room as his neighbors would have us thrown out because of the noise, but thankfully Raphaël allowed me to keep the set in the basement of my old building. It made practicing inconvenient, but at least I could still play.

Madison and I messaged only a few times in the days after I left, and part of me felt lighter for having less contact and creating some boundaries. Another, bigger part missed her, as well as our evenings spent on the sofa together watching trash TV or reading each other's horoscopes and rolling our eyes at how inaccurate they were.

Perhaps by thinking about Madison so often, I sent telepathic messages into the universe, because almost two weeks after I'd moved out, and was on my way to work, I ran into her three blocks from Theo's place.

"Hey," she said, looking at me with those huge green eyes. She moved in for a hug, which felt more awkward than anything else. "How are you?"

"Fine, fine. Heading to the restaurant. Were you on your way to see me?"

I sensed her bristle a little. "No. I'm meeting with a study group."

"Great. College okay?"

Madison nodded. "Not bad. How are things with Theo? Marital bliss?"

"Ha, less of the marital, but we're good."

"Really?"

"Yeah, really. I'm happy."

She shook her head, softly said, "You're another number for him, Vee."

"You know what?" I said, voice going up. "I'm tired of your jealousy crap."

"Excuse me?"

"Admit it, you're jealous."

"Of you and Theo? Don't be ridiculous. All I've done is try to warn you."

"That's not what it feels like."

"Isn't it?"

I stepped to my left so a woman with a baby stroller could pass by. "No. But I can't figure out if you don't want me to be with Theo because you can't stand me having any friends other than you, or if you're jealous of us because you can't commit to anyone."

"*Neither.*"

"Actually, whenever I made other friends in Portland you got pissed off."

"No, I didn't."

"You *did*. Remember the Valentine's date you begged me not to go on? What about when you told me Tessa Morris was trashing me behind my back? Was that true or did you say it so I wouldn't be friends with her?"

"Can you hear yourself?" Madison said, voice raised. "You're paranoid."

"Am I? And it's not just that. I bet you hate how I'm free to do whatever I want when you're tied to your parents' purse strings."

Madison put her hands on her hips. "Funny how none of this came up when you were living in the apartment they pay for."

"For which I gave you rent."

"Rent? More like Monopoly money."

"Which you happily spent on whatever booze you shoveled—" I pinched the bridge of my nose. "Okay, we need a time-out."

"Bit late, don't you think? Your gloves are off already."

I lowered my voice, pushed my anger away so I didn't ignite more of hers. "I don't want to fight, Madison. I'm going to be late for work. Maybe I'll see you around."

I didn't contact her for over a week, considered blocking her number but couldn't bring myself to do it. Good thing, considering what happened next. Exactly nine days after our argument in the street, she sent a message with the words *I'm sorry*, along with a photo.

It was Theo at a bar. His hands on another girl's ass.

When was this? I wrote back, fingers trembling.

The three bouncing dots appeared, followed by Yesterday.

Yesterday? Theo had said he'd been to the movies with his friends. Blood whooshed in my ears as I sent the picture to him with WTF??? My cell phone rang two seconds later.

"It was nothing, it didn't mean anything," he said, words tumbling out.

"You said you went to a movie with your friends."

"I did. Jeez, Vienna. I went for a few drinks after, what's the big deal?"

"The big deal, Theo, is you never mentioning it. Lying by omission. Now I know why."

"Do you give me a blow-by-blow account of your day?" he said, apparently on the hunt for enough wiggle room to worm his way out. Then he hit me with, "It's not my fault you don't trust me."

"Don't you dare turn this around, I'm not gullible," I said. "Did you sleep with her?"

"We kissed…"

"At the club?"

"Uh, no. I went to her place."

"But you didn't sleep with her?" When he hesitated a fraction too long, I said, "Screw you, Theo. We're done." I hung up, ignoring him when he called back and sent me a message insisting they'd only kissed, that was all. I didn't believe him.

Not long after, Madison phoned. "Have you dumped him?" she asked.

"Yup."

"Want your room back?"

"Please."

"Pack your stuff. I'll be there in twenty."

Not once did she say *I told you so* as she helped me shove my things into bags while I willed myself not to cry. He wasn't worth it. Madison had been right all along.

"How did you find the photo?" I said. "Were you stalking him?"

"Hardly," Madison said. "We were at the same bar. He didn't notice me—he was too busy with…you know. You deserve better than him."

"Thank you."

"Anytime. Okay, what's next? Cutting the crotch out of all his pants?"

Laughing, I shook my head. "No, thanks. Petty revenge isn't my style."

"Petty?" she said. "The scumbag cheated on you."

I was about to answer he'd told me all they'd done was kiss, but of course he would say that.

"Let's go home," Madison said before I could formulate another response. "Listen, from now on I'll be a better friend. First, I'm going to tell my parents you're living with me."

"For real? They'll be furious."

"Probably. But you were right when you said I was happy to let them hold the purse strings. If they cut me off, they can have at it. I'm tired of them dictating everything, and me being miserable about it. I'm getting a job as well. It's time for me to grow up."

"What about college?"

"I'll make an effort. I promise I'll party less. There are other ways I can rebel against Mom and Dad without messing up my future." Dropping on the bed, she grabbed my hand. "One more thing. I want to hear the songs you've written. What do you say?"

I pulled her in for a hug as I kissed her cheek. "Welcome back. I've missed you."

Two hours later we were in the basement's practice room, Madison playing the electric guitar, her face in the effervescent smile I remembered. We'd gone over two of the songs I'd written, and she'd helped me make a few tweaks. As we were on our third round, Guy called.

"Need me to come in for a shift?" I asked, hoping he didn't because I wanted to spend the evening with Madison playing music. "Or are you going to give me a hard time about Theo?"

"Theo? No. Things okay between you two?"

"I don't want to talk about it. Did you call me about work?"

"No, I've got it covered. Listen, are you busy tonight?"

"No, why?"

"Brendan, the owner of the FlatCat is here," he said. "The pub on—"

"Flatbush Avenue," I said. "I've been a few times. Great place. What about it?"

"In confidence, he also owns a craft brewery and he's been trying to get me to buy his stuff for the restaurant," Guy said. "Anyway, in the middle of our conversation he finds out one of the bands he'd lined up to play opening songs tonight has fallen through."

"Guy...is this going where I think it's going?"

The smile in his voice was audible, and my heart thumped in anticipation of his reply. "Yup. I mentioned one of my friends is a brilliant female drummer, and he got really excited. You're still in a band, right? Because I think I can get you this gig if you want it."

Grinning at Madison, I said, "Yes, I'm definitely in a band, and I guarantee we want to play at the FlatCat tonight."

"Us?" Madison said, pointing to her chest before waving her hands around. "No. No way. What are you doing?"

"Fantastic," Guy said. "Sit tight. I'll send Brendan's details."

17

The day of the accident

I SWEEP MY flashlight's beam across the dusty stairs leading to the upper floor, searching for signs of rotting wood before I put my foot down, easing my weight onto each step. Moving slowly, I hope I'm not about to encounter a colony of bats or other wildlife that have made this old cabin their home. The last thing we need is for one of us to be attacked by a rabid animal.

Images of Evelina and Isabel's broken bodies pepper my mind. When I reach the top of the staircase, I press my eyes shut, willing the tears away as I try to forget the protruding tree branch and missing hand. Although intellectually I know Isabel's dead, part of me wonders if she's cold, if she's scared lying out there in the darkening forest all alone.

I have to focus on everyone else, but more questions come.

When we're rescued, will Evelina recover?

What about Libby? Does she have a concussion? What if it's worse and she has a brain bleed?

No, these thoughts aren't helping. I need to concentrate on

our survival, which means finding objects to burn, lighting a fire, and keeping warm until the storm passes.

Holding up the flashlight, I take in the upstairs landing. Pine paneling reaches midway up the bare white walls. Four doors lead in different directions, and I pick the one closest to me. It's another bathroom, windowless, with a shower, toilet, and sink. I try the taps to see if there's running water but other than a regurgitative clanking noise from inside the bowels of the cabin, which scares me half to death, nothing else happens.

There isn't anything useful to make a fire with in here but as I look at the shower again, a thought occurs. There's a bath downstairs, proper plumbing. Whoever built this cabin hauled building materials to this location, and I doubt they did so on an ATV. There's a basement, meaning they excavated, requiring heavy machinery. Maybe a road or at least a much wider path isn't far away. Help could be only a few hundred yards from here.

Buoyed by the glimmer of hope, I move back into the hall and choose another door. It's a bedroom, similar in size to the one downstairs, and it's directly above the kitchen area. I can tell because of the damaged floorboards, through which I catch a glimpse of downstairs. There's a bedside table and a matching desk in here, both made from pine, and hopefully easy to break down and toss into the flames.

The other three rooms yield a broken rocking chair, dead mice, and a pile of musty books. The latter will be helpful. More hope spreads its wings in my belly. We're going to be okay. We'll survive this.

Except…the Bittersweet will never be the same. I instantly feel guilty for thinking about how this will change everything, how we'd been doing so well only for it to abruptly end. Can the survivors continue? Will we want to? Tragedies and trauma such as this can bring people together as much as they can rip them apart.

Thank goodness I wasn't driving, or everyone would blame me.

The thought comes from nowhere and makes me want to throw up. Gabi was behind the wheel, yes, but the roads were slippery, visibility near nil. It was an accident.

Which she caused.

No, I won't think this way. It wasn't Gabi's fault. As I chastise myself for my attitude, Madison's words about the two of us not returning to the crash site when we found the cabin try to squirm their way into my brain again. I refuse to give them entry, but it's enough to remember how people think— and sometimes say—all kinds of horrible things under duress.

As I pick up some of the old books, I glance out of the window. I've never witnessed such utter darkness. It's as if the cabin has been enveloped in an impenetrable cloak and is the only thing in the world. A shiver runs the length of my spine and I try to ignore this incessant, irrational fear about the house being a bad place. It's ridiculous.

I turn my thoughts back to Gabi, picture her walking through the woods, tying our scarves to trees on her way to the Tahoe. Hopefully she's already found Evelina's insulin and is coming back.

As far as I'm aware, Evelina never told any of us about her diabetes. It's her story to share, of course, but it makes me wonder what other secrets there might be between all of us.

No time for these thoughts either. What's crucial is my bringing the books first, then the furniture to Madison so she can work on a fire while I go find Gabi. As I navigate my way down the stairs, dusty novels in one hand, phone with the flashlight on in the other, I call out, "I got some great stuff to use."

When Madison doesn't reply, I dip my head into the bedroom at the back of the main floor, but it's empty. I walk to the living room, stop in front of the unlatched basement door, and open it wide.

"Madison?" I call out. "Are you down there?"

There's not a single sound save for the wind blowing outside, and the silence from the basement gives me another uneasy feeling so I slam the door shut and lock it. When I reach the main room, Libby's on the floor, in the same position as when I left her. Evelina is, too, but I immediately know something's terribly wrong. Madison stands over her. Immobile. Unblinking.

"Madison?" I whisper.

She lifts her head, slowly, almost trancelike, and says, "Evelina's dead."

18

1 year 9 months before the accident

TRANSCRIPT: *What's On NYC*: **Season 12, EP 11:
Most Anticipated Spring Shows**

MELODIE JOHNSON: Welcome back to *What's On NYC*. I'm
your host, Melodie Johnson, and I'm here with my
good friends Xander Roberts and Liam Felder. So,
we talked about the upcoming concert season and
which performers we can't wait to see. Now let's
chat about what happened yesterday. You folks seen
what's lighting up socials?

XANDER ROBERTS: Hmm. Give us a clue.

MELODIE JOHNSON: Brooklyn.

LIAM FELDER: (snaps fingers) I got it. The duo at
the FlatCat pub.

MELODIE JOHNSON: Excellent. Bonus points for their
name?

LIAM FELDER: Too easy. EmVee.

XANDER ROBERTS: Envy?

MELODIE JOHNSON: EmVee, you know, the letters *M* and *V*.

LIAM FELDER: What's my prize, Melodie?

MELODIE JOHNSON: I'll buy you a cookie.

LIAM FELDER: (laughs) Good enough. Chocolate chip?

MELODIE JOHNSON: Smart man. Did you catch the show at the FlatCat? I only saw the video, but I love that place. They have the best beer and the coolest bands.

LIAM FELDER: Man, I wish I'd been there because, as you said, social media's blowing up over this new duo. People loved them. And I mean *loved*.

MELODIE JOHNSON: Well, here's a scoop for you, gentlemen. EmVee, cool name, by the way, isn't new per se.

LIAM FELDER: No way. Where have they been hiding?

MELODIE JOHNSON: Nowhere. They haven't played in two years. Not since twelfth grade.

LIAM FELDER: Hold up. Did you say two years? And twelfth grade?

XANDER ROBERTS: You sound really surprised.

LIAM FELDER: Yeah, man, they were amazing. They've got this classic pop-rock with an attitude vibe going on. Their rendition of No Doubt's "Don't

Speak" is ridonkulous. One of the best I've heard. Their harmonies were perfection. It's as if they've played together for years. They remind me a little of the cool Canadian band called—

MELODIE JOHNSON: The Beaches.

LIAM FELDER: Yeah, exactly. They're fantastic, too.

MELODIE JOHNSON: They sure are. I love "T-Shirt" and "Money" in particular. In any case, we'll post our YouTube links to the EmVee videos on the radio station's website and socials. Truth is, we don't know much about EmVee. I think it's intriguing everybody more because they're a bit of an enigma.

XANDER ROBERTS: Sounds mysterious.

MELODIE JOHNSON: Exactly. Let me tell you what I found out about these women. They're originally from Portland, Maine, and now live in Brooklyn. Madison Pierce, the one with the amazing red hair, was on guitar and vocals. Vienna Taylor, she's the stunner with the black hair, was on drums and vocals.

LIAM FELDER: Their singing alone is impressive, but Vienna's drumming's extraordinary. I can't believe she's, what, twenty, if they were in high school two years ago?

MELODIE JOHNSON: Yup. We call that massive talent. But wait, there's more. She's self-taught.

LIAM FELDER: You've got to be kidding me.

XANDER ROBERTS: She's that good?

MELODIE JOHNSON: Oh, yeah. Like you wouldn't believe.

LIAM FELDER: Watching her is… I don't know, magic. I can't believe she learned by herself. She's fiercely talented, man, and I mean fierce.

MELODIE JOHNSON: Not to downplay Madison's guitar skills. Or her vocals, for that matter.

LIAM FELDER: Definitely not, although Vienna's got to be the driving force behind EmVee. It came across very clearly.

XANDER ROBERTS: Did they play covers last night?

MELODIE JOHNSON: There was one original. You could tell they hadn't rehearsed it as much, and they were a little raw, but you know what? It made them better. Less polished, you know? More authentic. If you read the comments online, the audience agrees.

LIAM FELDER: I think Vienna wrote their original. Add that to her list of talents.

MELODIE JOHNSON: I'm not at all going out on a limb with this prediction, but I believe a star was born last night. Vienna Taylor's going to be huge whether it's with EmVee or not. If she wants a career in music, it's all hers.

XANDER ROBERTS: What about the other one? What was her name again?

LIAM FELDER: Madison Pierce. I'm not sure Vienna needs her, specifically, so to quote some folks on Twitter, I'm #TeamVienna, not #TeamMadison. I mean, sure, they're great together, but remember what happened to Andrew Ridgley?

XANDER ROBERTS: Who?

LIAM FELDER: (laughs) Exactly.

MELODIE JOHNSON: Not sure this is a fair fight, Liam. Xander's only twelve.

XANDER ROBERTS: (laughs) Hey, I'll be twenty-four next week.

MELODIE JOHNSON: Still a baby. Anyway, to all our listeners, be sure to check out the clip of EmVee performing "Don't Speak." The link's now on our website and socials. We're going to keep tabs on EmVee. I, for one, am excited to see where they go from here. Surely, the only way is up?

LIAM FELDER: According to Otis Clay.

MELODIE JOHNSON: Or Yazz and the Plastic Population.

XANDER ROBERTS: (laughs) Who?

MELODIE JOHNSON: Oh, boy. If this were an episode of *Jeopardy!*, the question would be *Who are performers before Xander's time*. And on that note, yeah, yeah, sue me for the pun, here's Yazz's version of "The Only Way Is Up." Meanwhile, Liam and I will educate Xander in the brilliance of '80s music. We'll be right back after this. Stay tuned.

19

1 year 9 months before the accident

"WHAT A WILD NIGHT," Madison said. "I still can't believe it." We were in our living room the day after the FlatCat gig, dressed in our pjs, sipping coffee, and splitting a cream cheese bagel. We hadn't woken up until after lunch and it had been a complete miracle I'd slept at all considering my entire body still thrummed with excitement.

"Neither can I," I said. "It was incredible."

The FlatCat had truly been an extraordinary experience, the most invigorating set we'd ever played. No small feat considering it almost hadn't happened.

After I'd spoken with Guy and suggested to Madison that EmVee play at the venue, she'd gone into full-blown panic mode. "No, no, no, no," she said, waving her hands around. "It's not possible. We haven't practiced in forever. We'll sound horrendous. Everyone will laugh. It'll be a nightmare."

"They won't. It's not until nine tonight. We've got a few hours to rehearse."

"Are you for real? A few *hours*? I need months."

"You don't. I promise you sound as good as ever. Better than. We'd only do a couple of songs anyway. We can manage that."

She took a deep breath. "Okay, okay. If we do this, and it's a big if, what's the set?"

I knew I could coax her into performing if I chose the songs she was most comfortable with, the ones she loved that showcased her guitar and vocal skills, but even with Madison on board, things hadn't been straightforward.

I'd spoken to the FlatCat's owner, Brendan, on the phone, and somehow convinced him to give us a shot after telling him about the different bands I'd played with, and the music Madison and I liked. He agreed to let us do three songs, adding in no uncertain terms how he'd pull all the plugs if we sounded like shit.

We still had the issue of getting my drum set to the pub. Neither Madison nor I had a vehicle, on foot wasn't an option, when I checked out Uber it wasn't clear if everything would fit in one trip no matter the size of the car, and we needed as much time as possible to get our literal act together.

"I'll call my cousin," Guy said when I asked if he could help. "He owes me multiple favors. He's a florist and I bet you can borrow one of his old delivery vans. I'm on it."

We used the rest of the afternoon to rehearse each song as often as possible, and thanks to Guy coming through for us with transportation, we arrived at the FlatCat at eight o'clock.

It was an Irish pub with dark oak tables, a paneled bar, and slate flooring. "Beautiful Day" by U2 played on the sound system, and I decided to take it as a good sign until a man walked up to us with a quizzical look on his face and introduced himself as Brendan the owner. He was a big man, at least six-four and probably close to three hundred pounds of pure muscle. Someone who wouldn't take bullshit from anyone.

"You realize this is a favor?" he said, his voice gruff. "I'm not a fan of duos, but Guy vouched for you so I hope you're as good as he says you are. Come on, I'll show you the stage."

The place was already packed, most of the two dozen or so tables filled, more people mingling at the bar. I tried not to let Madison see my trembling fingers or hear the nerves in my voice as we ran over the set list while I assembled my kit. She hadn't performed publicly in so long, if she detected my trepidation she could balk and walk before the show began.

A bathroom break, a guzzled glass of water, and we took our places. I glanced around. People barely paid us any attention, though a few individuals sized us up, making an early judgment call on whether we'd be any good.

Guy had mentioned the FlatCat's crowd generally skewed older, "Mostly Gen Xers," he'd said, and Madison and I had chosen our tracks accordingly. We'd rehearsed songs by No Doubt, Maroon 5, Lush, Kate Bush, and Liz Phair, plus one of mine, which I felt we could pull off. After a bit of deliberation, we'd agreed we'd decide what to play depending on the crowd's vibe.

Immediately as we began the first bars of "Running Up That Hill," the energy in the place shifted. Heads swiveled and bobbed, eyebrows were raised with what I deciphered as a mix of surprise and approval. Feet tapped, and phones went up in the air, pointing in our direction.

By the time we broke into the chorus, Brendan, who'd stood by the bar watching us with his meaty arms crossed, gave us two thumbs up. It was the moment I knew we had the audience in our pockets, and I relaxed, closing my eyes as the beat filled my soul.

When we finished the last chords of the first song, the near deafening applause and whistles made my adrenaline pump so hard, I thought my whole body might explode. Madison gave me an eager nod, indicating she was ready for the second track, the joy on her beaming face mirroring mine. We crushed it, and after performing "Don't Speak," Brendan told us to play five songs instead of three.

Now, as I lay on the living room sofa, I could tell the energy from the show would feed me for days. Drumming had always felt exhilarating and exhausting at the same time. Sharing this renaissance-esque experience with Madison made it a billion times better. Music was what I wanted to do forever, full-time, and, as impossible and out of reach as it seemed for now, I needed to be able to support myself through my craft.

"EmVee has to get out there on a regular basis," I said, sitting up, my face and voice serious. "Last night, we—" I stopped when her head snapped up from her phone, her expression unreadable. "What's wrong?"

She let out a scream. "It's…it's… Holy shit. We're trending." *"What?"*

Breathless, she said, "EmVee's trending on Twitter."

"Very funny."

"I wouldn't joke about this stuff, Vee. It's true."

I snatched up my phone and flicked to the app, my mouth dropping as my eyes skimmed the comments.

Anyone know where I can hear more from EmVee? #EmVee

Who are these girls? They're amazing. #EmVee

If you weren't at the FlatCat last night you missed out #EmVee

Why aren't they on Spotify? #EmVee

I kept scrolling and reading, scrolling and reading until Madison interrupted me. "Someone called Melodie Johnson mentioned us on *What's On NYC*."

"Shut. Up. *The* Melodie Johnson?"

"Who is she? The name's familiar but I can't place it."

"Only one of the most iconic radio jockeys, ever," I said. "I've listened to her show for years. She's incredible. What did she say? Oh, God, I'm not sure I want to know. She can make or break an artist with a single comment."

"Hold on, I'll play the recording." She tapped the loudspeaker, and when we heard Melodie say "EmVee," I squealed like a five-year-old. I barely contained my excitement as I bounced on the sofa, suppressing another giggle so I could hear the rest of the conversation. Madison grinned, but her excitement slid from her face when the guy named Liam said he wasn't sure I needed Madison to have a music career of my own.

"He doesn't know what he's talking about," I said, as she switched off her phone. "EmVee needs both of us. It *is* both of us. The clue's in the frigging name."

"He's not wrong."

"Yes, he is."

"Not really. None of this would've happened if you hadn't pushed me. And it's what people in Portland thought. Remember the news article after the school's Winter Holiday concert? #TeamVienna followed us around for weeks."

"You can't pay attention to those comments. Without you, there's no em in EmVee." My cell phone rang, cutting off Madison's reply, but judging by her face she was about to disagree with me again. "You and me. Simple," I insisted before answering what I saw was Guy's call.

"Hey," he said. "Brendan's raving about EmVee's performance last night. Loved you. So did everyone else."

"Thank you. It was a fabulous night. Great crowd."

"Congratulations again." Pause. "Listen, I'm calling about something else."

I pulled a face, crossed my fingers. "Do you need me to come in?"

"No, uh, your mother's here."

Sitting up straight, I blurted out, "Did you say my mom?"

"It's what she said. Barb Taylor-Cole. Five foot six, long blond hair. Eyes like yours. Fingernails you could use for daggers." Definitely Mom. As I wondered what the hell she wanted, Guy added, "She said she was in town, saw stuff about the Flat-Cat gig online, and dropped in to say hello."

"How the hell did she figure out where I work?"

"Uh…it's my fault. I tweeted you're my best server."

I let out a groan. "Shit."

"Oh, crap. I remember you saying you don't get along. Want me to tell her I couldn't get hold of you?"

As tempting as it was, I couldn't expect Guy to deal with my mother. "Give her a drink on me, it'll soften her up when I tell her to leave. Whiskey sour with a twist. I won't be long."

20

The day of the accident

EVERY PART OF me feels numb. It's as if metal rods have been driven through the length of my body starting from my heels, going up through my legs, my spine, and out the top of my head, making it impossible to move.

"Evelina's dead," Madison repeats, and my head spins.

The books in my arms now weigh a thousand pounds and they clatter to the floor. I hear a moan, realize it's coming from my mouth. When I can finally manage to make my legs work, I take five steps and sink to my knees by Evelina's side.

My fingers shiver so much I can barely hold on to her wrist, and I'm trembling too hard to feel a pulse. After wiping my hands on my jeans, I push my fingertips to her neck, moving a fraction of an inch to the left, to the right, and back again. I'm desperate, searching, searching. There's nothing, but her skin's still warm. She looks asleep.

Evelina can't be dead.

"We have to do something," I say, scrambling to lift her chin, keeping her mouth open with my thumb as I tilt her head back.

Pinching her nose closed, I breathe into her mouth, notice how her lips carry a hint of strawberry lip balm.

Evelina can't be dead.

I put my hands to her chest. "How many compressions?" I ask Madison, and when she doesn't reply I catch her blank expression. "*Madison*, how many?"

"I heard her choking," she says, gesturing to her own throat. "She was making a gurgling noise and…and…"

I continue trying to resuscitate Evelina, suddenly remembering details about "Stayin' Alive" by the Bee Gees. It's thirty compressions and two breaths to the beat of the song. No, twenty compressions and three breaths. Or something else? Unable to remember I start anyway, attempting to count but getting confused. Was that eight or ten? Does it matter? Yes, it matters. Of course, it matters. I'm trying to save a life. I'm trying to save my friend.

Panic ebbs and flows, mixing with fear. I need to focus. *Focus.* I force air into Evelina's lungs again, see her chest rise and fall—a glimmer of life—until she stills once more. Another round, and another, but it's not working. Nothing's working.

Evelina can not *be dead.*

Madison puts a hand on my arm. "Stop," she says. "Vienna, you need to stop. She's—"

"Don't say it." Tears run down my cheeks, and I swipe at them. I'm bursting with so much anger, don't know what to do with it. I shake my hands to loosen them and gulp down the rage as I resume my efforts. "We've lost Isabel. We're not losing Evelina. Can you—"

"What's going on?"

Startled, I see Gabi in the doorway, clutching a polka-dot pouch in her gloved hands. Her hat, jacket, pants, and boots are covered in so much snow, she could be a Yeti. I don't know why, and my reaction is wildly inappropriate, but it makes me want to put my head back and laugh, and laugh, and laugh until I throw up or pass out.

"Tell me what the hell's going on," Gabi says, her voice loud, hard. *"Now."*

Madison slowly moves to her. "Gabi, I'm so sorry, but Evelina's... I'm afraid she... While you were gone, she..."

Madison can't finish her sentence but doesn't need to. A flicker of understanding crosses Gabi's face and she opens her mouth wide. A desperate wail escapes, filling the room, the cabin, the entire forest. She sounds more animal than human, full of disbelief, anguish, and pain. Dropping to her knees she crawls over, touches Evelina's face and intact hand. Next, she grabs her sister's shoulders, making Evelina's head loll to one side.

"Stay with me," Gabi shouts, pulling the insulin from the pouch, fumbling with the pile of clothes on top of her sister and finally plunging the needle into Evelina's belly. "Don't you die on me. Don't you dare." Another howl, another sob. She speaks again, her voice quieter this time, a gentle whisper from one sibling to another, desperate and pleading. "Wake up, Evie, please wake up. You can't go. Stay with me. Don't go. Please, please don't leave me. *Please.* I'm sorry. I'm so, so sorry."

I shuffle backward to give her space. Madison's still standing by the doorway but Libby, who's stretched out on the floor behind us, hasn't moved. Fear grabs me by the throat as I suddenly worry she's dead too, forgotten amid the chaos. I see her chest move but it doesn't stop my anxiety. If Libby has a concussion, her being this drowsy can't be good, but I won't draw attention to this until Gabi calms down. It might catapult her over the edge and, quite frankly, pull me with her.

As Gabi sobs, I get up and go to Madison, feeling like we're a pair of voyeurs, witnessing such a private moment of grief. I grab Madison's hand, promising myself I'll help Gabi through this. No matter how horrific the situation is for me, I must remember it's a trillion times worse for her.

Madison's the closest person I have to a sister, and I can't imagine losing her, never hearing her voice again. Living the rest of my life without her in it, unable to celebrate milestones and achievements, as well as dealing with failures and challenges together.

"Sweetheart," Madison says, her voice wavering as she lets go of me and kneels next to Gabi. She rubs her shoulders, making a circular motion with her palm. "We're here for you."

Gabi shrugs her off, anger faster, hotter, and more destructive than a lightning bolt. "We can't let this happen," she yells. "We've got to help her."

"It's too late." Madison's voice is calm, but when she reaches for Gabi's fingers, Gabi gives her a shove, almost making her topple over.

"I can't stay here," Gabi says, jumping up. "I won't. I have to get help. We can still save Evelina. I have to save my sister."

"You can't go outside, it's not safe." I try to keep my tone even, to not be condescending, but reassuring and gentle. Unsure if it's working, or if Gabi's registering the words, I keep going. "We don't know where we are. We've no idea how far away the next house is, or in which direction. Gabi, please. Stay here."

Her face crumples, her heart visibly shattering all over again because there's no hope left for Evelina. I bite my lip, will myself to stay strong for Gabi's sake as she collapses onto the floor and sobs. This time I'm the one who crawls over, and I softly ask Gabi if I can hug her. She allows it, and I rock her back and forth, back and forth, stroking her hair.

Madison looks at me. "Should...should we move Evelina to the other room?"

I'm not sure why she suggests this when Gabi's so distraught. Perhaps Madison's squeamish about being in the same place as a body but it feels rushed and insensitive. I'm about to speak when Gabi wipes her eyes.

"Yes, I don't think she'd want to be in this room with the rest of us—" she takes a gulp of air "—going about making a fire and whatever. I think she'd prefer to be alone."

Without saying a word, we do as she requests, moving the mattress and Evelina to the bedroom on the ground floor. Gabi goes to the main area to fetch Evelina's hoodie, taking so much time I wonder what she's doing. When she comes back, her eyes are wide, her expression filled with an emotion I can't decipher. Gabi insists on staying with Evelina, so Madison and I retreat, giving her the space she needs to start saying goodbye to her sister.

As soon as I'm back in the main room with Madison, I attempt to wake Libby. After gently shaking her shoulders and pinching her arm as hard as I dare, I can't rouse her. She won't open her eyes. I've never felt so helpless, guilty, too, because my head's no longer throbbing. I survived a horrific crash. Two of my friends didn't, and a third might be badly injured. Was there something I could've, *should've* done to save them? Am I to blame for any of it?

"We have to start a fire," Madison says with a shiver, and I know she's right. We need warmth to survive. It's only going to get colder as the night progresses.

"There's a bedside table and an old rocking chair upstairs," I say. "I'll tear pages from the books if you want to get the furniture and your lighter. You do have one?"

"Sure. I'll get the stuff."

"Be careful of the broken floor up there."

She doesn't answer as she disappears into the hallway. Once she's gone, I rip a few pages from the books and crumple them into balls, stacking them in the fireplace. I look upward, trying to see if anything's blocking the flue. From the little I know, lighting a fire could be precarious if anything is impeding the airflow. We'll have to leave a window open. Not tricky, considering half of them are broken.

When I hear Madison walking in the room above me, I decide to search the kitchen cabinets in case there's any lighter fluid or a flammable substance because we'll need all the help we can get, but there's only an old bottle of cooking oil, which I leave on the counter.

Back at the fireplace, I prepare more paper, and I'm halfway through destroying an old edition of *The Stand* by Stephen King, when I hear Madison coming down the staircase. Soon after, she's shouting my name. I jump up, run to the hall.

"Gabi," she says when I reach her, pointing to the open front door. "She's gone."

21

1 year 9 months before the accident

AFTER GUY AND I hung up, roots of curiosity about Mom being in town took hold and bloomed in the time it took me to get to Papa e Ragazzi. Madison offered to come, but I wanted to handle the situation alone, and as fast as possible. Find out what my mother wanted. Send her on her way, preferably without her making a scene.

As I walked down the street, I wondered why Mom had come here, and doubted she'd felt a maternal need to check up on me. The last time we'd spoken to each other was the day Grams passed and Mom had thrown me out of the house for punching Rick. Aside from the texts from her demanding to know if I'd taken Rick's car, which I hadn't answered, neither of us had bothered keeping in touch.

Why now? Probably because she thought I had money after she'd seen a semi-viral video of me, and figured she could cash in somehow. Or maybe she was sick. I thought about how I'd feel if she told me she was dying, and a jumble of conflicting emotions—fear, indifference, dismay—swirled around my insides.

Mom and I may have become estranged over the past sixteen months, but she was the only family I had left. Maybe that was why I found myself being pulled through the streets of Brooklyn by an invisible thread I thought had long been severed.

When I reached the restaurant, Mom sat on a barstool, her lean legs crossed. Her tight jeans hugged her curves, and despite it being cold outside, she'd worn a spaghetti-strap top smaller and lower-cut than the ones I remembered. Judging by the way she leaned in, she'd been flirting with Gino the barman. He'd plonked his elbows on the counter, his head bent toward her as if she were telling the most riveting story he'd ever heard. Too bad for him she was a lousy tipper.

"Mom," I said as I approached. "This is a surprise."

She smiled, a gesture lifting years off her features, and which seemed surprisingly genuine. "Well, well, well. If it isn't my brilliant little drummer girl." She hopped off the barstool and teetered in my direction on her high-heeled boots, arms outstretched. The hug felt stilted. A mother and daughter more than a little out of practice.

"I wish I hadn't missed your gig last night," she said. "I'd have come if I'd known you were performing."

The whole sweetness and light act was no doubt mainly for Gino's benefit, and when he moved away to serve another customer, I got down to it. "Why are you in town?"

She took a sip of her whiskey sour. "Came here for the weekend with some girlfriends."

"How nice."

"Yeah. Except I overslept this morning, and they got the bus to Portland without me. Some friends, eh? Anyway, your stepfather—"

"You know I don't consider him as my stepfather."

"Yes, well, *Rick* sent me a link about EmVee earlier, and when I saw a comment about where you work and found out it was in Brooklyn, I wanted to surprise you." The corners of her mouth fell. "I know we haven't communicated much—"

"More like at all."

"—but I'm still your mom. Unless it's not how you consider me, either."

I ignored the guilt trip bait, settled for, "What's your plan for getting home?"

"Bus leaves tomorrow, I couldn't get an earlier seat. Good thing I can use the ticket I already bought because I don't have cash for another. This city's expensive."

Now I knew where this was heading, but I still let her spell it out for me anyway, waited as she took another sip of her drink and patted my hand, her long fingernails sparkling with red glittery polish.

"I was hoping to crash at your place," she said. "Maybe we can talk a little and catch up?"

"What would we talk about, exactly?"

"What you've been up to for over a year. I had no clue you'd come to New York. You can tell me all about it."

"Okay…"

"Are you living with someone? Boyfriend? Girlfriend?"

"Madison."

"Ah, yes, of course." She paused for a moment. "Vienna, I'd like to talk to you about what Rick said the day you left. I owe you an apology."

I felt my eyebrows shoot to my hairline. This was definitely a first, because Mom barely apologized to anyone. While I didn't relish spending more time than strictly necessary with her, a tiny part of me, the one I'd figured was long dead and buried, still longed for a semblance of a normal relationship. Surely there was no harm in letting her stay the night.

I messaged Madison to ensure she was fine with us having a visitor, and after she replied with a shocked-face emoji and a thumbs-up, I led Mom back to the apartment.

"This is lovely," Mom said with a generous nod of approval as soon as she walked in. "It's good to see you again, Madison. Thanks for taking care of Vienna."

"Actually, Mrs. Taylor," Madison said, "it's been the other way around."

It was odd at first, spending time with Mom—as if we were at a high tea or fancy party, all of us on our best behavior. The dynamics had shifted. I was no longer the high school student living in her house on her terms. This was my home. I was a working woman and Mom had no choice but to accept I'd grown from child to adult, thereby making us equals.

"You can take my room," I said, for a split second wondering what I was doing. I didn't owe this woman anything but found myself unable to recant the offer. "I'll sleep on the sofa."

"Thanks," she said, pulling her dented, scuffed purple wheelie-bag behind her when I pointed to the bedroom door. "I'll freshen up a little, too, if you don't mind."

"The bathroom's the first on the left," Madison said. "Help yourself to whatever you need." She waited for Mom to disappear and for us to hear the sound of running water before turning to me. "Have we dropped into a parallel universe? Because this is weirding me out. She's being *nice*. I haven't heard a single criticism yet. What's going on?"

"I'm not sure. Are you really okay with her staying?"

"Yeah, plus it'll force me to tell my folks about you living here in case she spills the beans before I get the chance. But… it's only for one night?"

"Definitely."

When Mom returned to the living room, it quickly became apparent some things hadn't changed since we'd last seen each other. She walked over with two full bottles of wine— one red, one white—in her hands and wiggled them in the air with a grin.

"I have some Jack Daniel's, too," she said as she put the wine on the coffee table with a clunk, and I made a mental note to ensure I set my alarm for early the next morning, so she didn't oversleep and miss the bus again.

By the time we were waiting on our pizza delivery for dinner, Mom had downed a few shots of the whiskey, finished one bottle of wine almost entirely on her own, and was working her way through the other, blinking slowly as she talked, her speech getting a little fuzzy.

"I envy you two," she said, waving her glass around, a splash of red wine landing on the rug. "I envy you living here. Endless possibilities in front of you, as well as your youth."

"Worrying about making Brooklyn rent," I quipped.

"Money troubles never go away," she said. "I bet millionaires have sleepless nights about their cash. How they'll hold on to it, maintain their wealth." She finished her glass in one gulp and poured herself another. "You were right, Vienna."

"About what?"

"Getting out of Dodge. I wish I had the guts to say what I think to his face the way you did."

"Do you mean Rick? Things aren't good with you two?"

"Were they ever?" she said with a small, sad chuckle. "I never should've married him but it's too late now. Made my bed and all."

"Hardly," I said. "You can find someone else. Someone good. Or be alone for a while."

"At my age?"

Madison who'd been silent all this time said, "You're barely past forty, Mrs. Taylor. You're young. Better to be single than with the douche...I mean Mr. Cole."

Mom took another sip of wine and burst into tears. I'd rarely seen my mother cry and didn't know what to do. Wait for her to stop? Console her? I dithered before getting up and putting my arms around her. She smelled of patchouli and booze with a hint of sweat. I listened as she told us she'd suspected Rick had been seeing a much younger woman for months, how he took most of Mom's money, leaving her broke.

"I stashed cash for this trip for six months," she said. "Hid it with my tampons because it's the only thing I know he won't touch."

I tried to remain apathetic, but sympathy crept in around the edges. No matter what had happened between us, she was my mom, and I reminded myself she'd been dealt a crap hand she hadn't known how to play. Life didn't come with a manual, so I listened and tried to provide some form of constructive counsel.

She calmed down a little after we ate our pizza, and by eight she was fast asleep, stretched out on the sofa, snoring gently. I decided to leave her be and covered her with a blanket, stopping short of giving her a peck on the cheek.

When I got up the next morning, my mother had showered, done her hair and makeup, repacked her suitcase, and sat in the kitchen with a mug of coffee. Nobody would've guessed how much alcohol she'd had the evening before.

"You ready for the bus?" I asked.

"Yep. Just need to figure out where to get the subway."

"We agreed last night I'd get you an Uber. I'll order it now."

"Oh, yeah." Mom frowned, fidgeted with the zipper on her bag. "Before you do…" she whispered, glancing over her shoulder as she lowered her voice some more. "What I told you about Rick's cheating, please don't mention it to him."

"Don't worry. I've no intention of speaking with him. You know, maybe he's done you a favor. Given you a reason to leave and rebuild your life."

"We'll see."

"You have my number, if you want to talk."

"I do," Mom said. "Thank you. It, uh, it was good seeing you, Vienna. Really good. I hope we can do it again sometime."

Another sliver of animosity between us dissipated. We weren't best friends, we'd probably never be more than acquaintances bound by blood, but things were better than they'd been this time yesterday and for many years before. "So do I."

"Hey, guys," Madison said, walking out of the bathroom. "Have either of you seen my sapphire ring and tennis bracelet?" She pointed at the sideboard. "I put them over there last night and I can't find them."

"No," Mom said. "I haven't seen them."

"Me neither," I said. "We can help you search."

"What about my ride?" Mom said, glancing at the phone.

"I'll do it in a sec. Let's take a quick look for Madison's jewelry first."

We spent the next few minutes hunting through the living room, behind the sofa and under the sideboard, but nothing turned up. The kitchen and bedrooms didn't yield anything either. It was as if the items had vanished. After Mom had excused herself to go to the bathroom, Madison grabbed my arm.

"I know this sounds mean," she whispered, "but do you think your mom might've—"

"Taken your jewelry?" I tried to sound a little insulted but couldn't because the thought had already crossed my mind. Why wouldn't it? Last night, Mom had explained at length how badly she needed cash, expressed delight and jealousy at this apartment, openly wishing she could have a place like it. Was this why she'd contacted me? To see what she could steal? I didn't want to believe it, but my heart dropped as I understood her visit might've been a different kind of ruse all along, and I'd fallen for it.

With a furtive glance toward the bathroom, I picked up her bag, unzipped it and had a good poke around while Madison searched under the sofa again. As I stuffed my fingers into the bag's side pocket, my hand closed over an object wrapped in tissues. I unfolded them, a groan escaping my mouth at the exact same time as Mom opened the door.

"What the hell do you think you're doing with my stuff?" she said, storming over.

I held up Madison's tennis bracelet and missing ring, shoving the tissues in my pocket. "It isn't though, is it?"

"I've no idea how they got in there," Mom spluttered. "I didn't take them."

"Don't." I stood up and pressed the jewelry into Madison's hands, her eyes narrowing more than mine. "You know, Mom, you almost had me believing you were happy to see me. Did you plan this stunt from the beginning or make it up on the fly?"

"I didn't take anything," Mom insisted. "I *didn't*."

"Leave," I said. "Find your own way to the bus station and lose my number."

"You know what," Mom said, her back straightening, all the vulnerability gone. "It hurts me to think you believe I came here to steal from you, my own daughter."

"Are you serious? It didn't seem to hurt much when Rick took my money to spend on the two of you. Is that why you miss me? Because he's taking all *your* cash now?"

"You're being unfair. I think—"

"I don't care what you think," I said. "I honestly don't. Leave."

She clicked her tongue and a snide expression slid across her face as she made a sweeping gesture with one hand. "You can play posh around here all you want, Vienna, but you'll never belong in Madison's perfect world. You'll always have a chip on your shoulder, exactly like mine. The constant reminder you'll never be good enough no matter what you do or how hard you try."

"Get out," I said. "Now."

Mom moved closer. "We're one and the same, you and me. Destined to amount to nothing. You'll see."

"She told you to get out. You're a liar, a thief, and a terrible mother." Madison's voice trembled as she grabbed my mother's arm and yanked her to the front door. "You don't deserve a daughter like Vienna."

"Let go of me," Mom said, trying to pull away.

Madison held firm. "Show your face here again, and it'll be the last thing you do."

"Are you threatening me?" Mom shouted.

Madison's sneer reminded me of Rick's when I'd asked him the exact same question. "It's not a threat, Mrs. Taylor. It's not a promise either. It's a fucking guarantee."

22

1 year 9 months before the accident

NOT LONG AGO, my mother's stinging insults would've burrowed deep. Not this time. With the energy I had left from EmVee's FlatCat success, I spent the next few weeks trying to capitalize on the gig. Reality soon arrived, demonstrating whatever was trending one moment got discarded before you could blink. I was no stranger to the fickleness of social media. Had always known the different platforms chewed you up and spat you out, but I'd naively hoped it wouldn't happen to EmVee so quickly.

Despite Brendan (quote) *loving us*, the FlatCat's schedule was already full until mid-October. Although I managed to find another few venues for EmVee, they were tiny, dingy, with far less enthusiastic crowds. I found out places needed their bands to bring in a ton of people, and they expected a certain quota of tickets to be sold, which was easier said than done.

My attempts to contact Melodie Johnson to let her know where we were playing had been met with outright disinterest from her assistant. Not overly surprising. She probably had dozens of people vying for her attention every hour of every day. Undeterred, I built a website in my barely existent spare time, and set up social media accounts, but trying to grow an audience seemed impossible and I really didn't have much of a clue about marketing.

"What if you had more people?" Guy said one day as I helped lug the cases of beer and boxes of hard liquor into the restaurant.

"More people?"

"Yeah, you know, became a real band."

I opened the lid on one of the boxes, pulled out a bottle of Knob Creek and waggled it around. "This is expensive. I might drop it if you don't take your *real band* comment back."

Guy laughed, but quickly grabbed the booze and put it in the box. "Easy there, tiger. I'm not saying EmVee isn't a legit group, but remember how you told me about Brendan's reaction about you being a duo?"

"There are plenty of great duos. What about—"

"The White Stripes. All hail Meg White. She's your hero, I know."

"Don't forget Demetra Plakas and Sheila E. They inspired me as much as Meg."

"Whatever you say." He grinned. "Hey, I understand precisely squat about the music world but maybe having more members to beef up your act would give you more options, more possibilities in the long run? More people to pitch in with the promotional stuff and more—" he waved his hands around "—*presence.*"

"More headaches, you mean," I said. "Madison and I have known each other for years. We sound good. I'd have to hold auditions, practice with them to see if we work well together, for which we'd need a bigger space. It's so much hassle."

"Well, you won't know if you don't try. What about joining an existing band?"

"Been there, done that, hated it."

"Then put up some flyers or throw an ad on Craigslist for members. Vet them for industry connections. What's the worst that can happen? If you don't gel and they bring nothing to the table, kick 'em out."

"Our band, our terms?"

"Exactly."

After thinking about Guy's comments for a few days, I took his advice. Madison was okay with my looking for new members. To be quite honest, her enthusiasm for EmVee had waned again because of the quality of the gigs I'd found. I wished she could help, but she was struggling with her courses, a fact her parents tried to blame on my living with her. Predictably they'd been unhappy when she'd told them, but she'd refused to negotiate and for now, they'd given in.

My continued attempts to expand EmVee were more miss than hit. Some candidates never bothered showing up. Others arrived late, and many of those who got there on time could barely hold a tune. One woman asked what stage play we'd perform, and another guy kept talking about getting his big break on Broadway.

I was hopeful when I found two women and a man, a trio who went under the name the Obscures and played bass, keyboard, and guitar. We didn't sound terrible the first time we rehearsed, all of us somehow squishing into the tiny basement room in our building, but I wasn't sold on the five of us forming a band. When we met the following weekend, and the woman with the perpetual sniffle pulled a baggie of coke from her pocket, I saw Madison's eyes light up. I messaged them a few hours after they left and said we were done.

"Why did you cut them loose?" Madison said when I told her. "You should've talked to me. EmVee belongs to both of us. You and me, remember?"

"They weren't right, our sound was off."

"We barely got started. We'd have improved."

"We'll find someone better."

We thought we had when we met Wil, who hailed from Dublin and had a cheeky grin and gorgeous pillow lips I instantly wanted to kiss. Despite vowing I'd never get involved with a band member, three rehearsals in and we couldn't keep our eyes or hands off each other, making out in the basement as soon as Madison went upstairs to study. Wil played rhythm guitar like a god, but Madison wasn't happy when she found out he and I were seeing each other.

"It'll get messy," she said, hands on hips. "And you can do better."

"That's what you said about Theo."

"Which happened to be true."

Aside from stringing Guy along, Madison had dated a few guys at college, but nothing ever became serious. Maybe she didn't want me to be with Wil because none of her flings had lasted, although it seemed more her choice than theirs. Either way, things between Wil and me fizzled quickly, and he joined another band, turning EmVee back into a duo.

I didn't think Madison was upset, and her alleged commitment to us expanding the group wasn't the only thing I secretly questioned. The whole jewelry incident had been bugging me for months. After my mother had left our apartment, storming out, pulling her purple suitcase behind her, Madison had slammed the door, and turned to me.

"Can you believe she wrapped three grand of jewelry in tissues?" she said. *"Jesus."*

I'd dismissed the tiny alarm bell going off in the back of my mind. Ignored it until it rang harder, louder, making it impossible for me to think about anything else.

The tissues.

When I'd found the jewelry in Mom's bag, Madison had been searching under the sofa. She hadn't seen me unwrap the tissues, or stuff them in my pocket. I hadn't mentioned them and yet, somehow, Madison had already known.

The uncomfortable feeling she'd planted her own jewelry in my mother's bag for me to find swirled around my head no matter how hard I tried pushing it away. Madison had been there the night before, sitting on the sofa, observing as I'd told Mom she could call anytime, and maybe come back for a visit. She'd witnessed how our relationship had gone from subzero temperatures to frostbitten. Far from perfect, but progress, nonetheless. Had Madison been jealous about that, too? Had she done it out of love, to protect me from future disappointment?

Once again, I told myself I must've been mistaken and switched focus, deciding I'd increase my efforts to find new band members and give EmVee a fresh start. I had to move on, tackle my music career before I woke up one morning with nothing but wasted dreams. As it turned out, I should've let those dreams die.

If I had, the friends I was yet to make would still be alive.

23

The day of the accident

I'M STANDING IN the hall, freezing air blowing in through the open door. "What do you mean, Gabi's gone?" I ask Madison. "Gone where?"

She doesn't answer. Doesn't need to. We both know Gabi's disappeared into the night in the middle of a snowstorm, driven by her desperate need to help her sister. Except it's too late. Evelina's gone and nothing Gabi does will bring her back—but we have to find her before we lose her, too.

Without another word, Madison and I rush through the front door, the wind hitting us full force when we step onto the porch. It's snowing hard, thick flakes clouding our vision, making it impossible to see, and hard to breathe. I search the ground for footprints, but I can't tell which ones are fresh because of the lack of light, the intensity of the wind, and how much snow's being whipped around.

"Where is she?" I yell to Madison, cupping my hands to my mouth. "Which direction?"

"Let's split up," she says. "We have to find her before she gets too far. We'll circle the house."

Madison goes right and I turn left, trudging through the snow, stopping every so often as I hold up my phone and shine the flashlight into the trees and over the ground in case Gabi has fallen. This is futile, impossible. I can't see anything, but I force myself to keep going. One foot in front of the other, over, and over.

When I pass a pile of split logs, my brain registers I should come back for some for the fire. I've no idea how I'm still able to think logically given the circumstances, but I'm grateful for the moment of pseudo normalcy, however brief.

I go around the first corner of the house, try to see in through the window in case Gabi changed her mind and came back, but it's completely dark inside. Moving on, I reach the second corner, and expect Madison to come my way. She's nowhere.

Pulse pounding, I try breaking into a run, slipping, and tumbling to the ground. I push myself up and look around with my phone held high. "Madison," I shout, but my voice is no match for the weather. I call out again, coughing as thick snowflakes hit the back of my throat.

Willing myself to move, I walk around the cabin. Madison isn't anywhere so I venture farther from the house, shouting her name as well as Gabi's, shining the flashlight again. At this rate my cell battery will die soon. I can't let that happen. When I go for help in the morning—*please let it be in the morning*—I'll need to use my phone as soon as I make it to an area with cell service.

I'm not sure how long I'm out there, ten minutes, fifteen, more? I'm frozen. Logic tells me I must get back inside, get warm. Maybe Madison's already in there with Gabi, worrying where I've got to.

"Madison?" I call out as I reach the front door and enter the hall, almost crying from relief as I step out of the unrelenting winds. "Are you here?"

Stopping to listen, I think I make out the sound of movement. The basement door's slightly ajar, and as I reach it, I hear the noise again. A heavy object is being dragged across the floor. It makes no sense. Not unless Gabi never left the house after all or came back once we were outside. Maybe she went to the basement and fell on the steps. Perhaps she's been lying there all this time. Except…wouldn't we have heard?

I open the basement door, trying to ignore the musty smell as I shine my flashlight on the steep stairs and the walls. Glistening cobwebs hang from the ceiling in silky strands, moving gently in the breeze. There's no more noise. Not a single sound.

"Gabi? Madison?" I say, moving down one step, and then another, the wood cracking beneath my feet. The farther I descend, the more the damp scent intensifies, creeping up my nostrils, making me want to retch. At last, my feet touch the concrete ground below, and I hold up my phone again, turning in a circle, half a footstep at a time.

Something scuttles above me, and I jump, shine the light on the old joists above my head. A gray spider with a body bigger than a grape freezes mid-step, and a dishwater-brown millipede slithers back into the darkness, out of sight. Nobody else is down here, there's nothing but—

A body near the far end of the basement. I gasp, think it's Gabi, but as I move to her, my brain can't process what I'm seeing. I stop because I don't understand. This person has long blond hair. Gabi's is dark. As I try to grasp what's happening, my heart moves into my throat. The hair, the jacket, the pants. It can't be, but I know it's—

"Libby?" Although I whisper the word, it echoes around the room as if I've shouted. Maybe I did. I'm muddled, confused. What's Libby doing down here? She was upstairs, unconscious, and now she's in the basement. How?

Another noise, directly behind me this time. I turn, but only in time to see a wooden object speeding toward me. There's no opportunity to move, no way of avoiding the thick, heavy log that smashes into my temple. A blinding pain bursts across my skull as hot white stars explode in front of my eyes.

Stumbling backward, I try to catch myself but trip over my feet and fall. The pain in my head's so intense, my vision blurs, softening around the edges. Just like in the truck a few hours ago, I feel myself slipping into unconsciousness. I lose the grip on my phone. As it falls to the floor, plunging me into darkness, the last thing I see is someone standing over me.

A person with fiery red hair.

24

1 year 4 months before the accident

THROUGHOUT AUGUST, I stuck to my plan of finding new EmVee members and organized more auditions, which I decided to keep quiet about until I had a few viable options I could present to Madison. It was slow going at first, but things paid off once I posted an ad on a new website called JoinMy-Band, keeping it short and to the point:

> *Drummer seeks guitarist & bassist for existing pop-rock duo. Heavily influenced by 70s–00s music with a modern twist. Big ego? Love drama? Don't bother.*

A bassist named Isabel Riotto messaged me within an hour, and after we spoke on the phone, and I grilled her on her current playlist—almost identical to mine—we met for a drink. I liked Isabel as soon as she strolled through the door. About my age, she'd dyed her long blond hair a light shade of pink, wore ripped black jeans, and a yellow T-shirt brighter than sunshine. She also had a guitar case in her hand, and I loved the fact she'd come prepared.

After making quick introductions, she grabbed a coffee and took a seat. Elbows on the table and brown eyes sparkling, she said, "I'm in."

I burst out laughing. "You haven't heard me play yet."

"Sure have," she said with a grin wider than mine. "I was at the FlatCat the night you played. You were amazing."

"Thank you," I said, a sudden rush of exhilaration from being recognized for the first time flowing through my veins.

"You're welcome. As I said, I'm in if you'll have me." She smiled again. "I'm guessing you want to hear me first?"

"That would be great." I nodded to the case she'd propped up against an empty chair. "How long have you played?"

"Guitar since I was nine, bass since I was fourteen."

"Do you sing?"

"Sure, but lead vocals aren't my thing." She waved a hand. "I get too nervous."

"No problem, Madison and I have got it covered."

"Cool."

I'd initially planned on us talking a while longer, but I instantly took to Isabel. She seemed a no-fuss kind of person, exactly what we needed. "How do you feel about creepy basements?" I said with a chuckle.

She gave me a puzzled look. "I guess it depends."

"The rehearsal room is in my building's basement."

"Want to go now? I have time."

I laughed. "You're not worried I'm a serial killer?"

"Are you?"

"Not today."

"Good enough for me."

As we walked home, I learned this was Isabel's style—uncomplicated and direct, but never rude. She talked with her hands, had the most infectious giggle I'd ever heard, and was fiercely protective of her mom and younger sister, particularly since her father had died from prostate cancer a few years earlier. She was blatantly honest, too.

"I work in finance, and although I'm good at my job, I totally hate it," she said. "The ultimate dream is to be in a wildly successful band, filling arenas and going multi-platinum."

"When you dream, you dream *big*."

"Is there any other way?"

When we reached my building, we headed directly to the basement where I unlocked the storage room and flicked on the light. I felt embarrassed about my cramped quarters, and despite tidying up as much as possible, the metal shelving was still full of old dusty boxes with an eclectic assortment of stuffed animals, dishes, and fake flowers.

Isabel didn't seem to mind. "Wow, nice drums," she said, pointing to my kit as she set her case on the floor. "What shall we play? You said you like the Dragons?"

"Love 'em."

"Let's get to it."

Midway through "Shots" I already knew I wanted Isabel to join EmVee, but I didn't want to seem too eager, so we kept playing. Song after song, we fed off each other's rhythm and improvisation. It didn't feel clumsy or forced. She was a generous musician, comfortable to step back and let me lead but happy to take over at a moment's notice.

As far as I was concerned, bass players were often overlooked when it came to bands. They were, pun intended, the *unsung* heroes who brought the groove, and worked to hold everything together alongside the drummer, keeping everyone else on track. And this girl could sing—her voice had a low, husky quality, a cross between Dua Lipa and Florence Welch.

When we stopped for a break, we sipped water and munched our way through a couple of granola bars I'd stashed in a Tupperware and left on one of the shelves. The air felt electric, humming with adrenaline, joy, and the unspoken knowledge that we fit.

"You *can* carry an entire song by yourself," I said. "Your vocals are fantastic."

"Oh, no. I prefer being in the background."

"Maybe you'll change your mind."

"Maybe. When will I get to meet Madison?"

"Soon," I said. "Very soon."

After promising Isabel I'd be in touch within a few weeks to make introductions, I decided not to tell Madison about our meeting yet and continued to stay silent about my quest to find our fourth and final member, because I figured it might take a while.

Thankfully, it didn't. Three days after I'd jammed with Isabel, as I was on my way back from a double shift at Papa e Ragazzi, I walked past a coffee shop. The door was open, and I heard someone singing "What About Us" by P!nk, accompanied by an acoustic guitar.

I peered inside, saw a woman at the back. Tall, slim with shoulder-length, straight black hair, she was dressed in a light blue button-down shirt and stone-washed boyfriend jeans, which all somehow gave her a slightly edgy look.

Her rich, warm voice was captivating, but what struck me more was her guitar skills. Smoother than Madison's, clean and sharp, never missing a single beat.

Stepping closer, I stopped and listened. A handful of customers sat dotted around the place, and they gave a few half-hearted claps as the song ended, which I tried to make up for with three times the enthusiasm. Apathy could be the worst for an artist.

Another woman joined the first. Their features were similar, but this one had to be a little younger. Her curly hair was dark, too, and tied into a loose bun sitting at her nape. She wore a long purple dress and flat shoes, and as I settled into a chair, they sang "Perfect" together, another of my P!nk favorites. Whoever these two were, they had great taste in music, and judging by their perfectly timed harmonies, they'd played together awhile.

Once their set was done, I walked over to introduce myself. "I'm Vienna," I said.

"Evelina," the older one replied.

"I'm her sister Gabriela," the other woman said, her voice a lot softer. "But everyone calls me Gabi."

I gave them both a wide smile. "You sounded great. I love P!nk."

"Thanks, and she's awesome." Evelina slid her guitar into her case. "Glad you enjoyed it. Thanks for stopping in." Turning to her sister, she continued, "Gabi, we should—"

"Are there other people in your band?" I said quickly.

"No," Gabi answered. "We're a duo."

"Neat. I play the drums and write songs."

"Oh, how cool," Evelina said. "Are you in a band?"

"Yeah…actually, can I buy you both a drink?"

Evelina shook her head. "We're in a bit of a hurry."

"Won't take long," I said. "Promise. I might have a proposal for you."

Evelina and Gabi took a lot more convincing than Isabel to consider joining a new group, but by the time we said goodbye, we'd exchanged phone numbers and promised we'd get together for a session as soon as we could settle on a date.

I hadn't expected to find such talented musicians so quickly, and there was still a question mark about how we'd sound together. This wasn't what concerned me the most. The bigger obstacle now was Madison. She was the one person left to convince to take a chance on EmVee's future, and I suspected it wouldn't be easy.

I worried she'd freak out and her jealous streak would re-emerge because I'd talked to Isabel, Evelina, and Gabi without her, but in my defense, I didn't know if she'd want to participate in the band anymore, especially considering how she was supposed to be focusing on her studies. Barry and Lucinda had made their expectations clear over the summer, especially after they'd learned I was living there. They were the ones paying the exorbitant college fees, after all.

On the other hand, I had to give Madison the option of declining, and if she didn't want to move ahead with the group, I had three other potential members. We couldn't ever be EmVee without Madison, of course, but I had to explore opportunities, even if they didn't include my best friend. I hoped she'd understand. I was wrong.

"You did *what*?" she said when I explained how I'd met Isabel, Evelina, and Gabi. "You held auditions without me?"

"You were busy, and—"

"Doesn't mean you should go behind my back. We're a team, remember? You and me. We're supposed to do everything for EmVee together."

"No decisions have been made."

"Then why does it feel like it?"

I held my tongue as I thought about all the times I'd asked for input on my songs, and she'd brushed me off. How I'd been the one busting my ass, trying to organize gigs for us. Now we were co-responsible? Still, I could concede I'd overstepped some boundaries.

"I'm really sorry, Madison," I said. "I was honestly trying to help our band and I'm sure you'll love them. Isabel's fantastic. She's got this great vibe."

Madison didn't seem convinced. "What about the sisters? What are their names again?"

"Evelina and Gabi."

"Have you told any of them they're already in the band?"

"No, not at all."

"Good, because I don't want there to be five of us."

I frowned. "Why?"

Madison shrugged. "For one, as we saw with the other guys, the more people there are, the more complicated things get. Plus, the best rock bands have four people, not five. Anyway, from what you've said, Gabi only sings backing vocals. We don't need her."

"She plays rhythm guitar."

"So do I. And Isabel and Evelina, apparently."

"Gabi's great on the keyboard and synth."

"Okay…I play piano."

"Not for ages and you can't do both at the same time. Anyway, Evelina made it clear they're a package deal. If we want her, we have to include Gabi."

"See? They're strong-arming you already."

I wanted to roll my eyes, thought better of it. Why was Madison being so closed-off about this? Couldn't she see if we didn't progress as EmVee, I'd have to explore other avenues to move my career ahead? My smile felt forced as I said, "Let's meet and see how it goes. It may be a moot point if we sound awful."

A week later we squeezed into the tiny basement room. Introductions were made, instruments tuned, and Madison turned into her charming self. She warmed to Isabel and Evelina instantly, but I could tell she wasn't a fan of Gabi, who was more reserved than the rest of us.

"She has the image and personality of someone who belongs in a folk group," Madison whispered a while later. I never shared this tidbit with anyone, and I completely disagreed. I liked Gabi: she had a gentle side I felt balanced our band out more and gave our potential audience another person they could identify with. Plus her and Evelina's harmonies sounded incredible.

One thing Madison couldn't deny was the fact the five of us were awesome together. We all brought different things— background, skills, vocal talent, arrangement ideas—and all were hungry for success. Isabel, Evelina, and Gabi had never broken through either, be it alone, together, or with anyone else, and we were determined to make it happen.

After a few jamming sessions, as we were working through a couple of harmonies, Isabel put her guitar down, and said, "Who else thinks it's time to decide on a band name?"

Madison frowned. "What do you mean? We already have one."

"EmVee is the two of you," Isabel said.

"Exactly," Evelina jumped in. "It would be good to start fresh."

Madison looked as if she'd munched on a box of lemons. "But EmVee's our name."

"I understand why you're emotionally attached to it," Isabel said slowly. "And it would matter if you were hugely successful but there's no name recognition."

"Not to you," Madison said, turning to me. "You don't want a change, do you?"

I chose my words and tone carefully. "Well...Isabel's right. It's not like we've had a hit song or a million downloads. We haven't released anything. Nobody knows us."

Madison's eyes could've shot daggers at me, but before she could answer, Gabi spoke up, her soft voice marked with more than a hint of determination. "When we're asked why we're called EmVee, it makes the three of us—" she gestured to her sister, Isabel, and herself "—seem irrelevant."

"What would we call ourselves?" I held up a hand as Madison opened her mouth. "For sake of argument. Anyone got some ideas?"

"Go on," Evelina told Gabi. "Tell them."

Gabi's face flushed a shade of deep scarlet as she mumbled, "The Bittersweet." Nobody spoke and Gabi rushed on. "It doesn't matter if you don't like it. I mean—"

"No," Isabel said quickly. "It's awesome. I love it."

"So do I," Evelina added as Gabi grinned. "It's simple, effective, easy to remember."

"Agreed," I said. "I love band names starting with *the*."

"This is great," Isabel jumped back in. "We made our first decision as a team."

"Yeah," Madison said, her tone able to cut glass. "Fantastic."

25

11 months before the accident

A FEW MONTHS later and it was January again. Christmas had come and gone, as had the second anniversary of my arrival in New York, and my twenty-first birthday, which I celebrated at Papa e Ragazzi with the Bittersweet. Things were moving forward with the band, and I felt momentum growing that had never been there before.

We practiced as often as possible, which was difficult at times because of conflicting schedules. Isabel had a nine-to-five job, Evelina and Gabi were servers like me, and they did a bit of voice-over work on the side, recording jingles and radio commercials, making them dash off for an audition or booking without much notice.

Madison's study load was heavier than ever, and I tried to work as many shifts as I could because I needed the money. We still managed to squeeze a jam session in at least once a week, even if it meant starting late at night and being dead tired the next morning.

Despite Madison's initial frostiness, the Bittersweet had become our official name. She'd also gently warmed to the idea of there being five of us, although she kept any compliments for Gabi tucked away more safely than the secrets at Area 51.

One of the family traits Madison had inherited was the inability to admit when she was wrong. Along with the need for control. The Bittersweet name hadn't been Madison's idea, which had irked her profoundly, especially because everyone we talked to thought it was a great choice.

As always, I put her churlishness down to stress and pressure, hoped once she'd finished her studies in the spring she'd be back to her old self if only for the summer. She was partying less, at least, and I hadn't seen her high in ages. I took it as a definitive win.

One night as we gathered in the basement room, eating slices of pizza I'd brought from the restaurant, we started talking about band image.

"I've done some research," Madison announced. "I think we should each have a clearly defined role within the group. I don't mean the instruments we play, but an identity in which the fans can see themselves, you know? It makes us relatable."

"Isn't it a bit early?" Isabel said. "I mean, nobody knows who we are."

"Exactly my point," Madison answered. "We need a brand. Together and individually."

It all sounded a little forced to me, I just wanted to make music, cared less about the fame and glory it might bring, but Gabi seemed on board. "Perhaps we could come up with nicknames like the Spice Girls," she said. "You know, Scary, Posh, Ginger, Sporty, and Baby, although they didn't invent them. Mel B said it was a lazy journalist who couldn't be bothered remembering their names."

"Good to know," Madison said dryly. By now we'd all heard about Gabi's fascination with the girl-power group, an obsession passed down from her mom. I thought it was sweet. Madison thought it ludicrous. "My point is," she continued. "We need a cohesive image. Personas."

"Pretend to be something we're not?" Isabel said. "No, thanks."

"All right, listen." From the clipped tone of Madison's voice, I could tell she was on the wrong side of irritated. "I'm not suggesting we pretend to be anything, but what we can do is lean into who we are. Make it a bit more extreme. Like stage makeup." She pointed at me. "Take Vienna, for example."

"What about me?"

Madison laughed. "My parents always thought Vienna was a bad influence."

"What?" Isabel said. "Vienna's the sweetest."

I pulled a face. "I'd rather be branded a bad influence, thanks."

"Exactly," Madison said. "You could amplify it a lot more. Have fun with it. Give more attitude and sass. Be the badass drummer girl."

"A stereotype?" I said. "Then you should be the wholesome guitarist led astray. Prove your mom and dad right."

"Not a bad idea," she said. "I've always been the yin to your yang."

We didn't get anywhere with the whole assuming personas discussion as we kept going around in circles. Later that night, when the two of us were back at the apartment alone, Madison tried to convince me she and I should have the final say when it came to decisions involving the Bittersweet.

"We're the original founders," she insisted, glossing over the fact I'd instigated the expansion of the group and found the three others when she'd been on the precipice of giving up. "Our word needs to have more sway than theirs."

"Democracy is always best," I countered. "Whatever we disagree on, we put to a vote. With five of us there'll always be a majority decision."

The comment led to yet another debate about why she

thought Gabi shouldn't have joined in the first place. "Besides," Madison said, "too many cooks in anything never works. We need a leader, and I mean the two of us."

"What we need is collaboration," I insisted. "On writing music, arrangements, harmonies, the cover songs, the order we perform them in, the whole lot. I wouldn't want to be in a band where I was made to feel lesser than. Would you?"

She caved, and I think the more we rehearsed the covers and the songs I continued to fine-tune for us, the more she knew I was right. For this to work, for the Bittersweet to have a tiny hope in hell of becoming any kind of success, we needed to make space for one another, listen to each other, and have everybody's back. It was a concept I wasn't sure Madison could get used to.

Over the winter, the five of us networked at every opportunity, talked to anyone who'd stand still long enough to listen about our new all-female pop-rock group. We took gigs whenever we could, wherever we got them from, whether paid or—most often—for gas money or only the glory.

When we booked a few venues upstate, in New Jersey, and a little beyond, I spent most of the money I'd saved on an ancient, beaten-up Chevrolet Tahoe. Guy snorted when he saw it and called it a hunk of junk.

Undeterred, I made him feast on his words—adding a generous serving of humble pie—after I spoke to one of my best customers at Papa e Ragazzi, who owned a car detailing service. I offered for the Bittersweet to play at her son's bar mitzvah in exchange for the crappy old Tahoe to be deep cleaned. Granted, it was still a piece of crap, and trying to fit five people and the equipment inside was a human game of Tetris, but at least we were mobile.

With all of us plugging away at getting gigs and raising band awareness, Madison's studies came under more strain, and on multiple occasions we talked about her quitting so she could focus on music full-time. But the same thing always happened. She broached the subject of taking a gap year with her parents, they threatened to cut her off, she backed down.

At times it made living with her a challenge, her mood swings could be monumental, unpredictable, but I learned how to navigate the stormy waters as best as possible, making more excuses for her than I probably should've.

Slivers of success kept our drive high during those initial months. A two-line mention on a few blogs felt like a write-up in *Rolling Stone*. They were droplets, the smallest of indications we were moving ahead. Enough to light more hunger and give us another collective shove.

When we had a bit of praise, the fact every agent we'd contacted had ignored us, and that our online presence remained slim, all faded into the background. Agents were inundated with requests, and social media was an impetuous beast, a full-time gig for which none of us had time.

Our big break came from the unlikeliest of places. A friend of Isabel's cousin was getting married and was on the hunt for a band to play at their wedding. Isabel had sent her our recording, and we'd got the gig.

"It's a fancy golf club out in Newton," Isabel said.

"Newton?" Madison wrinkled her nose. "It'll take forever."

"I told them we want fifteen hundred bucks," Isabel said.

"What?" Evelina said.

Isabel gave us two thumbs up. "Plus gas. Are we in?"

Of course we were, and when we arrived at the upscale country club with its plush green lawns and sprawling, white clubhouse, I suspected we could've asked for more. With the amount of caviar, foie gras, and oysters served as appetizers alone, the food probably cost twenty times our fee. The guests were dressed in well-cut suits and long cocktail gowns, but those didn't stop them from getting up to dance.

The happy couple had requested "You Really Got Me" by

the Kinks as their first song, after which we played Pat Benatar, Oasis, and the Goo Goo Dolls. Like at the FlatCat, we had our audience exactly where we wanted them—in our palms and on their feet.

After playing half the set, we took a break and I headed for the bathroom. As I came out and walked into the plush hallway, my boots sinking into the pristine ruby carpet, I noticed a dark-haired bearded man standing twenty feet back from the door, his hands clasped in front of him.

I'd seen him inside the venue room, watching us. Hard to miss with his sharp charcoal suit and starched white shirt, an indigo tie slung loose around his neck. He stood a few inches taller than me, wore three silver rings on his left hand and had a cluster of freckles on his left cheek. He exuded confidence, and money.

"The Bittersweet," he said as I was about to walk past. "Have you played together long?"

I stopped, hoped this wasn't going to be a sloppy attempt—or any kind of attempt—to hit on me, but I supposed I had to suck it up and be nice to the wedding guests, providing they didn't try anything sleazy. "Not long. I hope you're enjoying the music."

"Very much," he said. "The last song was an original."

"Sweet Spot? Yes, it's one of mine."

"I knew it." He took a few steps toward me, held out a hand. "Roger Kent."

"Vienna Taylor," I said as we shook. "Good to meet you, Roger, but I'd better get back in there. Wouldn't want to disappoint the bride and groom."

"Okay, confession time." His chuckle had me groaning on the inside. He was at least twenty-five years older than me. Probably had a kid my age. As I opened my mouth to excuse myself a second time, he said, "I'm not actually a guest at your party."

"Oh?"

He gestured down the hallway. "Mine's an investment thing I was roped into against my better judgment. Food's not bad but their entertainment sucks. It's a string quartet."

I grinned. "I take it classical isn't your style?"

"Jesus, no. I mean, I appreciate the skill and all, but give me Green Day, any day."

I let out a surprised laugh. "Same. I really should—"

"Do the Bittersweet have a manager?" he asked. When I found myself unable to answer, he smiled, reached into his jacket pocket, pulled out a black-and-silver business card and held it out to me. "Excellent. Let's talk."

26

7 months before the accident

TRANSCRIPT: *What's On NYC*: **Season 13, EP 21: May Mayhem & Meet 'n' Greet The Bittersweet**

MELODIE JOHNSON: Welcome back to *What's On NYC*, folks. I'm your host, Melodie Johnson, and today I have the absolute pleasure of chatting with our great city's latest musical rising stars, the Bittersweet. Get this: their first single, "Sweet Spot," of which you just heard a snippet, has been streamed over five hundred thousand times since it dropped last week. This awesome all-female pop-rock band is comprised of Vienna Taylor, Madison Pierce, Isabel Riotto, and sisters Evelina and Gabi Sevillano. A huge welcome, ladies. It's great to have the Bittersweet in the studio today, and congrats!

MADISON PIERCE: Thank you, thank you. I can't believe we're chatting with the iconic Melodie Johnson. You're an absolute legend. I've listened to your show for years and years.

MELODIE JOHNSON: Ah, that's great to hear. I'm flattered, truly. Shall we begin with quick introductions, so our listeners can put names to your voices? Let's start with you, Madison. Tell us about yourself and your role in the Bittersweet.

MADISON PIERCE: Oh, me first? (laughs) Okay. I'm Madison Pierce. Originally from Portland, Maine. I'm a student at NYU's engineering program and I'm a lead vocalist, play guitar, and write music for the Bittersweet.

MELODIE JOHNSON: Impressive. I think we'll call that a quadruple threat. You go next, Vienna, then we'll keep moving around the table.

VIENNA TAYLOR: Sure. I'm Vienna Taylor. Same as Madison, I'm originally from Portland but I'm not an engineering student. I failed physics (laughs).

MELODIE JOHNSON: (laughs) Same. But you are the Bittersweet's sensational drummer.

VIENNA TAYLOR: Thank you so much, what high praise. Yeah, I play the drums, sing lead vocals, and write our original songs. Over to you, Isabel.

ISABEL RIOTTO: I'm Isabel Riotto. Originally from Holmeson, New Jersey, and I live in Queens now. I play bass and I'm another of your biggest fans, Melodie (laughs).

MELODIE JOHNSON: Put the sledgehammer down, please (laughs). And you, Evelina? Where are you from?

EVELINA SEVILLANO: Boston, now living in Brooklyn. I play guitar and sing backing vocals.

MELODIE JOHNSON: And last but by no means least, we have you, Gabi. You're Evelina's younger sister?

GABI SEVILLANO: Yes. I play rhythm guitar and sing backing vocals.

MELODIE JOHNSON: Wonderful. Now, as I mentioned in the intro, "Sweet Spot" is your first release and has already got a ton, and I mean a ton, of love. How does it feel?

VIENNA TAYLOR: I think I speak for us all when I say it's incredible so far, but let's see if it continues. I don't want to jinx anything.

ISABEL RIOTTO: Yeah. What she said (laughs).

MELODIE JOHNSON: I have a great feeling, trust me. You haven't signed with a label yet though. How come?

MADISON PIERCE: We felt we were ready to release the song now. Test the water, so to speak, and see what the reaction is.

MELODIE JOHNSON: Quite the gamble but I think it's paying off. Vienna, did it feel different when you wrote "Sweet Spot" compared to other songs you've worked on?

VIENNA TAYLOR: I loved the melody, and the lyrics came more easily. I put my heart into it as much as possible, which I always try to do when I write. If I'm not feeling a connection, how can I expect anyone else to? But with "Sweet Spot" it dug deep into my bones.

MADISON PIERCE: Same for me.

MELODIE JOHNSON: You and Madison write all the songs together?

MADISON PIERCE: Since we met in high school almost four years ago. We're a team.

MELODIE JOHNSON: And the Bittersweet is a new band. Not quite a year old.

VIENNA TAYLOR: Yes. Madison and I originally formed a duo called EmVee, but we never released any music or had any kind of success.

ISABEL RIOTTO: Not true!

MELODIE JOHNSON: Agreed. There was one notable show at the FlatCat pub in Brooklyn just over a year ago, and it got a lot of attention. It's when you first showed up on my radar, by the way. Why did you decide to expand from a duo? Were you always hoping for there to be five of you?

MADISON PIERCE: Oh, yes, no question. We find it adds depth and complexity to our sound. More variety to the harmonies as well. We hit it off and make all the decisions together. With five there's always a majority.

MELODIE JOHNSON: Obviously, it was meant to be. Let's get to the other members. Isabel, tell us your story.

ISABEL RIOTTO: Well, I moved to Queens for work last summer. I'm an associate at an auditing company.

MELODIE JOHNSON: Not to stereotype all you accountants out there, but you don't look like one, Isabel. For those of you who haven't seen a photo of the Bittersweet yet, she's the one with the long pink hair.

ISABEL RIOTTO: I scrub up well for the office (laughs).

MELODIE JOHNSON: So, you moved to Queens for your job. Were you in a band before joining the Bittersweet?

ISABEL RIOTTO: A couple here and there. Everything changed when I met Vienna.

MELODIE JOHNSON: Was it band love at first sight?

ISABEL RIOTTO: (laughs) It was for me.

MELODIE JOHNSON: Oh? Tell us how you met.

VIENNA TAYLOR: I put an ad on JoinMyBand and Isabel was one of the first to respond. We met, she played, I convinced her to join.

ISABEL RIOTTO: Trust me, with her skills I didn't need any convincing.

MELODIE JOHNSON: I'll bet. Vienna's drumming was one of the first things I picked up on when I saw a video of the FlatCat gig. And Evelina and Gabi, did you respond to the ad as well? Had you two been in a band together before?

EVELINA SEVILLANO: Yeah, we played in one in Boston for a while before I moved to Brooklyn. Gabi joined me here a few months later. But we met Vienna when we performed at a coffee shop, and she happened to walk by.

MELODIE JOHNSON: Sounds serendipitous.

GABI SEVILLANO: It totally was.

MADISON PIERCE: Vienna and I share an apartment, and I'll never forget the day she came home saying she'd found the perfect pair. Evelina's guitar skills are outrageous and Gabi's backing vocals are a fabulous extra. I knew we needed them to join our little family right away.

MELODIE JOHNSON: All-female pop-rock groups still aren't all too common, which I'm sure we can all agree is a travesty. Was it always your plan for it to be all women? Show the guys how it's done?

VIENNA TAYLOR: (laughs) I think it's the sound that matters most. Whether we work well together. I'm incredibly happy we found each other.

MELODIE JOHNSON: Fair point. Who are your musical influences?

MADISON PIERCE: Gosh, there are so many. I love older bands, thanks to a nanny I had years ago. The Go-Go's, Blondie, the Runaways, and U2. Lenny Kravitz, Pat Benatar, and Alanis Morrissette have always been favorites.

VIENNA TAYLOR: Same. Add in Snow Patrol, Prince, Imagine Dragons. Nirvana, too. And the Beaches from Toronto, is a more recent band that I love. I used to listen to music from the sixties and seventies with my grandmother, so she had a huge impact. Meg

White from the White Stripes, Demi Lovato, and P!nk have, too. They're the epitome of cool.

MELODIE JOHNSON: Agreed. P!nk's incredible and she's the nicest person you'll ever meet.

GABI SEVILLANO: (gasps) You've met her?

MELODIE JOHNSON: Multiple times. Trust me when I say I had a complete fangirl moment the first time, and I mean flappy hands, high-pitched voice, the works (laughs). Let's not get into it. Who did you listen to as a kid, Evelina, Gabi?

EVELINA SEVILLANO: Brit Pop was huge for me. I love Elastica, Lush, and Oasis. But Stevie Nicks is my favorite female singer.

ISABEL RIOTTO: I adore her.

GABI SEVILLANO: I adore the Bangles, Tina Turner, Taylor Swift, Miley Cyrus, and the Spice Girls.

MELODIE JOHNSON: Whoa. Didn't see that last one coming.

GABI SEVILLANO: Well, the power they exuded in the nineties, and still today, was incredible. They're legends. Ginger Spice was our mom's favorite. Quite sure she could sing "Wannabe" and do all the dance moves in her sleep.

MELODIE JOHNSON: (laughs) Couldn't we all? Okay, so you meet, put the band together, record "Sweet Spot" and here we are, with it taking off. Some say it'll be the song of the summer.

GABI SEVILLANO: (whispers) Wow.

MELODIE JOHNSON: How much pressure and expectation does it all put on you?

MADISON PIERCE: I think we're taking it day-by-day, trying to let what's happening sink in but not become distracted by it.

EVELINA SEVILLANO: I can't think about it, to be honest, or I feel paralyzed. We're focusing on new songs, which keeps us busy.

MELODIE JOHNSON: Did you always want to be in a band?

MADISON PIERCE: Most definitely.

GABI SEVILLANO: Same.

ISABEL RIOTTO: What they said.

VIENNA TAYLOR: (laughs) Me, too.

EVELINA SEVILLANO: I'd rather die than not be able to play.

MELODIE JOHNSON: Wow, intense. Okay, ladies, what does the Bittersweet's future hold? Where do you want the band to be next year, the year after, and beyond?

VIENNA TAYLOR: Signed by a record company, successful and together. Playing venues. Working on more tracks.

MELODIE JOHNSON: How's it going with the new songs?

EVELINA SEVILLANO: We're having an absolute blast. Vienna's such a great writer.

GABI SEVILLANO: And these ladies are awesome to be with.

ISABEL RIOTTO: There's such positive energy, you know?

MELODIE JOHNSON: I'm definitely feeling the vibe. Vienna, are you writing all the material for the album?

VIENNA TAYLOR: Well—

MADISON PIERCE: We're working on them together.

VIENNA TAYLOR: And there are a few songs we're happy with already.

MELODIE JOHNSON: Can you release them tomorrow? Because I can't wait. Will you come back to the studio for another chat in the future?

MADISON PIERCE: Are you kidding? We'd love to.

MELODIE JOHNSON: It's a date. In the meantime, let's play your sure-to-be-a-summer-hit-song. Everybody, listen up. This is "Sweet Spot" by the Bittersweet. But wait, there's more, as always. After the break I'll give you the skinny about a surprise concert scheduled next month at Radio City. Who is it? All will be revealed, and we have tickets to give away. Stay tuned.

27

The day after the accident

I DON'T KNOW how many hours have passed when I wake up. My eyes feel welded shut and the side of my head throbs so badly I want to pass out. It takes me a few seconds to remember what happened. Somebody assaulted me. The last thing I saw was…

Refusing to finish the thought, I force my eyes open and push myself to a sitting position. I'm still in the basement but it's no longer dark. Opaque light finds its way in through the windows. Two of them are fully blocked by a mound of snow, but another is almost clear. I crane my neck, see trees glistening in the distance, their branches sagging. Beyond them is a patch of blue sky amid white fluffy clouds. The storm has passed.

Heaving myself to my feet, pausing as the room spins, I recall I wasn't alone down here. Sure enough, Libby's lying in the corner, where she was when someone hit me over the head last night. Was it last night? I'm freezing cold, so cold it's as if my blood has solidified in my veins. I can't imagine she's doing any better.

"Libby?" I don't know why I'm whispering, there's nobody else in the basement, but my pulse accelerates, tap-tap-tapping in my neck. I'm afraid whoever hurt me is upstairs, and I'm terrified Libby's... I can't finish the thought. Why won't she wake up?

Slowly, I take a few steps in her direction, and as I approach, she groans and stirs. Her eyes flutter open, and I kneel beside her, take her hand in mine. Her skin's freezing, too, the color almost translucent.

"V-Vienna?" she says. "Wh-where am I?"

"We're at the cabin."

"Cabin?" she whispers.

"We were in a car accident yesterday. Do you remember the crash?"

"Isabel..." She stops, swallows. "Yes, I remember. You and Madison went for help."

"Yes, we found a cabin and came here," I say, deciding not to tell her about everything else that happened yet, and hoping she can hear me as her eyes close again. "Libby? The snow's stopped. We can go find help."

Her face scrunches up, and she shakes her head. "I'm tired."

"I know, honey, but you have to get up. We need to leave. Please?"

She shakes her head again, mumbles a few words I can't make out.

"Do you remember who brought you down here?"

"No," she whispers. "I'm tired. So, so tired."

Shit. This time, when I scramble to my feet, I ignore the throbbing in my head. My priority is Libby and me getting out of this cabin, together, but first I need to ensure we're safe.

The room's completely bare. I was hoping to find an object I could use to defend us with in case the attacker returns, but there's nothing here. My phone has disappeared, although it wouldn't be much use.

The last thing I saw after I was beaten resurfaces, and this time I can't push it away.

Red hair. *Madison's* red hair.

I must be mistaken, confused. Madison wouldn't hurt me or Libby. It had to have been someone else. Fear slams into me, almost making me stumble. Whoever brought Libby to the basement and assaulted me might've hurt Madison when the two of us were outside last night searching for Gabi. That's why I couldn't find her. Maybe it's why we couldn't find Gabi.

What if my assailant hurt them both?

What if they're upstairs with my friends right now?

What if splitting us up was a strategy to make us easier to handle?

The fear intensifies, and I force myself to take deep breaths in and out of my nose, trying to calm myself down.

Libby's eyes are still closed. Perhaps it's better to leave her for now, sneak upstairs and out of the basement. If anyone's in the cabin, maybe I can surprise them. Find anything I can use to smack them over the head with like they did to me. If I incapacitate them, we can escape.

Treading as quietly as I can, I head for the stairs, take them slowly, one at a time, wincing as the third step lets out a loud creak. I see the door at the top is closed. When it's within reach, I stretch out my arm, and my fingers close around the knob.

I push but the door doesn't move. More fear rises from my belly, wrapping around my chest like a giant snake. Breaths come in shallow gasps, faster and faster, my pulse racing out of control. My heart's going to tear itself from my chest if I don't stop and while I think this is some form of panic attack, and know I need to calm down, I'm powerless to stop it. I need to get out of here.

"Help!" I shout, pounding my fists against the door. "Somebody, help!"

I try the knob again, rattle and shove as hard as I can, hoping

I made a mistake, or the door will magically open, but it doesn't budge. My fists are hurting, red and raw, so I slap my palms against the wood, shouting and hollering, my voice reaching a deafening crescendo.

Nothing happens. Nobody comes. There's no gruff voice on the other side telling me to shut my mouth. Crouching, I peer through the crack underneath the door but can't see feet, shadows, or any kind of movement. When I listen for the tiniest of noises, all I hear is silence.

Defeat sets in and I slump onto the top step with my head in my hands. I want to cry. I feel so helpless, so alone, but tears won't help. Determination will. I have to take action. Libby's hurt, Gabi and Madison are out there somewhere. What if I'm their only hope left?

I get up, head downstairs, and examine the windows. Even if I stand on my tiptoes, the handle is out of reach, teasing me by four inches. If I can find something to stand on, maybe I'll have a way out. I scan the room once more despite knowing there's nothing here, and go to Libby, gently shaking her awake.

"I need you," I say. "Please, Libby. Please can you help me?"

She opens her eyes, winces as the light hits her face. "What can I do?"

"Give me a boost." I take her hand. "Come over by the window."

It's almost a miracle when she does as I ask. She can't stand without swaying, so I get her to kneel on all fours beneath the window and place my foot on her back. On the first try, her arms almost collapse so we go again, and this time I manage to release the latch and jimmy the pane, creating an opening wide enough for my body to fit through.

Libby's exhausted from the effort, so I give her a minute as I creep to the basement stairs and listen. Still no sound. Once I'm certain Libby can take my weight, I get her in place, swiftly step on her back and pull myself up.

The air outside's so crisp it instantly freezes the hairs in my nose. As the snow bites at my skin, I keep going, scrabbling against the inside wall with my boots to gain traction. My grip's slipping, and when I'm about to fall, Libby grabs my legs and pushes me up.

In one swift movement I heave myself out of the window—out of the cabin—and onto the icy ground. Relief flows though me, but I can't stay here. I roll onto my side, pop my head back through the window. Libby's already slumped on the floor, her eyes pressed shut.

There's no way she can attempt to climb to me, and if she gets up here, I doubt she can walk through the forest. It's a hard choice but the fact is she'll slow me down, which means a delay in getting her the help she needs. As distressing as it is, it's best to leave her.

Except, what if I get lost and don't find the cabin again?

What if whoever locked us up is still here or on their way back?

I wait for panic to fill my veins, but it doesn't come. Instead, it's anger. Sheer white-hot rage straightening my spine. I'm not leaving Libby, Gabi, or Madison here without first being certain there's nobody else in the vicinity. It means I only have one option.

I'm going inside.

28

6 months before the accident

THINGS HAD MOVED so fast in the past four months, at times it was difficult to keep track. On the drive back from the Newton wedding, I'd told the others about Roger Kent giving me his business card, and I think our yells and screams were audible all across the state. Isabel immediately pulled out her phone and googled him.

"Holy crap," she said. "He's got quite the pedigree."

I'd already taken a peek, knew Roger had been in the music industry for almost thirty years. He'd discovered and managed several high-profile artists who'd gone on to have multiple smash hits, and dozens of others who'd been successful.

There was no doubt Roger knew the industry, had connections on both coasts, in between, and beyond. Judging by the bands he represented, he made a point of keeping up with evolving tastes and trends. Another bonus point in his favor was that, no matter how hard Gabi, Madison, Isabel, and Evelina scoured the internet as we drove back to Brooklyn, we couldn't find a whiff of a scandal involving him.

I'd wanted to call Roger as soon as Madison and I got back to our apartment, but decided to wait until the next day, and we arranged for the Bittersweet to meet him at Dina's Diner on Ninth Street for brunch the following week.

"I've been hoping to find a band exactly like you for a while," Roger told us over plates of pancakes, waffles, and crispy bacon. "And I know a few A&R managers who are, too."

"What's an A&R manager?" Gabi said, and I caught Madison rolling her eyes.

"Artist and repertoire," Roger answered, his voice patient. "They work for the record label and liaise with the artists, and their manager, of course."

"You think we'll get a record deal?" Evelina said, practically bouncing on the royal blue pleather seat. "Do you *actually* mean it?"

"I can't guarantee it," Roger said. "But yes, I do."

The way he spoke to us—answering our questions about how the industry worked, what he could do for us, how he could help protect our rights—we all sensed what a genuine person he was. I also appreciated how he tempered our expectations, balancing keeping our dreams alive but not blowing smoke up anyone's ass.

We all liked how he listened to our concerns, answered incessant questions no matter how ludicrous they sounded, and treated us as equals. I put it to a vote after Roger left the diner, but it was no contest. The Bittersweet had a manager.

To celebrate, Roger invited us for drinks at his three-bedroom duplex near Madison Avenue, where we met his real-estate guru husband, Max, and their two spaniels, George and Michael, named after Roger's favorite artist of all time.

A while later, he helped us decide which songs to use for our updated demo and cashed in a few favors to get us two free sessions at a professional recording studio. We all gawped at one another, saying, "Pinch me, pinch me" a thousand times because we'd all dreamed about this day for eons, and now it was here it felt surreal.

Once our few original songs were recorded, we strategized about the best route to take, and Roger suggested releasing "Sweet Spot" independently to generate buzz. "It can be a gamble," he said when Madison questioned the tactic. "But I think the song will gain traction quickly, and when it does, it'll give us leverage to negotiate a better deal with a record label because we'll have demonstrable interest."

He was right, and a few days after our interview with Melodie Johnson on *What's On NYC*—another *pinch me* moment—Roger invited us for dinner at an exclusive French restaurant called La Tartiflette in Lenox Hill. Guy couldn't believe it when I told him where we were going, said there was a ridiculously long wait-list unless you had connections—another indication of Roger's influence.

We all settled around the table sipping Veuve Clicquot from dainty crystal flutes. The amount of food on the oversize plates the immaculately dressed waitstaff carried as they walked by was microscopic, and when I saw the astronomical prices on the menu, I wondered how they could justify charging so much for a bit of chicken.

Madison appeared to be in her element, talking about body, tannins, and acidity of wines as she and Roger perused the list, her pedigree and upbringing on full display. As I watched them, I thought about how much she'd got into the *persona* she'd assigned herself. She came across as the educated, sophisticated one, a good girl—the anomaly in a pop-rock band and thereby instantly recognizable.

Her ability to get everyone to like her really was uncanny. Guy still pined after her, taking the scraps she threw his way as he hoped it would lead to more. She'd enchanted Roger and Melodie Johnson, too.

"You didn't remember who Melodie was last year," I'd teased

Madison after our radio interview. "Not until she mentioned us on her show after the FlatCat gig."

Madison shrugged. "Tell people what they want to hear. Feed their ego, feed yourself."

Did she do the same with me, I wondered, thinking I'd always considered being fake synonymous with being a liar.

Since we'd got the Bittersweet together, and in particular during the time since we'd met Roger, agreed to him being our manager, and released "Sweet Spot," Madison had changed, becoming more and more obsessive about fame, about being well-known.

Not a day went by without her frantically checking our social media accounts, which Isabel had updated with Roger's guidance. She constantly monitored the amount of likes and comments, becoming despondent or going on rants whenever she felt the latter were unfavorable to her. Didn't much appreciate #TeamVienna getting more mentions than #TeamMadison, either, or how the two hashtags had reemerged. Of course, she only made these comments to me in private. Publicly she insisted we were all truly *blessed*, *charmed*, and *oh-so-grateful*.

"Overnight success?" she'd said before we'd left for La Tartiflette together, after she'd scrolled through socials for the past hour. "They don't have a clue. I've made music for years."

"Not as the Bittersweet."

She clicked her tongue. "Obviously, but my point is now everyone's giving the same amount of credence to the other three."

"Why does it matter?" I asked. "We decided we're equals, so who cares?"

Madison didn't answer. She didn't need to because I could see it in her eyes. *She* cared, and a whole damn lot. A voracious appetite for the spotlight to remain on her had developed. I wasn't sure if anything could feed it fast enough, but I knew for certain I didn't like what it was doing to her.

"Ladies," Roger said, bringing me back to the restaurant, the smell of the fresh bread rolls the server put in front of us wafting up my nose, making my stomach rumble. "I have news. Great news. The fact 'Sweet Spot' is trending on TikTok is one thing, but combined with the streaming downloads and views on YouTube…"

"The suspense is killing me," Isabel said. "Tell us, tell us, tell us."

Roger grinned. "Have your ears been burning? Because I spent most of my week talking to a few labels about what they can do for the Bittersweet."

Gabi let out a gasp, and Isabel squealed so loud, every patron at the surrounding tables glanced in our direction. "We're getting signed?" she gasped.

"If you want to be." Roger beamed. "Let me take you through the offers."

"Offers?" Evelina said. "There's more than one?"

"I have two," Roger said. "One from a larger label, the other's smaller. Let me lay out the pros and cons, and we can debate options. If you want to proceed with either, I suggest we meet the execs and if all goes well, we'll get the lawyers involved."

It took us a while to agree. I wasn't surprised Madison wanted the larger label, arguing they had the biggest budget, the deepest pockets, and therefore a better reach. Roger countered it wasn't necessarily true.

"Yes, Mooseman Records made a lower offer, and the company's smaller too," he said. "But it's more boutique. They're known for giving artists more creative control. The owner, Marvin Lavoie, is a friend of mine, and the producer they're suggesting teaming you up with is top-notch. If there's anyone out there with a finger on the pulse of what the public wants, it's her."

"A female producer?" Evelina said. "Done. Mooseman gets my vote."

"Same," Gabi said.

The discussion continued. Isabel and I were on board with Mooseman within an instant. Eventually, and reluctantly, Madison gave in. Didn't have much of a choice considering it was four against one.

I could tell she wanted me to side with her, but I wouldn't. I'd already agreed to letting everyone believe she and I had cowritten "Sweet Spot." I kept telling myself it didn't matter. We were moving ahead, this wasn't the time for petty arguments. However, getting a bit more money in return for less creative freedom? Not a decision I'd support, nor did I understand why Madison was so hung up on cash when she had her parents' financial backing.

Two days after our celebratory dinner with Roger, all became clear when I came home from a shift and walked in on Madison having a heated argument with her father over the phone.

"I'm taking a year off college, nobody died," she yelled, switching her cell to speakerphone as soon as she saw me, gesturing at me to come over and listen but stay silent. "I don't understand what the big deal is."

"Listen to me." Barry's voice could've frozen Portland harbor on a summer's day. "Your mother and I have stood by watching your grades fall. We've hired tutors and paid for you to retake courses."

"For which I'm thankful," Madison said.

"We've funded your life in Brooklyn," he continued. "Accepted how Vienna came to live with you despite our reservations about how it would affect your studies, which it clearly has."

Madison rolled her eyes. "Actually, she tries to keep me on track."

"Be that as it may," he said, "you're not dropping out—"

"It's a gap year."

"You're not taking a gap year to focus on music. We want

you to get your degree, have a good, respectable career, not bum around playing gigs. It's not the kind of people we are."

"What about what I want?" Madison said, the iciness in her voice matching her father's. "Do you ever think about that?"

"We haven't spent all this money for nothing, so I'll make this easy for you," Barry said. "If you don't continue at NYU, I'll sell the apartment. You'll be on your own."

"I'll pay you rent," Madison said quickly.

"You won't be able to come up with the amount I can command for the place or pay all your bills."

"Wait. Are you saying you'll cut me off completely?"

"Correct, or you can stay in college and live comfortably." He paused. "I'll consider increasing your allowance."

"You know what, Dad," Madison said. "I learned an important lesson a few days ago. Taking money in exchange for someone clipping your wings is a bad deal. Put the apartment on the market. We'll find somewhere else to live."

"Don't do anything you'll regret, Madison, because when your band fails—"

"*When?* Either that's a weirdly veiled threat or a complete lack of confidence in my abilities. Care to elaborate on which one you're going for?" When Barry hadn't answered a full ten seconds later, Madison lifted her chin, her face filled with steely determination I'd never seen in her before. "Bye, Dad."

29

I DIDN'T EXPECT Madison to go through with it, but she did. Two weeks after the phone call with her father, we moved into our new apartment in Bushwick, on the border of Brooklyn and Queens. Guy, who seemed to know everyone and their neighbor, helped find the place, which had one bedroom and a tiny den with no windows.

Madison and I flipped a coin, and she ended up in the smaller room. She wasn't impressed and didn't enjoy not having a doorman either, but she had no choice.

I kept reminding myself she came from an affluent family, didn't know what it was like to scrape and scrounge the way I'd been raised. The paperwork for the deal with Mooseman Records Inc. would take a few weeks to come through. The advance we'd receive wasn't terrible, but once split into five equal parts, there wasn't enough to live on. Definitely not in Brooklyn.

Guy offered Madison a job at Papa e Ragazzi, which she almost turned down until her credit card was canceled. Barry had made it clear if she didn't continue college, he'd cut her off. She'd called his bluff, and he'd called hers. She still had a bit of money left in her checking account, but it wouldn't go far.

Finally, one Monday in early October, Roger messaged, saying the contracts were ready to sign. The five of us could barely wait until the ink was dry before going out to mark the occasion, and we ended up in a dodgy karaoke bar.

"What shall we do to celebrate?" Madison asked after grabbing another round of tequila shots. They were all on their way to getting hammered while I was practically sober, having refused the last two drinks in favor of a Coke.

"Isn't that what we're doing now?" Evelina lifted the glass to her lips, making quick work of the contents before popping a lime wedge in her mouth and pulling a face. "Bwah, this stuff gets me every time."

"We should do something special," Madison said. "Go somewhere."

"I'd love to," Gabi agreed. "A girls' weekend."

"Works for me," Isabel said.

"But not far and it's got to be cheap," Evelina added.

I nodded and sipped my drink. "Somewhere we can drive to. We can take the Tahoe. It won't be as much of a squeeze without all our gear."

"What about the Hamptons?" Madison asked, and I wondered if she was thinking of trying to convince her parents to let us use their place. I couldn't see it happening.

"I've never been," Evelina said. "I'd love to go."

"Isn't it expensive?" I said, but Madison pulled out her phone.

"Not necessarily…" She turned her cell to us, and I gathered she must've planned this as she'd saved a few tabs on her browser. "This place is twelve hundred a night. Only two forty each."

"*Only.*" Evelina rolled her eyes. "Way too much."

"Hold on." Madison tapped her screen. "This one's half, but it's in Center Moriches."

"Doesn't mean anything to me," Evelina said. "But I'm cool with it."

"Me, too," Isabel added. "I'll be happy to get away."

"Perfect," Madison said. "There are three bedrooms so some of us will share. What do you think? What dates work for you?"

Didn't take long to decide and make plans, the booze probably giving our spontaneity a boost. Still, it made sense to go away. We'd met Marvin Lavoie, Mooseman's owner, Chris Wright, our A&R manager, and Freya Brown, our producer, and they expected us to have at least ten tracks recorded by next summer, preferably earlier. The next seven months would be busier than ever, working our regular jobs plus rehearsing, so going on a trip seemed to be a great idea.

Two weeks later, the five of us piled into my crappy old Tahoe and we got out of Brooklyn, trying to beat rush hour along with half the city. We arrived a few hours later, pulling up in front of the online gem Madison had found, a cozy three-bedroom house with a wraparound porch, wooden floors, and white picket fence.

We went into town, ate food rivaling Papa e Ragazzi's, although I'd never have admitted as much to Guy. A while later we ended up at a pub with a live local band called the Beach Macs, who played excellent covers of the Beach Boys' songs. About an hour in, Isabel tapped me on the shoulder, nodded to the stage.

"Want to play?" she asked, waggling her eyebrows.

"Huh? We don't have any gear."

"I got chatting with the singer at the bar, they said we can play if we want. Use their drums, guitar, and bass. Gabi said she'll sing backup."

"What about Madison?" I said, craning my neck as I tried to

find her amongst the crowd. I hadn't seen her in a while, had assumed she'd gone to the bathroom, but that had been ages ago.

"Last I saw her, she had her hands up a guy's shirt outside," Isabel said. "She winked at me when I walked past. I have a feeling we may not see her until tomorrow."

I couldn't pass up the opportunity to play, and so the four of us took to the tiny stage and delivered an impromptu three-song mini concert. When we played "Sweet Spot," a few people in the audience joined in the chorus. It was the first time I realized how well-known the song had become, and I wanted more for the Bittersweet—more recognition, success, and more engagement from our audience. I wanted to go on tour, perform at different venues, feast on the creative energy it all provided for weeks.

The cheers, whistles, and rounds of applause after our third song had begun to subside when Madison appeared in the doorway, her face an explosion of thunder. Her mouth fell, her eyes narrowed—especially at me—when the lead singer of the Beach Macs took the microphone and said, "Ladies and gentlemen, the Bittersweet from Brooklyn. Give it up for these four fantastic women."

Madison turned and walked out of the front door. I bolted from the stage, trying to make my way through the crowd as quickly as possible to find her. When I got outside, she stood twenty feet from the entrance, arms crossed and chest heaving.

"We didn't know where you were," I said before she had a chance to speak.

"And that makes it okay?"

"No. Yes. I mean—"

"Which one is it?" she said, hands on her hips as she took a step in my direction. "How would you feel if you walked in on the rest of us playing? You cut me out, Vienna. Like I didn't exist."

"It was three songs, Madison. Honestly, I don't think anyone will notice."

"You don't get it, do you?" she said. "Of course, they will. This kind of stuff ends up on social media. Remember the Flat-Cat gig? What if this performance goes viral and I'm not in it?"

"You're right," I said, shoulders dropping. "I'm really, really sorry. Thankfully the chances of this going viral are so tiny—"

"We don't know," she snapped. "Nobody does. You're the one who always says it's got to be a democracy. Then you pull this stunt, and I sure as hell don't appreciate you taking over."

"Taking over?" I said. "I'm not taking over."

She glared at me. "Whatever."

"Madison—"

"See you back at the house."

We remained frosty for the remainder of the trip but two days later, things were back to normal, as if our argument had never happened. Madison was good at glossing over things, but I knew untreated resentment could bubble for a long time, slightly beneath the surface. She didn't want to talk about the Hamptons, no matter how often I tried, so I decided to leave it, for now.

Later in the week, I sat at one of the tables at Papa e Ragazzi enjoying a caprese salad before my shift, idly flicking through the news on my phone. I was about to stuff my cell into my pocket when a short article caught my eye.

HOUSE DESTROYED IN HAMPTON FIRE

A detached, newly renovated beachfront property in Westhampton Beach couldn't be saved after a fire broke out late Friday night. The cause of the blaze is as yet unknown, there were no reported injuries, and nobody was home at the time. The owners, Mr. and Mrs. Pierce from Portland, Maine, are said to be shocked and saddened by the loss of their vacation property. According to the fire marshal, the extent of the damage will necessitate that the building be torn down.

Wait… Barry and Lucinda's house burned to the ground on the weekend our band visited the Hamptons? Throat running dry, I brought up Google Maps and plugged in the distance between the pub and Westhampton Beach. Less than a twenty-minute drive. Madison knew where I kept my car keys, and she'd disappeared for almost an hour, plenty of time to—

I tried to brush the thoughts away, stuff them down as I reminded myself the article didn't mention arson. If someone had torched the house, wouldn't they know by now? I stood, cleared my dishes away before thanking the chef, mind still whirring.

Working efficiently proved harder than I thought over the next few hours, and I was glad when Madison arrived so I could talk to her.

"Did you hear about the fire in Westhampton Beach?" I asked almost as soon as she walked through the restaurant door.

"What fire?"

I held my phone out to her, watched as she read the article. "What a shame," she said once she'd finished. "Especially after they spent so much money on the place."

As she turned, I swear there was a slight upward curve of her lips. Until now, I'd never believed Madison capable of hurting anyone, but as I stood in the middle of Papa e Ragazzi, watching the woman who'd been my best friend for years walk to the kitchen, I wasn't sure I knew her at all.

30

6 weeks before the accident

TEN DAYS WENT by and although I thought less about what happened in the Hamptons, I still checked the news for updates, but no cause of the fire was mentioned.

Madison messaged her parents, telling them how sad she was to hear of their beloved house burning down. While she received a single text from her mother saying Thank you, her dad remained silent. Madison didn't seem to care.

I talked myself into believing there was no way she'd commit arson, but the doubts crept in, the same way they had when I'd discovered her jewelry in Mom's bag. When those thoughts wouldn't go away, I began wondering about how Madison had *happened* to be at the same bar as Theo the night he'd gone home with another woman. Had she been involved somehow? I gave my head a shake because...*how*?

As much as I told myself to stop being paranoid, the nagging suspicions wouldn't leave me alone. For a few days I found myself watching Madison more closely, analyzing everything she said twice. I felt guilty, like a terrible friend, so I forced myself to stop.

Now the Bittersweet had a record deal, and we were expected to add nine tracks to "Sweet Spot" for our debut album, I was working harder than ever. I hummed and sang to myself all the time, woke up in the middle of the night to scribble a few lines of "Still Waters" and "Devil On My Shoulder." My mind wandered to the harmonies of "Over You, Under You" when I was supposed to take orders during my shifts. I couldn't help it. The words, the melodies were inside me, beguiling me. And obsessing me.

The cash from Mooseman had finally come through, and Roger helped us find a few local paid gigs—one of which Melodie Johnson attended—and a new rehearsal space in an old warehouse in Queens.

The heating didn't work properly, the radiators made loud clanging noises causing us all to jump periodically, and we had to clear a thick layer of dust from the floor. The payoff was great acoustics and rent cheap enough for us to pay four months upfront. We figured we'd soon be ready for the recording sessions Mooseman would book at a Midtown studio.

Things had shifted within all of us since we'd signed the deal. The Bittersweet had been focused before, but now instead of *what-ifs* and hopes of being signed, we had deadlines, meaning more pressure for everyone.

Every week we sat down, pulled out our phones, and went through our upcoming day job schedules, trying to find pockets of practice time. There was an energy in the room, an undeniable belief we were on the verge of...*something*. None of us wanted to say out loud what *something* might be for fear of jinxing it, but it was there, and it was growing.

More exhilaration came when Chris, our A&R manager, suggested we release another track in January. "I know it's not a lot of time," he said during a conference call with Roger attending from home, and the five of us Bittersweet huddled around my cell in the rehearsal room, "but let's not wait. We need to jump on the success of 'Sweet Spot' as quickly as possible. Give your fans another tidbit so they're excited for your debut album next summer."

"Got a track in mind, Chris?" Roger asked.

"'Bitter Pill,'" he said without hesitation. "It's a fantastic song and the fans will go wild for your drum solo, Vienna. It's intense, cool, exactly what we need, and—"

"What about 'Good Tomorrow'?" Madison cut in.

"Nowhere near as strong," Chris said. "It needs a lot of work."

Madison's face turned a deep shade of crimson. She performed lead vocals and had insisted on adding a guitar solo to "Good Tomorrow." None of us had wanted it, but she'd been defiant, and eventually we'd given in. Now I wished we hadn't.

"Trust me," Chris said. "'Bitter Pill' is fresh, authentic. It's the kind of song we signed you for. Shoot. Got another call. We'll talk soon."

After we said our goodbyes and Chris hung up, Roger spoke. "Talk things over and let me know what you think of the proposal. For the record, ha ha, I agree 'Bitter Pill' is the way to go. Now, there's another thing we—"

"The stuff we talked about yesterday?" Madison said.

They'd had a conversation? This was news to me. As far as I was aware, none of us had spoken to Roger since last week. We always made a point of the five of us being on each call. What was Madison doing?

"What stuff?" I said, frowning.

"I have ideas about our sales trajectory," Madison said, coolly. "And the venues we should play. I've done some research, so I sent Roger an email about advertising and merchandising ideas. He told me he'd look into it."

"Merchandising?" Isabel said. "Aren't you getting a bit ahead of yourself? I mean, we release one song, and you expect us to end up in a Happy Meal?"

"No," Madison snapped. "I'm thinking about what we can sell when we're on tour."

"What tour?" Evelina said. "There'll never be one if we don't focus on the album."

"Madison was planning ahead," Roger said, with his usual brand of diplomacy.

"Exactly," she huffed. "I'm trying to come up with strategies to ensure our success and get multiple revenue streams."

"Jeez." Evelina let out a groan. "I just want to make music."

"There's nothing wrong with having a wish list of things you want to see happen," Roger said. "But let's stay grounded and realistic. Work on nailing 'Bitter Pill' and I'll coordinate recording session options with Chris and get back to you. Agreed?"

"Agreed," everyone said quickly, except Madison, who stayed quiet.

"Excellent," Roger said. "Now, about the other thing I wanted to discuss. I had drinks with a filmmaker friend last night and told her about the Bittersweet. Funny thing is, she'd already heard about you from one of her staff."

"Really?" Isabel asked.

"Yes, she suggested making a documentary about you," Roger continued. "Following the journey of an up-and-coming all-female pop-rock band from Brooklyn is a neat project."

"You mean a movie?" Madison said. "Like for Netflix or Amazon?"

"No, no," Roger answered quickly. "A web series, most likely."

"I'm not sure," I said. "Do we want someone hanging around, shoving a camera in our faces?"

"It wouldn't be quite like that," Roger said. "Zeke, their lead researcher, would be assigned to shadow you on and off for a couple of weeks. We'd set limits as to when and where he can record."

"Sounds kind of interesting," Isabel said.

"I thought so too," Roger continued. "We envisage a fly-on-the-wall documentary, predominantly filmed as you're writing and rehearsing new material, plus a set of interviews about how the band came together."

"A *making of* series," Gabi said.

"Precisely," Roger answered. "It would be unique exposure and wouldn't air until the album's ready."

"I think it's a *fantastic* idea," Madison said. "Surely you all agree? It's amazing promotion. We can release snippets beforehand, generate more interest. Come on, can't you see how valuable this is?"

When I saw the enthusiasm in her face, I couldn't stop myself from grinning. "Yeah, okay, providing we set boundaries."

Madison beamed as Gabi, Isabel, and Evelina added their agreement.

"Wonderful," Roger said. "I'll be in touch."

A few days later, a young blond-haired woman slid the door to the rehearsal room open. We were in the middle of discussing our latest take of "Bitter Pill," none of us quite happy with the harmonies we'd been trying out for the last hour.

"The spin class is five doors down," Evelina called over, pointing to her left.

"No." The woman stepped a little farther into the room, her hand fiddling with the long ponytail draped over her right shoulder. She wore dark blue jeans, a pair of brown leather boots and a matching jacket that skimmed her narrow hips, plus a pristine cream turtleneck sweater. By the time she'd come a little closer, it seemed her face might burn up from blushing so hard.

"I'm Libby Alexander, the assistant researcher from City Slicker Productions," she said.

"Oh?" Madison frowned. "We were told to expect the *lead* researcher, Zeke."

"He's, uh, not available, so they sent me," Libby said. "I hope you don't mind. I'm a huge fan."

"Not at all." Isabel leaped up and bounded over, ushering Libby inside the room.

"I can't believe I'm meeting you," Libby said, her cheeks flushing harder. "I absolutely love your music and it's such an honor to be here."

"Grab a seat," Evelina said, nodding at an empty chair. "You can—"

"Tell us the projects you've worked on," Madison jumped in.

I wondered if I was the only one who felt Madison had suddenly turned this into an interview. And what was with the emphasis on *lead* researcher? What difference did it make?

"Okay," Libby said, setting her bag on the floor. "I'm originally from Albany and have a BA in Cinema and Media Studies."

"Nice," Gabi said. "Must've been interesting."

"It was." Libby nodded, smile wide. "I've worked a few jobs since graduating and have been with City Slicker for almost a year."

"What, exactly, is your role there?" Madison said.

"I'm a researcher." Libby sat up a little straighter. "Assistant researcher. I spend a lot of time fact-checking, interviewing, reading about the subjects of the documentaries we're making. I have lots of questions about the Bittersweet already."

"How does this work?" Evelina said. "Do you need us to do anything special?"

"I'll observe for a while, if it's fine with you," Libby said. "Pretend I'm not here. I'll make notes and film, and stay out of your way, I promise."

As the five of us headed back to the instruments, Madison whispered, "Can you believe they sent the *assistant*?"

If my eyes had been closed, I'd have thought I was speaking with her mother.

★ ★ ★

We soon learned Libby was far more than a research assistant, she was a talented documentarian in the making. Over the next two weeks, she stopped by our practice sessions, spent time with each of us asking intelligent questions about our backgrounds. She was easy to talk to, had a natural ability to turn what was essentially an interview into a chat with a friend. Most of the time I forgot her camera was rolling.

One evening when Libby and I were the only two left in the rehearsal room, we grabbed a beer and sat on the floor with "Linger" by the Cranberries playing on my phone. It was only the two of us because Madison had a date, Isabel had left early for her mom's birthday party, and Evelina and Gabi were both working.

I hadn't spent much time alone with Libby, but her knowing a lot about us when we barely knew anything about her felt odd. "What made you want to become a documentarian?" I asked, taking a sip of beer.

"My dad," she said. "He's obsessed with them, and we'd watch one every Wednesday night until I left for college. Mom and my brother, Linus, are more superhero movie fans, so it became our thing."

"Your dad sounds sweet."

"Oh, he is. Both my parents are great. I miss them."

"You don't get to see them much?"

"Not as often as I want, but I'm going home for the holidays. I can't wait. How about you? You haven't mentioned your parents a lot. I got the feeling it was a bit of a no-go zone."

I put the bottle to my lips, took another mouthful. "There's a can of worms I don't want to open."

"Fair enough," she said, confirming another thing I liked about Libby. She respected the boundaries we'd agreed on, didn't try to push her way in or trip us up with trick questions.

"How's working for City Slicker?" I asked.

"I love it, especially since Zeke left."

"Zeke? Wasn't he the lead researcher who was supposed to be here instead of you?"

"The one and only."

"You said he was unavailable. Was he sick?"

Libby pulled a face. "No. He sent dick pics to the boss."

"Whoa."

"Yeah. It happened the morning I came here. He claimed it was an accident."

"Of course he did."

"My boss won't put up with any of that stuff, accidental or otherwise, so she fired him on the spot and sent me. I thought flames would shoot from his nostrils when he found out."

"Well, we're all glad you're here. The Bittersweet loves you and your huge ambitions."

She smiled. "Yikes, are they so obvious?"

"What's wrong with being driven? Providing it doesn't turn you into an asshole, of course, as it does with some people."

"Exactly how I felt about Zeke. He doesn't know what collaborate means."

I wanted to say it was how I felt about Madison these days. She and I had clashed on several recent occasions—always in private—about our lyrics, style, and the way she constantly criticized Gabi, Evelina, and Isabel behind their backs. According to her, we could've recorded all of our songs without them, subbing in a few session musicians instead, in which case we'd have kept a whole lot more money to ourselves.

"We're the *real* Bittersweet," she told me. "You and me."

I disagreed and figured if the tiny taste of fame made Madison's head swell any more, she'd turn into a hot-air balloon. What would she be like when we released "Bitter Pill" in January and our album a few months later, and they were both the hits we all aimed for? What if they weren't?

How long until her attitude and surliness spilled from a closed circle of two, and into the group? This stuff could be poison, the kiss of death for a band, and we hadn't yet begun. I didn't say any of this to Libby. No matter how much I liked her, some things were not to be shared with a filmmaker.

"Do you have all the footage you need so far?" I asked her. "Anything you're missing?"

Libby hesitated before saying, "To hell with it. I'm going to ask. You can always say no."

"Okay…"

"I heard you all talking about the Mooseman party in the Catskills. The one at Marvin Lavoie's place."

"Oh, yeah." I finished my beer, set the bottle down. "Apparently, it's an annual thing he invites artists and managers to. Roger showed me some photos. It's quite the scoop to be on the guest list."

"Are the five of you going?"

"Uh-huh. We're leaving the day before. Roger gave us an extra night at the hotel and a spa day as a Christmas gift, so he'll meet us at the party the next evening." Excitement bubbled within me. "We don't know who else will be there yet. I hope I don't go into freaky fangirl mode but it's a distinct possibility."

"I wouldn't mind getting that on film," Libby said with another grin. "I know asking if I can come to the party is—"

"Oh, Libby, I'm not sure it would be appropriate."

"No, no, I get it, but do you think I could travel with you? I've mainly filmed you here plus a few locations for the individual interviews."

"I'm not sure…"

"Being on the road with you would add another layer, another dimension," she said quickly. "I'll pay for my room and, I don't know, get a massage while you rub shoulders with the rich and famous." She paused, looked at me. "Please? I know I'm being direct but…as you said, I'm ambitious. I want to show people like Zeke how it's done."

I thought about it for a moment. Where was the harm in her tagging along? "I'll have to check with the others, but I can't imagine it'll be a problem," I said. "Plus, we can make space for you in my old clunker as we're not lugging our gear with us. It'll be fun."

"Thank you," Libby said, reaching over and giving me a hug. "You won't regret it. This is going to be the best trip ever."

31

The day after the accident

THE SNOW SCRUNCHES and squeaks beneath my boots as I circle the cabin and wrap my jacket tight around my waist. As I sneak past each window, I slowly raise my head and peer inside. Nothing. Nobody. I keep going, step after step, expecting someone to jump out at me from behind a boulder, a tree, the pile of split logs. Nobody does.

As I approach the porch, I see a snowdrift piled so high it reaches a quarter of the way up the broken front door. There aren't any footprints leading in or out, and I don't know if it means whoever hit me has gone, or if they're still in the cabin.

I move closer and gently push the door open. When I'm inside, every nerve and muscle screams at me to turn and run, but I refuse. Libby's in the basement. I don't know where Gabi and Madison are, but I'll do whatever I can to find them before getting help. I'll never forgive myself otherwise.

After taking a few steps, I pop my head into the living area. It's empty, so I continue my search, creeping in stealth mode. Evelina's body is still on the mattress in the bedroom. I can't bring myself to look at her for long, bite my lip to stop the tears from falling as I think about losing her and Isabel, and the fact that, so far, Gabi and Madison are missing. It's the jolt I need to get it together.

Despite searching the cabin one floor and room at a time, I find nothing. There's nobody here but Libby and me. Back in the living room, I go through every bag and search underneath the sparse furniture for my cell phone, but I can't find it. Whoever assaulted me must've taken it. Evelina's and Isabel's are gone, too, and I have no clue where Gabi, Libby, and Madison's devices are.

More unease settles in my chest, and as I make my way into the hall, louder alarm bells ring in my mind, demanding attention. I backtrack to the living room, frowning as my gaze sweeps across the bags I rummaged through.

Madison's backpack has vanished. It's the only missing one.

I frown harder when I spot a shiny trail on the kitchen floor. I hadn't noticed it before because of the light, but from this angle it's glaringly obvious. Whatever it is, it's new, fresh.

Crouching, I touch the glossy liquid, bring my fingers to my nose. It's the old cooking oil I found last night, the bottle I left on the counter, I'm sure of it. My eyes follow the path, which travels all the way from the splintered wooden kitchen cabinets to the fireplace, where the torn pages of *The Shining* lie in a half-burned heap.

Logic wants me to connect the dots, but my heart refuses. Did someone try to set fire to the cabin with Libby and me locked in the basement, alive? Why would anyone do this? *Who* would do this? The answer slams into me, almost knocking me sideways.

Madison.

"No," I whisper, but the image of the red hair surges to the front of my brain again, screaming at me to pay attention. Madison's backpack is gone. So is she. Did she lock us in? Did she try to kill Libby and me? What else has she done? My mind fights itself over the questions.

No, she would never. Never.

Remember the fire in the Hamptons?

That was arson, this is attempted murder. She wouldn't.

Look at the evidence.

It's not something I can deal with. There's no time. I need to help Libby, try to find Gabi, who's likely out in the woods somewhere, hopefully sheltering in place. The sooner we get search and rescue out here, the better. Everything else has to wait. If I keep thinking about what might've happened here, I can't function.

The key's still in the lock when I reach the basement door. I turn it and put it in my pocket before going downstairs. Libby's where I left her, and when I try to wake her, she moves her head from side to side. Her skin feels colder to the touch, her face more ashen than before. I have to get out of here, find help. If—I can barely finish the thought—*if* Madison did this to us and ran, I can't imagine she'll be coming back here.

I dash upstairs, start moving Evelina off the mattress so I can give it to Libby but can't bring myself to touch the body for any length of time. Starting a proper and safe fire is impossible as Madison had the lighter, but I have to bring Libby upstairs where it's a little warmer than the basement.

After laying as many clothes as I can find on the floor, I coax Libby upstairs, which takes so much of my energy I worry I'll have none left to walk through the woods. I pile the rest of the T-shirts, pants, and sweaters on top of her. She's failing fast, barely responding. It's time for me to leave before she gets any worse.

"I'll be back as soon as I can," I say, squeezing her hand. "Hang on, okay? Please?"

Once outside, I try to get my bearings, stand with my back facing the way Madison and I came when we found the cabin.

There seems to be a clearing in the trees possibly indicating a path or a trail, but I can't be sure. I walk over, anyway, make it around a hundred yards before I reach the edge of another cliff. There's no way down, it's a dead end.

I put my head back, yell a dozen expletives at the sky, sending a few birds flying from the branches above. Pressing the heels of my hands into my eyes, I will myself not to cry. There's a way out of here, and I'll find it. I blow out my breath in a big steamy puff, am about to turn when an object thirty feet down catches my eye. I squint, trying to convince myself it's a tree branch, a log, a gnarled root.

It's a person.

Lying on a ledge below, one arm dangling over the side, the rest of the body almost entirely covered in snow, except for their shoes. I recognize the soft gray color immediately.

The shoes belong to Gabi.

I turn and run.

PART TWO

Beware: some liars tell the truth.

—ARABIAN PROVERB

32

42 days after the accident

Music Lovers,

This is a super brief update to my post from earlier today. In case you missed it, the cops took the Bittersweet's drummer, Vienna Taylor, in for questioning about band members Gabi and Evelina Sevillano's deaths, and—if the rumors are true—Madison Pierce's disappearance.

I still can't believe it. I've searched the internet and reached out to everyone I can think of, trying to find a whisper of an update. There's nothing but a whole load of speculation and tons of mean-girl #TeamVienna vs. #TeamMadison stuff, but so what's new?

Do *you* have info, peeps? This story's all I can think about. I'm getting the scoop no matter what. I swear, we *will* somehow get to the truth about what happened in the Catskills.

Stay tuned,
Melodie @musicalmelodiej

Comments (596—showing most recent)

@georgiaonmym_ Still can't believe they came for her during a memorial service!

> **@bellybean56** I can. She looked guilty af

>> **@georgiaonmym_** She looked terrified

>>> **@bellybean56** Because she's guilty af

@pretty_pete There's no way Vienna killed anyone. NO WAY #TeamVienna

> **@bellybean56** How the hell do you know? #TeamMadison forever

@harry_dude92_returns Who cares? The Bittersweet suck

> **@musicalmelodiej** @harry_dude92_returns FFS not you again

33

42 days after the accident

SOMEONE SET THE interview room's thermostat to chilly, and I wouldn't be surprised if it was deliberate. The walls are bare except for a plethora of scuff marks dotted around the chipped beige paint. I'm sitting at an old, dented, and scratched metal table, with the smell of burned coffee from a paper cup I've left untouched drifting up my nose.

My hands are in my lap, one palm on top of the other. It's a display of openness and honesty. I'm conveying to the two detectives who brought me here, and who've questioned me for the last few hours, I have nothing to hide.

Except, everyone does, including these detectives, no doubt, if I cared to dig deep enough. God knows I've had plenty of time to observe them since they came to Gabi and Evelina's memorial service and plucked me from the crowd.

"You're not being arrested, Ms. Taylor," they informed me.

It sure as hell felt like it.

I'd planned on going home after the service to continue writing my memoir about the Bittersweet, which I've worked on incessantly since the accident. Instead, I'm sitting in a freezing cold interview room with a cup of shitty coffee, two cops, and their relentless questions.

This discussion is voluntary. Apparently, I can leave anytime I want, but how will taking them up on their offer make me look? *Guilty* is how, and it's what they're hoping for.

Suppressing a smile, I think of how social media must be blowing up with this latest development about the Bittersweet. I itch to pull out my phone and check whether #TeamVienna's trending. Open Spotify and iTunes to see if the streams and downloads of "Sweet Spot" have had yet another surge. Call Roger and ask how many interview requests he's fielded.

Obviously, I can't do any of those. It would be bad form, not to mention the blow my reputation would take if I broke character now and appeared in any way happy about benefiting from the terrible tragedy that tore my band apart. Not that I'm happy, but I'm making do.

"Vienna, you do understand you can call your attorney at any time," Detective Laura Ashbury says with a smile, which doesn't quite make its way to her big brown eyes. I haven't met her before, but she doesn't like me. I can tell no matter how soft her approach has been, see it in the way she looks at me, although she does a semi-decent job of veiling her mistrust. I don't take it personally. It probably comes with the job.

Ashbury's an NYPD detective and sharply dressed, obviously a veteran professional. With her attire of a slick gray suit and white button-down blouse, she reminds me of a shark circling the waters, searching for a hint of blood. I'm ensuring there isn't a single drop to make her go for my jugular, and I'm playing this role to perfection.

"Thank you for the offer, but I don't need an attorney," I say. It's a fine balance between not displaying guilt but still showing nerves. Good thing I practiced nonstop in the six weeks since the accident in case things came to this.

I hoped they wouldn't. But I'm prepared. And convincing.

"Let's clarify a few more facts." This comes from Detective Isaac Newell. He's a Catskill PD cop and I met him before, talked to him at length in the days that followed the Bittersweet's accident. I guess he joined forces with the NYPD, was perhaps instructed to seek assistance given the scale of the case.

They're putting me through the classic good cop, bad cop routine, and it appears Newell has been assigned the latter. He's a little older than Ashbury but definitely less experienced and is way more direct, as if he has something to prove because he knows she's miles ahead of him.

Although he's dressed in cheaper clothes and has a Scottish accent, Newell reminds me of Damian Lewis from *Billions*. I love that show, most of all how manipulative and scheming the characters are, going after whatever they want, no matter the cost or fallout, even to themselves.

"Walk us through what happened the day of the accident," Ashbury says.

"Of course." I lean in and rest my hands on the table, relaxed and pointing at them. Crossing my arms could be construed as my being defensive, and I've made sure to watch my body language at all times. So far, neither Ashbury nor Newell has found a single inconsistency or crack in my story. They never will. "The six of us, Madison, Gabi, Evelina, Isabel, Libby and I, left Brooklyn late morning and—"

"Skip to the bit where you arrive at the cabin," Newell says, and Ashbury shoots him a quick glance, looking as if she's trying to telepathically order him to stay calm. Judging by the way he's tapping his pen on the yellow notepad in front of him more and more frequently, he's frustrated. We've already gone over what happened at the cabin multiple times today alone, as he and I did when I first spoke to him.

"We carried Evelina into the main room as soon as we arrived," I say, and Ashbury nods, sits back and smooths down her shirt. She wears her dark hair in a pixie cut, which suits her, giving more prominence to her cheekbones and making her mahogany eyes pop. "Libby had a wicked headache," I continue. "Madison gave her pills."

"Whose pills were they?" Newell asks.

"I assume they were my acetaminophen," I answer, frowning. "Same as the two pills I gave Libby at the crash site for her headache. Didn't I mention it?" Yes. Four times, in fact.

"What happened next?" Ashbury says, putting her arms on the table, mirroring mine.

I sit back and rest my hands in my lap to see if she'll mimic me. When she does, I suppress a smirk. "Gabi realized Evelina's insulin was missing."

"Why didn't she check before?" Newell says.

I shift my face into a startled expression. "Gosh, I don't think it's fair to blame Gabi for the oversight, Detective Newell. When you've been in an accident, seen a tree branch stuck through your friend's chest, and your sister's missing a hand, your focus is more than a little shot."

He writes a few words on his notepad. I hope it's *I must not ask pathetic questions.* "Then what?" he says, voice terse.

"We argued—"

"Who's we?" he says.

"Mainly Madison, Gabi, and I. We argued whether Gabi should go back for the insulin alone."

"And Libby?" Ashbury asks.

"She offered to help but she could barely stand at this point." Something else they already know. "Libby needed rest, and Gabi insisted Madison and I find whatever we could to start a fire." I take my time. "Gabi left the cabin, and Madison and I searched the place. I went upstairs, Madison stayed on the main floor. When I came back…" I gulp some air before continuing with a tremble in my voice. "Could I have a glass of water, please?"

Once my request has been granted, which I know has an-

noyed Newell because he's tapping his pen harder, I take a few
sips and go on. "As I was saying, when I walked into the living room after searching the upstairs level, Evelina was…she
was dead."

"What do you think happened to her?"

"I'm not sure I understand the question, Detective Ashbury."

"How do you think Evelina died?" she says.

"At first, I thought it was from losing her hand, but it didn't
make sense. I mean, she lost a lot of blood, but Libby managed to stop it. She was incredible." When neither Ashbury nor
Newell answer, I keep going. "Later, after we were rescued, I
wondered if it might've been because Evelina didn't have her
insulin, but I've since learned it would've taken much longer
for her to get that sick."

"You researched this?" Newell says.

"I'm trying to understand what happened to my friends," I
snap, only half pretending to be indignant because he's being
such an ass. "So, yes, I researched it."

"What else did you learn?" Ashbury asks.

"When there's a car crash there are three impacts." I make
sure they're looking at me before I continue, counting on my
fingers. "The first is the vehicle when it collides into something. The second is the person when they hit whatever stops
them from moving." I let my shoulders sag.

"And the third?" Newell asks, as if he doesn't already know.

"The internal organs crashing up against our bones because
there's still motion happening inside our body," I whisper.

My shudder isn't fake, I was truly sickened to learn these facts,
and they've kept me awake for hours as I picture Isabel smashing into the tree, and how Evelina had been thrown around
the truck like a rag doll. I press my eyes shut now because I
think I might throw up.

"Did I mention Evelina wasn't wearing a seat belt?" I say quietly. "Either way, it's completely horrifying. It's hard to imagine how much she suffered."

"Where was Madison when you found out Evelina was deceased?" Ashbury asks.

I take a deep breath, glance at them in turn before saying, "Standing over Evelina. Madison said Evelina was choking."

"Where was Libby?" Ashbury says.

"Lying by the living room door, unconscious. She didn't move."

"And Gabriela?" Newell jumps in.

"Gabi," I say. "She hated Gabriela."

He holds up a hand. "Where was Gabi?"

"She got back from the crash site when I was trying to resuscitate Evelina."

"By giving her CPR," Ashbury says.

"I can't forget the scent of her strawberry lip balm," I say, touching my lips as my eyes move above Ashbury's shoulder, staring off into the nonexistent distance. Snapping my gaze back to her and Newell, I add, "Gabi was devastated, we all were. She administered insulin, kept saying she had to get help, but we, I mean Madison and I, calmed her down. Afterward, we moved Evelina into one of the bedrooms on the main floor to give Gabi space with her sister. But then Gabi slipped out when we weren't paying attention."

"To get help," Newberry says, an eyebrow raised. "In the middle of a blizzard."

"Her sister died. She wasn't thinking straight."

"Uh-huh," Ashbury says. "Gabi leaves, so you and Madison search for her."

"What else should we have done?" I raise my voice a little before biting my lip. "We'd lost Isabel and Evelina. I suspected Libby had a pretty serious concussion, we needed to get Gabi back inside. Madison and I split up to look for her, but then I couldn't find Madison either."

"At which point you returned to the cabin and went up-stairs," Newell says.

He's going to have to do better if wants to trip me up. "No. I heard noises in the basement, where I found Libby. It made no sense because she'd been completely out of it. And then… the last thing I remember is being hit over the head."

"That's not what you said before," Newell says.

"Yes, it is." There's no way I've made a mistake so glaring.

He slowly flips a page on his notepad, a deliberate stalling tactic to give me the jitters. It doesn't work. "You said the last thing you saw was, and I quote, a flash of red hair."

I lower my eyes. "Yes, but I still don't want to believe Madison hurt me. I don't understand why she'd do this."

"Vienna." Detective Ashbury leans back, crosses her long legs and frowns at me. She must be changing tack. Going for a new angle after another unsuccessful fishing expedition. "These events must've been incredibly traumatic for you."

Wait for it. Just wait for it.

"And yet…"

Here it comes.

"The clarity of your recollection about what happened is astonishing."

I nod. "Honestly, Detective, it's so vivid in my mind, I don't think I'll sleep properly again. Libby probably won't either. And don't forget I'm working on my memoir."

"Ah, yes, the infamous memoir," Newell says, leaning back in his chair. I pretend not to notice the sarcasm lacing his words. He's really pissing me off now, but I won't let it show.

"Writing the Bittersweet story is incredibly…*therapeutic*," I say.

"Not to mention potentially…*lucrative*," Newell adds with a smirk.

Hopefully he's right because it'll mean everything that happened was worth it, but I give him a sad smile. "Who knows?

Anyway, isn't it common knowledge that writers don't make much money? It's not about that."

He lets out a snort. "I'm sure it won't hurt."

"Three of my friends are dead, Detective. One of them is missing. And yes, I'm counting Madison because she's my *best* friend." I put a hand to my mouth, take a shuddering breath. "Can you please tell me why you really wanted to talk to me? Why we're going over the same things repeatedly? Have you found Madison? Do you know where she is?"

"We got some results back," Ashbury says, ignoring my questions. "Libby's tox panel showed elevated levels of benzodiazepines."

"What's that?"

"She took Klonopin," Ashbury replies.

"I'm afraid I still don't know what that is," I lie.

"It's also known as clonazepam," Ashbury says. "Prescribed for anxiety, panic disorders, and so forth."

I frown a little. "But…I thought Madison gave her my headache pills."

"Did Madison have a prescription for Klonopin?" Newell says.

"Not that I'm aware of." This is true because she got the pills from a dealer at NYU, but I stop talking as I watch them exchange a glance before they go for a different angle yet again.

"We also have the results from Gabi's and Evelina's autopsies," Ashbury says, opening a folder in front of her and turning the pages to reveal a set of photographs. I prepare myself for what's coming, remember the reaction I've practiced. Shock, horror, disbelief. She closes the folder again, watching me, teasing me. "Evelina was suffocated."

I let my jaw drop. "She was…*what*? What do you mean? Are you…are you saying she was *murdered*?"

"We found signs of petechiae in the eyes, and fibers in her

throat and lungs," Ashbury says as she observes me. "Fibers from a sweater that also happens to have your DNA."

"*My* DNA? Is the sweater mine?"

"No," Newell says. "It was Gabi's."

"Then…Gabi's DNA must be on it, too."

Ashbury raises an eyebrow. "You said Gabi left the cabin to get her sister's insulin, and you've repeatedly mentioned how well they got along. Why would Gabi hurt Evelina?"

"She wouldn't."

"Who would?" Newell asks.

"I don't know, but…wait, do you think *I* hurt her? Am I a suspect?"

"We're trying to understand exactly what happened," Newell says.

I whisper, "Madison was standing over Evelina when I came downstairs."

"Yes, so you've said," Newell quips. "Except Madison has disappeared."

"Is *her* DNA on the sweater?" I ask.

They don't reply but they know they've reached another impasse because the answer's yes. Isabel's is probably on it, too. My reasons for choosing it.

"Detective," I continue, my voice low, a few tears making my eyes glisten. "If Evelina hadn't been…suffocated, would she have survived? Please, tell me. Would she have made it?"

"No," Ashbury says. "As well as losing her hand, she sustained significant injuries causing her to bleed internally. She would've died long before help arrived the next day."

"Oh, my God," I whisper. I could've waited.

Knowing I killed Evelina without needing to makes a big ball of gnawing guilt appear in my throat and I swallow it down, try to make it go away, but it grows and grows until I think it might burst out of my chest. I force myself to ignore it, focus on my breathing and pay attention to what Newell is saying.

"There were interesting revelations in Gabi's autopsy, too." He waits for my reaction, and I give him a widening of my eyes, a look of fear about what's to come. I'm back in control and I may as well throw him a bone. He puts his elbows on the table and steeples his fingers beneath his chin. "Bruising consistent with her being pushed." Pause. "And DNA underneath her fingernails."

"Your DNA," Ashbury says, opening the folder again. She pulls out a photograph and slides it to me with her fingertip.

I recognize the image instantly. It's not Gabi, not Evelina, but a close-up of my wrists. The left one has two angry red scratches about three inches long, the dark blood already dried. The picture was taken a few hours after I'd left the cabin and managed to get help from the house over a mile away, a place owned by an elderly couple. Once I told them about our accident and finding the deserted cabin, we immediately rescued Libby.

We were so grateful when they brought us back to their home, wrapped us in blankets, and pressed mugs of hot cocoa into our hands while we waited for the emergency services to arrive. A little earlier that morning I thought maybe I'd lose Libby, too, and that would've been very, *very* bad.

I lean forward, study the photo of my wrists. "I don't understand..." I tell the detectives.

"How did you get the scratches, Vienna?" Ashbury says, moving in for what she must hope will be an easy kill. She doesn't expect me to be a slippery fish, darting out of reach. "How did your DNA get beneath Gabi's fingernails?"

"I don't remember." Lie. "I know I held her back when she initially said she was going for help after Evelina died. It's probably when she scratched me."

"Is that in your memoir?" Newell says, deadpan.

Not yet, asshole, but it will be when I get home.

"I don't know what to tell you, but if you're insinuating I hurt Gabi—"

"Did you?" Newell says.

"No," I say. "I thought she fell. Are you saying it wasn't an accident? Was she…murdered, like her sister?" They look at one another and I press on. "You think I had something to do with it? You're making a mistake. Madison—"

"Madison is *missing,*" Newell says, raising his voice as he punctuates every word. "According to you, she left the cabin in the middle of the night, during a snowstorm."

"I never said that," I counter. "I can't tell you when she left. I was unconscious with Libby, locked in the freezing basement. Maybe she went a short while before I woke up. Or waited until the worst of the storm had cleared."

Ashbury jumps in. "Except there's no trace of her. Nobody has seen or heard from her in six weeks. No transactions on her credit cards or bank accounts. She hasn't used her phone." She waits. "Do you know why that might be, Vienna?"

I glance at Ashbury, Newell, and back to her again. "Yes, I think I do," I whisper, and expectation gleams in their eyes. "And I think I want to call my attorney."

34

42 days after the accident

IF ASHBURY AND Newell think they'll get a quick confession out of me, they're about to be disappointed. Torin Ryan, a ridiculously expensive defense attorney with whom Roger had already put me in touch, just in case, shows up within the hour. Lucky for me, he's taking this case pro bono because it's so high-profile, and I can almost hear Ashbury groan internally when she spots him. I've been told he's well known, highly competent, and very much respected.

Torin's in his midfifties, trim, with a full head of gray hair and a sharp goatee. He's handsome, evidently takes good care of himself. His tailored suit doesn't have a stray speck of lint, the creases in his blue shirt are freshly pressed, and the silver studs in his collar gleam, even under the police station's drab fluorescent lights. If I had to go up against him in court, I'd call in sick.

After another hour of discussions with the detectives, during which I'm mostly silent because Torin often says I don't need to answer the question, he sits back and exhales. Taking his time, he crosses one leg over the other and slowly lays his hands in his lap, palms facing upward, exactly as I'd done a few hours ago.

It's good for me to observe him in action. There's only so much I can learn from watching courtroom dramas and crime shows on TV, although so far, I've done a pretty decent job. Shame I'll never be able to share any of this preparatory work with Torin.

"Time to wrap things up," he says in a deep, rumbling voice. "My client has been more than cooperative, especially considering you approached her at her friends' memorial service, which by the way, was in exceptionally poor taste."

Newell looks as if he's been schooled but Ashbury brushes the scolding off by ignoring it completely. "One more question," she says, and Torin gestures for her to go ahead. She turns to me. "Vienna, before you called Mr. Ryan, you said you knew why there hasn't been any activity on Madison's credit cards, or bank account, and why her phone hasn't been used since the accident."

"Is there a question coming, Detective?" Torin asks, tone sharp. "Or are we going to sit here listening to you restating the facts?"

"Do you know why nobody has heard from Madison?" she asks me.

"You don't need to answer," Torin says, holding up a hand.

"I can answer," I tell him, then meet Ashbury's gaze. "Isn't it obvious?"

"Why don't you spell it out for us?" Newell's snide delivery is evidence of how I've depleted his patience this afternoon, drop by drop. The dusky circles under his eyes have slid halfway down his cheeks, his tie's hanging to one side like a thirsty dog's tongue. He looks as if he's longing to solve this case, get the hell out of here and go home to kick back and have a few beers. All in good time, Detective Newell, all in good time.

After waiting a beat, I say, "Guilty people run. Especially when they're trying to frame someone else."

I swear Newell wants to climb over the table, put his hands around my neck and give it a good throttle. Part of me hopes he does so I can sue his ass and get him thrown off the case simply for the hell of it.

"You think Madison Pierce is trying to frame you?" Ashbury says. "Why?"

"A question you need to find the answers to." Torin closes his notebook and gets up.

As I follow suit, I catch a glimpse of the label on the inside of his coat—Brunello Cucinelli—exclusive and expensive, exactly like him. Thankfully, Torin won't be billing me any hours to pay for another. Besides, I doubt I'll need him much after today if my plans work, although why they haven't yet is worrying.

"Should you wish to talk to my client again you know how to reach me," Torin says as he gives them each a curt nod. "Good meeting you, Detective Newell. Laura, always a pleasure."

Their mumblings don't sound like agreement as Torin and I leave the room. I remain silent until we're out of the building—I'm surprised there are no journalists—and have walked a good fifty yards down the road. You never know who's listening. Having a chat with your attorney, or anybody else for that matter, in front of a cop station is practically asking for trouble.

"Penny for your thoughts?" Torin says, an expression of concern taking over his face. His sudden shift to a fatherly demeanor makes me wonder if he has kids, and what kind of a dad he is. I imagine him strict but loving, helpful yet not overbearing. Then again, he could be a complete asshole who thumps his offspring if they disagree with him on anything. You never can tell who does what when nobody's watching.

"I'm fine, I think." I shudder a little. "That's a lie. Sorry. If I'm not honest with you then who can I be honest with."

"You've been through a lot, Vienna, it's okay to admit it."

Shaking my head in apparent confusion, I say, "They believe I hurt Evelina and Gabi. And why do they think I know where Madison is? I told the truth. We went over everything multiple times before you arrived, but they don't believe me."

"You can't take it personally," Torin says. "They're trying to solve the case, it's their job to examine it from all sides. You've got nothing to worry about."

"My DNA's on Gabi's sweater, and there's more of it under her nails."

He waves a hand. "Circumstantial. There were six of you in the truck, five at the cabin. It's not enough to pin one murder on you, let alone two, and they know it. Trust me, Vienna. There's no case. This won't go to trial, and if it did—"

"You just said it wouldn't."

"*If* it did, there'd never be enough to convict." He pauses, his hazel eyes filling with compassion. "You're one of the victims here, Vienna. Don't forget Libby remembers waking up with you in the locked basement, helping you climb out of the window so you could go for help. She can corroborate much of your story, exactly how you say it happened."

"Because it's the truth," I say. "I can give the police my memoir. It's only a draft, but—"

"Let them get a warrant. Until then, email it to me, as we discussed. Listen, don't you worry. If Ashbury, Newell, or anybody from the police contacts you, call me. Immediately."

"Thank you," I say. "It's good to know I have you on my side."

"My pleasure. Now, go home, get fed and rested. I'm giving you an order."

"Yes, sir."

Moments later, Torin's gone and I'm standing alone on Second Avenue. It's been a little over three years since I followed Madison to New York, meaning it's my fourth winter here.

You'd think I'd be used to the freezing winds blowing between the buildings, but I shiver, nonetheless. Maybe it's not only from the cold, but also because I should've been exonerated by now. I can't believe it's taking the cops this long.

I unzip my bag, yank out a navy beanie and pull it low on my head so nobody recognizes me. After Libby and I were rescued from the cabin, I gave multiple short interviews, which Roger arranged, and my face has been plastered all over the news and social media for weeks.

As expected, the press hounded me constantly, showing up on my doorstep and skulking around outside my building but I decided I'd wait until the evidence I'd left for the cops showed up before talking to journalists again. When things got so bad, I couldn't even get to my local deli, Roger asked his husband, Max, to find another place for me in Brooklyn.

Within twenty-four hours, Max had pulled some strings and I was living in a fully furnished two-bed apartment in Cobble Hill, far better than the one in Bushwick, and more glam than Madison's original place in Williamsburg.

"Mooseman and I have covered the three months' rent upfront so don't worry about money," Roger said, telling me not to argue and instructing me to only give the address to people I trusted. "Stay incognito," he added. "Always wear a hat and sunglasses whenever you're out. Better yet, keep a low profile. Get groceries delivered."

I gave Guy the address because he's a friend, and he visited the next day, his eyes red, face blotchy. "Please tell me Madison's okay," he begged. "Tell me she didn't do anything bad."

He didn't yet know the woman he'd been in love with for years would be branded a murderer. In a way, I'd done him a favor. He'd pined for her for so long without getting much in return. Now he'd be able to let her go and move on. Still, as he hugged me, I cried real tears for what I'd done to my best friend, and I told more lies to ensure I saved myself.

"I don't know what she did," I whispered as he held me. "I'm scared for her."

Shoving the memories away, I bow my head and walk faster to warm up, heading for the subway that'll take me back to Brooklyn. I'm glad I'm not returning to the Bushwick apartment I shared with Madison. *Share*, I remind myself. Such a seemingly innocuous slip could make the cops come running.

Same with my new cell phone. Although it's still burning a hole in my pocket, I don't look at it in case I have an uncontrollable, visceral reaction to whatever I find online. I've no clue if anyone here might recognize me and snap a photo, or if Newell and Ashbury have sent someone to tail me, and I'm not about to take the most microscopic of chances.

As soon as I get home and close the front door, I take off my boots and let my jacket fall to the floor. Madison always moaned when I did this, saying I was messy and asking why I couldn't use the closet because that's what it's for. I must add the detail to the memoir, but this is my place—temporarily at least—and she's not here anymore.

The fact she's gone, that I'll never hear her nagging me because she tripped over a bag I left by the door again stabs at my heart and makes the regret resurface. It's something else I'm going to have to learn to live with, and I already know from experience that it'll get easier with time.

Once I've made a cup of coffee and flop on the fancy slate-gray sofa, I grab my cell phone, see my social media has exploded. The number of new email notifications grows exponentially, too, Google and Talkwalker alerts flowing into my inbox as if a virtual dam has burst. All of them contain links to mentions of Vienna Taylor, the Bittersweet, and of course #TeamVienna.

I start sifting through it all, unable to keep up because as soon as I read one message or post, it's replaced by another ten. My pulse throbs in my temples, blood pressure rising.

The cops may have picked me up at the memorial service only a few hours ago, but I've long understood how quickly—and without adequate information—the court of public opinion casts its verdict. I've been guilty of doing the same in the past. Being on the other side, however, gives me a whole other perspective of how it feels to be so blatantly skewered.

Vienna Taylor's guilty af #TeamMadison

I used to be #TeamVienna but now I'm #TeamMadison. What a whack job.

Throw her in jail and lose the key forever

People like her make me want to bring back the death penalty

I hope she burns in hell

Fucking bitch #TeamMadison #TeamMadison #TeamMadison

For every ten comments like these, there's one supporting me, drowned out by the mass of insults. One of them, a certain @flip_flop_22 is particularly vocal, going up against those trying to defend me. I look at her profile picture, don't recognize the young woman with a head of dark curls and pouty pink lips. She could be anyone.

The vitriol from the #TeamMadison camp—and #TeamVienna people who've turned on me—will no doubt silence many of my remaining fans. Sure, they may still support me privately, but there's no way they'll say so out loud, which renders their voices useless.

I want to hurl my phone against the wall, smash it to pieces. It won't change anything. These comments will keep existing and continue to grow and propagate. Just because I don't see them doesn't mean they don't exist.

Time to refocus on what I *can* control. Thinking back to my conversation with Newell and Ashbury, I go over what I said and how I said it, evaluate whether they could trip me up with any of my answers. There's nothing, but I don't think either of them are done with me yet, making them dangerous opponents. For now.

I wonder if they've met Gabi and Evelina's family, made promises about bringing Evelina's killer to justice, voiced their suspicions about Gabi not having died accidentally. Maybe Newell has assured Madison's parents he'll find their daughter and bring her home.

There's a huge need for me to tread carefully. When cases like this go unsolved, they can get under a cop's skin, become an itch impossible to ignore, urging them to do whatever it takes to find answers, no matter the method. The trail may eventually go cold, but some cops don't forget. Ask the infamous Golden State Killer, Joseph DeAngelo. It took over forty years to catch him, but they got him in the end.

Fact is, I should never have been taken in for questioning, or an *interview* as Ashbury tried to have me think of it. They've had six weeks to search the goddamn cabin, although I know they were only there for one. Still, it's ample time to have found the evidence I left. Evidence to absolve me.

Where is it? Are they really this incompetent? If they don't uncover it soon, I'm in trouble. It won't necessarily be legal trouble. As Torin said, they've got nothing to pin the murders on me, but if I'm not one hundred percent cleared of having a hand in the demise of the Bittersweet and the deaths of my friends, then my future's royally screwed.

Also, while Torin doesn't believe the cops have a case, and I'll never stand trial, the possibility he's wrong does exist. Roger assured me Torin's the very best, but depending on whom he's up against from the prosecution, and the new DA's appetite for fast convictions, things might get sticky without my irrefutable proof.

What the hell was I supposed to do, leave Libby's camera beneath a flashing neon sign? Gift-wrap and hand deliver it to the cops with a bow on top and an explanatory note?

Frustration builds as I imagine myself in the courtroom, sitting next to Torin with my head bent, seeming approachable, definitely not guilty. Trying to convince twelve jurors and a judge of my innocence for weeks on end is far different than fooling the cops from the Catskills who'd already interviewed Libby and me in the days after we *escaped* from the cabin, and a NYPD detective for a few hours six weeks later. I'm not sure if I can pull off a performance of that magnitude, particularly when I've no clue what questions could be thrown my way in court, no matter how many hours Torin and I prepare.

From what I understand, Torin could bring in character witnesses to support my case, but the prosecution could do the opposite and go for character assassination. I bet Mom and Rick would love the opportunity to take the stand. Tell the world what a horrible, ungrateful daughter I am.

"She abandoned us the day her grandmother died," Mom would say, shedding fake tears.

"She torched my car," Rick would yammer. "Who does that?"

The press and the #TeamMadison fans would eat it all up.

I sit back, press the heels of my palms over my eyes and regroup. Getting away with murder, both from an emotional and technical standpoint, was never going to be easy, I knew that, but the latter remains wildly possible. The scratches on my wrist can easily be explained, as can the DNA on the sweater used to suffocate Evelina. *Circumstantial*, Torin had called it, exactly what I'd been going for.

As for Gabi's bruises, we were in a car accident, so was there really something there or were Ashbury and Newell trying to force a reaction? Surely there's no hard proof Gabi was pushed, and Madison will never be found. Never. Trying to charge, let alone convict, me without a body isn't without its complications, which Newell and Ashbury certainly know.

All I have to do is control my guilt, all my other emotions, and the narrative until the missing link surfaces. When it does, the #TeamMadison fanatics will have so much egg on their faces, they'll feast on nothing but omelets for the rest of their lives.

I take a sip of coffee, feel my shoulders fall away from my ears.

Let the games begin.

35

TWO DAYS AFTER my interview with the detectives, speculation about why I was hauled in for questioning is still rife. Roger called, asked if I wanted to give any interviews, but I declined. Torin suggested I stay quiet, and I agree. I'll have plenty to say when I'm cleared.

Libby texted earlier, asking if she can come to my apartment. We've seen each other a handful of times since the accident. While we'll never be anywhere near as close as Madison and I were, we've become friends, and she's been here on a number of occasions already.

I ordered lunch from Papa e Ragazzi and it's keeping warm in the oven. Pumpkin ravioli for Libby because it's her favorite, minestrone soup for me because I don't have much of an appetite.

Guy refused to charge me for the meal when I phoned in the order. I haven't worked a shift since December and when I suggested I return this week, Guy danced around the issue at first, under pretext the schedule was already done.

"Call me if someone drops a shift," I insisted. "Come on, Guy, I can work, I promise. It'll be a good distraction for me."

"And everybody else," he muttered, but I still caught it.

"What do you mean?"

"You being here isn't a good idea, Vienna."

"But I can work. I—"

"I meant for us, the restaurant. With all the negative press coverage—"

"Hold on, please tell me you don't believe what they say about me."

"No, of course not." His answer came a little too quickly.

"Then what is it? Why can't I come back to work?"

He let out a sigh. "Journalists have come sniffing. Hanging around the building, walking in and asking questions."

"Did they at least order a drink?"

Guy snorted. "Barely. But listen, everybody and their uncle knows this is where you had a job and it's putting our regulars off."

"Had?"

"Huh?"

"You said *had* a job. Am I fired?"

"No, course not. We need the dust to settle, is all."

"What *I* need, is money," I said. I wasn't lying, and once again felt grateful that Roger and Mooseman had covered a few months' rent for my temporary home.

"What about the memoir thing?"

"Why does everyone keep bringing that up?" I snapped. "It's not a sure thing, and if the manuscript sells it'll take time for contracts to be signed and an advance to come through."

"Really?"

"Yes. Publishers pay in installments. I haven't suddenly got a million dollars in my bank account."

"You think you'll get a million bucks?"

Hopefully, with all the trouble I've gone to. "No, and you're missing the point. I'm broke, Guy. I need to work."

This was the complete truth and it's frightening how little money I have. Sure, sales and streams of "Sweet Spot" have skyrocketed, exactly how I suspected they would after a catastrophe of such magnitude, but as with book advances, music royalties take eons to be processed and trickle into the hands of the artists. I won't see any cash for months and while I'm living here rent-free, I still have to cover the entire amount for the Bushwick place. Thankfully I have just about enough socked away for that, but it'll be tight.

"Please, Guy." I lowered my voice to make it seem like I was on the verge of tears.

I've cried for real exactly three times in the last five years. Once when I dropped Pepper off at the animal shelter on that freezing night, the second when Grams took her last breath, and the third… I can't bring myself to think about it. Guy didn't know any of this, of course, and it's another detail that can't make it into my memoir.

People might think I'm a freak but tears not coming easily doesn't mean there's no pain going on inside. Most of my grief is real. I survived the horrific crash Careless Gabi caused, and the dreadful things that happened thereafter weren't planned.

The Bittersweet's demise wasn't premeditated—why would it be when we were about to blow up—but after the accident I saw an opportunity, and when one of those comes along, you seize it with everything you've got. I just wish things hadn't taken an even darker turn. And I wish Madison were still here with me.

She wasn't supposed to die, Madison truly was my best friend since high school, exactly as I've described in my memoir. I think about her all the time. Whisper an apology each night before I fall asleep, hoping for respite, and her not visiting me in my dreams again.

"Working will help me forget what I've been through," I told Guy, hoping he'd come around because it's true, I do need to forget until I've managed to convince myself the lies I'm telling are reality. "If only for a while."

Evidently, it wasn't enough to convince him. "Maybe in a few weeks," he said. "Let's see how things go. In the meantime, if you need food, it's yours." He paused. "Have you, uh, heard anything about Madison?"

"No, I'm sorry."

"So am I," he whispered. "So am I."

When we hung up, I pondered whether Guy meant it when he said he didn't believe all the stuff being written about me, how I'm a murderer. He's always been kind, but he had—still has—a thing for Madison, getting by on the tiny tidbits of affection she fed him. In fairness, she'd always been perfectly clear nothing serious would ever happen between them, but he'd still hoped, going gooey-eyed whenever he saw her. This was my best friend all over. Madison could ensnare people simply by existing.

The doorbell rings and I walk over. Today, I'm dressed in black jeans and a simple sea-green shirt. My face is bare of makeup, and I've lost weight since the accident. I hate the way my ribs could be mistaken for a xylophone, but being a little on the hollowed out and emaciated side makes my story appear more believable.

I pull open the front door. Libby's face is paler than mine. Her blond hair hangs around her face, limp and lackluster, the sparkle gone from her big blue eyes. She's thinner, too, cheeks resembling scooped out jack-o'-lanterns.

She moves in for a hug, wrapping her spindly arms around my equally bony shoulders. Her hair smells of vanilla and berries, making me want to pull away because it's vaguely reminiscent of Evelina's lip balm but I hold on until she steps back.

"How are you doing?" she says.

"Truth?" I answer, already knowing whatever I offer will only be partially so.

"Always."

"Terrible, and I'm taking a break from social media," I say, ushering her inside and taking her coat. I hang it up, as Madison would've expected, and when Libby removes her boots, I point to the mat. "You can leave those on there, next to mine."

"Did the cops keep your boots, too?"

"Yeah, and I want them back at some point, they're my favorite," I reply as I walk down the hall. I've no idea if they'll do me the courtesy, and presumably they kept our footwear and other items to run tests or whatever. Thankfully Madison and I were the same size, so I've brought over some clothes and shoes from her Bushwick wardrobe. They make me feel closer to her.

"I read the disgusting things people are writing about you," Libby says as she follows me into the living room. "Are they why you're avoiding socials?"

"Uh-huh."

"I'm sorry you're going through this, Vienna. It's completely unfair. I wish you hadn't seen the posts."

"To be honest, they're hard to miss."

I sit in the armchair and Libby sinks onto the high-end sofa. A layer of discomfort spreads across her face, but I don't think it's from our seating arrangements.

"What's wrong?" I ask.

She hesitates, fiddles with the cuff of her shirt. "The police came to see me again yesterday," she says. "Detective Ashbury from the NYPD, and Detective Newell from the Catskills. I gather you met with them, too?"

"Yeah, day before last. Were they nice to you, at least?"

She gives an apologetic grimace, like she already knows how they were with me. "Yes, they were very kind. They wanted to go over what happened. I told them everything I could but I'm not sure it helped *you*."

My heart beats a little faster. "Why do you say that?"

"Because I still don't remember anything after arriving at the cabin and taking those pills. Nothing until the morning when we woke up in the basement, which is also on the fuzzy side." She sighs, wrings her hands. "They kept asking if I saw you climb out of the basement window, and if I saw you with a key. What's up with that? I told them I helped you escape, and if you'd had the key, we would've used the door."

Unlike Libby, I know exactly what Ashbury and Newell are doing. Trying to determine if I locked us in and tucked the key in my pocket. Yes, is the answer. It's exactly what I did after hauling Libby into the basement. That part was tough. She's smaller than Evelina, but I was moving her alone and those stairs are steep.

"When I try to force anything else to come back it feels like—" she spins her hand in a circle next to her head "—like my mind's made from cotton wool and it's all bunched up in there."

"Don't they understand you're not supposed to get stressed out with your concussion?" I say. "You have to be careful, Libby. Take care of yourself."

"They want to figure out what happened, and so do I. Anyway, you know my concussion turned out to be mild." She pauses again. "Did they mention I had benzos in my system?"

"Yes."

"I've never taken any. Never. It was the pills Madison gave me."

"Maybe it was an accident. It was dark in the cabin. Perhaps—"

"Stop," Libby says. "She dragged me into the basement, assaulted you, and tried to set the cabin on fire. She left us to die. Why are you still making excuses for her?"

"Because we don't know any of that for sure," I say. "Maybe someone else—"

"Come on, Vienna," Libby says gently. "There was nobody else. And what about Evelina? I'm guessing the cops told you she was…"

"Suffocated," I whisper.

"Do you think that was somebody else, too?"

"But why would Madison do this?"

"Jealousy?" Libby says, simply. "From what you wrote, she's been envious of you for years."

"Me?" I say, congratulating myself on how I've portrayed Madison in the memoir by making a few omissions, writing a subtle touch here, giving a small exaggeration there, building her into an unlikable character people will love to detest. "No, that can't be her motive."

"Why not?"

"Because…because…it would make all this my fault."

"None of this is your fault," Libby says, before rushing on. "Maybe there was an argument between her and Evelina. Maybe Gabi saw Madison hurt her sister."

She's on one of the paths I'm trying to lead the cops to, but I can't make it obvious. "Madison and Evelina got along fine, and I already told you, Gabi came back from the truck a short while after Evelina died. Besides, wouldn't she have said if she'd witnessed Madison murder her sister?" I stop, blink three times. "God, I can't believe those words came out of my mouth. It's surreal."

"Maybe Gabi suspected it. What if she accused Madison and Madison killed her?"

We go around in circles for a little while, trading theories. This was always going to be the riskier part for me because Libby's right—when there's murder, there's got to be motive.

Sometimes it's obvious, sometimes it isn't, and sometimes only the killer truly knows. I have to tread carefully, let the cops come to their own conclusions by leaving a tiny breadcrumb at a time, uncovering a plausible story so the entire blame lands on Madison's shoulders. Stand by while they endlessly congratulate themselves for figuring everything out. Deciding to sacrifice my best friend's reputation in this way wasn't easy, but she was already gone, and it's the only way for me to survive.

When my stomach growls, I get up and pull the food from the oven. We move to the dining table, both of us picking at our dishes with little appetite. Once we're done and the plates are cleared, Libby retrieves a blue binder from her bag. I recognize it immediately—it's a copy of the memoir she insisted on reading.

"I went over all the chapters again," Libby says. "The scenes at the cabin are…intense."

"I still can't believe you wanted to read them," I say, which is the truth, but I'm glad she asked. She feels she owes me for saving her by getting us help, and I'll use it to ensure she keeps telling the cops exactly what she's told them so far. Like Torin said, she's corroborating my story. Libby's my star witness.

She gives a small shrug. "I needed to know what happened while I was unconscious. It feels so strange to have been physically present, but AWOL otherwise. Does that make sense?"

"Perfectly, and I'd imagine it's terrifying."

"It is," she whispers. "I feel violated, and guilty."

"Guilty?"

"What if I hadn't mentioned my headache? What if I hadn't taken those pills from Madison? What if I'd never passed out from the benzos?"

"What if I hadn't given Madison the pills at the truck?" I say. "She wouldn't have had the opportunity to swap them out."

"Did you know she was taking Klonopin?" Libby asks, and I shake my head. Truth is she took them whenever she got overly stressed before an exam, or an important holiday party with the owner of Mooseman Records Inc. I saw them in her bag the day we left for the Catskills.

There was no way I'd write any of that in my memoir because the cops could accuse me of switching the meds. It had been easy enough. When Libby mentioned her headache at the crash site, my plans were already in motion.

The first two pills I'd given her were vitamins, and while I'd been at the truck I'd quickly swapped out the acetaminophen for Madison's benzos, which I'd plucked from her bag. With all the chaos going on, nobody noticed a thing. All I had to do was hope for Libby's headache to get worse, so I could put her to sleep for a while.

I don't say any of this, instead, I offer, "I feel ashamed, too."

"Of Madison? I—"

"No, of me. For not realizing she'd given you benzos."

When Libby continues staring at me, her eyes widen. "You can't feel bad for that."

"I can't help it. I feel guilty and ashamed for so many things," I answer, and not lying for an instant feels good, but it doesn't last because I have to spin more tales. "For one, I wish I'd known Madison was capable of doing what we *think* she did." I pause for a few beats, stare at my lap. "Mostly I feel guilty for surviving."

"You do?"

"Yeah. I've read about survivor's guilt but never understood it until now."

"Me, neither."

I brush away an inexistent tear with the back of my hand. "Thank you for reading my ramblings. As I told the cops, it's supposed to help make sense of it all."

"It's helped me, too, and...I'm sorry you had such a hard time with your mom and step... I mean Rick. I have to ask... did you secretly torch his car?"

"No, absolutely not," I say, pretending to look shocked because of course I did. Driving it to Falmouth and watching it burn had been exhilarating, and my parting gift to him. Vengeance for everything he'd done to me and for how he'd treated Grams. "Rick always left both sets of car keys right by the door," I add. "It was chaos at his house, but I'm not surprised they blamed it on me."

"Is it wise to include the news article in your memoir though?" Libby asks. "Aren't you worried it'll make you look guilty?"

"I was trying to show the breakdown of the relationship with my mother," I say.

While I've lied about stealing the car, about most of what happened after we got to the cabin, and I've amplified Madison's jealousy a touch in my memoir, I've told the truth about Mom and Rick's behavior, but Libby's right. There's little point handing them ammo they can fire back at me.

"I'll take it out," I say. "Although it's really important for me to tell my truth."

Libby looks at me, nibbles on her bottom lip. "But...you didn't mention what I told you about my colleague Zeke—you know, how I made sure he couldn't come for the initial meeting with the band."

"You shared that with me in confidence."

Libby puts a hand to her chest. "Thank you. I really don't want him finding out I emailed those dick pics to the boss. I promise I'd never have done it if he hadn't sent them to the admin assistant anonymously first. I'll never forget her face. She was mortified." She shakes her head. "We had a feeling it was him, but I couldn't confirm it until he left his cell unlocked. Anyway, thanks for not including those bits."

"I've got your back," I say.

"Also...I was wondering if you might change my name in the memoir, you know, to protect my anonymity. I can't tell you how glad I am that my lawyer managed to keep my name confidential. Being 'and another woman' in the news is fine with me."

"Of course, Libby, no problem."

"Thank you," she says.

"No need. It's what friends are for."

"My thoughts exactly, which is why—" Libby slides the binder to me "—I hope you don't mind but I kept a copy and added notes to this one. I'm no expert, obviously, but I love how you included newspaper articles and radio transcripts to give an additional perspective. And I have to say, writing the cabin scenes by hand made them so vivid, and raw." She presses her lips shut before adding, "And terrifying."

"My turn to thank you."

"You're welcome. You have beautiful penmanship."

My eyes meet hers. "I mean thank you for *everything*, Libby. For standing by me, for defending me, and supporting this memoir project. I know for some it seems like a cash grab."

"Not for me. I hope the discussions with the literary agents work out. You said Roger's lining some up?"

"Yes, once I polish these pages and plan the rest of the book. I want the world to know the truth about the Bittersweet. Understand what happened, what could've been. I'm grateful for the opportunity to be heard, and the book just poured out of me."

That's a fact. I've barely slept in the past six weeks, and I'm going to do whatever I need to keep my band's name in the news. I promised Madison fame, and it's a promise I'll keep.

I know I'll have to live with the lies for the rest of my life. At times I wonder if I'll be able to stand it, but I can't stop now. It's also too early to start planning the progression of my healing, but I'll have to ensure it's up and down to mirror the way a person would authentically try to recover from trauma like this.

I've looked into it, have been able to research the stages of grief from the comfort of my own home rather than one of the obscure internet cafés I've frequented these last few weeks to take care of things. If Ashbury or Newell get a warrant for my laptop or phone, I can easily say my searches were to prepare myself for the long and arduous journey ahead.

"Is everything all right?" Libby says, before her face falls. "What a ridiculous question."

I give her a tentative smile before letting my gaze drop again. "I'm scared about the online abuse. It's getting out of control."

"You can't listen to them."

"Somebody said they hope I burn in hell."

"Show me."

After I grab my laptop, we navigate to Twitter first. The insults haven't stopped. In fact, they've increased both in number and intensity, and they set my insides on fire with unadulterated rage. I make sure it translates to despair on the outside by turning my head away from the screen, but not before I glimpse some of the comments.

Vienna should be cut up into tiny pieces and fed to the dogs #TeamMadison

Kill the bitch #TeamMadison

She's fucked. She's going down for this #TeamMadison

She'll be fucked and going down in prison, but not by choice #TeamMadison

What a bunch of absolute pricks. They don't know me. They've no reason to believe I'm guilty, there's no proof whatsoever, and yet they want me raped, mutilated, and dead. It makes me wonder how genuinely innocent people feel when they're faced with this stuff.

"You should report these," Libby says. "Show them to Ashbury and Newell."

Her naivety makes me laugh. "They won't care. They think I killed our friends."

"They're wrong, and it makes me furious," Libby says. "I

asked them why I'm not a suspect. My attorney tried to shut me down, but I needed to know."

"What did they say?"

"The benzos," she answers, simply. "I wouldn't have been capable."

"I don't want anything to do with the cops," I say. "Given a little time, I'm sure everybody out there will find another scandal to direct their hatred toward. I'll have to keep my head down until it passes. At least there's been a gag order on my address."

"Yeah, I'm relieved about that, too." She looks at me. "Is there any way I can help?"

"Believing me is already a whole lot," I say. "I can't ask for more."

Except for the goddamn evidence to appear, but unless Libby has a magic wand up her sleeve, I'll have to sit tight and wait out the raging storm no matter what, because the lands beyond are beautiful, bountiful, and soon they'll be all mine.

36

45 days after the accident

THE GRAVEYARD'S EMPTY, a sliver of silver moon hanging in the dark skies. I'm completely alone, but there's a pungent smell in the air I can't ignore, and which I'm trying to believe is only coming from the damp leaves and wet grass beneath my feet.

Animals snuffle and hoot in the distance. The collection of eerie sounds should make me anxious in the dark, but they're not what I'm afraid of. What scares me is the grave ten steps ahead, and the fact I'm incapable of walking away.

It's as if roots have burst from the soles of my shoes and dug in deep, anchoring me to the ground, yet, when I look down, I'm barefoot, my toes tinged blue. I try closing my eyes but find my lids are frozen open, forcing me to watch what I know is to come.

Pale-as-pearl fingertips emerge from the loose dirt covering the grave, one first, then another, before all five scrabble and break the surface. Knuckles come next, followed by an entire hand reaching upward. It's impossible for me to blink, impossible to move.

"I'm sorry," I whisper. "I'm sorry. I'm sorry. I'm sorry."

A fraction of a beat passes and the hand's no longer in the grave, but on my neck, fingers pressing hard. Trying to pull it off, I weave my upper body left and right. It's no use. The grip is viselike, cutting off my air supply. I let out a choking noise as I hear Madison's voice in my ear, whispering, "I'm coming for you, Vienna. I'm coming for you."

Gasping, I wake up and reach for the bedside light, click it on, desperate to banish these demons back into the shadows. Considering Madison has haunted my dreams almost every time I've slept since returning from the Catskills, I should be used to her showing up, but the images are getting more vivid and disturbing with each passing night. Although the rational part of my brain knows none of it's real, the rest of me remains unconvinced.

It's only 4:17 a.m. but I'm unable to ignore the wild thumping of my heart. I swing my legs over the side of the king-size bed and head for the kitchen where I grab a tall glass of water and gulp it down, half of the liquid dribbling onto my sleep shirt.

After making a strong cup of black coffee I take a seat and slump onto the table. As I rest my head in my hands and close my eyes, more images of Madison return. This time it's not the graveyard in my dream, but the memories of what really happened at the cabin. All the details I left out or changed as I wrote my memoir, while trying to etch the fake images into my mind in lieu of reality.

For a little over six weeks, I've tried everything I can think of to forget or suppress the truth, push it aside, make it go away, invent a new story. It mostly works during the day, but at night, when my body rests, these efforts falter.

Maybe I can allow myself to give in this once. Perhaps by letting the recollection of what transpired at the cabin play out in my mind as if I'm watching a movie, I'll rid myself of it, get it out of my system. Afterward I'll read the pages of my memoir again and again, as if I'm spreading thick coats of paint on a wall until what's beneath isn't only hidden from view but ceases to exist.

Most of what I've written is accurate. Any skilled liar knows they need to anchor their tales deep in truths for their deception to stick. There's too much to remember otherwise, too many possibilities of being tripped up, too many people who can argue and contradict.

Writing everything down was also helpful for me to recall what I've told everyone—Libby, Roger, Ashbury, Newell, Torin, and the rest of the world. There is, as the expression goes, a method to my madness, and I intend to see it through, which means convincing myself a hundred percent what I've said is the absolute truth. There can be no lingering doubts in my mind, either, if I want to be believed.

I close my eyes, let myself travel to when I woke up after the crash. My body tenses as I hear Madison's voice, shouting at me to wake up. The images of Isabel's chest impaled by the tree branch, and Evelina's missing hand come next, thick, fast, and deeply horrific. It's as if I'm having an out-of-body experience, reliving the day from above, and I make myself observe, trying to remain detached and unemotional because this exercise won't work otherwise.

I see myself scrambling for the fire extinguisher, beating back the flames. Evelina being pulled from the wreckage, her injuries tended to. Gabi and Libby staying behind while Madison and I go for help.

This is where fact and fiction partially bid each other goodbye. I follow the factual trail, vowing this'll be the last and final time I travel this road. Once done, I'll barricade the virtual path in my head and eventually it'll fade and disappear. I'm good at compartmentalizing. This isn't my first time.

I remember Madison's exact words as the two of us stood in

front of the cabin we found, snow coming down so fast, our footprints had almost disappeared already.

"What if we get lost trying to find this place again? Maybe you and I should stay."

"What? We can't abandon them," I said.

"It's not a question of abandoning them."

"Sounds like it to me."

"I'm scared, Vee. I want to make sure the two of us survive."

"You stay here, then. I'll go."

"No, I—"

"It's okay. I'll lead them here."

"Vienna…"

I turned and headed back to the crash site, my mind spinning, the shock of what had happened to us turning to disbelief and despair. Isabel was dead. Evelina badly injured. It was anybody's guess how long she'd survive.

The Bittersweet were finished.

It was so unfair. We'd been on the cusp of success and Gabi had ruined it all when she'd lost control of the truck. When we'd stopped for coffee and she'd offered to drive, I'd warned her about taking it easy. The careless bitch hadn't listened, and now…now all of us could wind up dead.

My despair shifted and turned, transforming into gnarly anger. Gabi should've been the one lying in the snow with a missing hand, or a tree branch stuck through her chest, not Evelina and Isabel. I hated, no, barely strong enough, I *loathed* Gabi for it. Detested her for destroying the collective future we'd worked so hard for, especially after I'd fought with Madison about having her in the band in the first place. If I'd listened to Madison back then, maybe we wouldn't be in this mess.

A few yards later, I slowed my pace as a glimmer of an idea grabbed hold of me, pulling me in. I tried to brush it off and push it away, but it held tight, whispering at me to listen. The glimmer became bigger, a phoenix rising from the ashes. *Some-*

times, it whispered, *tragedy brings opportunity, providing you know where to look.*

Madison's words sped through my mind again. *I want to make sure the two of us survive.* I couldn't stop myself from thinking if we were the *only* survivors of our band, we'd have one hell of a story to tell. To *sell.* We wouldn't only survive. We'd thrive.

I ordered myself to stop thinking this way. In time, maybe we'd start a new band, and—

What if Madison didn't want to? What if she complied with her parents' wishes, went back to her studies, leaving me on my own? I couldn't let it happen. There was no way I'd let her abandon me.

I know how twisted it sounds, but Madison's and my relationship had always been complicated. Some might have tried to label it as toxic, but we loved each other, we were best friends. We infuriated each other, too, yet couldn't stand being apart, either. She had more of a jealous streak, but both of us found it impossible to stomach the other achieving more.

Sure, we celebrated respective successes, but she grabbed onto my coattails and hung on, either being pulled forward or holding me back, and I did the exact same thing. Over the years I'd realized it was a defense mechanism to ensure neither of us got left behind.

Maybe there was no need for that in our current desperate situation. Not if we could take a giant leap to another level of stardom together.

It was no secret Madison had become increasingly impatient since she quit college, wanting to show her parents how much she *didn't* need them, or their checkbook. We both knew they were keeping score just as much as she was, hence her drive and voracious craving for recognition, success, money, and fame because she felt she had so much to prove.

What if I could give her all that, and more? What if we could keep it for the two of us, exactly how she'd always wanted?

Once again, I made myself stop, but when I approached the crash site, and took one glimpse at Evelina's ashen face, saw her shallow breathing, I knew she wasn't getting out of here alive.

The gnarly temptress on my shoulder softly whispered about opportunity again. Because of Gabi, the Bittersweet barely had a pulse, but everybody knows how artists can become worth a significant amount more dead than alive. Sales go sky-high when there's an especially tragic ending, and that boost of fame can last for years.

My mind sped up, calculating, estimating. While we'd still have to split revenues from our existing songs five ways—the amount destined for the deceased members going to their inheritors—anything new would be shared between Madison and me. There'd be a feeding frenzy after such a gruesome tragedy.

I could see it playing out now. TV and magazine interviews, appearances on radio talk shows and podcasts, and if Netflix or Hollywood came knocking…well, the proverbial sky really was the limit. I didn't care for the fame part the way Madison did, but it would ensure I could work in the music industry for the rest of my life.

I didn't have much time to decide what I was going to do. This was one of those moments when a large but fleeting possibility presented itself, and I had to either grab hold of it, or let it go. Within seconds I understood the prospects this disaster offered us. Realized what our new situation could allow Madison and me to achieve together, fast, which was all too irresistible to ignore.

There was no way she'd go along with any of it, and only one of us having to lie ensured fewer risks of slipping up, so I engineered a plan to shield her from the truth. I'd shoulder the burden alone for our mutual benefit because she was my best friend, and I loved her.

For a moment I wondered if I should've stayed at the cabin with her. Told Madison she was right, it was too dangerous to return to the Tahoe, but whether or not the others survived overnight in the cold, abandoning them would be terrible optics. We'd be branded the devil.

If I was going through with this, if I was going to kill again, this time for different reasons, I had to find a way to first subdue Libby—she didn't need to be hurt, I wasn't a monster—then ease Evelina's pain before maneuvering Gabi out of the way. She didn't deserve to live considering Isabel was already gone and Evelina wasn't far behind. Given time, the guilt would probably kill Gabi anyway.

When I got back to the truck and Libby mentioned her headache, I gave her the vitamin pills. By the time we arrived at the cabin, her headache had worsened, exactly as I'd hoped. Madison gave Libby what they both thought was more acetaminophen, and once that was done, I made sure to put the real pills I'd saved back into the bottle.

I didn't know how long benzos might show up in Libby's system, but I could make it seem as if Madison had given Libby the wrong pills by accident. The cabin was dark, we were all in shock and panic, and my preparations for Libby to sleep through the night, completely unaware of what was going on around her, were set.

With Libby taken care of, I focused on Evelina. A few days earlier, I'd walked into the bathroom of our rehearsal room and found her clutching a syringe.

"What are you doing?" I demanded.

"It's not what you think," she said quickly.

"Whatever." I pointed at the door. "Get out. Don't come back."

"Vienna, listen—"

"No, I don't care."

"It's diabetes. Type one."

I rolled my eyes. "Sure it is."

"It *is*, I promise." Evelina moved toward me, her face plead-

ing. "It's why I've been losing so much weight and peeing all
the time. I was diagnosed last month."

"Really?" I said, thinking how I'd noticed her becoming
slim as a rake over the past couple of months. I'd thought it was
because we were so busy, and she mostly picked at her food.
"What's this?" I asked, nodding at the syringe in her hand.

"Insulin. It brings my blood sugar down because my body
can't do it on its own."

"Does it hurt?"

"Only my bank account," she said. "This crap's expensive,
and I'm going to have to use it for the rest of my life."

"I'm sorry," I said. "Really. I shouldn't have accused you of
doing drugs, I know you better than that."

"It's fine, don't worry," she said. "Please don't tell anyone.
Gabi knows, obviously, but I don't want the others to find out.
I can't deal with the fuss. Let's not mention this conversation
to Gabi either in case she lets it slip."

I'd agreed, and when I'd got home in the evening, I'd said
goodnight to Madison and headed to my room, read up about
the disease, learning how type one diabetics navigated the highs
and lows of their blood sugar, and what could happen if they
didn't have access to their meds so I had a better understanding of what Evelina was going through.

It had been easy to hide the insulin pouch at the crash site,
with gloved hands, of course. We were all busy with making
the jacket stretcher and packing up items to take to the cabin, so
I tucked the polka-dot pouch under one of the seats. Not having insulin wouldn't harm Evelina immediately, but it would
give Gabi a reason to leave the cabin, hopefully providing me
with an opportunity to be alone with her sister.

I didn't think it would happen so soon after we got to the
cabin. Libby had only taken the pseudo-acetaminophen about
half an hour before Gabi saw the alert from Evelina's blood sugar
monitor, but the pills knocked Libby out faster than I expected.

After Madison suggested we find stuff to burn and Gabi went to the truck, I pretended to head upstairs, and doubled back to the living room. Libby was completely out of it, lying by the door with her face turned away from me, but my next move was risky, so I draped a jacket over her head.

"Help me," Evelina whispered, as I approached her, voice raspy as her eyes fluttered open. "The pain. The *pain*. Please, help me."

"Shh," I said, stroking her hair as I picked up Gabi's sweater. "I'm here now. Everything's going to be okay."

Evelina's eyes closed as she gave a little nod and passed out again. Keeping my eyes on Libby at all times in case she moved, I gently put the sweater over Evelina's mouth and nose, quietly whispering her suffering would soon be over. It didn't take long. Her body twitched a few times, but she was soon still.

Anyone who judges me might not understand it was peaceful, she didn't struggle, she didn't know what I was doing. It was a mercy killing, like Grams, whom I couldn't leave with Mom and Rick—it had been the only way to set us both free.

Later, when Detective Ashbury said Evelina would've died from her internal injuries, I balked so hard. While I tell myself I could've waited for her to die of natural causes, on the other hand I feel glad to have shortened her pain. Gabi had caused her death. I'd provided deliverance. During our interview with Melodie Johnson, Evelina insisted she'd rather die than not be able to play music. That fact alone eases my remorse.

After I was certain Evelina had passed, I'd stood up, taken a step back, heard Madison's footfalls on the basement stairs, so I'd removed Gabi's sweater, and the jacket covering Libby's face before darting into the hall, quietly moving to the upper level.

I didn't think Madison would realize Evelina was gone so quickly. I thought I'd have time to say I was going to help Gabi, that I was worried about her, but Madison screamed my name, and I couldn't leave. Not that it mattered. Gabi came back, freaked out and left again, and as Madison and I went outside, I spotted Gabi in the distance, but pretended I hadn't seen her.

"You go right," I told Madison. "I'll go left, and we'll circle the cabin, okay?"

Once I was sure she'd turned the corner I ran after Gabi, following her footprints in the snow, managed to catch up with her about a hundred yards later, when I saw her standing still.

"Gabi," I said as I reached her. "What are you doing?"

"It's another cliff," she said. "This is a dead end. I have to find a way around." She started to sob. "Evelina's dead. She died because of me. It's all my fault, isn't it?"

She expected me to placate her, reassure her it had been an accident, which was true, but she'd caused it by being careless. I didn't have time to play games. Madison would've gone around the cabin by now, she was probably searching for me.

Without another word, I shoved Gabi. Her eyes went wide, mouth falling open. As she fell, she reached for my arms, grabbed hold of my left wrist. She wasn't wearing her gloves, I've no idea why. Maybe she'd taken them off or she'd run out of the cabin without them. Either way, her nails dug into my flesh as she fell backward and disappeared from view with a piercing scream.

I'd never known it could be this simple, so fast and easy to kill someone. Terrifying. But not as terrifying as the fact I didn't feel guilty this time. I felt relieved. She'd caused Isabel's and Evelina's deaths, and the Bittersweet's demise. She'd ruined everything for us, everything we'd worked so hard for and the bright, exciting future ahead of us. It was only fair for her to pay.

As I stood by the edge, peering at Gabi's immobile body on the ledge below, I heard a shout.

"What did you do?" Madison yelled. "Vee, what did you *do*?"

"Nothing," I said, spinning around. "Gabi jumped. She—"

"No, she didn't," Madison screamed, taking a step back. "I saw you."

"No, I promise. I think she killed Evelina, and—"

"*Liar!*" She let out a moan of disbelief. "I thought I heard someone running upstairs when I was on the basement steps. Was it…was it *you*? Oh, my God. Did…did you hurt Evelina?"

"No, I—"

"I don't believe you. I don't believe anything you're saying."

I moved to her, taking one step at a time as if she were a wild animal, going as slowly as I could so I didn't startle her. "You said we should leave them at the crash site."

"I didn't want them to *die*."

"It's too late," I said. "They're gone now. Let me explain why I did this for us."

"No," Madison said. "No, no, no."

"It's for you and me, don't you understand?" I said, imploring her to listen. "They'll think Gabi killed Evelina because she couldn't cope with the guilt of the accident, and then killed herself by jumping from the cliff. Don't you see?"

"No, I—"

"A murder-suicide," I said. "And when all this gets out, everyone will know who we are. *Everyone.* We'll be famous. Really, *really* famous. Just like you wanted."

"Are you kidding me?" Madison said, teeth clenched, spittle landing on her lips. "If you think I'm going to have anything more to do with you—"

"Madison, please—"

"No. No fucking way. As soon as we get out of here, I'm calling the cops. I'm telling them everything."

"You wouldn't."

"Oh, no? Try me."

"I'll go to prison."

"Which is where you belong, you murderer."

"You can't. You need me."

"Need you?" She let out a piercing laugh. "I've never *needed* you. Stay away from Libby and me. In fact, stay out of the cabin. You can freeze to death out here for all I care."

There was nothing left anywhere in my body other than rage. After everything I'd done for Madison, right from the start.

I'd taken the blame for our altercation at Principal Mason's office.

Encouraged her to keep playing the electric guitar.

Propped her up as she'd fought with her parents about us forming a duo.

Lied about her whereabouts.

Got gigs for EmVee.

Taken a beating from Rick.

Come to New York.

Encouraged her to study.

Put the Bittersweet together and included her, even when she'd flaked and partied and been drunk so many times, I'd lost count.

She'd taken songwriting credits she didn't deserve, and I'd said nothing.

I'd introduced Roger to the band.

Slipped out the night we'd been in the Hamptons and set fire to her parents' house—*because she'd asked me*. I didn't want to, but she insisted, telling me about the utility room in which her parents ran a space heater nonstop because of the damp basement they hadn't yet fixed.

"It'll be easy," she said, pressing a spare key to the house and her lighter into my hands. "The alarm system isn't monitored, there won't be a record of anyone being there. All you have to do is unlock the door and enter the code. Go to the basement. Mom always leaves a few towels hanging in the utility room so drop them over the heater and set them on fire. There's no smoke detector down there, and nobody will know it's arson. It'll be our secret."

"Why don't you do it?" I asked.

"You owe me," she said. "After the stunt you pulled with the impromptu concert, you have to make it up to me." She smiled. "Besides, you're good at burning stuff. Rick's hand with the cigarette. His car when you left Portland. Remember?"

"Was this your plan all along?" I asked. "Is it why you suggested coming to the Hamptons?"

I swear her eyes twinkled as she said, "Won't you be happy to get revenge for how my parents have treated you all these years? I know I will."

Of course, I'd torched the place for her. I'd always been there for her, and now she wouldn't listen to why I'd done what I'd done, she was simply going to turn me in?

Madison had suggested abandoning the others at the crash site, not me. She was the one who'd continually dissed Gabi, told me she wished we'd kept more of a say in the Bittersweet, had more control, made more money than the others, that my trying to be fair and equitable was a bad idea. If she'd organized the auditions, she'd said, she'd have ensured we could veto any decision.

It was a pile of bullshit that she hadn't thought how Gabi and Evelina dying out here might be beneficial to us both as the two survivors. The difference between her and I was that she didn't have the guts to make it happen.

All these thoughts sped through my mind as Madison turned and stomped toward the cabin. My heart ached as it tore itself in half. If I wanted the career I'd always dreamed of, the one I was so close to now because of my actions, I had to do whatever it took to make her listen.

37

MY HANDS TREMBLE as I resurface from the past. The mug of coffee has long turned cold, and I want to go back to bed, sleep for a hundred years. I can't. As difficult and painful as remembering this next part will be, I must force myself to continue. Get these final memories of the night at the cabin and what I did afterward to the forefront of my mind so I can pull them out of my brain and discard them forever.

When Madison turned her back on me and walked off, I knew nothing would ever be the same again. If our friendship had crumbled when she'd witnessed me propel Gabi from a cliff, it had received the ultimate death blow when she understood I'd hurt Evelina. Whatever lies I spun now, however I tried to protect her from the truth, it wouldn't be enough.

Why couldn't she understand my actions were for us? For our careers? Our future? EmVee reborn?

Rage mixed with disbelief and hurt, jealousy, too. From the outside it may have seemed unreasonable that I expected her to defend me, but given our history, the fact she chose Evelina and especially Gabi over me was torture. Her saying she didn't need me was a million times worse. Of course, she needed me. She'd needed me since we met in Rosemont's cafeteria on the first day of twelfth grade. We'd been bound together from that moment, for better or worse.

Over the years, she hated me being friends with anyone but her. Detested it when I had a serious boyfriend in Brooklyn, too. I'd long figured out what had happened with Theo. Madison had run into him at the bar the night he'd gone home with someone else, that part was true, but the woman he'd ended up with was a friend of hers from college.

I knew this because a few weeks after my split with Theo, when I joined Madison and her friends for a few drinks, Theo's squeeze had been in the group. When Madison introduced her—Delilah—I'd pretended to have no idea who she was, to have already forgotten her face from the picture Madison had long instructed me to delete off my phone, saying it would only serve to annoy me.

"You look so familiar," I said to Delilah when Madison went to the restroom. "Are you…Theo's girlfriend?"

"Theo?" she said, her porcelain face crinkling before she waved a hand. "Oh, no, definitely not. He was a one-night thing. Madison thought we'd hit it off, but he wasn't my type in the end. Do you know him well?"

"No, barely at all."

I'd swiftly changed the subject, and I wasn't angry. Madison had sent Delilah in as bait for Theo, a loyalty test toward me. He'd failed, and he'd lied, sworn nothing had happened between him and Delilah aside from a kiss. Madison had been right all along—he would've cheated on me—she'd just helped speed things up to save me some heartbreak, kept quiet about her methodology because I might've taken my rage out on her.

Madison and I looked out for one another, we always had. Now she wanted to tell the world I was a killer. I had to convince her to lie for me, *with* me. Somehow, I needed her to listen to my idea of telling the police Gabi had suffocated Evelina in a mercy killing and then taken her own life out of guilt. I had to make her see how we could overcome this, together.

I rushed to grab her wrist. "Madison, please."

"Get off me," she shouted, but I held on, pulling her to me. "I said get *off*." She yanked her arm away with so much force, when I let her go, the momentum spun her in a semicircle.

Everything seemed to slow down as time stretched out like a rubber band. I was unable to react when Madison lost her footing, boots shooting toward me as her legs came out from underneath her. Her arms spun like a windmill, flailing as she tried to keep her balance, but she toppled backward with a dull thud.

"Madison?" I willed her to jump up, shout at me and try to stomp off again but she didn't move. Neither did I, and as I watched her lying completely still with her eyes closed, thick snowflakes swirled in the air before settling on her long lashes. She didn't flinch.

"Madison? *Madison!*"

Dropping to my knees, I shook her shoulders, called out her name again and again. Leaning over, I held my ear a fraction of an inch over her mouth. Nothing, no sound save for the wind in the trees. I tore off my gloves for just long enough to search her wrists and neck with my freezing, trembling fingers for any sign of a pulse. It wasn't until I grabbed her coat and pulled her limp body against mine as I sobbed and screamed that I saw the jagged rock jutting from the snow, the one the back of her head must've landed on full force.

There was no blood, no open wound like the one in Isabel's chest, no missing hand like Evelina's. Madison being dead didn't feel real, it couldn't be possible. I wanted to shout for help, but self-preservation took over, telling me to assess and manage this situation. Urging me to take care of myself because it was too late for her.

What if the police thought I'd killed Madison? What if they then suspected me of killing Evelina and Gabi, too? I was the only band member left, and Libby couldn't tell them any different. Madison's pills—

Madison's pills.

The thought made my racing mind slow down, giving me time. Nobody was coming to help us, nobody knew we were here. I had at least until daybreak to find a way out of this mess, and I'd use every bit to plan the tiniest of details. Go over them all again another twenty times.

Could I weave more narrative around the Klonopin? Make Madison responsible for all this? I wrestled with the thoughts of saving myself by framing my best friend, pushed away the guilt nagging at my sides. She'd take the blame, yes, but what if I could give her what she'd craved? The one thing she'd desired so much?

Fame.

Not the kind she wanted, but as the path ahead formed in my mind, I knew I could protect myself and ensure nobody ever forgot her name. Or mine, albeit for different reasons.

I fought with the decision, struggled with the lies and implications, but not for long. If I didn't do this, I'd be locked up forever, which was what Madison had said she wanted. I kept reminding myself of the fact as I knelt beside her, removing her hat and blue gloves which I stuffed in my pocket before taking off her coat, whispering apology after apology.

Back at the cabin, Libby was still fast asleep on the living room floor. She hadn't moved, hadn't seen anything. I dimmed the lamp after fetching another two Klonopin from Madison's bag. Kneeling behind Libby so she couldn't see my face if she opened her eyes, I shook her shoulder.

"Libby?" I whispered, changing the tone of my voice as best I could. "It's Madison. Your head hurts. You said you wanted more pills. Come on, Libby, they'll help you feel better."

It took a while to coax her awake and get her to swallow the meds, but after waiting for them to kick in, I pulled her to the empty room on the main floor, and locked her in.

Knowing I could work undisturbed, I went to the other bedroom. I hauled Evelina's body and the mattress back to the living room, sweating from the effort. Madison's bag held another item I needed—the clip-in extensions she wore to make her hair seem fuller.

Next, I turned my attention to Gabi's belongings. With my red gloves still on, I swiped a few of the beaded bracelets she had in her backpack and slipped them on my wrist before retrieving Libby's camera, the one she'd shown Gabi how to use earlier in our trip, before we swapped places and Gabi had taken the wheel.

When I checked the memory card, I saw some footage Libby had taken during our rehearsals, but she'd barely filmed during our drive to the Catskills. She'd been asleep for some of it and suffered from car sickness the rest, meaning there were only a few snippets she'd taken while sitting in the back of my Tahoe. It wasn't much, but the coat Madison had worn all day was clearly visible, and it would do. Eight minutes of filming time remained on the memory card, more than I needed, but I'd make it work.

I set up the camera with the volume turned off, trying out different places and angles that worked with what I hoped to achieve. In the end, I left the camera under one of the old armchairs, pointing directly at Evelina's torso, angled slightly upward. I had no idea if an investigator could tell how many times a memory card had been recorded on, which meant I'd have a single attempt at getting this right. If it didn't work, I'd need to come up with an alternate plan, which I didn't have.

Gabi had worn a white hoodie all day, and Evelina had an identical one, so I pulled it over my head. With the camera in place, I switched it on, muted the sound and hit Record. I removed my gloves and pretended to adjust the camera's angle a little, making sure the only things visible were the sleeve of Gabi's hoodie and her beaded bracelets dangling in front of the lens. Just enough for whoever would watch this to believe Gabi had set up the camera.

Explaining why she'd done this was a problem I'd have to figure out later. Or not. Investigating was a job for the cops, after all, and I could always throw out a bunch of theories to keep them busy.

After tying my hair back and clipping in Madison's extensions, I slipped on her coat, blue gloves, and hat, making sure a few fake red locks dangled forward. With less than a minute to go before the space on the memory card ran out, I grabbed Gabi's sweater and got into position, pressing the fabric over Evelina's mouth and holding down, making her body twitch like it had when I'd given her the release she'd asked for.

There had been a little more movement than when I'd used a pillow on my darling Grams, but not by much. I'd given Grams an extra sleeping pill the night she'd left us, and she'd barely moved at all. There were no signs of struggle, no bruising or anything to raise suspicion. The family doctor had seen my grandmother the week before, increased her heart medication and told Mom she might not have much longer. Although the cops came to Rick's house because Grams' death was unattended, the doctor signed it off as *natural causes* because nobody said any different. No one ever came looking for me.

I stopped thinking about Grams and played the video back. It was darkish and grainy, but Madison's coat came through clearly, as did her gloved hands with Gabi's sweater and the strands of hair dangling from above as Evelina took what were supposed to be her last breaths.

It would be enough evidence to make everyone believe Madison had suffocated Evelina before propelling Gabi from a cliff. They'd conclude that fame-hungry Madison had wanted to benefit from the Bittersweet tragedy by making Gabi's and Evelina's deaths appear like a murder-suicide. Alas, on her way back to the cabin after killing Gabi, Madison had accidentally hit her head and died.

Meanwhile, I'd say I'd come back to the cabin to warm up for a few minutes when I couldn't find Madison after we'd headed out to search for Gabi outside, but had fallen asleep from exhaustion. They wouldn't be able to prove otherwise.

"Madison Pierce got what she deserved," people would say. "Justice was served."

I was the only one to survive. Give it a few days, and the Bittersweet would be on everyone's lips. The band I'd worked hard to create would survive despite—and because of—this tragedy.

Everyone would remember Madison. And everybody would want to work with me.

38

I GET UP and stretch, make myself a fresh coffee. It's only 6:00 a.m., still dark outside, but I know I won't sleep again until tonight. Hopefully with all this reminiscing, Madison won't visit me in my dreams.

There are a number of things I'd change about what happened at the cabin. Madison seeing me push Gabi from the cliff is one. The other is the fact I'd been forced to kill my best friend to survive.

After recording the fake evidence, and for the cops to believe the narrative I'd created—Madison killing Evelina and pushing Gabi from the cliff—I still had things to take care of. I returned Evelina to the main floor bedroom and brought Libby back into the living room, so she'd wake up where she'd fallen asleep.

Once done, I took Libby's camera to the bathroom, tucked it into the hole behind the missing bathtub tiles after making sure the spot was dry. I figured if Gabi had really set up the camera and found the footage of her sister being murdered, it was a semi-logical thing to do. There was no absolute guarantee the elements wouldn't get to the device, but it was a gamble I'd have to take for a few days until Libby realized her camera was missing, and the cops located it.

Having checked that everything inside the cabin fit with my story, I pulled on my own coat and hat, picked up Madison's clothes, and trudged through the snow to her body, fighting back the tears when I saw her.

I hadn't wanted her to die. Seeing her lying there, most of her blanketed by snow, almost made me change my mind—wait until morning and confess what I'd done. But I couldn't. I was already in way too deep.

As I gently lifted Madison to slip her coat back on, she let out a moan, making me gasp. "Vienna," she said, her voice slurred. "What did you do? Where did you go?"

I laid her down, and she struggled to sit up as she reached for the lapels of my jacket. "You left me to die," she said, eyes rolling into the back of her head. "Y-you're a m-murderer. You're a f-fucking murderer."

She pulled me toward her, was a lot stronger than I expected, especially considering she'd knocked herself unconscious and the amount of time she'd been in the cold. What choice did I have? If I didn't shut her up, and she survived, everything I'd done inside the cabin was for nothing.

I reached for my scarf, remembered both Madison and I had given them to Gabi to tie around trees to mark the path back to the cabin, and so I used my hands instead, pushed myself on top of Madison, pinning her down as I squeezed the life out of her. The fight she had left soon gave way, and I cried long after it was over, couldn't believe what I'd done.

Afterward I sat for a while, holding her close and cradling her body, whispering more apologies as I tried to decide what to do now all my plans were coming undone.

There was no way they'd believe Madison died in this spot

from an accidental fall. There'd be too much evidence to the contrary, all of it rightly pointing at me.

Could I say I'd seen the footage of Madison killing Evelina, had then witnessed her shoving Gabi from a cliff and Madison had attacked me? That I'd killed her in self-defense?

No, my music career, my entire future, would be over. To save it, I had to build more lies. It was the only way I'd come out the other end.

My mind clicked and whirred. In this fictional story—the one which would become my truth and everybody else's—when the fake footage was found, it would reveal how Madison had killed Evelina when I'd gone upstairs to search for things to burn.

"Why would she do that?" the cops would ask.

"I don't know," I'd whisper. "It doesn't make sense."

"Did you ever witness them fighting?"

"Sometimes," I'd say. "Evelina didn't care about being famous, but Madison did."

They'd roll their eyes, say, "Well, she found fame all right."

"Do you…" I'd stop, give my head a shake, and when the cops urged me to go on I'd say, "Do you think Madison planned on murdering Gabi all along? Make it look like Gabi killed her sister and then herself somehow?" I'd shake my head again, whisper a quiet, "No, that doesn't make sense either, does it? Except Madison never liked Gabi, right from the start."

The cops would think Gabi had set the camera up—we'd perhaps never know the reason why—before she'd gone to the Tahoe for Evelina's insulin. When she returned and retrieved the camera from underneath the chair, she'd watched the recording in horror, freaked out, and insisted on going for help. She hadn't meant help for Evelina. She'd meant help because Madison was a killer.

What Madison hadn't known at first, the cops would assume, was how Gabi must've found out what Madison had done to her sister.

"I saw you," Gabi would've shouted when Madison caught up to her near the cliff, after Gabi had run from the cabin and Madison and I had gone looking for her. "I saw you kill her, and everybody else will see it, too."

Left with no choice, Madison shoved Gabi, thinking she'd solved the problem, but as she'd returned to the cabin, she'd have remembered Gabi's words. *Everybody else will see it, too.* She may have suspected a phone or a camera, torn through the cabin to find them while I was still outside, searching for her and Gabi in the storm.

Psychosis, paranoia, anxiety—maybe a combination of all three had set in when Madison couldn't find the evidence. She couldn't search Gabi's body because she was thirty feet down a cliff. In a panic, Madison had decided to torch the cabin to get rid of everything, including Libby and me, and disappear forever.

For them to believe this version of the truth, I had to add a few layers. First, I'd press Madison's fingers on Gabi's beaded bracelets before walking to the cliff, ripping the bracelet apart, and scattering some of it in the snow before dropping the rest over the ledge, indicating a struggle between Madison and Gabi.

For the apparent fire, I'd use the rancid cooking oil from the kitchen, splashing a trail of it across the floor, already knowing it wouldn't ignite when I used Madison's lighter. Hopefully it would be enough to make it seem as if she'd tried to burn the place down.

"But why didn't Gabi show you the video of Madison killing Evelina?" a police officer might ask.

I'd hang my head. "I don't know. She must've been terrified. Madison was my best friend, maybe Gabi thought I was involved."

"Were you?" they'd probe.

I'd gasp at the indignance of this, say, "Madison left me in the cabin to *die*."

The cops would investigate, maybe come to a different version closer to the truth. How perhaps initially in Madison's warped brain she'd thought by killing Evelina and finding an opportunity to make Gabi appear responsible by having her death seem like a suicide, all without my knowing, the fame of the Bittersweet would soar. But her plans had been thwarted, and she'd decided to kill us all.

It would be an incredible story, and this was when the idea about writing a memoir hit me. If I told the cops about it, they might think making money on the publishing deal was motive for me to kill everyone, but even to me that seemed a bit of a stretch. In case they wanted to read the manuscript, I'd work in a few untruths, and some exaggerations about Madison's character, things nobody could dispute.

I'd include a transcript of the Bittersweet's conversation with Melodie Johnson, during which Evelina had said she'd rather die than not be able to play her guitar. I could leave things out, too. Madison's hair extensions. Gabi's beaded bracelets. How I'd known about Evelina's diabetes.

I'd stood still for a while, shivering as I went over the details, poking and prodding to see what holes I could make, and how to fix them. Snow swirled outside, over a foot already with more on the way tonight. Another storm was forecast for the day after tomorrow and it would add ten more inches. The subzero temperatures would last at least ten days beyond. Ideal conditions for stashing a corpse.

I'd have to hide Madison somehow, which would be tricky with the snow, cold ground, and no tools, and I couldn't use my hands because the cops would question any damage I made to my skin by digging.

I remembered seeing a rusty old poker in the basement. If I found a good hiding spot for Madison's body, the poker combined with a couple of logs of wood from the pile outside might be enough to get the job done and it would only be a temporary grave.

Working quickly, I went back to the cabin where I changed

into clothing I took from everybody's bags because digging would make mine dirty, grabbed the poker and wood, pulled on a spare pair of Evelina's gloves, and headed back out.

A natural depression in the ground turned out to be the ideal location about two hundred yards from the cabin, in the opposite direction from the ogre boulder, and right next to a tree with a heart-shaped knot, which I'd easily find again.

Once I'd removed enough snow and dirt, I fetched Madison's body, ordering myself not to break down again. I pressed the basement key I'd brought with me into her hands to ensure her DNA would be found on it.

Next, I gently placed her body into what I knew would be a temporary resting place, added our switched-off phones, her backpack, the poker, the wood, her hair extensions, and the soiled clothes I'd changed out of, before covering everything up as best I could.

Madison's body would stay frozen—and hidden—until I returned, but there were no guarantees the K9 unit wouldn't be brought in before I had the opportunity to come back. I'd have to hold it together until then and stick to my story. And if Madison was found before…game over.

Back at the cabin and out of the freezing cold, I locked myself in the basement with Libby, and tried to sleep despite the bitter cold. My intention had been to wait for her to wake up first, for us to escape from the cabin together, but when I finally opened my eyes, she was still unconscious. I must've given her too much Klonopin, suddenly wondered if four pills could be in any way fatal.

I panicked because if she died from the meds or hypothermia, I wouldn't have someone to confirm a single part of my story. Finally, I managed to wake her, got her to help me climb out of the window, pretended to search the cabin and find the basement key, and brought her upstairs before going for help.

The snowplow, cops, and ambulance arrived at the neighbor's house, took a stunned Libby and a fake-stunned me to the hospital before asking us questions for hours about what had happened. I never wavered, didn't slip up a single time as I silently begged Madison and Evelina for forgiveness.

While all our friends, including Guy, Roger, and Marvin, Chris and Freya from Mooseman, were devastated when they heard the news, Mom didn't attempt to contact me, not once. Madison's parents called multiple times a day, demanding details of any new developments, getting angry when I said I had none. I stopped picking up in the end. I already felt guilty enough about what had happened, I didn't need them to remind me of what they'd lost. Although to be frank, they seemed to care more about Madison after she was gone than when she'd been alive.

The cabin was released less than a week later, after the second storm had blanketed the area with another thirteen inches of snow, and the cops decided anyone who'd left the cabin on foot had long perished.

"We'll work to locate our missing person when the weather conditions are more favorable," one of the investigating police officers said, adding they couldn't stretch the already beyond limited K9 resources to find someone who had practically a zero chance of survival.

By then I'd found an obscure internet café and completed my research on where to lay Madison to rest. I took garbage bags, a set of fresh clothes and shoes from the apartment and left the new phone Roger organized for me behind.

Using the fake ID Madison had given me the day I arrived in Brooklyn, which said Janet Jenkins, not Viola Smith, I donned a baseball cap and sunglasses, and rented a car from a tiny place in Teterboro.

After driving fifty miles, I visited five different stores in five different locations, picking up a plastic tarp and a bucket, duct tape, a shovel, a collapsible ladder, and a battery-operated hacksaw. I didn't want to use the last item, I truly didn't, but dismembering a body makes it easier to carry, and when it's frozen solid, there's no blood.

All I needed was time once I reached the cabin, the road to which was now accessible thanks to it being plowed to give the emergency services access. Once I put Madison into the bags and stowed them in the trunk of the rental, I waited for nightfall, shaking as I sat in the car, sobbing every few minutes as I thought about what I'd done before reminding myself I'd come so far, I only needed to bury Madison properly now, and the worst part would be over.

A funeral was to be held the next morning, in a town fifteen miles away, for an elderly gentleman named Samuel Zurcher who'd died in his sleep aged ninety-six. His freshly dug grave was located on the outskirts of town, far away from prying eyes.

Under the moonlight, I used the collapsible ladder to climb into the hole. Removed the plywood before digging deep enough to hide Madison's remains, backpack, the phones, dirty clothes, hair extensions, and the rusty poker, adding the extra earth to the graveside pile hidden beneath a blanket of fake grass.

There was no better place for her to stay undetected. Madison Pierce—a famous missing person and suspected criminal, who was presumed to either be on the run or to have died somewhere in the Catskills forest.

I would've attended Mr. Zurcher's service, said a silent prayer, and whispered another apology as they lowered his coffin on top of her, but didn't dare in case someone recognized me. Instead, once I'd finished hiding Madison a second time, I stood by her grave under the moonlight and whispered words of comfort to her, told her again that I was sorry, how I wished things were different, and that maybe I'd see her again someday.

Over six weeks have passed now, and ever since, every morning when I wake up, I wonder if today's the day the cops will locate the footage, especially considering Libby told them her camera was missing early on in the investigation.

What the hell are they doing? Ashbury and Newell are breathing down my neck, stirring up controversy and more support for #TeamMadison, which is exactly what I worked so hard to avoid.

Now I've let myself remember what really happened at the cabin, it's time to let it all go, but I find I can't, not until the video surfaces. I drum my fingers on the table, wonder if I can return to the cabin, retrieve the camera, and somehow get it to the cops. No. If I deliver it to them, it will be suspicious, far too convenient. Ashbury in particular is smarter than that. But if someone else finds it...

I grab my phone.

"Libby?" I say when she answers.

"Is everything all right?" Her voice sounds muffled, and she stifles a yawn. I've forgotten how early it is, although for me it could be the middle of the afternoon.

"I need your help," I say. "I'm freaking out."

"I'm coming over," she answers immediately. "Give me half an hour."

As soon as she arrives, she rushes to hug me, and in her haste, knocks my bag off the sideboard, spilling the contents across the floor. "Whoops," she says, scrambling to retrieve my gloves and wallet, hesitating a little. "The police didn't keep these?" she asks, holding up my gloves.

"I bought a duplicate pair," I say, wondering why she's asking, before remembering the conversation we'd had about our boots being taken by the cops. "I haven't got the others back yet." I bite my lip. "The original ones were a gift from Madison. Red's my favorite color."

"Sorry about knocking your stuff over," she says, giving me a tight smile as I gesture for her to move into the living room. "Tell me what's going on with you. What can I do?"

"I'm scared the police don't believe me," I say as we settle in.

"I can't sleep or eat. I'm worried they'll show up, break down the door, and arrest me."

"But—"

I rush on, my nerves shot because the truth is, I *am* getting scared. "What if they somehow manage to blame me for what Madison did?"

"Remember how Torin said there's no chance of that?" Her voice is kind, reassuring. I'm glad I have her as an ally. "You have to trust him."

"I know, but…and I get this is hard for you, but have you remembered anything else? Any details about the cabin?"

"No," she says slowly, blinking hard. "Nothing. It's all still fuzzy."

I pretend I'm working up the courage to ask what I think will be a difficult question for her, say, "Would you…could you come to the cabin with me?"

"What?" she whispers. "You want to go back?"

"Yes, only to see if it helps with your memory," I say, which is a lie. If we're both there I can somehow get her into the bathroom, point out the broken tiles and get her to see what's behind them. Discreetly, of course. "Maybe it'll spark a useful detail for you to share with the police," I say, openly begging now. "Please, Libby. I'm desperate and terrified. People get wrongly convicted all the time. What if it happens to me?"

"I…I don't know," she says. "I'm not sure I can face it."

I want to shout at her, rant and rave and scream how we need to drive to the Catskills *now*, but I stay calm. Over the past six weeks I've told myself I must remain in control at all times, which means I can't push her too hard, not yet.

The trouble is, if she won't go to the cabin, it means I'll have to go by myself.

39

49 days after the accident

FOR THE PAST three days I've stood by my window and observed the street, making notes of the cars parked outside, writing down license plates and vehicle makes, barely sleeping as I keep watch. It doesn't seem as if anyone from the press has found my Cobble Hill address, or that the police are keeping watch, but I can't be too careful.

Another sleepless night, and once again, I leave my phone at home and slip out of the building, hoodie pulled low over my face, dark glasses covering my eyes despite the cloudy, late January skies. A different town, a different rental car place, and I'm on my way to the Catskills for what will hopefully be the last time. I never want to come back here. Ever.

I'm exhausted, wish this were all over so I can move on, get rid of this feeling of Madison never letting me go, even in death. She'll have to once the video of her killing Evelina surfaces, when the public sees her as the ultimate villain. I make myself focus on the thought, pushing away all my remorse as I park the car on an isolated path a mile from the cabin, and trek through the woods.

Temperatures have been mild over the past two weeks, leading to a big snowmelt. It makes it easier for me to walk through the forest. Still, I stopped to buy a new pair of boots on the way, a size larger than what I usually wear, paid for in cash, and which I'll dispose of somewhere random once I'm done.

As the cabin comes into view, I hold my breath. Torn yellow crime scene tape dangles from the doorframe, fluttering in the breeze. I wonder how many people have been here since the news broke. Dozens? Hundreds? Some adoring Bittersweet fans have posted pictures of this place on social media, and I spot what appears to be a makeshift memorial on the porch.

The heady smell of decaying flowers reaches me from twenty yards away, and as I get closer, I see candles, teddy bears, and handwritten notes covered in plastic. I stop and read a few.

We miss you, Madison xo

Madison, please come home safe

Gabi & Evelina, we love you xxx

I'm sorry #TeamMadison forever

It takes a while to find one about me. The dead are more popular, it seems. For now.

I push open the front door, make my way straight to the main floor bathroom where I get on my knees. I need to work quickly so I can get out of here before anybody else arrives. Sticking my gloved hand into the gap behind the tub, I reach around.

My breath hitches.

The space is empty.

Gut lurching, I lay flat on my stomach, peer inside. There's nothing. *Nothing.*

Panic sets in before I remind myself this is possibly a good thing. The cops must've found the camera. But why are they waiting so long to give an update about the evidence? Can it really be taking them this long to go through everything they've found at the crime scene, including a hidden camera?

Of course, it's a possibility, and I want to kick myself for being so naïve. Reality is completely different from crime shows on TV, where autopsies are performed the same day, DNA results take a matter of seconds, and crimes are conveniently solved within the hour.

I exhale, trying to collect myself. This is a game of strategy, of perseverance. Waiting until the cops follow the breadcrumbs and catch up to what I'm feeding them, letting them gobble down the distorted truth straight from my hand. Patience is what's required, and not only to keep up my façade, but to reinforce it, turn it to steel.

Coming here wasn't smart. One mistake like this, particularly if I'm being watched despite my precautions, will land me in trouble. The fewer lies I have to tell, the less I have to explain and talk my way out of, the better. I need to keep moving in the direction I set myself from the outset. The cops will look for inconsistencies, and me panicking and being hasty or inattentive could be one of them.

It's almost 6:00 p.m. by the time I get home, and the pep talk I gave myself at the cabin isn't working anymore. No matter how much I try to reassure myself, I'm still freaking out, consider stuffing my things into a bag and running.

Guilty people run.

It's what I told Ashbury and Newell when I sat in their bland interrogation room, drinking burned coffee and answering their questions for hours. I won't run. I don't need to. Yet.

I switch on my phone and leave it to power up, deciding I'll have a shower before I'm ready to comb through social media. As I reach the bathroom, my cell dings a few times and I backtrack. There's a dozen missed calls from an unknown number, as well as four voice mails. Curious, I listen to the first one.

"Hi, Vienna. This is Darlene McMillan. I'm a lead investigative reporter with the *New York Times*. I'm hoping to speak to you about the Bittersweet. Please call me. My number's—"

I know the name. Darlene was in the room when I gave one of the short interviews Roger arranged. I've read her articles, and know crime is her specialty. How the hell did she get my number?

Delete.

I skip to the next message.

"Vienna, this is Darlene McMillan. I really need to speak to you. My number's—"

Delete.

"Darlene again. Please call me. I'd love to have a quote from you in my piece."

I bet you would, but only so you could try to spin it against me.

Delete.

"Vienna…in confidence, what if I told you there's irrefutable evidence you're innocent? Please call me."

This time I listen to her number, snatch up a pen and jot the digits down. It might be a trap, so I'm wary when she answers on the first ring, her voice smooth and soft as silk. She thanks me for calling, tells me I can trust her, she won't print anything I say without my permission. She's a journalist. I put zero value on her promises, but I need to know what she's talking about.

"What did you mean by irrefutable evidence?" I ask, forcing myself to slow down. "Has Madison been found? Did she confess?"

Darlene clicks her tongue. "No, and after this goes public, she'll never want to be found."

"After *what* goes public?"

She hesitates, takes her time. It makes me want to put my

hands into my phone and out the other end so I can pull the words from her mouth. I wait a beat, say, "Can you please tell me what's going on?"

"I received an anonymous email this morning with a video attachment."

My heart jumps into my throat. "What video?"

"This might be hard to hear, so please, if you're not sitting down, I suggest you do." Darlene pauses, continues with, "The video shows Madison...killing Evelina."

"What?" I whisper, surprise, joy, and elation all filling my veins at the same time, and it's such a strange combination considering it's the video I was looking for earlier today, and what I did to my best friend, but I can't help it. "What are you talking about? Who sent you this? How do you know it's real?"

"We don't know who sent it, not yet. As for authenticity, we showed it to a few contacts and sources. I promise you it's real, not a deepfake or anything. It was taken at the cabin, and it's Madison."

I want to jump up and punch the air, but I force myself to quietly say, "I can't believe it. All this time I thought...I don't know what I thought, but it wasn't...it wasn't...*this*."

"I understand," Darlene says, gently. "Listen, I'm running with this story and it's dropping at midnight. Care to provide me with a quote? Did you honestly believe she could be innocent?"

"I wanted to," I whisper. "But I guess I never knew her at all."

I hang up, drop the phone on the table and let out a shriek before jumping up and doing a little dance across the kitchen. This is what freedom feels like. It's phenomenal, and I take a moment to absorb it all. My plan worked. It actually *worked*. I let out another yell, leap into the air, dance, and spin to the living room where I collapse on the sofa. I have to figure out what I'll do and say next, but until then, one thing's for sure.

Otis Clay got it right when he said the only way is up.

40

50 days after the accident

FOR THE FIRST time since the night at the cabin, Madison doesn't visit me in my dreams. It's as if I've created a protective barrier around me, impenetrable to her memory. Although I wake up early, I feel rested, almost serene as I pick up my phone. I smile when I see the amount of email alerts and social media notifications, grin when I read the contents.

I always said she didn't do it #TeamVienna

Eat your words, you hating bastards #TeamVienna

Madison can run but she can't hide. She'll get what's coming to her #TeamVienna

There are pages and pages filled with comments supporting me, more of them pouring in, filling my feed, my bones, feeding my ego. This is what being a celebrity must be like, and suddenly I'm here for it, all of it.

I can't get enough, drink it all in. I navigate to the *New York Times* website, see Darlene's article on the main page, and snuggle underneath the covers as I read. One paragraph in particular catches my attention.

Although it remains unclear who sent the video of Madison Pierce allegedly murdering Evelina Sevillano to the *New York Times*, a Catskill PD police officer who worked the case was recently suspended with pay and is under investigation. Sources confirm she's suspected of stealing cash, jewelry, and electronic items from crime scenes. One colleague who asked to remain anonymous speculated the suspended officer wanted the Bittersweet case to be solved and sent the video to the press anonymously to avoid implicating herself in more crime scene thefts. Catskill PD refused to comment as both investigations are ongoing.

My stomach clenches when I think about how lucky I am. How my video could've been lost forever if this opportunistic officer hadn't realized what she'd found, or if she didn't have a conscience.

Ultimately it doesn't matter how Darlene got the footage—it's out there, proving me innocent one view at a time. What it tells me though, is that in the future I can't and won't leave such things to chance. I'm responsible for my own destiny, and this is a stark reminder of how depending on anyone could mean my downfall.

I try calling Libby, but she doesn't pick up so after leaving her a message I go to the kitchen and eat. Toast and jam, bagel with cream cheese, almonds and apple slices—with my appetite returning, I wolf down enough food to last me a week.

As I stuff another piece of fruit into my mouth, I look around the kitchen, take in the smooth granite worktops and high-end appliances, wondering how much a place like this costs, and how long it'll take before I can afford one.

Then I wonder how much time needs to pass before I can ask Roger about the sales numbers and my projected royalty payments. A month? Two? Surely by then it won't be unreasonable, uncouth, or suspicious to ask him where I stand financially. At that point he'll understand I need money to live.

I pop another piece of bread in the toaster, spread it thick with jam. I'm watching the news—checking to see how many channels are talking about the Bittersweet—and enjoying my food along with another large cup of coffee when Torin calls.

"Good morning, Vienna," he says, his voice light and breezy. "Actually, I mean *great* morning. I presume you've seen the news?"

"Yes, Darlene McMillan from the *New York Times* called yesterday."

"Yesterday?"

"She wanted a quote."

"I wish you'd spoken to me first," he says, and chuckles when I explain what I told Darlene. "I won't give you a hard time considering the developments. Anyway, Ashbury and Newell would like to see you."

"I'm not going to the station."

"I don't blame you, but we should listen to what they have to say."

"Tell them I'll meet them here, at my apartment."

"Are you sure? We could easily go to my office."

"Here's fine. I'll be home all day."

"Very well, I'll text you the time as soon as I've made arrangements." I hear another smile in his voice. "Now do you promise you'll stop worrying?"

"I promise," I say, making sure to suppress my own grin.

The detectives show up a few hours later, a good quarter hour after Torin gets here and reminds me to let him do the talking. Seems Newell may not have slept in a month. His green shirt's rumpled, and his jeans have a coffee stain below the knee. I wonder if he's stayed somewhere local for the past ten days, living out of a suitcase.

In contrast, Ashbury's more polished and professional than the last time I saw her. Another classic-cut gray suit and white shirt, hair freshly trimmed, her pixie cut sharp enough to cut my fingers on.

I've deliberately chosen to look like hell. I'm not wearing makeup and I pulled on a pair of old jeans along with a shirt more rumpled than Newell's. If I was telling the truth and had learned my best friend was a murderer, I'd be far too distressed to worry about my appearance.

They greet me with smiles and handshakes. Their entire demeanor may have done a one-eighty, but I still don't trust them as I usher them into the living room where they say hello to Torin.

"Can I get anyone a drink?" I ask, sounding nervous. "Glass of water or coffee?"

Newell starts to nod, but Ashbury interjects. "No, thank you, Vienna. Let's get down to business, shall we? We don't want to take up much of your time. I'm sure you're busy."

"Quite," Torin says, leaning back and crossing his legs in a display of nonchalance. "We've seen the news, but why don't you give us the nitty-gritty details about the new evidence the press got hold of before you did."

Ashbury ignores the dig and gives Newell a nod.

"We'll show you instead," Newell says as he pulls out an iPad, turns it in our direction, and gently adds, "This will no doubt be incredibly distressing—"

"I'm okay," I say. "Please, I need to see."

Another nod from Ashbury, and he presses Play. Torin and I lean forward. I swear my attorney's eyes are about to burst from his skull and bounce across the carpet when he sees *Madison* holding the sweater over Evelina's face.

I only watched the video once, and in the weeks since then I've worried about whether I did a good enough job. Clearly, I did. Madison's coat and blue gloves, Gabi's sweater, the strands of fake hair. If I didn't know better, I'd swear it was my best friend, too.

I cover my eyes with my hands and get up. "It's...it's...Madison."

"Yes," Ashbury says. "We showed this to Libby. She confirmed it, too."

I spin around. "When did you see Libby? I tried to call her. I left her a message."

"This morning," Ashbury says. "We asked her not to contact you until we had this discussion."

"Discussion?" I snap. "You mean this is no longer an interrogation?"

Torin gestures at me to calm down, and I sink back into my seat. My infuriation is genuine. I really am pissed at them for suspecting me and plucking me from the memorial service, unleashing a deluge of online hate. Although those who were on my side will feel vindicated, too, voices loud, ready to fight my battles by my side forevermore.

"What, exactly, did Ms. Alexander say when she saw the video?" Torin asks.

"She identified Madison immediately," Ashbury says. "Categorically. We also matched the bracelet you see in the beginning of the video as belonging to Gabi. We found parts of it on the ledge with her body. Madison's prints were on them."

I let my shoulders drop. "Do you finally believe me? You don't think I had anything to do with Evelina's murder or Gabi's fall?"

"We believe you," Ashbury says.

"*Did* Gabi fall?" I ask quietly.

"We're working on it," Newell says. "We're trying to understand Madison's motive for killing Evelina."

"I've no clue," I say.

"My client already told you Madison was obsessed with becoming famous," Torin says. "Maybe it's something for you to examine."

"You think she did this for fame?" I say, pretending to consider the possibility. "I guess it was all Madison talked about. Merchandising and venues and—" I make air quotation marks "—multiple revenue streams. It was getting a bit much." I shake my head. "I told her the weather forecast the day before the party was supposed to be terrible, but she insisted on us going. Said we couldn't miss an opportunity to mingle with the *other* stars. I mean, as if *we* were stars."

Ashbury nods, and I can almost hear the cogs in her brain turning. A fame-obsessed woman who's presented with an opportunity to become well-known overnight. She's on the right track, following the correct path, but I'm not the one standing at the end of it.

"What might have been her reason for killing Gabi?" Newell asks.

I make myself appear lost in thought. "When Gabi came back and found Evelina dead, she freaked out. I assumed it was because her sister had died. What if it was more? What if she watched the footage and it's why she ran to get help?"

"You think Gabi confronted Madison, and Madison pushed her?" Ashbury says.

"Or maybe Gabi fell," I say with an apologetic grimace to convey they're the specialists, and I have no business making up theories.

"Detectives," Torin says. "Clearly, you have a different person to focus your investigative efforts on. No doubt you'll be busy searching for Ms. Pierce, especially considering the head start she now has."

"You think she's still alive?" I let out a gasp. "Am I in danger?"

"There's no indication Madison made it out of the forest,"

Ashbury says. "My guess is like you suggested, she waited for the storm to clear a bit before she left the cabin. We'll search for her, of course, put BOLOs out and so forth. But I have to be honest, if she's lying somewhere in the Catskills, we may not find her until spring."

"Or at all. You know—" Newell makes a tearing gesture with his hands "—because of the animals."

Vomit rises to the back of my throat when I think about how she's already dismembered, and I quickly push the images of my doing that to her away. At least where my best friend is buried no wild animals will ever get to her.

"How awful," I whisper. "Poor Madison."

"However—" Ashbury looks at me "—*if* she's alive and makes contact with you for any reason, you must tell us immediately."

"Of course, but why would she contact me? She tried to set fire to the cabin with me and Libby inside. She killed at least one of our friends."

"We checked Madison's bank accounts," Ashbury says. "No movement. Our guess is if she's alive she'll have gone into hiding. She'll need money."

"Her parents are wealthy," I offer.

The detectives exchange a knowing glance. "How would you say they get along?" Ashbury asks.

"Madison and her parents?" I say, glad I'd anticipated this question and know exactly what to reply. "Not well at all. They didn't approve of us being friends. Hated it, actually."

"Why?" Newell says, leaning in.

I roll my eyes. "They're rich, I'm poor and from the wrong side of the tracks and all. They thought I was a bad influence. Hated us being in a band in high school, and only wanted Madison to have a respectable career." I take my time in delivering the next delicious morsel, placing it straight into the detectives' mouths. "They must be freaking out about what this scandal will do to their reputation."

"Reputation?" Ashbury says, eyebrows raised.

I get up, retrieve a brand-new blue binder from the kitchen island. It's a copy of the memoir I had made. Torin has already speed-read the pages, told me to make a few edits, including removing the article about Rick's car, before giving my gesture of good faith toward the cops the go-ahead. I hand the folder to Ashbury.

"You'll get a better picture of the Pierces if you read this," I say. "Barry and Lucinda Pierce are defense attorneys. They'll do anything to try and salvage this situation, to keep things quiet and make them go away, and Madison knows it."

"We're giving you this manuscript in strictest confidence, of course," Torin adds.

Ashbury nods, eyes eager. This isn't a drop but a pint of blood for her. In an instant, I see her mind is off circling the waters again, hunting her prey. But this time, I'm not the one swimming in the deep.

41

51 days after the accident

TRANSCRIPT: *What's On NYC*: Season 14, EP 9:
The Bittersweet update

MELODIE JOHNSON: Welcome back to *What's On NYC*. I'm Melodie Johnson, here with Xander Roberts and Liam Felder. If you've just tuned in, the three of us are discussing the latest development in the Bittersweet saga. Frankly, it's the only thing people can talk about. It's trending everywhere.

XANDER ROBERTS: I'm not surprised, and my mind's blown. Truly.

MELODIE JOHNSON: Same, my friend. Same.

LIAM FELDER: I know you always believed Vienna was innocent, Mel, but I mean…did you expect anything like this to happen? This story has more twists than a frigging corkscrew.

MELODIE JOHNSON: I need a corkscrew, along with the bottle, please, or make it bottles (laughs). But seriously, of course I'm thrilled Vienna's been exonerated. Can you imagine what she's gone through?

LIAM FELDER: Honestly? No.

MELODIE JOHNSON: Right? I mean, how do you begin to recover from this? Social media vilified her, in particular these last ten days or so, since the cops took her in for questioning. In social media years, that counts as at least a decade.

XANDER ROBERTS: Well, #TeamMadison are for sure eating their words. Some are in denial, no surprise there, but the new evidence is a hundred percent clear. The by now infamous video, of which a lot is blurred out for obvious reasons, was enough for anyone to clearly identify Madison as Evelina's killer.

MELODIE JOHNSON: Alleged killer.

LIAM FELDER: Yeah, sure.

MELODIE JOHNSON: Why do you think she did it?

XANDER ROBERTS: There's so much speculation. I'm telling you, this story's going to be in the news for weeks. No, I take it back. Months. Mark my words, there's going to be a TV series about it, whether they catch Madison Pierce or not.

LIAM FELDER: If she's still alive.

XANDER ROBERTS: Yeah, and it's a big if, considering how she left an abandoned cabin in the Catskills in the middle of a snowstorm. Duh. But, hypothetically at least, she's been on the run for weeks. Imagine the advantage. She could be anywhere by now, literally.

MELODIE JOHNSON: Let me read you part of the statement Vienna released yesterday afternoon. "I'm relieved and grateful my name's been cleared. My heart goes out to Evelina and Gabi's family, and Isabel's, during this awful time, and Madison's, too. Thank you to everyone who believed and supported me. Music has always helped me in the past and it's what I'm going to focus on, not only to heal, but to help others and to thank my loyal audience." My gosh, she's so gracious, so caring. She went on to say, "Madison, if you hear this please turn yourself in. We all need to understand what happened. Let us help you."

XANDER ROBERTS: (laughs) Yeah, no chance. As if the biatch, I mean *woman*, will give herself up. She's probably on a beach somewhere sipping margaritas, cackling.

MELODIE JOHNSON: Not everyone agrees she did it, including her parents.

LIAM FELDER: What, they don't trust their eyes? The evidence is in front of them.

MELODIE JOHNSON: I'll paraphrase what they said, but the gist of it was their daughter would never commit murder and they'll do whatever they can to clear *her* name. I remember this part vividly. Madison's mother, Lucinda Pierce, peered straight into the camera and said, "We're going to fight with everything we've got." Man, she gave me the shivers.

LIAM FELDER: Jeez. She's delusional. Speaking of

potentially delusional people, do either of you think Vienna has a future in music?

MELODIE JOHNSON: Good grief, I hope so. It would be so unfair if her career was over because of what her supposed best friend did.

XANDER ROBERTS: Ha. Best friend, my ass. Anyway, even if she doesn't, "Sweet Spot" has raced up the charts and is blowing up on downloads. Did you know it's the fastest selling single in the last twenty years? Not only in the US but also in Canada, the UK, Ireland, and Switzerland. It's off the charts. Well, at the top of the charts, ha.

LIAM FELDER: I'd say she's set, financially.

MELODIE JOHNSON: Yeah, but I'm pretty certain she'd rather her friends were alive.

LIAM FELDER: Oh, for sure.

MELODIE JOHNSON: Well, gentlemen, are you with me on #TeamVienna?

XANDER ROBERTS: (laughs) What kind of a question is that?

LIAM FELDER: How can you not be? I wish her much success in everything she does. She deserves it.

MELODIE JOHNSON: One hundred percent agreed. Okay, peeps, we're taking a quick break, but first, we want to play you "Sweet Spot" by the Bittersweet. I don't know about anyone else, but from the first time I heard this track, it gave me goose bumps. Even more so now. We'll be right back after this. Stay tuned.

42

IT'S BEEN TWO days since the news broke with the video of Evelina's murder, and both nights I slept soundly. The outpouring of genuine love and support from my fans has almost been overwhelming—the complete opposite online experience compared to when I was taken in for questioning.

There are still some who doubt Madison's capable of murder—conspiracy theorists #TeamVienna calls them, and they defend me whenever #TeamMadison attacks. It's like having my own pack of pit bulls.

Poor Guy's a mess, which is to be expected. It's going to take him a while to process he was in love with a killer. In time he'll move on and find someone else. Shame we were never interested in one another, or we could've tried to make a go of things, but at this point he's more brother than potential partner.

It's late morning. Roger and I have agreed he'll stop by in an hour. He said we need to discuss a few things and as I get dressed, I wonder what's on his agenda. Deciding how and when we'll relaunch my music career is top of mine.

Until Roger arrives, I decide to scroll through the news and socials, check if #TeamVienna's still trending. It is, and it makes my heart leap around in my chest. I thought I wasn't interested in fame, but it turns out I was wrong. I've had some and now I want—no, *need*—a bit more.

I head to the bathroom where I reapply my makeup, choosing a clear gloss on my lips and dark gray kohl to frame my eyes, making them appear bigger. The result is understated, someone who's been through trauma but fighting hard to come out the other end.

I'm used to being onstage, used to performing. This role is no different, just longer, more intense, and I need to give the #TeamVienna fans snippets of how I'm feeling to keep them on my side and interested until I have news about a music or memoir release. Preferably both.

Back on the living room sofa, I position my mandatory ring light on the coffee table and click my phone in place. I open Instagram, do a double take when I see my followers have grown again, almost doubling in the last two days alone to more than sixty thousand.

"Hello, everyone," I say, giving a shy smile and pausing. "I'm Vienna Taylor, and I'm the Bittersweet's drummer." I stop again, blink three times and press my lips together as I bring my hand to my neck and add, "I *was* the Bittersweet's drummer."

I've barely spoken three sentences, but in an instant, there are over six hundred viewers.

"I want to express my gratitude to you all for your kindness and love."

A thousand people are watching now, and the number's growing and growing. Strangers wondering what I'm going to say.

Comments, heart and hug emojis rise up my screen so fast, they become a blur. I exhale a quivering stream of breath, imagine my viewers clutching their devices, anxiously waiting for what comes next. They may have loved the Bittersweet before, but now they're here for me, and only me. All of them, mine.

"The past seven weeks since the…*accident* have been horrific. The worst time of my life." I bend my head, act as if I'm considering whether I can continue before I peer straight into the camera again. "There's no doubt what got me through this is your loyalty and messages of support. I know it'll take time for all of us to recover, if recovery is at all possible, but please know this: you were here for me, and I'll never forget it. I'm so grateful, and I'll get back to making music for you all soon. You and my art are what will help me survive. I promise."

A constant stream of reactions keeps coming. ILUs, more hearts, and praying hands. #TeamVienna, #Warrior, #Survivor. Viewership has grown exponentially. I'm at almost six thousand people now, and that's only those watching live. This video's destined to go viral—the first of many if I get my way—putting the name Vienna Taylor on everyone's tongue. Madison's too, of course, but she can't make new music. I can.

"Thank you," I say, tilting my head a little and looking up at the camera. "I'll see you soon."

I stop broadcasting and flop back. This is excellent. I'm the last standing member of the Bittersweet. Wrongly suspected, almost accused, and definitively, unequivocally cleared. My story's an absolute gold mine.

The doorbell rings thirty minutes later. Roger stands on the doorstep dressed in a pair of jeans, a black turtleneck sweater and a long charcoal overcoat. He stomps his boots on the mat before taking them off without being asked. When he catches my quizzical expression he smirks, says, "When I was nine, my grandmother made me clean the floor with a toothbrush after I traipsed through her house with muddy shoes."

"Oof. Harsh."

"Maybe, but I've never forgotten." He follows me to the living room and sits in the armchair to the left of me. "How are you holding up?" he asks.

"I'm not sleeping well," I lie. "Nightmares."

"Want to talk to someone about it? They can prescribe—"

"No, I don't want to take anything. Not after seeing Libby… you know."

Roger grimaces. "Apologies."

"Don't, it's fine. I'll be fine."

He looks around the apartment. "You're settled here? All okay?"

"It's great," I say, preparing to cast my bait. "Thank you again for being so generous and covering the rent for a while. I wish I could afford a similar place."

"About that." Roger stops, and I force my face to remain neutral. My hands are in my lap, so I squeeze my left thumb between my fingers as a reminder to stay calm. "You mentioned you're not working, so I'd imagine you might be getting strapped for cash. I want to help."

"You already have." I gesture around the living room.

He smiles. "Time to do more. You know 'Sweet Spot' has exploded?"

"I saw it's trending on TikTok. To be honest I haven't paid much attention to what's going on online. I did a quick thank-you video before you arrived, but otherwise it's…it's too much, you know?"

"I understand. Let me fill you in. 'Sweet Spot' isn't only blowing up TikTok, it's everywhere. Streaming and sales have gone bananas."

"Really?" I say, acting as if I had no clue.

Roger pulls a folded piece of paper from his jacket pocket and holds it out to me. "I spoke to Marvin and negotiated a partial advance on your royalties. I hope this'll tide you over for a while."

I take the check, unable to suppress a genuine gasp as I read the number. It's huge. Enough to comfortably live on for at least six months, longer if I'm careful. This is far more than I anticipated, and it's a *partial* advance, meaning there's more to come.

"Th-thank you," I say.

"My pleasure. This way you don't have to worry about going back to the restaurant."

"I liked working there, and Guy's been good to me."

"I'm sure, but the thing is, Vienna, I don't think you'll have much free time."

"Why not?"

"Because I've had twenty-three interview requests since yesterday. Actually—" he pulls his phone from his pocket and glances at the screen "—make it thirty-seven. On top of the dozens I already got on Saturday."

I wonder if I misheard. "Are you joking?"

"Not even slightly."

"What are they for? TV?"

"And radio, and podcasts, and blogs. You name it, your presence is in high demand. I'm looking at what we can get you in terms of appearance fees."

"You want me to get paid for interviews?" I do, too, but I want him to think he needs to convince me first.

"Sure, for some. We can choose a charity for you to donate to if it makes you more comfortable. That's good for optics, too, but you don't owe anyone anything for free."

"What about my memoir?" I ask. "Won't telling my story on TV or whatever defeat the purpose of writing the book?"

"No, because it's far more detailed, and you already know I think it's utterly compelling. If anything, the short interviews you do will drum up interest for the book." He smiles. "I spoke with three top New York literary agents yesterday."

"Really?"

"Uh-huh. They almost fell over themselves when I told them you're already working on something, and it's incredible."

"Thanks, but I…I don't know, Roger," I say. "I'm not sure it should be published."

"Why? It's well-written," he says, voice reassuring. "You'll have an editor at the publishing house and the manuscript will go through a whole process before it gets released. They'll make recommendations about changing names to protect the innocent. Or not so innocent. Here's looking at you, Barb and Rick."

"It's not that," I say, my voice soft. "I can't help thinking financially benefiting from what happened is awful." I hesitate, voice a concern that's been pulling at my guts. "What's everybody going to think about Madison?"

"Probably nothing they don't already," Roger says. "But I hear you, and it's a decision only you can make. Personally, I think you should complete the memoir before anyone else pens a biography about the band, which someone is bound to do, by the way, and they'll get it wrong."

He's right, of course, but I tentatively say, "You really think I should tell my story?"

"Yes, but why not talk to the agents, at least on the phone? You know my starting position is to always be open to conversations because you never know where they might lead, exactly like when you and I chatted in Newton." His jovial expression falters. "Although things would've turned out differently if I hadn't been there at all."

I search his face. What I find isn't entirely surprising, but it still touches me. "You feel bad for sending us to the Catskills."

Roger sighs. "Yes. Every single goddamn day."

His discomfort unexpectedly makes my own levels of unease and regret about what happened and what I did surge, and I force myself to push them all down. Roger's a good man. Generous, kind, and honest. A gem in the music industry—or any industry. I'm having trouble seeing Roger grieve because I genuinely like him.

"What happened wasn't your fault," I say.

"My logical side hears you," he replies. "But my heart isn't doing much listening. I need to work through this, and part of my journey is helping you. Let me show the literary agents the first few chapters of your memoir, see what they think."

"Okay," I say. "I emailed Libby an updated version so I could wait for her feedback. Actually, she said she'll stop by later this afternoon with some notes."

"Hmm…is that wise?"

"Her coming over?"

"Her helping you with the manuscript. Do you think she's angling to be coauthor?"

"She hasn't mentioned anything."

"Okay, let's wait and see." He pauses. "It's good you're in touch. It must be helpful to have someone who understands." When I nod, he continues. "I really am deeply sorry about what happened. I only knew Madison for a short while and I can't imagine what you're going through because of her betrayal."

"Thank you," I murmur, trying not to think about how I betrayed her. "It's why I need to work, you know? Yes, it's a distraction but that's the whole point. What else am I supposed to do? Sit around here?" I pull a face. "No offense, this place is gorgeous."

He rubs a hand over his chin, seemingly contemplating what he's about to say. "There's one more thing, but I don't want you to feel obligated or under any pressure. You can say no to any and all of these proposals."

"Go on…"

"Fleur de Lizzie have a few upcoming dates booked at The Chord."

"Oh…?"

"Yeah, and their drummer broke his elbow. Their manager called. Asked if you—"

"Yes," I say immediately. "I'd love to play with them."

Roger grins. "I've got homework to do. I'll get the details and cross wires with you."

As we get up, I notice how his face has turned serious, and he quietly says, "The Bittersweet could've been one of the most successful bands in the next decade, and it would've largely been because of you. I know things are hard, but with your tenacity and drive, I see incredible things in your future. Huge things. Hang in there."

After we say goodbye and Roger leaves, I pick up the check he gave me, immediately deciding how I'll spend a teeny fraction of it. Excitement builds in my chest as I grab my coat, pull on my boots, hat, scarf, and sunglasses, and head outside.

Libby arrives a few hours later and lets out a squeal when I open the door. "Oh my gosh, who's this?" she says, reaching out to pet the tiny gray cat in my arms.

"This is Pepper," I answer, cradling the kitten I picked up at a local pet shelter earlier in the afternoon. He's almost identical to the one Mom and Rick forced me to get rid of a few years ago, the kitten Grams and I fell in love with, and for which I trudged through a snowstorm to ensure his survival. It felt like kismet when I walked into the third Brooklyn shelter and saw him at the back of the cage, big inquisitive eyes staring at me.

"Are you sure you don't want to hold any of the others?" the lady had asked.

"No," I said. "This little guy's perfect."

I bought all the supplies on my way home. A fluffy bed, toys, food, bowls, a litter box. Pepper loves me already, I can tell by the way he cries when I leave the room, if only for a minute. Maybe I should've asked Roger if I could have a pet in this apartment, and I hope Pepper doesn't scratch anything too expensive before my three months are up.

Libby and I settle at the kitchen island, and I offer her a beer, which she refuses. "I'm still a bit wary of booze because of my concussion," she says, pointing to her head. "I feel fine now, but…" She waves a hand.

"Go on," I say. "Tell me what's wrong."

"I've been having nightmares," she says. "Of the cabin."

It takes a split second for me to decide how to react to this news because of course it worries me. I put myself in Libby's headspace. She knows she was in the cabin with a murderer—Madison—and would've burned alive if the fire had taken. I put my hand on her arm. "Do you want to tell me about them?"

"There's not much to tell. I keep feeling someone pulling me into the basement. It's Madison, obviously, but I was unconscious, and I never saw her so it's terrifying. I still don't remember a thing." She pauses. "It's getting so bad, most of the time I don't want to sleep because I'm too anxious of the dreams. I'm exhausted."

I tread carefully, tiptoeing as much as I dare because unconscious or not, is it possible she registered something? "I wish I could've protected you."

"What?" Her eyebrows shoot up. "Oh, God, Vienna, no, don't think that way, please. You saved me." She hesitates, says she'll take a beer after all. Once she's had a sip, she says, "I saw a therapist this morning."

"Did it help?"

"Kind of, I guess. She said my dreams are probably my mind trying to fill in the gaps with the things I've been told happened that night."

"I guess it makes sense considering you don't know what went on."

"Exactly, and as I've said to you before, that's what bothers me the most. I'll never remember anything."

I'm safe. My story's unshakable, indestructible, and so is my future. After I've been to the bathroom, I join her in having a beer and we talk for a while longer, going over the new notes she made on my memoir.

"I don't think you should read more if it's potentially contributing to your anxiety," I tell her, remembering what Roger said earlier about Libby potentially fishing to be coauthor.

Clearly, she hadn't thought that far because she immediately agrees, and seems quite relieved by my proposal. A short while later we head for the door where she gives me a hug.

"I'm so glad you're okay," she says. "And thank goodness you've got tons of public support again. Never let the haters get you down. The truth always wins."

Not this time, I think, but keep my mouth shut.

Once Libby's gone, I can't resist looking at my Instagram video, diving into the comments people have left. Mild annoyance rapidly grows into my being mightily pissed off when I see the #TeamMadison trolls are refusing to accept defeat. They call me a witch, a bitch, and worse. I spot a comment on a Facebook post that reads *Vile Vienna's a lying c**t #TeamMadison*. It's been liked over eight thousand times. *Justice for #TeamMadison* isn't far behind.

Before I give in to the temptation to throw my phone across the room, I smack it down on the table. What will it take to convince them I'm innocent? Why hasn't the—albeit fake—evidence been enough? Libby said I shouldn't let the haters get me down. I'm not going to. Instead, I'll show them what I'm made of.

43

58 days after the accident

THE LAST WEEK went by in a blur of activity. Roger and his PR person organized a press conference, as well as more interviews for TV, radio, and beyond. I've spoken to countless journalists and show hosts, answering the same questions so often I can now do it in my sleep.

I don't mind the repetition one single bit. It's electrifying, energizing—a natural high I can't get enough of. Neither can my fans. "Sweet Spot" is flying at the top on the *Billboard* Hot 100, downloads and streams holding steady.

Every time I feel guilty about what I did at the cabin, I remind myself this level of success is what we all wanted. Maybe we could've achieved it without the tragedy, but it would've taken far longer, if we'd got there at all. Bands split up all the time and who knows? Maybe we would've, too.

Madison was getting too controlling, moody, and temperamental, and her secretly calling Roger to discuss revenue streams and so forth had upset us all. I'd worried there'd be mutiny, that the others would either leave or want to get rid of her, and then what would I have done? I don't need to worry about any of that now.

It's Sunday. Roger has arranged three conference calls with literary agents for tomorrow and I decide to take the day off to lounge around with Pepper. He's adorable and full of energy, which I attempt to use up with the help of the dozen cat toys I brought home. His favorite is a mouse made from red-and-blue string with a green feather for a tail, and I laugh as he throws it in the air and pounces before it hits the ground, sinking his little teeth deep.

Once he's exhausted and snuggled in my lap, I pull out my phone and scroll through apartments for rent and sale to get an idea of what's out there, debating how much I want to spend. I've never had enough money for a down payment on my own place before, not even close, but if the advance Roger gave me is any indication of what my financial future holds, it won't be long before I can, especially when I release new music.

I've decided I want to write songs for other artists, too. It's where the serious money is. Roger thinks it's a great idea, said to let him know when I've got something to pitch. I'll have to be careful as I don't want people thinking I'm bouncing back abnormally well after what happened. Thankfully I've maintained in numerous interviews how music, my art, and my audience are the only things getting me through each day.

Still, I'm not used to having cash, and I don't want to squander it. The check has mostly been deposited, although I ordered a snare bag and a new throne for my drum kit, which I've brought back to Cobble Hill from the Bittersweet's rehearsal space and set up in the spare bedroom. Playing again feels incredible, and every chance I get, I'm practicing Fleur de Lizzie songs as I'll be gigging with them soon and want to impress them at our first rehearsal.

Not wanting to be the asshole neighbor—which would also mean drawing attention to myself and potentially alerting the press to where I live—I left letters for the people in the apartments directly above, underneath, and next to me, saying they should put a note in my mailbox if the noise is too much. So far, I've only practiced during the day, and nobody has complained. The building is high-end, with great insulation, which I add to the wish list for my own place.

Pepper hasn't been impressed with my music. The last time I picked up my drumsticks he dashed to the bedroom and leaped into his basket. Ever since, whenever I practice, I pop him in the bedroom and close the door.

He purrs as I stroke his fuzzy head and tickle his chin. Hopefully he'll love the scratching post I ordered when I bought my snare bag and stool. There was no way I could buy stuff only for myself. I'd have felt terrible.

All the items were sent to my Bushwick apartment, and I emailed the super, asked her to watch for my parcels. She told me she'd let me know when they arrive so I can pick them up from her place.

Maybe involving her was a bad idea—obviously, she knows who I am—but I've managed to stay anonymous in the Cobble Hill building, and I want to keep it that way. There's a doorman here who receives all deliveries, and we don't yet have the same rapport I enjoyed with Raphaël. I've no idea about this man's discretion levels, or lack thereof, and much the same as with everyone else who lives here, the fewer interactions, the better.

When I tap on the tracking link for the snare bag, it comes up as delivered. A few swipes, and I get the same notice for the stool, and Pepper's fancy scratching post—all of them have supposedly arrived in Bushwick over the past two days. There are photos of the three parcels in front of my apartment door.

Annoyed by my (soon to be prior) super's lack of urgency, I decide I could do with a walk. I slide Pepper off my lap and onto the couch, pull on my boots and jacket, grab my bag and head out, donning my usual disguise of beanie and glasses.

When I get to the lackluster building, I go upstairs, but my doorstep's empty. Back in the equally drab lobby, I check my scuffed and dented mailbox for a note from the super. There's nothing other than flyers for a new hair salon and a local juice bar.

Chastising myself for not calling ahead, I walk to her main floor apartment and ring the bell. We only met briefly when Madison and I first moved in, haven't had any interaction since because the rent's paid electronically. If memory serves, she's somewhere in her early sixties, with curly gray hair and a dancer's body. Her name's Julie, I think.

"Hi, I'm in 23B," I say, pointing upstairs. "Do you have the deliveries for me?"

"I don't think so," Julie says, her voice raspy. She stares at me a fraction of a second too long as curiosity takes over her face. "You're the drummer. I thought so when I checked your name."

I wish I could frown and say, "I get that a lot. It's the hair, apparently," before adding how I work in finance and complaining how nothing dramatic ever happens in my life, but what's the point?

"Yes, I am," I say. "About those deliveries—"

"Terrible business," Julie says, giving me the once-over. "I guess you're really famous now."

"I guess. Anyway, the packages—"

"I don't have them," Julie says, her voice curt. I can't tell what she's thinking, but from her face I don't want to know because she seems more of a #TeamMadison fan. Or maybe I'm being a bit paranoid.

"Someone must've taken them."

Julie shrugs. "Or they're delayed."

"No." I show her the photos on my phone. "See? They were definitely delivered."

"Have you asked your neighbors?"

"Not yet."

"Try them," she says. "If they don't have 'em, there isn't much I can do."

"Isn't there any security footage inside the building?"

"Nope, no budget for cameras."

Clearly, I'm not getting anywhere with Julie. Annoyed at her and whoever swiped my things, I walk away. My neighbors aren't home, so I debate leaving a note in their mailbox, asking them to give the parcels to Julie if they happened to pick them up, but I don't want to interact with them. I call the company I bought the snare bag from.

"It was delivered," the man says once he's searched for my order reference.

"Did anyone sign for it?"

"No, ma'am. You didn't pay the extra."

My old habits of trying to save a buck are dying hard, but not before they've taken a bite out of my ass. "What happens now?"

"I can send you the photo the driver took of the item in front of your door."

"I already have it."

"Did you ask your neighbors or superintendent? Maybe they received it for you."

Fed up with going around in circles, I mutter a thank-you and hang up, contact the other suppliers, and have two similar conversations.

A quick text, and Roger agrees to my using his address for deliveries. I re-order everything, paying extra for signature upon delivery and cursing myself for not doing so before. By the time I get home, my irritation has subsided a little. I tell myself to chill out, it was only a few hundred bucks, and spend the rest of the afternoon playing with Pepper. Three missing parcels might be annoying, but it's nothing I should spend time worrying about.

It's only early February, the wind blustery and cold, so after having a shower the next morning, I bundle up and head out for groceries, grateful for the fresh air. Once I reach the store, I take my time selecting fresh fruit and veggies, organic chicken breasts and a loaf of crusty, delicious-smelling bread fresh from the oven.

I spot a bag of tuna kitten treats, which Pepper will love, and grab it too. It's strange to not have to stop and think about whether I can afford a seven-dollar item, and the smirk it puts on my face lasts until I get home and open the front door.

There's a chill in the air, a slight breeze coming from the bathroom, and my heart almost stops. I rush over, confused to find the window's ajar. When I was a kid, Grams taught me to always open the bathroom window after a shower to let out the humidity and prevent mold, but I thought I closed it before I left. Didn't I?

"Pepper?" I call out. "Pepper, where are you?"

He doesn't often come when I say his name, so I head to the bedroom first, drop to my knees and search under the bed. Empty, and he's not curled up in his basket, either. Frantic, I tear through the apartment, searching every nook and cranny I can think of, under cushions, down the back of the sofa, inside every closet and cabinet, the tub and shower, underneath every piece of furniture. Pepper isn't here.

I stand still, try to calm down as I strain to listen, hoping for the tiniest of meows, but all I'm greeted with is silence. Heart pounding, I run back to the bathroom and throw open the window again, check the sill before staring all the way down to the private courtyard.

Pepper's tiny. It's enough of a drop for him to be seriously hurt—or worse—if he fell. My gaze sweeps across the paving stones, but aside from wilted planters left over from the fall, four chairs and two rectangular mosaic tables, I don't see anything.

Pepper isn't anywhere. He's gone.

44

IT'S BEEN A week and there's still no sign of Pepper despite Libby helping me put missing cat flyers with his picture on them in all the building's mailboxes, after which we plastered them around the neighborhood. We stuck them on lampposts, she handed them to staff at coffee shops and restaurants, took them to launderettes and delis. Nobody has seen him anywhere.

I only had Pepper for a few days, but whenever I walk into the apartment, I hope to find him curled on the sofa or asleep in his basket. The red-and-blue string mouse is in my bag, and I'm on the verge of tears whenever I see it. I wonder what happened to Pepper, if he plummeted from the window ledge or slipped by me when I left to get groceries, and found his way out of the building. Either way, I'll never forgive myself for being so careless or for losing him.

"Would you consider getting another cat?" Libby had asked as we'd dropped off the flyers the other day. She'd raised a hand when I opened my mouth to tell her Pepper wasn't a pair of jeans or a shirt, easily replaced. "I don't mean now, but in time. When you're ready." She'd hesitated a little. "I read about the first Pepper in your memoir and I'm sorry. It must've been so hard."

Unimaginably so. My heart broke when I wrote the chapter as I remembered walking all the way to the pet shelter and dropping the kitten off. It took another stab when Grams had mentioned him a week later, unexpectedly asking, "Where's our cute little kitty-cat?"

It all makes me wonder what might've been if Rick hadn't told me to get rid of Pepper, if it could've somehow slowed Grams' dementia. I try shoving the memories away because I don't like thinking about what I did to my grandmother, no matter the reasons for my actions.

When I switch on the TV to distract myself, I land on a true crime series, which instantly reminds me of a show I watched. An uncomfortable sensation slides through my bones when I remember how one criminologist said individuals who take the lives of three or more people on separate occasions with a cooling-off period in between are considered serial killers. Those who take three or more lives at the same place and time are mass killers. Three lives.

Grams. *One.*

Evelina. *Two.*

Gabi. *Three.*

Madison. *Four.*

There wasn't a distinct cooling-off period between the last three, and more discomfort slinks up my legs, twists itself around my gut. I get up and go to the bathroom where I examine myself in the mirror. Although my cheekbones are still prominent, my eyes are less sunken because I'm eating properly again. There's no doubt my hair could do with a cut soon—not sure how I'll do it without being recognized, maybe Roger can help me find a discreet stylist—but I can't help thinking: Is this the face of a serial or mass killer?

I don't think so. There's no voracious appetite deep within me to dispose of another human being. Grams' transition was facilitated to keep her safe. If Gabi hadn't caused the crash, I wouldn't have touched any of the others.

Turning away, I switch off the bathroom light. Focusing on my music, career, and future is what matters now, not the past.

With my parcels and Pepper going missing, I'd almost forgotten about the conference calls Roger and I had with the literary agents. All of them said they wanted to sign me after reading a few sample chapters of my memoir, but Roger and I decided to first give them the rest of the manuscript to read. I'm keen to hear what they suggest doing with it, if they can engineer a bidding war with publishers, which two of them indicated is a strong possibility.

It's not the only exciting prospect. Roger has arranged for me to play two dates with Fleur de Lizzie at The Chord, off Broadway. It's not a huge venue, but it's well known, generally has a great crowd and atmosphere, and we're rehearsing there a few times over the coming week. I've been practicing more since I lost Pepper, taking out my frustrations on my drums, and I'm prepared. Our first session is this afternoon, so after having a shower and throwing together a quick sandwich, I head out.

Despite the upset these past few days, I'm excited to play with a band again. I check socials, see Fleur de Lizzie's accounts have already mentioned my joining them for rehearsals and the two concerts. The response is mainly positive save for the #Team-Madison brigade, which I force myself to ignore. Seems everyone else is excited I'm joining as a special guest, and tickets are sold out for both nights, which further bolsters my mood.

As soon as I get to The Chord, the lead singer and band's founder, Lizzie Neuhaus, walks over. She's gorgeous, a little taller than me, with long brown hair twisted into a loose bun, and a badass dragon tattoo, complete with golden wings wrapped around her bicep. Her pink muscle shirt skims her taut midriff and shows off her defined arms, and when she smiles, broad and welcoming, I like her right away.

"Vienna," she says, pulling me in for a hug, which is unexpected yet oddly comforting. I haven't had much physical contact with anyone these last two months. "We're so glad you're able to join us. Let me introduce you."

Aside from Lizzie, who sings and plays lead guitar, the band's made up of Kes on rhythm guitar and Drake on bass. Before my arrival, I'd wondered if there might be any kind of wariness or hostility toward me after everything involving the Bittersweet, but all I detect is eagerness for me to be here. I feel included, at ease, part of a group again.

They ask a few gentle questions about how I'm doing following what happened in the Catskills and extend their deepest sympathies. It feels a little planned, as if they've talked about what they'd say before I arrived, but I'm glad we get it out of the way so we can focus on what I'm here for.

"How did you make out with our songs?" Lizzie asks once she's introduced the crew handling the stage, lighting, and sound, who all seem kind and as eager to get to work as I am. "Did any of them give you any trouble?"

"No, I think I know them off by heart."

A bewildered expression takes over Kes's face as he rubs his stubble. "Already?"

"Yeah, I believe so."

"All ten?" Drake adds. He has a hexagon-shaped birthmark on his right cheek, dark brown hair, and the cutest dimples I've seen in a long time. I wonder if he's single.

"Yes," I say. "I'm a big fan and I've been practicing."

Lizzie grins. "Total pro. Great. Let's see what you've got."

Their drummer Mitch, who's taken his family on vacation while his arm heals, left behind his kit, which is already set up. His gear's great, at least as good as mine, and we play for the next hour and a half, going through their set list, including a few covers. We sound good together, our voices blending well.

Although I falter on two of the tunes, they're generous with their feedback, gracious in their approach. As we take another song from the top, I close my eyes and lose myself in the rhythm, thinking how everything's perfect. The bliss lasts until a deafening crash and the sound of breaking glass fill the air.

As I leap backward and open my eyes, Lizzie lets out a small shriek. One of the spotlights hanging above us now lies next to the drum kit, smashed to pieces. By the looks of things, it bounced off the bass drum, thankfully not breaking it, although the wooden stage is dented and gouged.

"What the hell?" I say, peering up, half expecting another spotlight to come flying.

Lizzie, Kes, and Drake all start talking at the same time, trying to ensure I wasn't harmed. The stage manager, a young guy wearing four leather bracelets and an Aerosmith shirt, runs over, offering profuse apologies, saying he'll get the mess cleared up and the spotlight replaced.

"We'll have to go over safety checks before you continue," he says.

"Thanks, Joe, but I think we'll call it a night," Lizzie says, before looking at Kes, Drake, and me. "Same time tomorrow, guys? Does that work for you, Vienna?"

"For sure," I say. "I had fun. Well, until the light almost took off my head."

After Joe offers another apology and chats with Lizzie and Kes about the next rehearsal, Drake turns to me. "We're heading out for drinks. Want to come with?"

The answer's yes, and from the look he's giving me, I already know I won't be sleeping alone tonight. He's exactly what I need.

Drake leaves my apartment midmorning the next day. It's Tuesday, but I've got nowhere to be until I play with Fleur de Lizzie again, so I stay in bed, exhausted from being up for hours with Drake. He's sexy as hell, hugely talented—not only in music—but I've no intention of what happened between us leading to anything serious. Never mind how great it felt to be touched and wanted, I don't need any kind of complication in my life.

I check emails, see one from Roger with the subject Literary Agents, and tap my screen.

Hi Vienna,

Great news. Georgina already got back to me. She devoured your memoir and has fantastic ideas about getting it ready for submission to publishers. I think she'd be a perfect fit. She'd like to schedule another chat with us soon. I told her you were busy with Fleur de Lizzie so when you have a moment, can you send me some dates? No rush, we can wait until we hear from the other two agents.

Hope the rehearsals are going well. Let me know if you need me.

Cheers,
Roger

I spend the next twenty minutes reexamining Georgina's client list, which is impressive. She specializes in nonfiction and has brokered many six-figure deals, plus a couple of larger ones. Roger's right, she does seem the best fit and I'm keen to hear her ideas. I reply to his email and ask him to set a date after my gigs with Fleur de Lizzie are done the week after next. I don't want to appear too eager.

As I wonder what the #TeamVienna fans will think of my writing a memoir, I decide if I truly want to know, I should ask. It might not be a good idea to post about this from my own profile in case I'm branded a sellout, so I create a fake one on Instagram, spend a little time posting about music and books, and following people with these interests. After an hour of padding my feed so at first glance it doesn't seem brand-new, I use a graphics app to make a cool photo of a drum set and write the caption.

Is it true there's going to be a book about the Bittersweet? I'd LOVE to read more about the band and what happened, especially if Vienna writes it. How about you? #TeamVienna #TheBittersweet #ViennaTaylor #Tragedy #nonfiction #books #bookstagram #TVShow #GrabItNetflix

It doesn't take long for a few comments to pop up and they're incredible.

Yes, yes, YES to a #TeamVienna book! #booksta #bookworm

Hands up if you can't wait #TeamVienna #ReadersOfInstagram #Books

Holy shit! Is this really happening???? #gimmegimmegimme

And then the trolls arrive.

Not if it's written by Vienna. She should stfu already #TeamMadison

I'm not reading a word that bitch writes

Murdering asshole. Fuck her. #TeamMadison

On the one hand I detest these comments because they're a slant against me, but part of me remains comforted to see Madison's fans still supporting her. She'd definitely get a kick out of knowing she hasn't been forgotten, exactly like I promised.

I read more comments, see how #TeamVienna pushes back full force, felling the enemy with comments and takedowns better than I could've ever imagined. Satisfied by having a loyal army on my side, too, which evidently wants to read whatever I have to say, I drop my phone on the table.

With how elated I'm feeling, and all this energy flowing through my body, I may have to bring Drake home with me again sometime soon after all.

45

68 days after the accident

BITTERSWEET PARENTS CONFRONT
SURVIVING BAND MEMBER

by Eleanor Willis of the *Maine Daily*

A verbal altercation took place last night outside The Chord, a concert venue in Queens, NY. The incident involved Vienna Taylor, the controversial North Deering drummer and one of two possible survivors of the pop-rock group the Bittersweet, and the parents of the band's missing guitarist Madison Pierce, who are also from North Deering.

It's alleged Barry and Lucinda Pierce, who are currently staying in New York, waited for Taylor to leave The Chord, where Taylor's currently rehearsing with the band Fleur de Lizzie for two upcoming gigs. When Taylor stepped outside shortly after 9:30 p.m., Mr. and Mrs. Pierce confronted her, denying her access to her rideshare.

In a video of the altercation, which has been widely circulated online, Mrs. Pierce tells Taylor, "We want the truth about what happened to Madison. Stop lying to the whole world about what you did to our daughter."

Madison Pierce has been missing since Taylor's former band the Bittersweet was involved in a car crash in the Catskills last December, which killed Isabel Riotto outright. When forensic evidence later determined Evelina Sevillano was murdered at the cabin where the band sought refuge for the night, Taylor was taken in for questioning. Subsequent footage of Madison Pierce suffocating Evelina Sevillano emerged, and Taylor was cleared of all suspicion. The cause of death of Gabriela Sevillano remains unclear and no trace of Pierce has yet been found despite "considerable" efforts by the authorities.

Police weren't called to the scene outside The Chord and no charges were laid.

Comments (25—showing most recent)

@sandie_j56 OMG why can't they leave poor Vienna alone? #TeamVienna

@flip_flop_22 Stop the video at 0m54sec and look at Vienna's face. It's demonic! Still and always #TeamMadison

@maplesyrup_12 Pretty sure you're the only whack job here!

@sandie_j56 I dunno. Her face is kind of scary…

@flip_flop_22 You can tell she did it. It's obvious.

@sandie_j56 Why don't you flip_flop off!

46

FRIDAY NIGHT, AND I'M on Libby's couch, nursing a beer. She suggested going out to grab a bite to eat but after the way the Pierces accosted me two nights ago, and the video one of the rubbernecking bystanders took and shared, I'm not going anywhere in public. Besides, my appetite has vanished again, plus when Roger called as soon as he saw Lucinda going off at me, he suggested lying low for a few days.

I hadn't seen Barry and Lucinda coming when they stormed up to me outside The Chord. The rehearsal with Fleur de Lizzie had been perfection, and as I walked out of the building, I felt vibrant, thriving off the energy playing with the band gave me. I'd been alone. Drake hadn't suggested spending the night with me and I didn't offer. He could chase me if he was interested. His loss if he didn't.

I'd stood waiting for my Uber, with my phone in one hand. The next second, Lucinda and Barry were in my face. I barely recognized Lucinda. She'd always been slim, but now she was almost skeletal, a lollipop with sinkhole cheeks and shadowy circles around her eyes. It took me a moment to connect her appearance to her grief for Madison, or, more likely, for their sacred reputation. Barry wasn't faring any better, looking rougher than Newell had when he'd taken me in for questioning.

"You!" Lucinda shouted, pointing a finger in my face as Barry unsuccessfully attempted to hold her back. She shook him off, came so close I could smell her acrid breath. "Tell us what happened to Madison," she said, grabbing hold of my sleeve. "Where is she? What did you make her do?"

"I don't know what you're talking about," I said, trying to move away, glancing around to see how many people were already watching. There were a few, so I lowered my voice. "I didn't do anything."

"Liar," Lucinda yelled, her eyes wild.

"Where is she?" Barry added, his jaw making tiny sinewy movements, as if he were grinding his teeth down to nubs.

I yanked my arm away, remained silent as I watched a gray Mazda pull up. I moved to check the license plate, ensuring it was my rideshare, but both Lucinda and Barry got between me and the vehicle. Lucinda's expression was filled with so much hatred and disgust, she seemed borderline unhinged.

"Don't try to walk away from us," she said. "Not until you tell the truth."

"I've nothing to say to you." I tried keeping calm, but I could feel the pressure building in my head, searching for an escape hatch. "You must've seen the video. You know what she did."

"You made her do it," Lucinda screamed, coming closer. "This is all your fault. We always knew you were trouble. I wish you'd never been born."

Hearing the words my mother had spat at me countless times made uncontrollable rage shoot from my mouth. "Fuck you," I shouted back, getting right up in their faces, pointing a finger at Lucinda's chest as I felt spittle collecting in the corner of my mouth. "Go to hell."

"Tell us what happened," Barry insisted, grabbing my arm.

I shook him away. "Get off me," I yelled. "Both of you. Don't come near me ever again or I'll have a restraining order slapped on your asses. I don't owe you *anything*. I don't care about you. Fucking stay away from me."

Pushing past them, I managed to slip inside the car, slam and lock the door as Lucinda banged on the glass, still shouting while Barry looked like he might cry. I meant what I'd said. I didn't owe the Pierces anything, and I didn't give ten shits about them. They'd been awful to me, and worse to their daughter. All this posturing was for show.

It wasn't until I saw the online recording of our spat that I'd realized someone had captured the entire confrontation. Inevitably it landed online, and I'd seen the freeze-frame where I looked like a woman possessed, or *demonic*, as some had called me.

I'd messaged Libby and asked if she was free this evening, so I'm forced to take a break from obsessing about what's being said online, but as I sit on her couch with my beer, the comments are still making the rage build inside me, no matter how hard I try to ignore them.

"Are you all right?" Libby says.

"Thinking about the Pierces," I answer, truthfully for once. "I can't forget what they said. It's playing on my mind in a loop."

"If you can, try not to judge them too harshly," she says. "They don't have anywhere for their grief or animosity to go, so they're lashing out at you."

"Yeah, I guess."

I fall silent as I look around the room. Libby's apartment on Ralph Avenue is quite different from the upscale one Roger got for me. This place is a cozy one-bedroom on the fourth floor, with twinkling fairy lights strung up above a wooden sideboard, and old movie posters on the walls, along with photos of Libby's family.

Her brother, Linus, is handsome and resembles Libby with his blond hair and blue eyes. She told me he's gone most of the year as he's an underwater photographer and specializes in shipwrecks. I wonder what it must be like, working where the only noise is the sound of your breathing. A sense of longing for peace and stillness—particularly in my head—washes over me, and I brush it away.

I set my beer on the Knob Creek coaster, which immediately makes me think of Guy and the time I pretend-threatened to drop a bottle of the stuff after he'd made a comment about getting more people to join the Bittersweet, create a *proper band*, as he put it.

I haven't heard from Guy in three weeks, ever since the fake video of Madison was found. If he's seen the footage of my freaking out at Lucinda and Barry, I wonder if he'll be in touch anytime soon, because I know to the outside world it made me seem like an uncaring monster.

"I love your apartment," I tell Libby, needing to get out of my head. "How long have you lived here?"

"Two years," she says. "It's a bit of a dump. It can get chilly at night."

"It's cute though. Lots of potential."

Libby lets out a laugh. "Yeah, we'll call it that. Although I hate the yellow walls."

"Nothing a coat of paint can't fix."

"God, maybe. My landlord said I could go ahead providing I stick to neutral colors, but I wouldn't know where to start."

"Easy. Pick a small space first. Maybe the hallway."

"Well, I've always imagined it in off-white." She looks at me. "Do you like decorating?"

"Love it. I did tons with my grandmother. She changed the color of her kitchen so often the room shrank." I smile at the memory of the two of us. When I was eight, Grams had decided she was sick of pastel pink, so we'd played a dozen rounds of tic-tac-toe, scribbling all over one of the walls. After the last game, when Grams was in the basement fetching some ice pops, Mom arrived.

"What the hell have you done?" she said, yanking the pencil from my hands and slapping me across the face. "I'll have to get this repainted. Do you have any idea how much it's going to cost?"

"But—"

She gave me another slap for trying to back talk, and when Grams rushed in, Mom turned to her and pointed at me. "This little shit drew all over your walls. See what she did when you left her alone?"

"We were playing a game, Barb," Grams said, calmly. When she glanced at my cheek, she narrowed her eyes. At this point my face felt as if it was on fire, and I bowed my head, letting my hair fall forward. "I'll keep Vienna here this evening. I'm sure you'll enjoy a night off."

Mom didn't apologize. Once she'd stormed from the house, Grams handed me the pencil, and said, "Your turn to start. Let's cover every single wall."

God, I missed her. I missed sharing stories about Grams with Madison, too.

Libby has been talking all this time, and I tune in. "…and I think some redecorating would certainly take my mind off things. Would you…would you mind helping me pick a color and give me some tips about the supplies I need?"

"Sure," I say, thinking it would be a welcome distraction for me, too. "When?"

"Now?" Libby says. "I've got time to paint this weekend."

Decision made, we head to a hardware store a few blocks away where I help her choose a tin of cotton-white paint, brushes, rollers, masking tape, a screwdriver, and a roll of plastic tarp because she doesn't have any old sheets to protect the floor with.

It feels odd to be out doing something so mundane, but I'm enjoying myself and Libby's great company. She's easy to talk to, I don't have the sense of endless competition like I did with Madison. As we chat, I find myself hoping our friendship will last long-term. I've missed having a friend.

Back at her apartment, we carefully fix the masking tape around the front door and baseboards, remove the light switches, and the few posters from the walls, which we roll up and set on the kitchen table. I use the screwdriver to open the tin of paint and dip my brush into the silky liquid.

"Ready for some favorite tunes while we work?" Libby asks, holding up her phone. P!nk's "Raise Your Glass" comes out of the speaker in the living room, making me grin. We work quickly, efficiently, and the first coat is done in forty minutes.

"Wow, it's much brighter already," Libby says, giving me a hug. "Thank you."

I go to the bathroom while she fetches glasses of water and some chips to snack on. When I return, she's standing in the kitchen, her fingers trembling as she stares at her phone, water overflowing from one of the glasses set in the sink.

"What's going on?" I say, and when she doesn't answer, I turn off the tap and ask again.

She holds out her cell without speaking. One of her social media apps is open. My eyes see what's on the screen, but my brain refuses to accept the implications.

The photo is of Libby and me at the hardware store barely two hours ago. Although I'd worn a hat outside, I'd taken it off as we'd walked down the shop's aisles, and my face is easily recognizable in the picture. That's not the worst part, because I have a roll of plastic tarp clenched under my arm. I scan the comments.

WTF are you doing, Taylor? #TeamMadison

Is this your next victim? #TeamMadison

Who's the woman with Vienna Taylor?

Research assistant for @CitySlickerProd named @Libby_Alexander_171

"The last comment's from Zeke," she says. "He tagged me, and the company."

"Dick pic Zeke, your former colleague?" I ask, and she nods as she swears under her breath, then another time, more loudly.

"He's such an asshole," she says. "What if everyone connects the dots and realizes I'm the other survivor from the Bittersweet crash. *Shit.*"

We watch as the comments keep piling in. #WheresLibby fills the screen, appearing over and over, and I feel her entire body trembling beside me while her face flushes, heavy with anxiety.

"They know who I am," she whispers. "Everybody knows."

"It'll pass," I say. "Trust me, they'll soon stop."

"Really?" she says, not sounding hopeful. "Because it hasn't for you."

"Don't worry," I say. "They'll get bored after a while. Anyway, it's not as if you're—"

"Famous?" she says. "Exactly, and I don't want to be. There's a reason why I'm behind the camera, Vienna. I want my privacy. I can't deal with this. Things have been bad enough as it is these past two months."

"It'll pass," I tell her again. "I swear they'll move on."

She sets her phone on the table as she sinks into one of the chairs. "I…I think I need to be alone now if you don't mind? Get my head around this."

"What about the decorating?" I say. "We haven't done—"

Libby looks away. "It's best if I finish it on my own."

She doesn't say much else. Not long after, I'm standing in the street in front of her building, wishing I wasn't quite so alone.

47

72 days after the accident

THE VIDEO FROM the hardware store and the she-devil memes people made with my face have circulated everywhere all weekend. Not only on social media but on the news, too, both online and on screen.

Turns out I was wrong when I told Libby it would all pass. It's Sunday night and #WheresLibby hasn't gone away but blown up. When I call to see if she's okay, she sounds awful.

"Reporters have been calling nonstop," she says, voice thick with tears. "When I didn't answer, they contacted my boss, and my friends. And *Zeke*. I'm taking unpaid leave and driving to Albany in the morning. I've no idea if I'll have a job when I get back."

"I'm sorry, Libby," I offer, meaning it. Hurting her more had never been my intention.

"Me, too. It was my dream job, especially after Zeke left. I was going places at City Slicker, now I'm on unpaid leave." She heaves a deep, shuddering sigh. "Call me if you need me. I won't be on social media for a while. I'm letting my accounts go dark."

Unlike Libby, I can't stay away. Every chance I get I'm opening the apps, constantly refreshing my screen to see the ongoing war between the #TeamVienna and #TeamMadison clans.

It's addictive—I can't stop scrolling, and when I see the hatred being thrown my way, animosity churns my stomach. Roger texts again, asks if I'm up for being interviewed, and I tell him to answer *no comment.* If I go on the record now I'm not sure what I'll say.

I lie on my sofa, wishing I had Pepper here for comfort. When my phone rings, I hope it's Libby, but it's a private number, so I let it go to voice mail. As soon as I hear the ding of a message, I grab my phone and listen. It's my mother, her voice high-pitched and grating, bordering on screechy.

"Vienna, how dare you think about writing a memoir. One of my friends saw a post about you working on a book. No way in hell will I let you. I know it'll be full of lies and nasty things about me and Rick. I can't believe you'd try and sell our lives this way. You're disgusting. A waste of space. I should've got rid of you when—"

I'm breathing hard as I hit Delete. My mother's last three sentences dig deeper than they should because I thought I was immune to her venom by now. While everything I've written about her in my memoir is true, I'll make sure to add more unsavory details to annihilate her.

My nerves are shot but I have a final rehearsal with Fleur de Lizzie tonight before our first gig at The Chord tomorrow. Being with them will take my mind off things. I'm excited to see Drake as well, and this time I'm definitely bringing him home with me.

A few hours of watching mindless TV go by, during which I can't focus. At last, it's time to head out. Fleur de Lizzie had other meetings today, so we're not playing until almost 8:30 p.m. The sun has already set when I step outside of the Cobble Hill apartment, and when I cross the road, I hear the rumbling of an engine.

I glance right, see a silver car speeding my way. Everything happens fast. I'm expecting the car to slow down but instead, it accelerates. Comes straight at me. I leap out of the way, land on my side between two parked cars, cry out as my hand and elbow hit the sidewalk.

Adrenaline makes me jump to my feet. The silver car has already sped by and is about to turn the corner. I crane my neck, try to catch a make or model or licence plate, but in the relative darkness I only see the number seven.

My heart's pounding in my throat as I try to work out what happened. I want to believe it was an accident, a distracted or impaired driver, but from the way the hairs on the back of my neck are tingling, it didn't seem like it.

Although I can't be certain, I think the driver saw me. Do they know who I am? Could this have been deliberate? An attempt on my *life*?

As I wonder if I should call Roger or Ashbury, I spot a police cruiser driving by and flag it down.

"I think someone tried to run me over," I say to the baby-faced officer whose name badge reads Christie, and my words immediately get his attention. He and his partner get out of the car, and I rush to explain what happened, my voice trembling.

"Did anyone else see this?" Christie asks, his head tilted upward because he's at least three inches shorter than me.

"I was alone."

"Did you get a video?"

"I was too busy jumping out of the way," I snap, which doesn't do me any favors and he raises an eyebrow. "Listen," I continue, lowering and softening my tone. "I think it might've been deliberate."

"Why would you think that?" the female cop, Bollani, asks.

"I'm Vienna Taylor," I say, putting a hand to my chest, but

they don't react. "The Bittersweet drummer from the accident in the Catskills."

"Oh yeah," Christie says as he rubs his cheek. "You seemed familiar."

"Maybe someone followed me," I say. "People have been posting stuff about me online. Nasty things."

"Do you want to file a police report?" Bollani says.

"About the online abuse?"

"The accident."

"I told you it might not have been an accident." I'm almost yelling, so I stop, force the air from my lungs. "What will filing a report do?"

Bollani shrugs. "We might investigate."

My annoyance levels shoot back up ten notches, and then another ten. *"Might?"* When Christie heaves a small sigh, my stretched nerves snap. "Let me guess," I say with a small, dry laugh. "You're #TeamMadison."

Bollani gives me a confused look. "I've no clue what that is."

"Are you being dismissive of me because you support *her?*" I ask, taking a step.

Christie raises a hand. "You need to calm—"

"Don't tell me to calm down," I say. "Someone almost ran me over and you don't seem to give a shit."

"Ma'am," Bollani says. "That's enough."

"Fine, whatever. I guess we'll forget about it. Thanks a lot."

Because I don't mean what I say, and so much frustration has built within me, when I bend over, pick up my bag and throw it over my shoulder, I swing too hard. Christie's still standing close to me, too close as it turns out, because my bag—and the weight of everything inside it—smacks him underneath his chin.

In an instant my hands are behind my back, and I feel the cold steel of handcuffs clicking into place. They think I did this deliberately, and the more I try to explain, the less they want to hear. With the way they're handling me, they must be Madison fans, and it makes me want to gouge their eyes out with my drumsticks.

"It was an accident," I say, trying to make eye contact with one of them as they push me against the cruiser. "I didn't mean to hit you."

They won't listen. Tell me I'm being arrested for assaulting a police officer and read me my Miranda rights before hauling me to the station. It takes over an hour to clear everything up. I avoid being charged because Torin shows up and works his magic, tells them about my extenuating circumstances.

I decline filing a police report about the silver car. I can't imagine they'll do anything other than throw it in the trash anyway and I'm still not sure if I was overreacting about the whole thing.

"How are you feeling?" Torin says as we leave the station.

"What do you think?" I answer, before pinching the bridge of my nose, willing myself to take it easy. If I'd done so with Christie earlier, none of this mess would've happened. "Thanks for your help, Torin. I really am grateful."

Once he's gone, I summon an Uber and call Lizzie. It's well after 10:00 p.m., meaning I'm beyond late for our rehearsal. I'm surprised she hasn't tried to contact me yet. I'd have expected a missed call or two, or a message, but there's nothing.

"Lizzie, I'm sorry," I say when she picks up. "There was an incident."

"We know," she says, an iciness in her voice I've never heard before, and which I don't like one bit.

"What do you mean?"

"Your arrest," she says. "You're in the news. *Again*."

"How?" I gasp. "Did someone film that, too?"

"Apparently you assaulted a *cop*?"

"It wasn't like that. It was a misunderstanding after somebody tried to—"

She cuts me off. "Listen, Vienna, we've spoken to our publicist and we're getting some major bad press here. Lots of pressure from our fans, comments all over Instagram and TikTok questioning why we're working with you."

"Wait, I—"

"No, I'm sorry," Lizzie says, and despite the fact I know what's coming, it flips another angry switch inside me, especially when she adds, "I'm sure you understand we can't have you performing with us."

"You're not being fair. I'm a great drummer, and—"

"I'm not disputing that," she says. "You're fantastic, no question. But the whole whacky where's Libby thing and now you being arrested for assault? No, we can't associate with this. Don't worry, we'll pay you for—"

"Fuck that, I want to perform."

"With respect," Lizzie says. "It's not about what *you* want. This is our band and we've agreed, so—"

I hang up, seething, but in an instant, an uncomfortable feeling snakes its way up my spine and positions itself on the back of my neck. I'm standing in the middle of the sidewalk, in front of the police station, yelling into my phone.

Did somebody get this on video, too? Is someone following me, watching my every move? Using whatever they find against me? Trying to run me down in the middle of the street? I shiver as I think about the spotlight crashing onto the stage a foot in front of me during my practice with Fleur de Lizzie. Was it really an accident?

Another shudder tears through me when I consider if someone wanted to hurt me, I'd have no idea who was behind it. With the thousands upon thousands of #TeamMadison fans who are all my sworn enemies, it could be anyone.

48

72 days after the accident

IT TAKES OVER forty minutes to get back to my Cobble Hill apartment. During the entire trip I walk with my hood up, sunglasses on, and head bent, avoiding eye contact with anyone coming my way.

I consider taking an Uber, but the driver might recognize me. The subway's out of the question. All I need is for someone to glance up from their phone, realize who I am, and post a photo online.

Rage builds and warps my insides as I think about the disgusting comments online. My carefully constructed video recording of Madison killing Evelina hasn't worked as well as I'd hoped. Sure, it got the cops off my back, but not everybody else. I berate myself for being naïve. Some people will hate me no matter what I say or do because it's what they decided from the outset, no matter their reasons why.

I let out a sigh of relief as I get to my street, but the feeling quickly fades when I see a small crowd gathered in front of the building. There are at least a dozen people. I wonder what's going on, and as I get closer, I see some of them are wielding posters and chanting words I can't yet make out. One woman with curly black hair turns to the side, and as the streetlight catches the sign she's holding, I read the angry red letters.

Murderer! #TeamMadison

What the fuck is going on? How do these people know where I live? This isn't my apartment. My name isn't on the paperwork, Roger and Max made sure of it to protect my anonymity.

I want to confront the crowd, march over and rant and rave, but truth is I'm scared. There are more than enough people to hurt me if they choose. There's another entrance at the rear of the building but I'm flustered and panicking. I can't remember the code Roger gave me, and there's no way for me to sneak inside without it.

As I retreat, I debate what to do. Phone Roger or Torin? They'll advise me to call the cops. I may as well get a head start. I'm definitely not contacting Christie or Bollani, and I'm grateful when Ashbury picks up instantly.

"It's Vienna Taylor," I say.

"Vienna," she says, her voice soft. "Is something wrong?"

"Yes. I think…I think someone's trying to hurt me."

"Where are you?" she asks, her tone urgent. It's so unexpected, it almost makes me cry. "Are you in immediate danger?"

"I'm near my apartment. I can't get inside. There are people outside the building."

"The one in Cobble Hill where we met you and Torin?" she says, and when I confirm this and describe the signs the people are walking around with, she adds, "I'll be there in twenty. Is there someplace nearby you can go while you wait? Somewhere quiet?"

"There's a launderette."

"Great. Text me the name and I'll meet you there. Lie low. If you feel threatened at any point, call 911."

I do as I'm told, hunker down in the warm launderette that smells of dryer sheets. From my vantage point I can see the crowd outside my building has grown, and once I pull out my phone, I learn from socials I've been doxed. The address of the Cobble Hill apartment Roger organized for me—and the address of the place in Bushwick where I lived with Madison—have been made public. *Shit.*

I think about this for a moment. Some bastard released these details. But who? Was it someone who recognized me in the new building despite my being so careful? Or was it someone I know? I flick through the list of people who have my new address and find it's not long. Roger and Max, Torin, Libby, Drake, and...Guy.

Neither Roger nor his husband would betray me, neither would Torin, or Libby for that matter, not when all it would do is keep our names in the news. Drake? To what end? Because he's pissed they have to find another drummer? Perhaps. As for Guy...

I freeze. I haven't heard from him in forever. Almost two years ago, my mother showed up at Papa e Ragazzi. While Guy hadn't shared my address back then, he had posted about my being employed at his restaurant, prompting Mom to come searching for me.

Is it possible he's involved this time? It doesn't take a genius to figure out I'm about to cash in a ton of money with how well "Sweet Spot" is doing, and with the rumors I started about writing a memoir, which are turning out to be true, people must anticipate more cash coming my way.

Theories swirl in my mind. I never called Mom back after her nasty voice mail about my memoir. Could she have contacted Guy again and asked where I live? Would he have told her because he's angry with me? Maybe that's why he hasn't been in touch. He's got something to hide—his treachery. He always did love Madison. No way is he #TeamVienna, despite everything.

I call him. "Did you release my address?" I bark when he picks up.

"What are you talking about?"

"Did you give anyone my new address?" I say. "My mom, for example. Did you?"

"I don't know what's going on with you," Guy says, "but you're way out of line."

"How would you know what I am?" I demand. "You haven't been in touch for ages."

He pauses, says nothing until I ask him why. "Because it's too hard," he finally says. "All you do is remind me of her and I can't stand it. I miss her."

"Why? All *she* did was use you."

"I know," Guy answers, and hangs up.

When Ashbury arrives fifteen minutes later with a colleague I've never seen before named Brennan, I breathe a little easier, but not by much.

"It might be best if you don't spend the night here," she says as we huddle in the launderette, telling me Newell has gone back to the Catskills to work the investigation, which somehow makes me feel sad because I'd got him on my side. "We can escort you inside to pick up a few things," she adds. "Let's find someplace else for you to stay. Is there a friend you can call?"

My list of friends is shorter than those to whom I gave my address. Torin's my attorney, Roger my manager. I want to call Libby, but people now know who she is. There's no way I can go to her place.

I don't want to tell Ashbury any of this because it's pathetic. I simply give her a nod as we walk to the building, both of them flanking my sides, jackets tucked behind their badges, visible for everyone to see. Heart thudding, I find myself waiting for the moment when someone in the crowd recognizes and lunges at me, but as we approach, the group goes silent, all eyes staring.

I find myself glancing at everyone I pass wondering if they're the person who tried to run me over, manipulated the stage light, or released my address. Is it the tall guy with the spacer earrings and neck tattoo? The short woman with the Canadian flag hat? It could be any one of them, all anonymous faces, people I've never seen before and may never see again, but who all know—or think they know—me. For the first time in my life, I'm almost paralyzed with fear.

"Where's Madison?" a woman shouts. She's tall, slim, with red hair cut in the same style as Madison's was. The similarities are so striking, I do a double take because it's almost as if I'm staring into the face of a ghost. "Where is she, you murderer?"

"Stand back," Ashbury says, holding out her arms. "Move away from the entrance."

"This is public property, we're not doing anything wrong," the redhead shoots back. "We're totally allowed to be here."

"Stop harassing me," I yell, incapable of keeping myself in check despite knowing I should shut my mouth for the next twenty yards. "I didn't do anything. I'm not a murderer."

"Sure, you're not," the man with the spacer earrings says, and a few of the others laugh, visibly emboldening him. "Show us the lie detector test and maybe we'll believe you."

"I'm not lying," I say, my voice on edge. I glance around, noticing how at least half a dozen phones are pointing in my direction, each of them recording my every move, my every word, waiting for me to make a mistake.

I dip my head, walk to the entrance, and unlock the door. Ashbury and Brennan follow. I'm about to slip inside when I hear a voice calling my name and I spin around, my knees suddenly weak. It's Libby.

"Vienna," she says, and I feel a rush of gratitude and relief when I see her face full of concern. "I saw what's happening online. Are you okay?"

"Let's talk upstairs," Ashbury says, and the four of us shuffle through the door and into the lobby, making sure nobody follows us.

As the elevator reaches my floor, Ashbury insists on exiting first, while Brennan, who must be close to seven feet tall and half as wide, stays at the back. I'm expecting to find an angry mob camped on my doorstep but the hall's empty, not a soul—angry or otherwise—to be found.

"Don't switch on the lights," Ashbury says as I slide the key into the lock. "We don't want anyone outside knowing the exact location of your unit if we can help it."

We file into the living area, and I slump onto the sofa. There's enough light coming in for me to see everyone's facial features, and I try to keep mine neutral, try not to show how frightened I'm feeling. I can't let my façade crack in case I break down and admit details I'd best keep quiet.

"Can you get rid of those ridiculous people?" Libby asks.

"I'll make a phone call," Ashbury replies. "Problem is the woman downstairs was correct, the sidewalk's public property. Aside from asking them to move along, there's little we can do."

"Are you serious?" I say. "I live here."

Ashbury tilts her head to one side, and I almost cry when her sympathy seems authentic. "As I mentioned earlier, I suggest you stay somewhere else. For a while, if possible."

"I'd offer you my sofa," Libby says. "But…"

"Best if you don't," Brennan jumps in, his voice empathetic, his demeanor kind, protective. I decide I like him.

"Definitely not with the recent video of you two at the hardware store," Ashbury adds.

"But we didn't do anything wrong," Libby says.

"Unfortunately, the people downstairs don't care," Ashbury says.

"It's fine, I'll go to a hotel," I say. "I'll ask my manager to help me find a new place in the morning. His husband works in real estate."

"We'll wait while you make hotel arrangements," Brennan says. "Drive you there and ensure you're safe. I suggest checking in under a different name. Go somewhere reputable and tip the person at the front desk really well in return for privacy."

I feel the axis of my world shift and tilt. Everything's spiraling. I'm getting closer and closer to the edge of a precipice, and I don't know if I can stop myself from plummeting over the edge. How has everything gone so wrong?

For a brief second, I consider spilling my guts. Confessing to everything I've done. Would I get any release? Maybe, but then I imagine what would happen to me, hear the sound of a prison cell door slamming, and I back away from the thought as fast as I can.

"Are you okay, Vienna?" Libby asks.

"This is unreal," I answer, truthfully, and she nods.

"Could you go home for a while?" Ashbury asks.

"Home?" I say.

"Back to Portland," she offers. "Not with your mother, I know from your memoir you don't get along, but perhaps stay with someone else?"

Ashbury's comment stirs up more possibilities in my mind. My mother's vitriol toward me when she learned about my potential memoir was like nothing I'd ever experienced from her. Before that, Madison's parents showed up at The Chord. Is it a coincidence? They all live in Portland. They all detest me.

Could Mom and Rick have joined forces with the Pierces, determined to make my life a misery? Madison's parents have the means to find out where I live. Maybe they followed me after I left The Chord or had me followed by a private detective. I was too riled from our confrontation to have noticed. Alternatively, if Guy told Mom where I live, she wouldn't have thought twice about releasing my address, particularly if she'd got money for it.

Trouble is, Mom won't tell me anything if I call. She may not even pick up. But if I have the chance to look her in the eyes when I ask the questions, I'll know for sure. She may be a good liar, but she's not as skilled as me.

"There's nothing left for me in Portland," I say. "I vowed I'd never go back."

I already know it's a promise I'm about to break.

49

73 days after the accident

THE POSH HOTEL I checked into last night is near Times Square, a suggestion Brennan made.

"You want me to go to the busiest place in the City?" I asked, wondering if he was trying to set me up, if he had anything to do with all the strange stuff going on. I found myself speculating if he drove a silver car before realizing I hadn't listened to his answer. "Sorry, what?"

"Going somewhere busy is the whole point," Brennan said. "The crowds give you the cover you need. It's when you walk down a near empty street that you might be recognized, not where there's tons of hubbub going on and you can blend in."

His theory made sense on one level, and when Ashbury backed him up, I relented, too tired to argue. Libby hugged me and left, and when the detectives dropped me off at the hotel, I followed Brennan's other suggestion.

Sliding a hundred-dollar bill across the counter, I asked for the room to be booked for three nights under the random name of Nick James. I added they were not—under any circumstances—

to give my real name to anyone. Reassurances were offered, which I had no choice but to believe, and I'd fallen asleep almost as soon as I lay on the bed fully clothed.

It's morning now, and Roger calls to ask how I'm doing, and says he'll talk to Max about finding another apartment for me. He reminds me of the security code for the back entrance to the Cobble Hill building, but I tell him I'll lie low at the hotel for the next few days.

I spend the rest of the morning trying to avoid the urge to check social media and the news, wondering if there are still #TeamMadison supporters hanging around outside either of my places. Part of me wants to go and check, potentially have a confrontation with anyone who's there. It's not a good idea, I know, but my anger is at a boiling point.

My usual cure of blasting a favorite playlist isn't helping. When I feel this way, the only thing that truly works is playing my drums hard enough to make my hands bleed but my gear isn't at the hotel. I pace the room, watch the clock tick by, wish it would speed up.

Shortly after noon and an overpriced room service lunch, I get dressed and prepare myself to pay my mother a visit. It's a five-hour drive to Portland which turns into seven by the time I've rented a car with my Janet Jenkins ID.

When I get stuck in heavy traffic, inching ahead a few yards at a time, I debate turning around and calling Mom instead, demanding to know whether she was involved in releasing my address. I remind myself I can't trust anything she says without looking her in the face, and the thought keeps me going.

I wonder if I should tell her I know she didn't attempt to steal Madison's bracelet and ring the day she came to Brooklyn. Perhaps I'll tell her it wasn't Madison who planted the jewelry in Mom's bag. It was me. She'd deserved it. Mom had cried on my shoulder the night before, told me she wanted us to rekindle our relationship, for us to have a future. I let her believe

I wanted the same thing, only to snatch it away from her by planting Madison's things. It was punishment for the way Mom treated me, and while it wasn't nearly severe enough, my secret made me smile whenever I thought about it.

When I finally arrive in Portland, I put the first part of my plan into action by stopping at Maine Mall where I park the car and circle back on foot, scanning for an area without cameras.

Working quickly, I locate a vehicle parked in a cluster of others, wait until nobody's around, and remove the plates. Back in the rental, I find a discreet spot near St. Hyacinth cemetery where I swap out the plates, hoping to blend in a little more now I've removed the out-of-state ones.

It's almost 9:00 p.m. when I get close to Rick's house. The sun has long set, giving me the advantages darkness provides. After parking a couple of streets away, I pull my hoodie over my face, put on my gloves, and set off. When the house I only lived in for a little over a year comes into view, I clench my teeth. There are few happy memories here, all of Grams, and I decide this will be the absolute last time I see this place.

I don't know what Rick replaced the Mustang I destroyed with, but Mom's old Toyota is the only vehicle parked in the driveway. Good, because I'm not interested in seeing him. I came here for her, and this conversation will be easier if she's alone.

As I approach, I see the TV flickering though the bedroom window and I take a peek inside, see Mom stretched out, watching an episode of *60 Minutes*, a generous glass of amber liquid in one hand. When I press my finger on the doorbell, I already know she'll be pissed at the interruption, wondering who's disturbing her at this time of night.

It takes another three rings for her to answer the door, her footsteps slow and labored, like a woman twice her age. When she sees me, her eyes widen.

"Vienna," she says. "To what do I owe this pleasure?"

I hesitate, almost ask if I can come in but I don't want to play nice, so I go straight for the throat. Taking a step, I ask, "Did you tell people where I live?"

This time her eyes narrow, becoming cold and hard. "What are you talking about?" she says, her words a little slurred, and I catch the scent of booze. She was already well on her way to passing out before the end of *60 Minutes*.

"People came to my apartment," I say. "I had to stay in a hotel."

She lets out a caustic laugh. "A hotel? Oh, boo hoo. It must be so hard."

"It's not funny, Mom," I snap. "Did you give anyone my address?"

"I don't know your address."

"Did you contact Guy?"

"What guy?"

"Guy, from the restaurant where I work."

Her face transforms, her expression becoming snakish and evil. "From what I've heard, you don't need to work, Madam Moneybags."

"Someone released my address on social media," I say, fists clenched by my sides. "People were outside my building. I had to get the cops involved."

She shrugs, and the nonchalance reignites my fury. "I guess it's the price you pay for fame."

"How much did they pay *you*?" I insist, still unsure if she's involved.

Mom leans in. "Trust me, if I had your address, I'd give it to everyone for free if they promised to harass you. It's what you deserve, what with your shitty memoir plans." She comes closer, grabs my wrist and pulls me to her, her face almost touching mine. "If you say anything bad about me or Rick, we're going to sue you for everything you have, you ungrateful bitch."

She lets me go, and I will myself to take a step back. Mom's not worth getting arrested over, and all I see now is a stranger. This woman is no longer my mother. Considering how she's treated me, she was never more than the woman who happened to push me out of her body, and who has regretted it ever since. Very soon the world will know what a despicable person Barb Taylor-Cole is, and there's nothing she can do to stop me.

As I turn and walk away, she calls after me. "Our roof needs redoing. Any chance you can spare a few grand from your new-found fortune?"

I stop, keep my back turned, waiting for her to continue, as I know she will. Sure enough, she takes a few steps onto the porch, says, "What kind of a kid won't help her mother keep a dry roof over her head? Maybe I'll see how much I can get for that story. Make up for all the things you're going to say about me in your *memoir* or should I call it me-me-*me*-moir?"

Thrusting my hands into my pockets, I don't look back, and by the time I reach the car I'm shaking. Why hadn't I properly considered this before? My mother and Rick are a threat. When my book publishes, which it will, she'll cry foul, lie and kick and scream about what I've written.

I could ask Torin if she'd have grounds to sue, but whether she does or doesn't, whatever she says will stoke the #Team-Madison fanatics. I won't let it happen. I can't let this woman help bolster that crowd more than she perhaps already has.

It doesn't take long to know exactly what I'll do to shut her mouth forever, and how I'll get away with it. I turn on the engine and drive away, park on another quiet and badly lit street with barely any houses before doubling back on foot and cutting through the wooded area behind Rick's house.

It's almost 10:00 p.m., and Mom will be snoring in front of the TV before long, although I hope Rick's at the bar for another while. It's Monday night, so I'd best not wait long.

After settling in, I let another twenty minutes pass before

I creep through the yard, checking every few steps to ensure neither of the neighbors are standing at their windows.

When I lived here, there was always a spare key in a broken flowerpot next to the back door and sure enough, it's still there. With gloved hands I slide it into the lock and turn, gently moving inside the house.

When I hear Mom's loud snores coming from the bedroom, I tiptoe to the gas fireplace. I gently pull out the insert, remove the clamp from the exhaust pipe fitting, and misalign the pipes before sliding the insert back into place. From what I remember seeing on a true crime show, overnight will be plenty of time for the leak to work, especially as Rick refuses to sleep with any windows open.

As I'm making sure Rick hasn't added a carbon monoxide detector anywhere—he never had any when I lived here— gravel crunches at the front of the house, and I hear the sound of a car engine shutting off.

Douchebag's home.

My heart's pounding so hard by the time I make it to the back door, I'm almost certain Rick will hear it when he walks in. I manage to lock up and slip the key into the broken flowerpot as the hallway light flicks on.

"Hey, Barb," Rick shouts. "What's for dinner? I'm starving."

I back away, search my heart for signs of regret for what I've done but find nothing. As I hold out my hands, I see they're steady. I've no qualms about what will happen here. Rick has no idea whatever leftovers he's about to devour will be his last meal.

As I slink away, I decide perhaps I'm a serial killer after all.

50

DOUBLE NORTH DEERING DEATHS ACCIDENTAL

by Eleanor Willis of the *Maine Daily*

Portland police confirmed Barbara Taylor-Cole (43) and Richard Cole (49), the couple found in their home on Alice Street late Tuesday afternoon, are suspected to have died from accidental carbon monoxide poisoning. There is no indication of foul play.

Taylor-Cole was the mother of Vienna Taylor, the known surviving member of the Bittersweet pop-rock band involved in a fatal Catskills car crash last December. In a statement released via her manager, Vienna Taylor said while she and her mother had endured a difficult relationship at times and had mostly been estranged for the past few years, she was "shocked and devastated" to learn of the deaths. She has requested the public to respect her privacy while she mourns another loss.

When asked for a comment, Portland Police Officer

Amelia Cortez said, "Unfortunately, we see tragedies such as these far too often, and it's even more unfortunate because they're largely preventable."

She added this is a reminder for everyone about the importance of installing and maintaining carbon monoxide and smoke detectors in their homes, and to check the batteries minimum twice yearly to help prevent such devastating consequences.

Comments (11—showing most recent)

@flip_flop_22 Anyone else think it's odd how everyone around Vienna keeps dying?

@sandie_j56 Seriously? She lost her mother and stepfather!

@flip_flop_22 She's a total fake, phony, and DMA

@cherub_smiiile DMA?

@flip_flop_22 Devastated, my ass. Still #TeamMadison

@cherub_smiiile LOL. Agreed!

@sandie_j56 You're both way out of line

@cherub_smiiile Whatever. Tell someone who cares.

51

76 days after the accident

IT'S BEEN TWO days since my mother's and Rick's lifeless bodies were discovered, and I've been inundated with interview requests, which I've asked Roger to handle. We provided a statement saying I'm too overwhelmed to speak to anyone, and asking people to please respect my privacy, give me time to grieve, because if I weren't responsible, it's what I'd do.

What a joke, because of course the online trolls came for me. *What did #VileVienna do* was the first tweet, and the hashtag spread. On Instagram alone it's been used thousands of times already and I haven't checked the other platforms for fear of what I'll see.

At least my mother won't be giving my enemies any ammunition to fight their battles with. Neither she nor Rick will have the chance to contradict what I write about them, either, despite all of it being true. I may rework the chapter where I hinted at Rick being involved in Grams' death, make it clearer how I believe he killed her. Let everyone think he's not only an asshole, but a murderer, too. Not that he could be. He'd never have the balls to do what I've done.

It's early Thursday morning and I'm on the phone again with Portland Police. Officer Cortez already called late afternoon on Tuesday to inform me about the most recent tragedy in my life.

Apparently, Rick's twenty-eight-year-old lover made the gruesome discovery when he didn't answer his phone or go to their secret rendezvous. When she peered through the window, she spotted Mom and Rick in bed, got in through the back door using the spare key, and when she couldn't rouse them, promptly spewed her guts on the bedroom floor.

"I'm sorry for your loss," Officer Cortez gently says now, and I recall her kindness from the night Grams went missing a few years back.

"Thank you." I wait for what she'll say next. I've seen the article about no foul play being suspected in Mom's and Rick's deaths, but I want to hear her say those words. I know better than anyone how whatever someone writes isn't necessarily true.

"I wanted to give you this update personally," Officer Cortez says. "This information was supposed to be kept confidential until I spoke to you this morning, but unfortunately that didn't happen."

"I saw the news," I say. "About the carbon monoxide poisoning."

"My sincerest apologies for you finding out this way," she says with a heavy sigh.

"It's fine," I mumble, which it really wouldn't be if I didn't already know what had happened. "Can you give me more details?"

"We've established there was a misaligned gas pipe in the living room fireplace," Cortez tells me. "It may have been leaking carbon monoxide all day. Unfortunately, there's no smell, so your mother and stepfather wouldn't have detected it before they went to bed."

"A misaligned pipe?" I say, letting the stepfather comment slide as I make myself sound bewildered. "I think it's the original fireplace, and I don't remember Rick ever having anyone in to inspect it when I lived at home."

"That can sometimes be part of the problem, I'm afraid," Cortez says. "Unfortunately, pipe fittings corrode, and leaks are an all-too-common occurrence." She pauses. "When there's no carbon monoxide detector in the house—"

"Are you blaming them?" I lace my tone with indignance but keep it from being over the top.

"No, not at all," Cortez replies, her voice calm. "This was an accident, and I'm truly very sorry for your loss. We'll keep you informed if there are any other developments. In the meantime, I wish you all the best, Vienna. You have my deepest sympathies."

After we hang up, I call a funeral home, make arrangements for Mom's cremation next week, which I guess I'll have to attend. I don't do anything for Rick because I'm not officially his next of kin and have never considered myself as such anyway. Whatever family he has left can sort things out. For all I care they can dump him and my mother in the same urn, let them argue for all eternity about his infidelities.

I stretch out on the hotel bed, a feeling of guarded contentment spreading through me. Maybe I should be scared by how easy it's been for me to literally get away with murder, but I promised myself I wouldn't dwell on the past.

Now I've got rid of all these distractions, I want to look to the future, figure out my career path and where it'll take me. Starting now, I'm done with my sordid history. I'm stuffing it into a tiny box and packing it away at the back of my mind, only to be reopened when I'm discussing my memoir.

When I spoke with Roger this morning, he asked what I wanted to do about the lunch with Georgina, the literary agent.

"Let's meet week after next," I told him. "I need to handle the funeral first."

"You're sure you don't want to wait a while longer?"

"No," I said, lowering my voice. "You know how work helps me heal."

In reality I wish we could meet today and get things moving. The two other agents want to represent me as well, and I'm hoping we'll receive offers from multiple publishers and generate a bidding war. I've decided I'll expand the book, end on a hopeful note about personal growth and staying resilient in the face of tragedy. People love that feel-good stuff.

I decide to treat myself to lunch downstairs—there's a restaurant with discreet booths I can hunker down in—but first I have a shower, do my hair and makeup before changing my mind and ordering room service again.

Ten minutes later there's a knock on the door but when I open up, it's not a server standing in front of me, but Roger. "Oh, hi," I say, frowning. "Did we agree to meet today?"

"No, but I thought it best to have this conversation as soon as possible."

"What conversation?"

"May I come in?"

"Sure," I say, closing the door behind him as he makes his way to the sitting area. "What's going on?"

He turns around. "First of all, how are you? I know I've already said this, but I'm sorry about your mother and Rick."

"Thank you," I say, when what I really want is for him to skip the niceties and tell me what's happened. He seems subdued, upset, and it's making me nervous.

Roger sits in one of the armchairs, gestures for me to do the same. His demeanor transforms my nerves to anger, which bubbles up my throat. I swallow it down, still can't tell what Roger's about to say except for the fact this visit isn't good.

"Tell me what's happened," I say, perching on the edge of my seat.

"I spoke to Georgina after our call," he says slowly.

"What did she say? Is everything all right?"

"Not exactly."

Frustration boils over and I throw my hands in the air. "Come on, Roger. Tell me what's going on."

"She's putting the offer to represent you on hold."

"What? *Why?*"

He raises his eyebrows. "Come on. There's been a lot of negative publicity about you recently. The video in the hardware store, the altercation with Madison's parents—"

"Those weren't my fault."

"Georgina understands that."

"Then what's the problem?"

"Optics."

"Okay, fine. Let's go with one of the other two."

He sighs. "I already tried. They both feel the same way as Georgina. It sucks, and I know how hard you worked on the manuscript. There are other agents we can try."

"But they were our top choices."

"Yes, and perhaps in a few weeks or months they'll feel differently."

Okay, this isn't great but it's not the end of the world. It'll give me time to work on the manuscript. It's fine. I sit on my hands, dig my nails into my thighs as I ask, "What else do you have for me? Are there any gigs with other bands on the horizon?"

"Not at the moment."

"What about Marvin? Has he got back to you about what's next with Mooseman?"

"He doesn't want to commit to anything."

"What does that mean?" I say. "My friends died, Roger. Madison killed them. I've lost my mother. Now I'm being punished? Why is there no interest when everyone knows who I am, and with the story I have to tell?"

"Being top of mind isn't necessarily a good thing," he says, voice calm. "Sit tight and lie low for a month or three, okay?

Work on your music, write some songs. The video of you outside The Chord was really quite damaging."

"Then do damage control," I shout, leaping up. "You're my manager. Do what you're paid to do and manage this mess. That's your job. Or do I need to find someone else?"

"I get you're under a lot of stress," Roger says evenly. "But don't threaten me. It's not something I've ever responded well to."

"Let's see how you respond to being fired," I shoot back, temper out of control.

He lets out a laugh. "Come on, Vienna, we both know you don't mean it and you're proving my point. Your behavior's a little on the erratic side."

"Are you calling me hysterical?"

"I said *erratic*. There's a difference."

"Are you sabotaging my career on purpose?" I ask.

"Excuse me? What the hell would I do that for?"

"Did you release my address?"

"Whoa, where's all this coming from?" Roger asks, but I don't think he's expecting a reply. "Listen, here's the truth. Your obvious volatility is why nobody wants to work with you."

"Fuck you, Roger."

"I'm going to pretend you didn't say that. I know your friends and family have died. We all understand how much you're hurting, but—"

"Understand this," I say, my voice glacial. "Get me a literary agent, some gigs with other bands, and a new deal with Mooseman or another record label. Otherwise, you're fi—"

"Enough," Roger says as he stands. "I'll see myself out. We'll talk more when you're receptive to having a calm conversation and not throwing accusations around."

I watch him leave, shut my mouth before I fire him properly, which I know I'll regret. But I'm furious, rage burning bright inside every part of me. Yes, "Sweet Spot" has blown up, but it's not enough. I didn't do all this to be a one-hit wonder. I need more. There *must* be more or Isabel's accidental death and what happened to Evelina and Madison won't have been worth it.

Despite every precaution I've taken, my carefully constructed plans for a successful post-Bittersweet life are collapsing. I don't know where to turn or how to stop it all from crumbling. I wish Madison were here so I could talk to her, tell her what's going on, flop on the sofa, put on our favorite Blondie album and listen to it with my best friend.

Except I barely have any friends. There's nobody I can trust, nobody except for Libby. She's called me every day since I texted her about Mom and Rick, offering condolences and her help, asking if there's anything I need. I grab my phone and when she hears the desperation in my voice, she immediately asks what's going on, and I tell her about my conversation with Roger, how I can't afford to alienate him, too.

"What do you want to see happen?" she asks. "Let's strategize."

"I want people to listen to my story," I say. "It's what the book was for, but without a literary agent, it's not going to happen."

"What if it wasn't a book?" she says.

"I've already given interviews."

"No, that's not what I mean." She takes a breath. "Okay, hear me out. From what I gather, publishing a book can take forever."

"Yes, that's what I heard, too. Probably a year at least, often longer."

"Right, well, if you want to get the story out there now, what about making a documentary?"

"With you?"

"With me."

"But I thought you wanted to stay out of all this? Keep your head down."

"You're my friend," she says, simply, and it fills my heart with unexpected affection. "I want to help you and I'll be behind the camera. We can do this alone, and once we've edited it and you approve, I'll show it to my boss at City Slicker."

"You'd do that?"

"It's a little self-serving, to be honest," she says with a small laugh. "I could do with some extra points after needing to take leave to get my head around things, which has helped immensely, I must say."

I think about her suggestion, fall in love with it immediately and wish I'd thought of it. Then again, Libby needed to be ready for this project. There's nobody else I'd trust with this but her. "Okay…where should we film? Here at the hotel?"

"Hmm…I'd recommend somewhere impactful, somewhere people can't ignore."

The answer comes instantly. "The cabin."

"What? No. No, I can't possibly—"

"Please, Libby. It's the best place. What if we get some footage there? Not necessarily the whole thing."

"I can't," she whispers, and I try hard not to get annoyed.

"Please, Libby," I coax, crossing my fingers. "I know it's a big ask but I need your help."

It feels like forever until she speaks again. "I can be there Sunday at noon. I'll go back to Albany afterward, edit from home and let you know when I have something to show you. Maybe you can come here? A break upstate might do you good and my parents would love to meet you. They're good people."

"That works," I say, adding, "I probably don't need to tell you this, but let's not post anything on social media about our plans—you know, in case someone shows up."

"Of course," she replies. "I'm not telling anyone anything."

52

79 days after the accident

BY 8:00 A.M. on Sunday morning, I've rented a car from the closest place in Brooklyn, and this time I don't use my fake ID because I've nothing to hide. Besides, the older woman behind the counter barely looks at me, and when she sees my driver's license there isn't a flicker of recognition in her eyes. She snaps her gum as her ruby-red nails fly across the keyboard.

I'm glad to be out of the hotel. I spent Friday and Saturday in my room save for a quick trip back to the Cobble Hill apartment. Thankfully nobody was hanging around the entrance, but I didn't linger, only stayed long enough to pick up a few clothes, toiletries, and a belt because since losing weight again, my jeans are falling off.

When I saw my drums, I played a few songs, but as soon as I broke into "Running Up That Hill" I had to stop because it reminded me of when Madison and I found the kit in the pawnshop. Moments later, I put down my drumsticks and left. I felt broken.

"Here you go," the car rental lady says after doing whatever she needed to do in the system, and once I've signed the paperwork and given her my credit card, she hands me a set of keys. "Out the door and turn left. Spot six."

The basic blue Ford Escape has a gazillion miles on the clock but runs well enough, and it's only for the day. I didn't bring much with me. Libby called yesterday to confirm our plans, and said she'd handle the equipment we'd need so there's little for me to do other than rehearse what I want to say.

As I drive upstate, I practice the answers to the questions I've prepared for Libby to ask. I'll talk a little about my childhood, about survivor's guilt, how I miss my friends and the difficulties in coming to terms with what Madison did, and how music has saved me.

I haven't quite decided but I might sing a couple of verses of the songs we'd worked on before the accident—which I haven't touched since—and ask viewers for their input. My regrets over threatening to fire Roger on Thursday are huge, and I hope when he sees a snippet of the documentary we're making, we can put our argument behind us, and I'll get him back on my side.

Maybe we can show an excerpt to the literary agents and get them to reconsider representing me. Perhaps we leapfrog them and generate interest directly from publishers if Roger can use his connections. Things will come together and work out in the long run. They have to.

The drive to the cabin is uneventful, except when I pass the signs for the town where Madison's buried. As soon as I see the name, chills zap up and down my spine, and I chase the gruesome images of what I did to her and my bandmates from my head.

My life feels like it's free-falling, and I need to regain control. I remind myself now is no time for those regrets because without some of my unsavory choices, I'd be in prison. Still, while the decisions I made brought fame and recognition, part of me wonders if it was worth the cost. If I'd made different choices the day of the accident, we may have had less success with "Sweet Spot," but I'd be celebrating it with the friends I had left.

I bite my lip, will myself not to cry and before too long, sadness gives way to bitterness followed by a feeling of resentfulness. I didn't cause the crash. If Madison hadn't seen me standing at the edge of the cliff, I'd have been able to spin the story about Gabi killing Evelina, and then herself.

Madison would've believed it, and the evidence would've backed me up. Libby would've thought her headache was from her concussion and if she'd been subjected to blood tests, I'd have suggested Madison gave Libby the Klonopin by accident. We'd have been the two surviving members of the Bittersweet, always there to support and rely on each other, bonded even more by unspeakable tragedy. I loved Madison enough to kill for her. I miss her.

Loneliness snakes into my core and curls up there, whispering I'd best get used to the sensation sticking around because with everything I've done, and the person I've become, I might be incapable of having a true relationship with anyone. Years ago, Bon Jovi recorded "Lonely At The Top." I'm beginning to understand how true those words are.

Telling myself to snap out of it, I refocus on the road because there's no sense dwelling. When I drive down the deserted track and the cabin comes into view, I try hard not to shudder, silently vow that after this trip, like Portland, I'll never return here.

There's no vehicle in front of the cabin. Libby isn't here yet. It's almost noon, the sun's shining bright in a cloudless sky, and although there's not been any recent snowfall, the temperatures are as crisp as one might expect in late February.

I get out of the car and stretch, see the remnants of the makeshift memorial that was here last time. Most of the flowers are long dead, the trinkets scattered to the winds. Instead of wait-

ing for Libby, I decide to go inside the cabin and do some tests
on my phone to see in which room it's best to film.

Floorboards creak beneath my shoes as I step into the hall.
The air smells musty and damp, instantly bringing back mem-
ories of the night I spent here. Trepidation slips into the pit of
my stomach, and I tell myself there's nothing to be afraid of.
Although I've never believed in ghosts, and this isn't *The Blair
Witch Project*, there's no way I'm going into the basement.

I turn right and head for the main room, hoping to throw
open a window to get rid of some of the smell. As soon as I
walk in, an object on the floor by the fireplace catches my eye.
Frowning, I head over and pick it up. It's a sweater. Not any
sweater. It's Gabi's—the one I used to kill Evelina.

Wait, that can't be right because the cops took it. It's stuffed
in a bag somewhere and locked in an evidence room at a police
station. My heart pounds, moves into my throat as I tell myself
it's a coincidence. There's nothing special about the sweater,
there must be tens of thousands of them in the state of New
York alone. It's a *coincidence*, nothing more.

When I hear a noise in the hall, my shoulders sag, and I expect to see Libby walk in through the doorway, but then I frown
because I didn't hear a car arrive. As I peer out of the window,
the hairs on my arms stand sentry, my flesh turning to goose
bumps when I see my blue rental is the only vehicle here.

There's a noise again.

Was that the sound of footsteps?

Is someone else in the cabin?

I slowly walk to the door and peer into the hall. Despite the
sun outside it's dim in here, and my heart almost stops when I
think I catch a glimpse of a shadow disappearing up the stairs
to the second floor.

"Hello?" I call out, blinking hard as I refuse to believe I saw
a flash of long red hair. Could it be…?

My mind screams it's not possible. Madison's dead. I strangled her. Hid her by the tree with the heart-shaped knot. Took her dismembered body to the graveyard and buried her beneath Samuel Zurcher's coffin.

She's dead, I tell myself, followed by *I don't believe in ghosts*.

I repeat these two statements over and over, scrunch my eyes shut and open them again. There's nobody standing there, in the hall or near the stairs. When I hear another noise in one of the rooms above me, I decide it's an animal. A raccoon or a rat, maybe a squirrel. With the shattered windows, it would be easy enough for any of those to get into the house and claim it as their own.

Except there are more noises, unmistakable footsteps this time.

I need to be sure my mind is playing tricks on me. Prove to myself the memories of what happened here are making me see and hear things that aren't there. I put one foot on the bottom step. Freeze when I hear humming. Someone's singing "Sweet Spot." No. No that can't be.

I move up, slowly, carefully, making as little noise as possible. When I reach the landing, I see one of the doors slowly swinging shut. I've had enough of these games, so I dart forward and crash into what I now remember is the upstairs bathroom.

I was wrong. Nobody's in here. There are no raccoons, rats, or squirrels. Instead, a blue pea coat, exactly like the one Madison wore that night, hangs from a hook on the far wall. What looks like a red wig protrudes from one of the pockets. I press my eyes shut, want to get rid of this apparition—because that's all it can be—but when I open them again, the coat and wig are still there.

I take a step farther into the room to get a better look, and as soon as I do, the door slams shut behind me.

"Hey," I yell, banging on the door, rattling the handle, but it won't give. It's locked. I'm trapped. "Hey!" I shout again, louder this time. "Open up. Who's there?"

Who's doing this? Has an obsessed Madison fan followed me here? No, that doesn't make sense. Whoever did this arrived before me. I exhale when I remember that Libby will get to the cabin soon, and when she does, she'll help me.

I hear someone moving around and fear grabs me by the throat. "Hello?" I say again, more quietly this time. "Who are you? Why are you doing this?"

A long moment goes by. I crouch, peer underneath the door, and through the small crack I spot a pair of boots. I'm immediately confused. I've seen these shoes before, including at my apartment. What the…?

"Libby?" I say. "Is that you?"

"Hello, Vienna," she answers, her voice calm, steady, and freezing cold.

I try to understand what's happening, but I can't grasp what she's playing at or why she's locked me in. "Libby, can you let me out now, please?"

"No, I'm not doing that," she says. "Not until I've got what I came for."

"What are you talking about? You were going to film me and I'm in here, so—"

"An audio recording will do fine," she says with a click of her tongue.

"A recording of what?" My impatience surges and I slam my palm against the door, give it a kick but it's solid oak and barely moves. All it does is hurt my toes. "Come on, Libby. Let me out."

"Tell me what you did with Madison first," she says.

"What?"

"Tell me, Vienna, or I swear I'll leave you here."

Panic balloons in my chest as I look around. I pull my phone from my pocket, hoping for reception but I already know there's none. Fuck. What am I going to do? Why is Libby doing this now? Why here? Has she suspected something all along? Did she see me hurting Evelina that night? It makes no sense. Why wait so long to do anything about it?

I need to get out of here, and fast. Taking a moment to calm down, I examine the door, notice its hinges are on the inside. Maybe if I can find something to take the pins out of the hinges, the entire door will come off. I'll need something small and flat. A dime or a nail.

My pockets yield nothing. Neither does the bathroom. There are nails in the floorboards, but I can't pry them out. My breathing accelerates again, and as I put my hands on my stomach to ground myself, I feel my belt. I touch the buckle, trace its thin prong, and my heart leaps.

As quietly as I can, I remove my belt. The prong barely fits under the pin of the door hinge but after a bit of effort it comes loose and I'll bet I can jimmy it out, hopefully the other two as well.

And then what? I don't know yet. I'm taking this one step at a time.

"Libby?" I say as I work on the pin again. "I don't know why you're doing this, but I loved Madison. I'd never hurt her."

Libby chuckles, and the sardonic sound irritates me so much I think I might scream.

"Tell you what," she says. "I'll sit here until you decide to tell the truth. I don't care how long it takes. I'm not the one trapped inside an old bathroom with no food or water. I brought supplies."

The first pin slides out, and I keep talking to stop Libby from hearing what I'm up to. I insist I haven't done anything, try to get her to tell me what she knows or what she thinks she knows, but she refuses. At one point she goads me, saying it's not an episode of *Scooby-Doo*.

That comment and the way she thinks she's so clever make me lose it completely for a moment. I bang on the door again, yell, "I'm going to fucking kill you when I get out of here," before regretting it, but it's too late, the words are already out, and she may have captured them on her phone.

Two pins are in my hand now, and as the third one follows, I lean against the door to keep it in place until I'm ready. From the sound of her voice and what I can see beneath the door, I think Libby's sitting against the wall directly opposite the bathroom. I hold my breath as I put my fingers around the knob and give it an almighty yank.

The heavy door falls toward me, the weight of it surprising me. When I spot Libby, her face has filled with shock, eyebrows raised, eyes wide, mouth open. She leaps up but I'm almost in the hallway now, and she dashes into one of the bedrooms.

I manage to shove my boot in the doorway and when I push the door open, Libby's walking backward by the window, her hands up, palms facing me. She has nowhere to go. She looks terrified, as she should be, because I'll do whatever it takes to get her to tell me what she knows.

"Stay away from me, you murderer," she says, her voice shaking. "I remember. I know what you did."

I lunge forward to grab her, not noticing the old dusty beige rug I've never seen before until my feet land on top of it, and it gives way beneath me.

53

I THROW OUT my arms to stop myself from crashing straight through the floor. Broken pieces of wood gouge into my legs, scrape my torso, making me yell out in pain. The hole isn't huge, big enough for my entire body to now be dangling down from my armpits but small enough for me to grasp the surrounding planks of wood, sending sharp splinters beneath my fingernails and into my skin.

I try to climb up, but the floorboards dig into my thighs as soon as I move, making me cry out again. I'm hanging with nothing but air beneath my feet, trapped and vulnerable, and it only takes a second to comprehend this was no accident. The hole was here in December, but the rug wasn't.

"Gotcha," Libby whispers.

"Help me." I say this as a command, but Libby doesn't move. My arms and shoulders already ache, and the scratches in my sides throb harder as she stares at me. There's a smile on her lips, and a coolness in her eyes I've never seen before. How am I going to get out of this?

"What are you doing?" I say.

She doesn't answer but points her phone toward me and says, "I told you. I'm here for your confession."

I can't help the laughter from exploding out of my mouth, immediately wince as I feel a stabbing pain from the jagged boards digging into my right side. "Have you gone completely—"

"Start with how you killed Evelina."

"I don't know what you mean," I say. "Pull me up. Let's talk about things."

"Let me kick things off," Libby says, ignoring my request. "You switched the painkillers with the Klonopin. You killed Evelina while I was unconscious. How am I doing so far?"

I don't react, keep my face completely under control. If she was unconscious that night, she doesn't know anything.

"You followed Gabi and pushed her off the cliff," she says. "I'm guessing Madison saw you, and you killed her, too. What did you do with her body?"

My shoulders are burning, my sides screaming as my body sags. Libby steps over, grabs the collar of my jacket and holds on. I want to claw at her face, but the respite from her pulling me up a little is immense, and I breathe out hard. I hadn't noticed how much I'm sweating.

"If you had proof of anything, you'd have gone to the cops," I say quietly. "And you're wrong. I didn't kill anyone. Why are you buying into the conspiracy theories? You read my book, you know what happened. I thought you were my friend."

"As did I," she says, letting me go, and my body drops again. "And I believed everything. Right up until I saw the video of you killing Evelina."

"It wasn't me, Libby," I say. "It was Madison. Please help me up."

She holds the phone toward my face again. "Tell me what you did with Madison."

"You brought me here and trapped me like this on purpose?" I ask her, flinching as the splintered wood scrapes my flesh again. "What do you think the cops will make of that?"

"Tell me what you did with Madison," she repeats.

"I didn't kill her."

Libby sighs. "Suit yourself." She bends down and pulls up one of my arms, lifting it above my head. I can't hang on. If she lets go, I'll fall. My mind speeds up. A confession given under duress will never hold up in a court of law, but I don't think that's her angle. If she shares anything I say on social media, I'm done. The bar for irrefutable evidence doesn't exist there.

"Wait," I say, buying myself some time as I calculate my next move. "I'll tell you."

Libby lowers my arm and I hold myself up as she points her phone at me. I see the eagerness in her eyes, the absolute greed and desperate hunger for my confession.

She's not getting one. But I need her phone. All she might have is a recording of me locked in a bathroom, yelling that I'm going to kill her but it's enough to do me more damage. I need to destroy it. Libby had better not try to stop me, or she's going to get hurt. I'll figure it out. I always do.

Without another word I lift my arms above my head and let myself go. I don't move at all for a second, but suddenly I feel my upper body slip as gravity does the rest. I expect to land on the wooden floor beneath, and while I do at first, it's pure horror when I keep going. I scream as the main floor gives way with a crack, and I tumble into the basement.

My entire right side slams into the concrete floor. The bones in my leg make snapping noises, and the searing agony in my thighs, hips, and abdomen is so intense, I think I'm going to vomit. When I try to move, hoping I can roll over and crawl my way up the stairs, I cry out in pain.

Footsteps approach, and by the time I manage to turn my head to the basement steps, Libby's kneeling next to me. "Remember you told us to be careful of the rotten floorboards in the kitchen?" she says. "I guess you forgot."

I can't help but smile, because she's smart. Maybe smarter

than me after all. "How did you know I did it? Tell me how you figured out it was me."

Libby points to my hands. "Your favorite color is red."

She doesn't elaborate, only asks me again to tell her what I did with Madison, saying she wants to give Lucinda and Barry the opportunity to bring their daughter home.

"They're not why you're doing this," I say, wincing as the pain in my side increases hundredfold, burning me from the inside out.

"Yes, they are," she says, and I laugh softly.

"Bullshit. Remember you told me how ambitious you are?" I have to stop and catch my breath, but all I can manage is a shallow inhale because it hurts too much. Everything hurts. "You want my confession to further your career. You want to use me to give yourself a boost." I pause again, whisper, "You and I are exactly the same."

"No, I—"

"I get it," I whisper. Speaking has become so difficult it takes all my strength to push my next words out. "I don't blame you. Trust me, I've done far worse."

"Tell me where she is," Libby insists, and this time I see myself in her eyes, my own gnarly, beastly desire.

"I'll tell you, if it's what you want," I wheeze. "But be warned, even a small taste of fame will do stuff to you that you won't like. It'll change you, make you ruthless." I let out a small chuckle, which I immediately regret as it makes me cough, and another searing pain shoots through my entire abdomen. I can taste blood. "It already has."

I grab her hand and squeeze tight as she records my murmured details of Samuel Zurcher's grave. My life's slipping away but as it does, I feel some of my soul latching itself onto Libby's.

This isn't the end for me, not really. By giving her this secret, this gift, she'll make me more well-known than I could've ever dreamed of. Vienna Taylor will be notorious. Not as good as famous, perhaps, but I guess it doesn't matter when you're dead.

54

10 days later

SURVIVING MEMBER OF THE BITTERSWEET DEAD

by Eleanor Willis of the *Maine Daily*

A final and shocking twist in the Bittersweet tragedy played out this afternoon during a standing-room-only press conference held by the New York Police Department.

Detective Laura Ashbury confirmed Vienna Taylor, the North Deering drummer of the pop-rock band the Bittersweet, which was involved in a fatal car accident last December, was found dead late Monday morning after being reported missing by her manager.

Taylor's body was located at the isolated Catskills cabin where her fellow band members had perished after seeking refuge following their vehicular crash. She's said to have died accidentally, and there are no persons of interest sought in this case.

Detective Ashbury provided the analysis of a letter found

near Taylor's body, which was authenticated by experts as having been handwritten by Taylor. Given the note's details, authorities believe she returned to the dilapidated cabin with the intention of dying by suicide but fell to her death before she had the opportunity to take her own life.

The following excerpt of Taylor's letter was released to the press:

The guilt and pain of what I've done is suffocating me. I have to make it stop, but I can't take this burden with me, wherever I go next.

There's no excuse for what I did to the people who thought I was their friend, and I don't expect anyone to understand why I hurt Evelina, Gabi, and Madison. None of it was planned. All of it was because of my limitless need for fame. Fame and recognition, no matter the cost.

By framing Madison for the murders, I hoped to benefit from the interest I knew being the only survivor of the Bittersweet would bring, but the guilt is killing me. It's feasting on my soul, not that I had much left.

Every day I see a monster in the mirror, and it's impossible to continue.

Living with what I've done is unfathomable.

I thought I wanted to be famous. Not anymore. This is to be my final appearance, the last gig. From now on, I want to disappear into the background, be erased from everyone's memories. Forgotten forever.

Taylor's note included details of the location of missing band member Madison Pierce's body. Detective Ashbury confirmed Pierce's remains have been recovered, and she's no longer considered a suspect in the deaths of Gabriela or Evelina Sevillano. The investigation into Taylor's involvement is ongoing.

Rumors about an upcoming memoir by Taylor have been circulating online for weeks, but Taylor's manager, Roger Kent, confirmed there are no plans for any publication. When asked when music by the Bittersweet might be released posthumously, Kent responded with, "Never."

Comments (87—showing most recent)

@sandie_j56 Holy shit! I always was and will forever be #TeamMadison

@maplesyrup_12 Nobody won here

@juicy_froot16 You're so wise! I don't understand what could drive anyone to do this, it's so awful.

@sandie_j56 Yeah it really is. BTW if you're missing the Bittersweet's music, there's a new and similar band called Sapphire Hearts. Check them out. I'm #TeamJade. How about you?

@juicy_froot16 I know them! They're fantastic but I'm #TeamAnnie. She kicks ass and is a far better singer. And cuter!

@maplesyrup_12 Are you two for real right now?

EPILOGUE — LIBBY

14 days after Vienna's death

SUNLIGHT STREAMS IN through my bedroom windows and I glance at the time. It's almost 10:00 a.m. but I don't want to get up yet. If I move, I'll disturb Pepper, who's nestled next to me, fast asleep and purring gently. I'll give him another little while before I wake him.

For now, I'm content scrolling through my phone and reading articles about the Bittersweet. As I lie here reminiscing, I'm wildly grateful everything's over.

Back in November, I was ecstatic when my boss agreed that creating a documentary about the Bittersweet was a great idea. Not so much when she assigned Zeke as lead researcher. The guy was talented, but he was a prick and a pig. He didn't deserve to work for City Slicker, let alone manage the project I'd suggested.

Sending Zeke's dick pics to our boss was simple enough. All I had to do was wait for an opportune moment when he left his phone unlocked. When he got fired, I felt powerful, invincible, not in the least bit apologetic because he had it coming.

When the boss agreed to send me to meet the Bittersweet, I thought I might explode with happiness. I'd been a huge fan ever since "Sweet Spot" was released, fell in love with the band's image, dynamic, and the way they supported one another. An illusion, as I soon learned. The Bittersweet were rotting from the inside, but it would take another while for me to see it.

I decided I'd go further than following the band around and taking notes. I wanted to put together a fifteen-minute short, the best my boss had ever seen. I'd earn a much larger part in the project, bolstering my career, and I could already imagine watching the documentary with my dad, who'd be so proud.

Looking back, I wish I'd never set foot in the Bittersweet's rehearsal room. I should've listened to the adage about never meeting your heroes because Vienna was mine.

Excited, I was desperate to make a good impression, and when I heard about the party in the Catskills, I practically begged her to let me travel with them.

When the Tahoe went off the side of the road, I thought for sure we'd all die. In those few seconds as the truck rolled and our screams filled the air, I pictured my parents and brother, how I'd never see them again, and my heart broke.

After we ended up at the bottom of the hill, with Isabel dead and Evelina badly injured, I found hope the rest of us would survive. I had no idea how bad things would get.

Much later, as I read through Vienna's manuscript because I needed to know what had happened while I'd been unconscious, I bought into the subtle and not-so-subtle clues portraying Madison as manipulative, increasingly dangerous, and someone who could kill. I was grateful Vienna had saved my life. Felt I owed her everything.

Until I knocked over her bag and saw the gloves.

Red's my favorite color.

A detail jostled at the back of my mind, demanding attention, but I couldn't place it, not until I got home and lay in the dark, thinking things through. Wisps and fragments of memories swirled around my brain, gradually clicking together like a broken jigsaw puzzle.

First came the recollection of Madison's voice. It had sounded off when she'd given me the second batch of pills at the cabin, but I'd blamed my confusion on the Klonopin.

Red's my favorite color.

I hadn't seen Madison's face when she drugged me, but I had seen her gloves, remembered them clearly. Red gloves, exactly like the ones that fell out of Vienna's bag when I knocked it over. Red. Not blue, the color of the pair Madison had worn all day.

For the next twenty-four hours I'd lived in denial, talked myself into believing I was mistaken, that Madison had killed the others, but in my heart, I knew it wasn't true. Vienna had manipulated me along with everybody else for weeks. I'd been a good little puppet, doing exactly as she'd hoped, supporting her narrative as she'd pulled me into her lies.

But…why had she begged me to go back to the cabin? What possible reason could there be for her to want to return? I no longer believed she thought it might jog my memory. She wanted me there to use me for something else. What was I missing?

The question clicked more things into place. What *was* I missing?

My camera.

I'd asked the cops multiple times if it had been found, but they always said no. I assumed Madison had taken it with her, although I couldn't fathom why. Was that why Vienna wanted me at the cabin? It didn't make sense, but the next day I drove to the Catskills anyway, spent hours searching each room, almost gave up countless times before I finally found my camera tucked away behind some broken tiles in the bathroom.

I cried when I watched the video, didn't believe for one second it was Madison although Vienna had done an excellent job of making it seem that way. She was behind this, all of it, I was certain, but there was no way for me to prove it.

For a short while I thought about handing the camera to the cops, but they'd think Madison was guilty. Case closed. For me, there was no longer any doubt Vienna had killed Evelina, and as I spent the night rereading her memoir, the more I suspected she'd done the same to Gabi and Madison, shifting the blame onto her best friend.

What good would giving the footage to the cops do? It wasn't enough for Ashbury and Newell to arrest Vienna, let alone charge and convict her. Any decent defense attorney would tear me to shreds if I took the stand and said I remembered the red gloves, no matter how much I argued. But my confidence in what I knew grew stronger, and while one path was to cut Vienna out of my life forever, there was an alternative.

I couldn't let Vienna get away with murder, and if I managed to prove she was guilty…

After scouring the internet, I found the story about the Catskills cop who'd recently been suspended for stealing stuff from crime scenes, and who'd been at the cabin. If I could make this connection, an investigative reporter could, too, so I anonymously emailed the video of pseudo-Madison killing Evelina to the most well-known *New York Times* reporter I could find. The cop might deny sending it, but that didn't matter as long as nobody suspected me.

The rest of my plan quickly took shape in my mind, feeding my drive and ambition. I had the footage I'd taken while shadowing the Bittersweet, plus all my notes. Now, the short film I'd planned on putting together would culminate in a confession from Vienna. Somehow, I had to make her tell me what she'd done. I imagined the breaking news and Vienna's demise leading to my career going stratospheric. It was all I could think about, my ambition driving me forward, pushing me harder.

Now Vienna believed she was free from all suspicion, that

everyone bought into her lies, her guard would slip, particularly if I maintained the illusion of our friendship. Isolating her became a game. Vienna was so desperate for fame and recognition, always checking social media for the latest updates, getting angry when people made derogatory comments about her.

I was happy to stoke those with a number of fake accounts I logged into via a VPN, in case anyone happened to check. People get into heated online arguments so quickly, waiting for their nemesis to write something they can immediately tear to pieces and throw back in their face, so I goaded people who openly detested Vienna. My favorite one to rile was @flip_flop_22, who I easily set off with a few well-placed barbs.

Next, when Vienna mentioned ordering a few things online and had them sent to her Bushwick apartment, I called in sick at work for a few days and hung out around her building, swiping the parcels.

I took an imprint of her house key while she was in the bathroom on my next visit to Cobble Hill, so I could come back and search for more clues. Maybe I'd find discarded pages of her memoir or notes of some kind, not that I thought she'd be careless enough.

Trouble was, I couldn't be sure for how long she'd leave her place, and if she caught me, it was over. Then I met Pepper, and the sight of Vienna so besotted with a kitten sparked another idea of how to destabilize her.

The next morning, I kept watch at her apartment building. As soon as she left, I slipped in and stole Pepper, leaving the bathroom window ajar, making her believe he'd used it to escape.

She loved Pepper, but she didn't deserve him, didn't deserve anyone, so I took him home and asked my neighbor to look after him the evening Vienna and I painted the hall—the night I quietly alerted #TeamMadison about Vienna Taylor being in a hardware store. It's truly amazing what you can do with a few taps and swipes.

Messing with the spotlight at The Chord wasn't my idea. I'd genuinely thought it was an accident until I found a chat room called *#VileVienna*, where people speculated about what she'd done to the Bittersweet members, and how to exact revenge. Nobody confessed to loosening a few screws, but I had no doubt at least one of them was responsible. Assholes. It could've killed her before I got what I wanted.

Same with Vienna almost being run over. I've no idea if it was deliberate or a genuine accident, nothing ever surfaced online, but I was the one who released her address, pretending to be concerned for her safety when I dashed to her side.

Coincidences, accidents—I gave Vienna enough to know she had enemies everywhere, enough to lead her to the edge. I wanted to get her to the cabin, let her think it was her idea for me to film her there for the documentary, and that was when I'd get her true confession.

I bought a red wig and the same jacket as Madison's to use as bait and trap Vienna in the upstairs bathroom, but I knew she was smart and I needed a backup plan in case things got messy. After manipulating the floorboards in the upstairs bedroom a little more, I covered the hole with an old rug I'd brought, and which was almost the same color as the floor. I bought the same hoodie she'd used to suffocate Evelina and left it on the living room floor, ensuring she wouldn't notice the hole above her head, either.

My strategy was risky, perhaps, and I wasn't entirely sure if I'd get into trouble if anyone realized Vienna got trapped in the ceiling deliberately. Then again, plenty of people had been to the cabin since the accident. The place was old, decrepit, and it was a chance I had to take.

The one thing I'd miscalculated was Vienna landing in the basement if she let herself drop. I knew the floorboards underneath were rotten, but I thought they'd hold, maybe trap a leg. I was wrong, and when I rushed to the basement and saw the bone sticking out of her thigh, I felt despicable for what I'd done.

But as Vienna confessed and the life seeped from her body, I understood what I'd captured on film was better than I'd anticipated. I could spin this story. Tell the cops the almost-truth.

First, I'd delete the recording from my phone of when Vienna had been in the bathroom, threatening to kill me, and the one when I'd trapped her in the bedroom floor. I'd say we'd come to the cabin because Vienna wanted to record a message for her fans, how she was getting so much online hate she wanted to walk people through what had happened here, and that I'd believed her.

As we'd walked around the cabin, she'd gone upstairs to figure out where to record, at which point she'd accidentally crashed through the floor. She must've known she didn't have much time left—the autopsy would later reveal Vienna had three shattered ribs, a punctured lung, and a serious laceration to her liver, killing her within twenty minutes—and her dying wish was to confess.

The guilt soon dissipated, and I felt giddy, elated. The story, the film I'd put together, would be huge. Except, as I left the cabin to make a fake-panic 911 call, I couldn't leave some of her last words behind.

You and I are exactly the same.

No, we were absolutely not. She was a murderer. I'd obtained justice. I hadn't meant for her to die. I kept walking, but still her voice wouldn't leave me alone.

But be warned, even a small taste of fame will do stuff to you that you won't like. It'll change you, make you ruthless. It already has.

As I took another few steps through the woods, I thought about how I'd felt when she'd tumbled two floors down. I hadn't been scared because I'd hurt her. I'd been terrified because I thought I wouldn't get the confession I desperately wanted. My actions and manipulation had taken her life, which didn't bother me nearly as much as it should have, no matter what she'd done.

What price had Vienna paid in her quest for fame?

Was I really prepared to pay the same for mine?

It didn't take long to decide. Vienna had brought a copy of her memoir with her, including her handwritten notes because she'd planned on me filming her reading an excerpt. Once I'd forged her suicide letter, I went to the cabin, wiped down the pen I'd used before pressing it into her hands and returning it to her car.

As I stood in front of the cabin, thinking about all the terrible things that had happened here, I swiped my finger across my phone's screen and deleted Vienna's final appearance without a single regret. Finally, it was over.

Lying in my bed now, I let myself resurface from the memories, put my phone on the bedside table, and as I stretch, my movement wakes Pepper. He blinks a few times, peers up at me and yawns, his little pink tongue licking my fingers as I switch on the TV. The story of the Bittersweet still dominates the news, and when I turn it off again, my phone rings.

It's *What's On NYC*. Along with the dozens of other outlets, Melodie's research assistant has called for days, leaving messages, asking me to phone back. This time, curiosity gets the better of me and I answer. Melodie was a huge #TeamVienna fan, too, and I wonder if she regrets meeting her hero as much as I do.

"Hi, Libby, it's Melodie Johnson," she says when I pick up, and I'm surprised to hear her voice instead of her assistant's. "I'm calling from—"

"*What's On NYC*," I say.

"We're hoping to have you on my show this Sunday," she says, her voice eager. "I'd love to speak to you about your experience with the Bittersweet. How would you feel about coming to the studio for an on-air interview Sunday afternoon? We want to hear your story."

My resolve to keep quiet falters, but I manage to say, "Thanks, but I'm not speaking publicly about what happened."

"I might have some information to change your mind," Melodie says, and when I don't respond, she continues. "I've heard the supposed accidental deaths of Vienna's mother and stepfather are being reexamined. Apparently, the cops have reason to believe Vienna may be responsible. I've heard rumblings about a request to exhume her grandmother's body, too."

I'm not entirely surprised, but I still lean back, sink into my pillow as Pepper nibbles my fingers. "That's truly awful."

"Yes, it is. We'd really like to have your insights into Vienna's character. I understand you spent lots of time with her recently. You're a documentarian and were shadowing the Bittersweet? It must've been fascinating."

The tiny amount of bait works, as I'm sure she knew it would. Fame and glory slink onto my shoulders, their velvet voices purring in my ear how this is my chance. Doors which would otherwise take years for me to get through will slide open with ease, welcoming me inside. All I have to do is share my story. Embellish a little. Tell a lie or ten. My parents and brother would be so proud. Where's the harm? I open my mouth to accept her invitation.

You and I are exactly the same.

"No, my decision's firm," I blurt out. "I'm not talking to anyone."

Melodie makes a mmm-hmm sound, says, "I respect your decision. Let me know if you change your mind, okay? I mean, jeez, you're the only person to have escaped the Bittersweet tragedy. You must feel incredibly lucky."

I close my eyes, whisper, "More than anyone will ever understand."

★ ★ ★ ★ ★

For free bonus material including a playlist, the Bittersweet
song lyrics, author interview, and a reader's guide,
visit HannahMaryMcKinnon.com.

ACKNOWLEDGMENTS

For me, one of the best parts of being a novelist is writing this section. Not only does it mean I've completed another novel (hurrah) but it's also the moment to reflect upon and express my gratitude to the most incredible individuals who've helped me. It's a big list!

I always start with you, the reader, because there are millions of books out there and I'm fortunate you decided to read this one. Whether you chose the novel in a professional or recreational capacity, I'm grateful you decided to give *Only One Survives* a chance and follow the Bittersweet's rise and ultimate demise. I hope you enjoyed the ride and perhaps felt a sense of nostalgia for some of the bands mentioned and/or discovered musicians entirely new to you.

To all the book reviewers and bookstagrammers, who are incredibly creative and wonderfully talented—thank you for your continued love and support, and for sharing my books in such astonishing ways. You're amazing!

To Carolyn Forde, my terrific agent. We've worked together for over six years and I'm so thankful for your advice and guidance, as well as our friendship. Here's to many more books, projects, and years of superb collaboration.

A huge thank-you to my talented editor Dina Davis for brainstorming *Only One Survives*'s plot for hours and calmly answering my panicked *gah, this still isn't working* email. You gave me exactly what I needed to pull the story together. Thank you for your steady hand!

Harlequin, HarperCollins, HTP, and MIRA's outstanding teams are a dream to work with—including Cory Beatty, Peter Borcsok, Nicole Brebner, Randy Chan, Heather Connor, Emer Flounders, Brenann Francis, Olivia Gissing, Miranda Indrigo, Sophie James, Amy Jones, Sean Kapitain, Puja Lad, Ana Luxton, Ashley MacDonald, Leo MacDonald, Margaret Marbury, Lauren Morocco, Jennifer O'Keefe, Pamela Osti, Lindsey Reeder, Nora Rawn, Reka Rubin, Loriana Sacilotto, Justine Sha, Elita Sidiropoulou, Colleen Simpson, Alice Tibbetts, Christine Tsai, Evan Yeong, and colleagues. Thank you for all you do!

To HarperAudio, BeeAudio, and Amy Hall—I'm always in awe of how my characters are brought to life and how voice actors make them their own. Thank you for handling them with such delicate care and outstanding talent.

To Jennifer Hillier and Samantha M. Bailey—thank you for your input when this book was at its most embryonic stage. Sam, the words "you could make them a band" changed everything. To Sonica Soares, who read an early version and excitedly messaged to tell me what she thought—thank you for your boundless enthusiasm. Breakfast with Jenny soon, please.

My brilliant friend Roger Guntern—thank you for our stellar call about the music industry and band management, and for reading an early version of the novel to ensure I hadn't messed it up. We rarely see each other now we live on different continents, but I treasure our friendship and can't wait to see you again. Thank you for letting me base the wonderful and dashing Roger Kent on you. George Michael forever, darling!

Hank Phillippi Ryan and Jonathan Shapiro—thank you for the legal advice and for stopping me from writing myself into a corner (or Vienna into a prison cell), and Hank, thank you for being such a great and trusted friend.

For years now, I've been getting away with (fictional) murder with the help of my go-to specialists: fellow crime author and retired Detective Sergeant Bruce Robert Coffin, and Forensic Detective Ed Adach who assisted with all things police and crime scene related. You make me a better criminal, ha ha. But seriously, chatting with you is a highlight of my writing process, and always lends more depth and complexity to my stories. Thank you.

More hugs and thank-yous to Cool A.F. Brady for the input about New York, Dr. Ali Kopelman for the medical advice, Lynn McPherson for the music ideas and early feedback, and Rowly McPherson for the additional diabetes details. A huge thank-you to Lisa Quinlivan for bidding on my prize offered during the 2022 *www.diversebooks.org* auction and suggesting the superb name Torin Ryan for my character.

Sometimes I make what might be perceived as oddball phone calls and I'm often amazed how people just roll with it. When I contacted Richards Funeral Home in upstate New York to inquire how I might hide an (cough, cough) *extra* body in a graveyard, John Martin not only humored me when I swore I was a crime author, not a murderer, but he also ensured I had what I needed to get the fictional job done. John—thank you for not hanging up and calling the cops.

To all the musicians, singers, and songwriters whose work inspired mine. Listening to your music was instrumental (pardon the pun) to shaping *Only One Survives* and I had a blast. Nothing can lift my mood faster than a few bars of my favorite tunes. Thank you!

To all my author friends, of whom there are many, I'm so thankful for you all. Sure, we write about dark stuff, and we bump off countless characters, but you're the funniest, warmest, kindest, and most generous people I know. I can't wait to hang out with you again.

To Dad, Joely, Simon, Michael, and Oli; my in-laws Gilbert and Jeanette; and my extended family everywhere—thank you for sharing my work far and wide. I appreciate everything you do, and all the encouragement you provide.

And finally, to Rob, Leo, Matt, and Lex, my fantastic husband and our three awesome sons. Thank you for supporting me once again as I disappeared into another of my fictional worlds, for humoring me when I told you about my whacky and murderous research, and for never doubting that I could pull off writing another book. I love you with all my heart. You've been my everything for over two decades. May it always be so.